Love Me Little, Love Me

By
Charles Reade

Love Me Little, Love Me Long

CHAPTER I.

NEARLY a quarter of a century ago, Lucy Fountain, a young lady of beauty and distinction, was, by the death of her mother, her sole surviving parent, left in the hands of her two trustees, Edward Fountain, Esq., of Font Abbey, and Mr. Bazalgette, a merchant whose wife was Mrs. Fountain's half-sister.

They agreed to lighten the burden by dividing it. She should spend half the year with each trustee in turn, until marriage should take her off their hands.

Our mild tale begins in Mr. Bazalgette's own house, two years after the date of that arrangement.

The chit-chat must be your main clue to the characters. In life it is the same. Men and women won't come to you ticketed, or explanation in hand.

"Lucy, you are a great comfort in a house; it is so nice to have some one to pour out one's heart to; my husband is no use at all."

"Aunt Bazalgette!"

"In that way. You listen to my faded illusions, to the aspirations of a nature too finely organized, ah! to find its happiness in this rough, selfish world. When I open my bosom to him, what does he do? Guess now—whistles."

"Then I call that rude."

"So do I; and then he whistles more and more."

"Yes; but, aunt, if any serious trouble or grief fell upon you, you would find Mr. Bazalgette a much greater comfort and a better stay than poor spiritless me."

"Oh, if the house took fire and fell about our ears, he would come out of his shell, no doubt; or if the children all died one after another, poor dear little souls; but those great troubles only come in stories. Give me a friend that can sympathize with the real hourly mortifications of a too susceptible nature; sit on this ottoman, and let me go on. Where was I when Jones came and interrupted us? They always do just at the interesting point."

Miss Fountain's face promptly wreathed itself into an expectant smile. She abandoned her hand and her ear, and leaned her graceful person toward her aunt, while that lady murmured to her in low and thrilling tones—his eyes, his long hair, his imaginative expressions, his romantic projects of frugal love; how her harsh papa had warned Adonis off the premises; how Adonis went without a word (as pale as death, love), and soon after, in his despair, flung himself—to an ugly heiress; and how this disappointment had darkened her whole life, and so on.

Perhaps, if Adonis had stood before her now, rolling his eyes, and his phrases hot from the annuals, the flourishing matron might have sent him to the servants' hall with a wave of her white and jeweled hand. But the melody disarms this sort of brutal criticism—a woman's voice relating love's young dream; and then the picture—a matron still handsome pouring into a lovely virgin's ear the last thing she ought; the young beauty's eyes mimicking sympathy; the ripe beauty's soft, delicious accents—purr! purr! purr!

Crash overhead! a window smashed aie! aie! clatter! clatter! screams of infantine rage and feminine remonstrance, feet pattering, and a general hullabaloo, cut the soft recital in two. The ladies clasped hands, like guilty things surprised.

Lucy sprang to her feet; the oppressed one sank slowly and gracefully back, inch by inch, on the ottoman, with a sigh of ostentatious resignation, and gazed, martyr-like, on the chandelier.

"Will you not go up to the nursery?" cried Lucy, in a flutter.

"No, dear," replied the other, faintly, but as cool as a marble slab; "you go; cast some of your oil upon those ever-troubled waters and then come back and let us try once more."

Miss Fountain heard but half this sentence; she was already gliding up the stairs. She opened the nursery door, and there stood in the middle of the room "Original Sin." Its name after the flesh was Master Reginald. It was half-past six, had been baptized in church, after which every child becomes, according to polemic divines of the day, "a little soul of Christian fire" until it goes to a public school. And there it straddled, two scarlet cheeks puffed out with rage, soft flaxen hair streaming, cerulean eyes glowing, the poker grasped in two chubby fists. It had poked a window in vague ire, and now threatened two females with extinction if they riled it any more.

The two grown-up women were discovered, erect, but flat, in distant corners, avoiding the bayonet and trusting to their artillery.

"Wicked boy!"

"Naughty boy!" (grape.)

"Little ruffian!" etc.

And hints as to the ultimate destination of so sanguinary a soul (round shot).

"Ah! here's miss. Oh, miss, we are so glad you are come up; don't go anigh him, miss; he is a tiger."

Miss Fountain smiled, and went gracefully on one knee beside him. This brought her angelic face level with the fallen cherub's. "What is the matter, dear?" asked she, in a tone of soft pity.

The tiger was not prepared for this: he dropped his poker and flung his little arm round his cousin's neck.

"I love YOU. Oh! oh! oh!"

"Yes, dear; then tell me, now—what is the matter? What have you been doing?"

"Noth—noth—nothing—it's th—them been na—a—agging me!"

"Nagging you?" and she smiled at the word and a tiger's horror of it.

"Who has been nagging you, love?"

"Th—those—bit—bit—it." The word was unfortunately lost in a sob. It was followed by red faces and two simultaneous yells of remonstrance and objurgation.

"I must ask you to be silent a minute," said Miss Fountain, quietly. "Reginald, what do you mean by—by—nagging?"

Reginald explained. "By nagging he meant—why—nagging."

"Well, then, what had they been doing to him?"

No; poor Reginald was not analytical, dialectical and critical, like certain pedanticules who figure in story as children. He was a terrible infant, not a horrible one.

"They won't fight and they won't make it up, and they keep nagging," was all could be got out of him.

"Come with me, dear," said Lucy, gravely.

"Yes," assented the tiger, softly, and went out awestruck, holding her hand, and paddling three steps to each of her serpentine glides.

Seated in her own room, tiger at knee, she tried topics of admonition. During these his eyes wandered about the room in search of matter more amusing, so she was obliged to bring up her reserve.

"And no young lady will ever marry you."

"I don't want them to, cousin; I wouldn't let them; you will marry me, because you promised."

"Did I?"

"Why, you know you did—upon your honor; and no lady or gentleman ever breaks their word when they say that; you told me so yourself," added he of the inconvenient memory.

"Ah! but there is another rule that I forgot to tell you."

"What is that?"

"That no lady ever marries a gentleman who has a violent temper."

"Oh, don't they?"

"No; they would be afraid. If you had a wife, and took up the poker, she would faint away, and die—perhaps!"

"Oh, dear!"

"I should."

"But, cousin, you would not want the poker taken to you; you never nag."

"Perhaps that is because we are not married yet."

"What, then, when we are, shall you turn like the others?"

"Impossible to say."

"Well, then" (after a moment's hesitation), "I'll marry you all the same."

"No! you forget; I shall be afraid until your temper mends."

"I'll mend it. It is mended now. See how good I am now," added he, with self-admiration and a shade of surprise.

"I don't call this mending it, for I am not the one that offended you; mending it is promising me never, never to call naughty names again. How would you like to be called a dog?"

"I'd kill 'em."

"There, you see—then how can you expect poor nurse to like it?"

"You don't understand, cousin—Tom said to George the groom that Mrs. Jones was an—old—stingy—b—"

"I don't want to hear anything about Tom."

"He is such a clever fellow, cousin. So I think, if Jones is an old one, those two that keep nagging me must be young ones. What do you think yourself?" asked Reginald, appealing suddenly to her candor.

"And no doubt it was Tom that taught you this other vulgar word 'nagging,'" was the evasive reply.

"No, that was mamma."

Lucy colored, wheeled quickly, and demanded severely of the terrible infant: "Who is this Tom?"

"What! don't you know Tom?" Reginald began to lose a grain of his respect for her. "Why, he helps in the stables; oh, cousin, he is such a nice fellow!"

"Reginald, I shall never marry you if you keep company with grooms, and speak their language."

"Well!" sighed the victim, "I'll give up Tom sooner than you."

"Thank you, dear; now I am flattered. One struggle more; we must go together and ask the nurses' pardon."

"Must we? ugh!"

"Yes—and kiss them—and make it up."

Reginald made a wry face; but, after a pause of solemn reflection, he consented, on condition that Lucy would keep near him, and kiss him directly afterward.

"I shall be sure to do that, because you will be a good boy then."

Outside the door Reginald paused: "I have a favor to ask you, cousin—a great favor. You see I am so very little, and you are so big; now the husband ought to be the biggest."

"Quite my own opinion, Reggy."

"Well, dear, now if you would be so kind as not to grow any older till I catch you up, I shall be so very, very, very much obliged to you, dear."

"I will try, Reggy. Nineteen is a very good age. I will stay there as long as my friends will let me."

"Thank you, cousin."

"But that is not what we have in hand."

The nurses were just agreeing what a shame it was of miss to take that little vagabond's part against them, when she opened the door. "Nurse, here is a penitent—a young gentleman who is never going to use rude words, or be violent and naughty again."

"La! miss, why, it is witchcraft—the dear child—soon up and soon down, as a boy should."

"Beg par'n, nurse—beg par'n, Kitty," recited the dear child, late tiger, and kissed them both hastily; and, this double formula gone through, ran to Miss Fountain and kissed her with warmth, while the nurses were reciting "little angel," "all heart," etc.

"To take the taste out of my mouth," explained the penitent, and was left with his propitiated females; and didn't they nag him at short intervals until sunset! But, strong in the contemplation of his future union with Cousin Lucy, this great heart in a little body despised the pins and needles that had goaded him to fury before.

Lucy went down to the drawing-room. She found Mrs. Bazalgette leaning with one elbow on the table, her hand shading her high, polished forehead; her grave face reflecting great mental power taxed to the uttermost. So Newton looked, solving Nature.

Miss Fountain came in full of the nursery business, but, catching sight of so much mind in labor, approached it with silent curiosity.

The oracle looked up with an absorbed air, and delivered itself very slowly, with eye turned inward.

"I am afraid—I don't think—I quite like my new dress."

"That is unfortunate."

"That would not matter; I never like anything till I have altered it; but here is Baldwin has just sent me word that her mother is dying, and she can't undertake any work for a week. Provoking! could not the woman die just as well after the ball?"

"Oh, aunt!"

"And my maid has no more taste than an owl. What on earth am I to do?"

"Wear another dress."

"What other can I?"

"Nothing can be prettier than your white mousseline de soie with the tartan trimming."

"No, I have worn that at four balls already; I won't be known by my colors, like a bird. I have made up my mind to wear the jaune, and I will, in spite of them all; that is, if I can find anybody who cares enough for me to try it on, and tell me what it wants." Lucy offered at once to go with her to her room and try it on.

"No—no—it is so cold there; we will do it here by the fire. You will find it in the large wardrobe, dear. Mind how you carry it. Lucy! lots of pins."

Mrs. Bazalgette then rang the bell, and told the servant to say she was out if anyone called, no matter who.

Meantime Lucy, impressed with the gravity of her office, took the dress carefully down from the pegs; and as it would have been death to crease it, and destruction to let its hem sweep against any of the inferior forms of matter, she came down the stairs and into the room holding this female weapon of destruction as high above her head as Judith waves the sword of Holofernes in Etty's immortal picture.

The other had just found time to loosen her dress and lock one of the doors. She now locked the other, and the rites began. Well!!??

"It fits you like a glove."

"Really? tell the truth now; it is a sin to tell a story—about a new gown. What a nuisance one can't see behind one!"

"I could fetch another glass, but you may trust my word, aunt. This point behind is very becoming; it gives distinction to the waist."

"Yes, Baldwin cuts these bodies better than Olivier; but the worst of her is, when it comes to the trimming you have to think for yourself. The woman has no mind; she is a pair of hands, and there is an end of her."

"I must confess it is a little plain, for one thing," said Lucy.

"Why, you little goose, you don't think I am going to wear it like this. No. I thought of having down a wreath and bouquet from Foster's of violets and heart's-ease—the bosom and sleeves covered with blond, you know, and caught up here and there with a small bunch of the flowers. Then, in the center heart's-ease of the bosom, I meant to have had two of my largest diamonds set —hush!"

The door-handle worked viciously; then came rap! rap! rap! rap!

"Tic—tic—tic; this is always the way. Who is there? Go away; you can't come here."

"But I want to speak to you. What the deuce are you doing?" said through the keyhole the wretch that owned the room in a mere legal sense.

"We are trying a dress. Come again in an hour."

"Confound your dresses! Who is we?"

"Lucy has got a new dress."

"Aunt!" whispered Lucy, in a tone of piteous expostulation.

"Oh, if it is Lucy. Well, good-by, ladies. I am obliged to go to London at a moment's notice for a couple of days. You will have done by when I come back, perhaps," and off went Bazalgette whistling, but not best pleased. He had told his wife more than once that the drawing-rooms and dining-rooms of a house are the public rooms, and the bedrooms the private ones.

Lucy colored with mortification. It was death to her to annoy anyone; so her aunt had thrust her into a cruel position.

"Poor Mr. Bazalgette!" sighed she.

"Fiddle de dee. Let him go, and come back in a better temper—set transparent; so then, backed by the violet, you know, they will imitate dewdrops to the life."

"Charming! Why not let Olivier do it for you, as poor Baldwin cannot?"

"Because Olivier works for the Claytons, and we should have that Emily Clayton out as my double; and as we visit the same houses—"

"And as she is extremely pretty—aunt, what a generalissima you are!"

"Pretty! Snub-nosed little toad. No, she is not pretty. But she is eighteen; so I can't afford to dress her. No. I see I shall have to moderate my views for this gown, and buy another dress for the flowers and diamonds. There, take it off, and let us think it calmly over. I never act in a hurry but I am sorry for it afterward—I mean in things of real importance." The gown was taken off in silence, broken only by occasional sighs from the sufferer, in whose heart a dozen projects battled fiercely for the mastery, and worried and sore perplexed her, and rent her inmost soul fiercely divers ways.

"Black lace, dear," suggested Lucy, soothingly.

Mrs. B. curled her arm lovingly round Lucy's waist. "Just what I was beginning to think," said she, warmly. "And we can't both be mistaken, can we? But where can I get enough?" and her countenance, that the cheering coincidence had rendered seraphic, was once more clouded with doubt.

"Why, you have yards of it."

"Yes, but mine is all made up in some form or other, and it musses one's things so to pick them to pieces."

"So it does, dear," replied Lucy, with gentle but genuine feeling.

"It would only be for one night, Lucy—I should not hurt it, love—you would not like to fetch down your Brussels point scarf, and see how it would look, would you? We need not cut the lace, dear; we could tack it on again the next morning; you are not so particular as I am—you look well in anything."

Lucy was soon seated denuding herself and embellishing her aunt. The latter reclined with grace, and furthered the work by smile and gesture.

"You don't ask me about the skirmish in the nursery."

"Their squabbles bore me, dear; but you can tell me who was the most in fault, if you think it worth while."

"Reginald, then, I am afraid; but it is not the poor boy; it is the influence of the stable-yard; and I do advise and entreat you to keep him out of it."

"Impossible, my dear; you don't know boys. The stable is their paradise. When he grows older his father must interfere; meantime, let us talk of something more agreeable."

"Yes; you shall go on with your story. You had got to his look of despair when your papa came in that morning."

"Oh, I have no time for anybody's despair just now; I can think of nothing but this detestable gown. Lucy, I suspect I almost wish I had made them put another breadth into the skirt."

"Luncheon, ma'am."

Lucy begged her aunt to go down alone; she would stay and work.

"No, you must come to luncheon; there is a dish on purpose for you—stewed eels."

"Eels; why, I abhor them; I think they are water-serpents."

"Who is it that is so fond of them, then?"

"It is you, aunt."

"So it is. I thought it had been you. Come, you must come down, whether you eat anything or not. I like somebody to talk to me while I am eating, and I had an idea just now—it is gone—but perhaps it will come back to me: it was about this abominable gown. O! how I wish there was not such a thing as dress in the world!!!"

While Mrs. Bazalgette was munching water-snakes with delicate zeal, and Lucy nibbling cake, came a letter. Mrs. Bazalgette read it with heightening color, laid it down, cast a pitying glance on Lucy, and said, with a sigh, "Poor girl!"

Lucy turned a little pale. "Has anything happened?" she faltered.

"Something is going to happen; you are to be torn away from here, where you are so happy—where we all love you, dear. It is from that selfish old bachelor. Listen: 'Dear madam, my niece Lucy has been due here three days. I have waited to see whether you would part with her without being dunned. My curiosity on that point is satisfied, and I have now only my affection to consult, which I do by requesting you to put her and her maid into a carriage that will be waiting for her at your door twenty-four hours after you receive this note. I have the honor to be, madam,' an old brute!!"

"And you can smile; but that is you all over; you don't care a straw whether you are happy or miserable."

"Don't I?"

"Not you; you will leave this, where you are a little queen, and go and bury yourself three months with that old bachelor, and nobody will ever gather from your face that you are bored to death; and here we are asked to the Cavendishes' next Wednesday, and the Hunts' ball on Friday—you are such a lucky girl—our best invitations always drop in while you are with us—we go out three times as often during your months as at other times; it is your good fortune, or the weather, or something."

"Dear aunt, this was your own arrangement with Uncle Fountain. I used to be six months with each in turn till you insisted on its being three. You make me almost laugh, both you and Uncle Fountain; what do you see in me worth quarreling for?"

"I will tell you what he sees—a good little spiritless thing—"

"I am larger than you, dear."

"Yes, in body—that he can make a slave of—always ready to nurse him and his foe, or to put down your work and to take up his—to play at his vile backgammon."

"Piquet, please."

"Where is the difference?—to share his desolation, and take half his blue devils on your own shoulders, till he will hyp you so that to get away you will consent to marry into his set—the county set—some beggarly old family that came down from the Conquest, and has been going down ever since; so then he will let you fly—with a string: you must vegetate two miles from him; so then he can have you in to Backquette and write his letters: he will settle four hundred a year on you, and you will be miserable for life."

"Poor Uncle Fountain, what a schemer he turns out!"

"Men all turn out schemers when you know them, Miss Impertinence. Well, dear, I have no selfish views for you. I love my few friends too single-heartedly for that; but I am sad when I see you leaving us to go where you are not prized."

"Indeed, aunt, I am prized at Font Abbey. I am overrated there as I am here. They all receive me with open arms."

"So is a hare when it comes into a trap," said Mrs. Bazalgette, sharply, drawing upon a limited knowledge of grammar and field-sports.

"No—Uncle Fountain really loves me."

"As much as I do?" asked the lady, with a treacherous smile.

"Very nearly," was the young courtier's reply. She went on to console her aunt's unselfish solicitude, by assuring her that Font Abbey was not a solitude; that dinners and balls abounded, and her uncle was invited to them all.

"You little goose, don't you see? all those invitations are for your sake, not his. If we could look in on him now we should find him literally in single cursedness. Those county folks are not without cunning. They say beauty has come to stay with the beast; we must ask the beast to dinner, so then beauty will come along with him.

"What other pleasure awaits you at Font Abbey?"

"The pleasure of giving pleasure," replied Lucy, apologetically.

"Ah! that is your weakness, Lucy. It is all very well with those who won't take advantage; but it is the wrong game to play with all the world. You will be made a tool of, and a slave of, and use of. I speak from experience. You know how I sacrifice myself to those I love; luckily, they are not many."

"Not so many as love you, dear."

"Heaven forbid! but you are at the head of them all, and I am going to prove it —by deeds, not words."

Lucy looked up at this additional feature in her aunt's affection.

"You must go to the great bear's den for three months, but it shall be the last time!" Lucy said nothing.

"You will return never to quit us, or, at all events, not the neighborhood."

"That—would be nice," said the courtier warmly, but hesitatingly; "but how will you gain uncle's consent?"

"By dispensing with it."

"Yes; but the means, aunt?"

"A husband!"

Lucy started and colored all over, and looked askant at her aunt with opening eyes, like a thoroughbred filly just going to start all across the road. Mrs. Bazalgette laid a loving hand on her shoulder, and whispered knowingly in her ear: "Trust to me; I'll have one ready for you against you come back this time."

"No, please don't! pray don't!" cried Lucy, clasping her hands in feeble-minded distress.

"In this neighborhood—one of the right sort."

"I am so happy as I am."

"You will be happier when you are quite a slave, and so I shall save you from being snapped up by some country wiseacre, and marry you into our own set."

"Merchant princes," suggested Lucy, demurely, having just recovered her breath and what little sauce there was in her.

"Yes, merchant princes—the men of the age—the men who could buy all the acres in the country without feeling it—the men who make this little island great, and a woman happy, by letting her have everything her heart can desire."

"You mean everything that money can buy."

"Of course. I said so, didn't I?"

"So, then, you are tired of me in the house?" remonstrated Lucy, sadly.

"No, ingrate; but you will be sure to marry soon or late."

"No, I will not, if I can possibly help it."

"But you can't help it; you are not the character to help it. The first man that comes to you and says: 'I know you rather dislike me' (you could not hate anybody, Lucy,) 'but if you don't take me I shall die of a broken fiddlestick,' you will whine out, 'Oh, dear! shall you? Well, then, sooner than disoblige you, here—take me!'"

"Am I so weak as this?" asked Lucy, coloring, and the water coming into her eyes.

"Don't be offended," said the other, coolly; "we won't call it weakness, but excess of complaisance; you can't say no to anybody."

"Yet I have said it," replied Lucy, thoughtfully.

"Have you? When? Oh, to me. Yes; where I am concerned you have sometimes a will of your own, and a pretty stout one; but never with anybody else."

The aunt then inquired of the niece, "frankly, now, between ourselves," whether she had no wish to be married. The niece informed her in confidence that she had not, and was puzzled to conceive how the bare idea of marriage came to be so tempting to her sex. Of course, she could understand a lady wishing to marry, if she loved a gentleman who was determined to be unhappy without her; but that women should look about for some hunter to catch instead of waiting quietly till the hunter caught them, this puzzled her; and as for the superstitious love of females for the marriage rite in cases when it took away their liberty and gave them nothing amiable in return, it amazed her. "So, aunt," she concluded, "if you really love me, driving me to the altar will be an unfortunate way of showing it."

While listening to this tirade, which the young lady delivered with great serenity, and concluded with a little yawn, Mrs. Bazalgette had two thoughts. The first was: "This girl is not flesh and blood; she is made of curds and whey, or something else;" the second was: "No, she is a shade hypocriticaler than other girls—before they are married, that is all;" and, acting on this latter conviction, she smiled a lofty incredulity, and fell to counting on her fingers all the moneyed bachelors for miles.

At this Lucy winced with sensitive modesty, and for once a shade of vexation showed itself on her lovely features. The quick-sighted, keen-witted matron caught it, and instantly made a masterly move of feigned retreat. "No," cried she, "I will not tease you anymore, love; just promise me not to receive any gentleman's addresses at Font Abbey, and I will never drive you from my arms to the altar."

"I promise that," cried Lucy, eagerly.

"Upon your honor?"

"Upon my honor."

"Kiss me, dear. I know you won't deceive me now you have pledged your honor. This solemn promise consoles me more than you can conceive."

"I am so glad; but if you knew how little it costs me."

"All the better; you will be more likely to keep it," was the dry reply.

The conversation then took a more tender turn. "And so to-morrow you go! How dull the house will be without you! and who is to keep my brats in order now I have no idea. Well, there is nothing but meeting and parting in this world; it does not do to love people, does it? (ah!) Don't cry, love, or I shall give way; my desolate heart already brims over—no—now don't cry" (a little sharply); "the servants will be coming in to take away the things."

"Will you c—c—come and h—help me pack, dear?"

"Me, love? oh no! I could not bear the sight of your things put out to go away. I promised to call on Mrs. Hunt this afternoon; and you must not stop in all day yourself—I cannot let your health be sacrificed; you had better take a brisk walk, and pack afterward."

"Thank you, aunt. I will go and finish my drawing of Harrowden Church to take with me."

"No, don't go there; the meadows are wet. Walk upon the Hatton road; it is all gravel."

"Yes; only it is so ugly, and I have nothing to do that way."

"But I'll give you something to do," said Mrs. Bazalgette, obligingly. "You know where old Sarah and her daughter live—the last cottages on that road; I don't like the shape of the last two collars they made me; you can take them back, if you like, and lend them one of yours I admire so for a pattern."

"That I will, with pleasure."

"Shall you come back through the garden? If you don't—never mind; but, if you do, you may choose me a bouquet. The servants are incapable of a bouquet."

"I will; thank you, dear. How kind and thoughtful of you to give me something to occupy me now that I am a little sad." Mrs. Bazalgette accepted this tribute with a benignant smile, and the ladies parted.

The next morning a traveling-carriage, with four smoking post-horses, came wheeling round the gravel to the front door. Uncle Fountain's factotum got down from the dicky, packed Lucy's imperial on the roof, and slung a box below the dicky; stowed her maid away aft, arranged the foot-cushion and a shawl or two inside, and, half obsequiously, half bumptiously, awaited the descent of his fair charge.

Then, upstairs, came a sudden simultaneous attack of ardent lips, and a long, clinging embrace that would have graced the most glorious, passionate, antique love. Sculpture outdone, the young lady went down, and was handed into the carriage. Her ardent aunt followed presently, and fired many glowing phrases in at the window; and, just as the carriage moved, she uttered a single word quite quietly, as much as to say, Now, this I mean. This genuine word, the last Aunt Bazalgette spoke, had been, two hundred years before, the last word of Charles the First. Note the coincidences of history.

The two postboys lifted their whips level to their eyes by one instinct, the horses tightened the traces, the wheels ground the gravel, and Lucy was whirled away with that quiet, emphatic post-dict ringing in her ears,

Remember!

Font Hill was sixty miles off: they reached it in less than six hours. There was Uncle Fountain on the hall steps to receive her, and the comely housekeeper, Mrs. Brown, ducking and smiling in the background. While the servants were unpacking the carriage, Mr. Fountain took Lucy to her bedroom. Mrs. Brown had gone on before to see for the third time whether all was comfortable. There was a huge fire, all red; and on the table a gigantic nosegay of spring flowers, with smell to them all.

"Oh how nice, after a journey!" said Lucy, mowing down Uncle Fountain and Mrs. Brown with one comprehensive smile.

Mrs. Brown flamed with complacency.

"What!" cried her uncle; "I suppose you expected a black fire and impertinent apologies by way of substitute for warmth; a stuffy room, and damp sheets, roasted, like a woodcock, twenty minutes before use."

"No, uncle, dear, I expected every comfort at Font Abbey." Brown retired with a courtesy.

"Aha! What! you have found out that it is all humbug about old bachelors not knowing comfort? Do bachelors ever put their friends into damp sheets? No; that is the women's trick with their household science. Your sex have killed more men with damp sheets than ever fell by the sword."

"Yet nobody erects monuments to us," put in Lucy, slyly.

She missed fire. Uncle Fountain, like most Englishmen, could take in a pun by the ear, but wit only by the eye. "Do you remember when Mrs. Bazalgette put you into the linen sponge, and killed you?"

"Killed me?"

"Certainly, as far as in her lay. We can but do our best; well, she did hers, and went the right way to work."

"You see I survive."

"By a miracle. Dinner is at six."

"Very well, dear."

"Yes; but six in this house means sixty minutes after five and sixty minutes before seven. I mention this the first day because you are just come from a place where it means twenty minutes to seven; also let me observe that I think I have noticed soup and potatoes eat better hot than cold, and meat tastes nicer done to a turn than—"

"To a cinder?"

"Ha! ha! and come with an appetite, please."

"Uncle, no tyranny, I beg."

"Tyranny? you know this is Liberty Hall; only when I eat I expect my companion to-eat too; besides, there is nothing to be gained by humbug to-day. There will be only us two at dinner; and when I see young ladies fiddling with an asparagus head instead of eating their dinner, it don't fall into the greenhorn's notion—exquisite creature! all soul! no stomach! feeds on air, ideas, and quadrille music—no; what do you think I say?"

"Something flattering, I feel sure."

"On the contrary, something true. I say hypocrite! Been grubbing like a pig all day, so can't eat like a Christian at meal time; you can't humbug me."

"Alas! so I see. That decides me to be candid—and hungry."

"Well, I am off; I don't stick to my friends and bore them with my affairs like that egotistical hussy, Jane Bazalgette. I amuse myself, and leave them to amuse themselves; that is my notion of politeness. I am going to see my pigs fed, then into the village. I am building a new blacksmith's shop there (you must come and look at it the first thing to-morrow); and at six, if you want to find me—"

"I shall peep behind the soup-tureen."

"And there I shall be, if I am alive." At dinner the old boy threw himself into the work with such zeal that soon after the cloth was removed, from fatigue and repletion, he dropped asleep, with his shoulder toward Lucy, but his face instinctively turned toward the fire. Lucy crept away on tiptoe, not to disturb him.

In about an hour he bustled into the drawing-room, ordered tea, blew up the footman because the cook had not water boiling that moment, drank three cups, then brightened up, rubbed his hands, and with a cheerful, benevolent manner, "Now, Lucy," cried he, "come and help me puzzle out this tiresome genealogy."

A smile of warm assent from Lucy, and the old bachelor and the blooming Hebe were soon seated with a mountain of parchments by their side, and a tree spreading before them.

It was not a finite tree like an elm or an oak; no, it was a banyan tree; covered an acre, and from its boughs little suckers dropped to earth, and turned to little trees, and had suckers in their turn, and "confounded the confusion."

Uncle Fountain's happiness depended, pro tem, on proving that he was a sucker from the great bough of the Fontaines of Melton; and why? Because, this effected, he had only to go along that bough by an established pedigree to the great trunk of the Funteyns of Salle, and the first Funteyn of Salle was said to be (and this he hoped to prove true) great-grandson of Robert de Fontibus, son of John de Fonte.

Now Uncle Fountain could prove himself the shoot of George his father (a step at which so many pedigrees halt), who was the shoot of William, who was the shoot of Richard; but here came a gap of eighty years between him and that Fountain, younger son of Melton, to whom he wanted to hook on. Now the logic of women, children, and criticasters is a thing of gaps; they reason as marches a kangaroo; but to mathematicians, logicians, and genealogists, a link wanting is a chain broken. This blank then made Uncle Fountain miserable, and he cried out for help. Lucy came with her young eyes, her woman's patience, and her own complaisance. A great ditch yawned between a crocheteer and a rotten branch he coveted. Our Quinta Curtia flung herself, her eyesight, and her time into that ditch.

Twelve o'clock came, and found them still wallowing in modern antiquity.

"Bless me!" cried Mr. Fountain when John brought up the bed-candles, "how time flies when one is really employed."

"Yes, indeed, uncle;" and by a gymnastic of courtesy she first crushed and then so molded a yawn that it glided into society a smile.

"We have spent a delightful evening, Lucy."

"Thanks to you, uncle."

"I hope you will sleep well, child."

"I am sure I shall, dear," said she, sweetly and inadvertently.

CHAPTER II.

A LARGE aspiration is a rarity; but who has not some small ambition, none the less keen for being narrow—keener, perhaps? Mrs. Bazalgette burned to be great by dress; Mr. Fountain, member of a sex with higher aims, aspired to be great in the county.

Unluckily, his main property was in the funds. He had acres in ——shire; but so few that, some years ago, its lord lieutenant declined to make him an injustice of the peace. That functionary died, and on his death the mortified aspirant bought a coppice, christened it Springwood, and under cover of this fringe to his three meadows, applied to the new lord lieutenant as M'Duff approached M'Beth. The new man made him a magistrate; so now he aspired to be a deputy lieutenant, and attended all the boards of magistrates, and turnpike trusts, etc., and brought up votes and beer-barrels at each election, and, in, short, played all the cards in his pack, Lucy included, to earn that distinction.

We may as well confess that there lurked in him a half-unconscious hope that some day or other, in some strange collision or combination of parties, a man profound in county business, zealous in county interests, personally obnoxious to nobody, might drop into the seat of county member; and, if this should be, would not he have the sense to hold his tongue upon the noisy questions that waste Parliament's time, and the nation's; but, on the first of those periodical attacks to which the wretched landowner is subject, wouldn't he speak, and show the difference between a mere member of the Commons and a member for the county?

If anyone had asked this man plump which is the most important, England or ——shire, he would have certainly told you England; but our opinions are not the notions we repeat, and can defend by reasons or even by facts: our opinions are the notions we feel and act on.

Could you have looked inside Mr. Fountain's head, you would have seen ideas corresponding to the following diagrams:

[drawing]

Mr. Fountain courted the stomach of the county.

Without this, he knew, an angel could not reach its heart; and here one of his eccentricities broke out. He drew a line, in his dictatorial way, between dinner and feeding parties. "A dinner party is two rubbers. Four gentlemen and four ladies sit round a circular table; then each can hear what anyone says, and need not twist the neck at every word. Foraging parties are from fourteen to thirty, set up and down a plank, each separated from those he could talk to as effectually as if the ocean rolled between, and bawling into one person's ear amid the din of knives, forks, and multitude. I go to those long strings of noisy duets because I must, but I give society at home."

The county people had just strength of mind to like the old boy's sociable dinners, though not to imitate them, and an invitation from him was very rarely declined when Lucy was with him.

And she was in her glory. She could carry complaisance such a long way at Font Abbey—she was mistress of the house.

She listened with a wonderful appearance of interest to county matters, i.e., to minute scandal and infinitesimal politics; to the county cricket match and archery meeting; to the past ball and the ball to come. In the drawing-room, when a cold fit fell on the coterie, she would glide to one egotist after another, find out the monotope, and set the critter Peter's, the Place de Concorde, the Square of St. Mark, Versailles, the Alhambra, the Apollo Belvidere, the Madonna of the Chair, and all the glories of nature and the feats of art could not warm. So, then, the fine gentleman began to act—to walk himself out as a person who had seen and could give details about anything, but was exalted far above admiring anything (quel grand homme! rien ne peut lui plaire);and on this, while the women were gazing sweetly on him, and revering his superiority to all great impressions, and the men envying, rather hating, but secretly admiring him too, she who had launched him bent on him a look of soft pity, and abandoned him to admiration.

"Poor Mr. Talboys," thought she, "I fear I have done him an ill turn by drawing him out;" and she glided to her uncle, who was sitting apart, and nobody talking to him.

Mr. Talboys, started by Lucy, ambled out his high-pacing nil admirantem character, and derived a little quiet self-satisfaction. This was the highest happiness he was capable of; so he was not ungrateful to Miss Fountain, who had procured it him, and partly for this, partly because he had been kind to her and lent her a pony, he shook hands with her somewhat cordially at parting. As it happened, he was the last guest.

"You have won that, man's heart, Lucy," cried Mr. Fountain, with a mixture of surprise and pride.

Lucy made no reply. She looked quickly into his face to see if he was jesting.

"Writing, Lucy—so late?"

"Only a few lines, uncle. You shall see them; I note the more remarkable phenomena of society. I am recalling a conversation between three of our guests this evening, and shall be grateful for your opinion on it. There! Read it out, please."

Mrs. Luttrell. "We missed you at the archery meeting—ha! ha! ha!"

Mrs. Willis. "Mr. Willis would not let me go—he! he! he!"

Mrs. James. "Well, at all events—he! he!—you will come to the flower show."

Mrs. Willis. "Oh yes!—he! he!—I am so fond of flowers—ha! ha!"

Mrs. Luttrell. "So am I. I adore them—he! he!"

Mrs. Willis. "How sweetly Miss Malcolm sings—he! he!"

Mrs. Luttrell. "Yes, she shakes like a bird—ha! ha!"

Mrs. James. "A little Scotch accent though—he! he!"

Mrs. Luttrell. "She is Scotch—he! he!" (To John offering her tea.) "No more, thank you—he! he!"

Mrs. James. "Shall you go the Assize sermon?—ha! ha!"

Mrs. Willis. "Oh, yes—he! he!—the last was very dry—he! he! Who preaches it this term?—he!"

Mrs. James. "The Bishop—he! he!"

Mrs. Willis. "Then I shall certainly go; he is such a dear preacher—he! he!"

"Just tell me what is the precise meaning of 'ha! ha!' and what of 'he! he!'"

"The precise meaning? There you puzzle me, uncle."

"I mean, what do you mean by them?"

"Oh, I put 'ha! ha!' when they giggle, and 'he! he!' when they only chuckle."

"Then this is a caricature, my lady?"

"No, dear, you know I have no satire in me; it is taken down to the letter, and I fear I must trouble you for the solution."

"Well, the solution is, they are three fools."

"No, uncle, begging your pardon, they are not," replied Lucy, politely but firmly.

"Well, then, three d—d fools."

Lucy winced at the participle, but was two polite to lecture her elder. "They have not that excuse," said she; "they are all sensible women, who discharge the duties of life with discretion except society; and they can discriminate between grave and gay whenever they are not at a party; and as for Mrs. Luttrell, when she is alone with me she is a sweet, natural love."

"They cackled—at every word—like that—the whole evening!!??"

"Except when you told that funny story about the Irish corporal who was attacked by a mastiff, and killed him with his halberd, and, when he was reproached by his captain for not being content to repel so valuable an animal with the butt end of his lance, answered—ha! ha!"

"So, then, he answered 'Haw! haw!' did he?"

"Now, uncle! No; he answered, 'So I would, your arnr, if he had run at me with his tail!' Now, that was genuine wit, mixed with quite enough fun to make an intelligent person laugh; and then you told it so drolly—ha! ha!"

"They did not laugh at that?"

"Sat as grave as judges."

"And you tell me they are not fools."

"I must repeat, they have not that excuse. Perhaps their risibility had been exhausted. After laughing three hours a propos de rien, it is time to be serious out of place. I will tell you what they did laugh at, though. Miss Malcolm sang a song with a title I dare not attempt. There were two lines in it which I am going to mispronounce; but you are not Scotch, so I don't care for you, uncle, darling.

'He had but a saxpence; he break it in twa,

And he gave me the half o't when he gaed awa.'

"They laughed at that; a general giggle went round."

"Well, I must confess, I don't see much to laugh at in that, Lucy."

"It would be odd if you did, uncle, dear; why, it is pathetic."

"Pathetic? Oh, is it?"

"You naughty, cunning uncle, you know it is; it is pathetic, and almost heroic. Consider, dear: in a world where the very newspapers show how mercenary we all are, a poor young man is parted from his love. He has but one coin to go through the world with, and what does he do with it? Scheme to make the sixpence a crown, and to make the crown a pound? No; he breaks this one treasure in two, that both the poor things may have a silver token of love and a pledge of his return. I am sure, if the poet had been here, he would have been quite angry with us for laughing at that line."

"Keep your temper. Why, this is new from you, Lucy; but you women of sugar can all cauterize your own sex; the theme inspires you."

"Uncle, how dare you! Are you not afraid I shall be angry one of these days, dear!!? The gentlemen were equally concerned in this last enormity. Poor Jemmy, or Jammy, with his devotion and tenderness that soothed, and his high spirit that supported the weaker vessel, was as funny to our male as to our female guests—so there. I saw but one that understood him, and did not laugh at him."

"Talboys, for a pound."

"Mr. Talboys? no! You, dear uncle; you did not laugh; I noticed it with all a niece's pride."

"Of course I didn't. Can I hear a word these ladies mew? can I tell in what language even they are whining and miauling? I have given up trying this twenty years and more."

"I return to my question," said Lucy hastily.

"And I to my solution; your three graces are three d—d fools. If you can account for it in any other way, do."

"No, uncle dear. If you had happened to agree with me beforehand, I would; but as you do not, I beg to be excused. But keep the paper, and the next time listen to the talk and unmeaning laughter; you will find I have not exaggerated, and some day, dear, I will tell you how my mamma used to account for similar monstrosities in society."

"Here is a mysterious little toad. Well, Lucy, for all this you enjoyed yourself. I never saw you in better spirits."

"I am glad you saw that," said Lucy, with a languid smile.

"And how Talboys came out."

"He did," sighed Lucy.

Here the young lady lighted softly on an ottoman, and sank gracefully back with a weary-o'-the-world air; and when she had settled down like so much floss silk, fixing her eye on the ceiling, and doling her words out languidly yet thoughtfully—just above a whisper, "Uncle, darling," inquired she, "where are the men we have all heard of?"

"How should I know? What men?"

"Where are the men of sentiment, that can understand a woman, and win her to reveal her real heart, the best treasure she has, uncle dear?" She paused for a reply; none coming, she continued with decreasing energy:

"Where are the men of spirit? the men of action? the upright, downright men, that Heaven sends to cure us of our disingenuousness? Where are the heroes and the wits?" (an infinitesimal yawn); "where are the real men? And where are the women to whom such men can do homage without degrading themselves? where are the men who elevate a woman without making her masculine, and the women who can brighten and polish, and yet not soften the steel of manhood—tell me, tell me instantly," said she, with still greater languor and want of earnestness, and her eyes remained fixed on the ceiling in deep abstraction.

"They are all in this house at this moment," said Mr. Fountain, coolly.

"Who, dear? I fear I was not attending to you. How rude!!"

"Horrid. I say the men and women you inquire for are all in this house of mine;" and the old gentleman's eyes twinkled.

"Uncle! Heaven forgive you, and—oh, fie!"

"They are, upon my soul."

"Then they must be in some part of it I have not visited. Are they in the kitchen?" (with a little saucy sneer.)

"No, they are in the library."

"In the lib—Ah! le malin!"

"They were never seen in the drawing-room, and never will be."

"Yet surely they must have lived in nature before they were embalmed in print," said Lucy, interrogating the ceiling again.

"The nearest approach you will meet to these paragons is Reginald Talboys," said Fountain, stoutly.

"Uncle, I do love you;" and Lucy rose with Juno-like slowness and dignity, and, leaning over the old boy, kissed him with sudden small fury.

"Why?" asked he, eagerly, connecting this majestic squirt of affection with his last speech.

"Because you are such a nice, dear, sarcastic thing. Let us drink tea in the library to-morrow, then that will be an approach to—"

With this illegitimate full stop the conversation ended, and Miss Fountain took a candle and sauntered to bed.

In church next Sunday Lucy observed a young lady with a beaming face, who eyed her by stealth in all the interstices of devotion. She asked her uncle who was that pretty girl with a nez retrousse.

"A cocked nose? It must be my little friend, Eve Dodd. I didn't know she was come back."

"What a pretty face to be in such—such a—such an impossible bonnet. It has come down from another epoch." This not maliciously, but with a sort of tender, womanly concern for beauty set off to the most disadvantage.

"O, hang her bonnet! She is full of fun; she shall drink tea with us; she is a great favorite of mine."

They quickened their pace, and caught Eve Dodd just as she took a flying leap over some water that lay in her path, and showed a charming ankle. In those days female dress committed two errors that are disappearing: it revealed the whole foot by day, and hid a section of the bosom at night.

After the usual greetings, Mr. Fountain asked Eve if she would come over and drink tea with him and his niece.

Miss Dodd colored and cast a glance of undisguised admiration at Miss Fountain, but she said: "Thank you, sir; I am much obliged, but I am afraid I can't come. My brother would miss me."

"What—the sailor? Is he at home?"

"Yes, sir; came home last night"; and she clapped her hands by way of comment. "He has been with my mother all church-time; so now it is my turn, and I don't know how to let him out of my sight yet awhile." And she gave a glance at Miss Fountain, as much as to say, "You understand."

"Well, Eve," said Mr. Fountain good-humoredly, "we must not separate brother and sister," and he was turning to go.

"Perhaps, uncle," said Lucy, looking not at Mr. Fountain, but at Eve—"Mr.—Mr.—"

"David Dodd is my brother's name," said Eve, quickly.

"Mr. David Dodd might be persuaded to give us the pleasure of his company too."

"Oh yes, if I may bring dear David with me," burst out the child of nature, coloring again with pleasure.

"It will add to the obligation," said Lucy, finishing the sentence in character.

"So that is settled," said Mr. Fountain, somewhat dryly.

As they were walking home together, the courtier asked her uncle rather coldly, "Who are these we have invited, dear?"

"Who are they? A pretty girl and a man she wouldn't come without."

"And who is the gentleman? What is he?"

"A marine animal—first mate of a ship."

"First mate? mate? Is that what in the novels is called boatswain's mate?"

"Haw! haw! haw! I say, Lucy, ask him when he comes if he is the bosen's mate. How little Eve will blaze!"

"Then I shall ask him nothing of the kind. Do tell me! I know admirals—they swear—and captains, and, I think, lieutenants, and, above all, those little loves of midshipmen, strutting with their dirks and cocked hats, like warlike bantams, but I never met 'mates.' Mates?"

"That is because you have only been introduced to the Royal Navy; but there is another navy not so ornamental, but quite as useful, called the East India Company's."

"I am ashamed to say I never heard of it."

"I dare say not. Well, in this navy there are only two kinds of superior officers —the mates and the captain. There are five or six mates. Young Dodd has been first mate some time, so I suppose he will soon be a captain."

"Uncle!"

"Well."

"Will this—mate—swear?"

"Clearly."

"There, now. I do not like swearing on a Sunday. That wicked old admiral used to make me shudder."

"Oh," said Mr. Fountain, playing upon innocence, "he swore by the Supreme Being, 'I bet sixpence.'"

"Yes," said Lucy, in a low, soft voice of angelic regret.

"Ah! he was in the Royal Navy. But this is a merchantman; you don't think he will presume to break into the monopoly of the superior branch. He will only swear by the wind and weather. Thunder and squalls! Donner and blitzen! Handspikes and halyards! these are the innocent execrations of the merchant service—he! he! ho!"

"Uncle, can you be serious?" asked Lucy, somewhat coldly; "if so, be so good as to tell me, is this gentleman—a—gentleman?"

"Well," replied the other, coolly, "he is what I call a nondescript; like an attorney, or a surgeon, or a civil engineer, or a banker, or a stock-broker, and all that sort of people. He can be a gentleman if he is thoroughly bent on it; you would in his place, and so should I; but these skippers don't turn their mind that way. Old families don't go into the merchant service. Indeed, it would not answer. There they rise by—by—mere maritime considerations."

"Then, uncle," began Lucy, with dignified severity, "permit me to say that, in inviting a nondescript, you showed—less consideration for me than—you— are in the habit—of doing, dearest."

"Well, have a headache, and can't come down."

"So I certainly should; but, most unfortunately, I have an objection to tell fibs on a Sunday."

"You are quite right; we should rest from our usual employments one day-ha! ha! and so go at it fresher to-morrow—haw! ho! Come, Lucy, don't you be so exclusive. Eve Dodd is a merry girl. She comes and amuses me when you are not here, and David, by all accounts, is a fine young fellow, and as modest as a girl of fifteen; they will make me laugh, especially Eve, and it would be hard at my age, I think, if I might not ask whom I like—to tea."

"So it would," put in Lucy, hastily; she added, coaxing, "it shall have its own way—it shall have what makes it laugh."

Long before eight o'clock the Fountains had forgotten that they had invited the Dodds.

Not so Eve. She was all in a flutter, and hesitated between two dresses, and by some blessed inspiration decided for the plainest; but her principal anxiety was, not about herself, but about David's deportment before the Queen of Fashion, for such report proclaimed Miss Fountain. "And those fine ladies are so satirical," said Eve to herself; "but I will lecture him going along."

Dinner time, and, by consequence, tea time, came earlier in those days; so, about eight o'clock, a tall, square-shouldered young fellow was walking in the moonlight toward Font Abbey, Eve holding his hand, and tripping by his side, and lecturing him on deportment very gravely while dancing around him and pulling him all manner of ways, like your solid tune with your gamboling accompaniment, a combination now in vogue. All of a sudden, without with your leave or by your leave, the said David caught this light fantastic object up in his arms, and carried it on one shoulder.

On this she gave a little squeak; then, without a moment's interval, continued her lecture as if nothing had happened. She looked down from her perch like a hen from a ladder, and laid down the law to David with seriousness and asperity.

"And just please to remember that they are people a long way above us—at least above what we are now, since father fell into trouble; so don't you make too free; and Miss Fountain is the finest of all the fine ladies in the county."

"Then I am sorry we are going."

"No, you are not; she is a beautiful girl."

"That alters the case."

"No, it does not. Don't chatter so, David, interrupting forever, but listen and mind what I say, or I'll never take you anywhere again."

"Are you sure you are taking me now?" asked David, dryly.

"Why not, Mr. David?" retorted Eve, from his shoulder. "Didn't I hear you tell how you took the Combermere out of harbor, and how you brought her into port; she didn't take you out and bring you home, eh?"

"Had me there, though."

"Yes; and, what is more, you are not skipper of the Combermere yet, and never will be; but I am skipper of you."

"Ashore—not a doubt of it," said David, with cool indifference. He despised terrestrial distinction, courting only such as was marine.

"Then I command you to let me down this instant. Do you hear, crew!"

"No," objected David; "if I put you overboard you can't command the vessel, and ten to one if the craft does not founder for want of seawomanship on the quarterdeck. However," added he, in a relenting tone, "wait till we get to that puddle shining on ahead, and then I'll disembark you."

"No, David, do let me down, that's a good soul. I am tired," added she, peevishly.

"Tired! of what?"

"Of doing nothing, stupid; there, let me down, dear; won't you, darling! then take that, love" (a box of the ear).

"Well, I've got it," said David, dryly.

"Keep it, then, till the next. No, he won't let me down. He has got both my hands in one of his paws, and he will carry me every foot of the way now—I know the obstinate pig."

"We all have our little characters, Eve. Well, I have got your wrists, but you have got your tongue, and that is the stronger weapon of the two, you know; and you are on the poop, so give your orders, and the ship shall be worked accordingly; likewise, I will enter all your remarks on good-breeding into my log."

Here, unluckily, David tapped his forehead to signify that the log in question was a metaphorical one, the log of memory. Eve had him again directly. She freed a claw. "So this is your log, is it?" cried she, tapping it as hard as she could; "well, it does sound like wood of some sort. Well, then, David, dear— you wretch, I mean—promise me not to laugh loud."

"Well, I will not; it is odds if I laugh at all. I wish we were to moor alongside mother, instead of running into this strange port."

"Stuff! think of Miss Fountain's figure-head—nor tell too many stories—and, above all, for heaven's sake, do keep the poor dear old sea out of sight for once."

"Ay, ay, that stands to reason."

By this time they were at Font Abbey, and David deposited his fair burden gently on the stone steps of the door. She opened it without ceremony, and bustled into the dining-room, crying, "I have brought David, sir; and here he is;" and she accompanied David's bow with a corresponding movement of her hand, the knuckles downward.

The old gentleman awoke with a start, rubbed his eyes, shook hands with the pair, and proposed to go up to Lucy in the drawing-room.

Now, it happened unluckily that Miss Fountain had been to the library and taken down one or two of those men and women who, according to her uncle, exist only on paper, and certain it is she was in charming company when she heard her visitors' steps and voices coming up the stairs. Had those visitors seen the vexed expression of her face as she laid down the book they would have instantly 'bout ship and home again; but that sour look dissolved away as they came through the open door.

On coming in they saw a young lady seated on a sofa.

Apparently she did not see them enter. Her face happened to be averted; but, ere they had taken three steps, she turned her face, saw them, rose, and took two steps to meet them, all beaming with courtesy, kindness and quiet satisfaction at their arrival.

She gave her hand to Eve.

"This is my brother, Miss Fountain."

Miss Fountain instantly swept David a courtesy with such a grace and flow, coupled with an engaging smile, that the sailor was fascinated, and gazed instead of bowing.

Eve had her finger ready to poke him, when he recovered himself and bowed low.

Eve played the accompaniment with her hand, knuckles down.

They sat down. Cups of tea, etc., were brought round to each by John. It was bad tea, made out of the room. Catch a human being making good tea in which it is not to share.

Mr. Fountain was only half awake.

Eve was more or less awed by Lucy. David, tutored by Eve, held his tongue altogether, or gave short answers.

"This must be what the novels call a sea-cub!" thought Miss Fountain.

The friends, Propriety and Restraint, presided over the innocent banquet, and a dismal evening set in.

The first infraction of this polite tranquillity came, I blush to say, from the descendant of John de Fonte. He exploded in a yawn of magnitude; to cover this, the young lady began hastily to play her old game of setting people astride their topic, and she selected David Dodd for the experiment. She put on a warm curiosity about the sea, and ships, and the countries men visit in them. Then occurred a droll phenomenon: David flashed with animation, and began full and intelligent answers; then, catching his sister's eye, came to unnatural full stops; and so warmly and skillfully was he pressed that it cost him a gigantic effort to avoid giving much amusement and instruction. The courtier saw this hesitation, and the vivid flashes of intelligence, and would not lose her prey. She drew him with all a woman's tact, and with a warmth so well feigned that it set him on real fire. His instinct of politeness would not let him go on all night giving short answers to inquiring beauty. He turned his eye, which glowed now like a live coal, toward that enticing voice, and presently, like a ship that has been hanging over the water ever so long on the last rollers, with one gallant glide he took the sea, and towed them all like little cockle-boats in his wake. From sea to sea, from port to port, from tribe to tribe, from peril to peril, from feat to feat, David whirled his wonderstruck hearers, and held them panting by the quadruple magic of a tuneful voice, a changing eye, an ardent soul, and truth at first-hand.

They sat thrilled and surprised, most of all Miss Fountain. To her, things great and real had up to that moment been mere vague outlines seen through a mist. Moreover, her habitual courtesy had hitherto drawn out pumps; but now, when least expected, all in a moment, as a spark fires powder, it let off a man.

A sailor is a live book of travels. Check your own vanity (if you possibly can) and set him talking, you shall find him full of curious and profitable matter.

The Fountains did not know this, and, even if they had, Dodd would have taken them by surprise; for, besides being a sailor and a sea-enthusiast, he was a fellow of great capacity and mental vigor.

He had not skimmed so many books as we have, but I fear he had sucked more. However, his main strength did not lie there. He was not a paper man, and this—oh! men of paper and oh! C. R. in particular—gave him a tremendous advantage over you that Sunday evening.

The man whose knowledge all comes from reading accumulates a great number of what?—facts? No, of the shadows of facts; shadows often so thin, indistinct and featureless, that, when one of the facts themselves runs against him in real life, he does not know his old friend, round about which he has written a smart leader in a journal and a ponderous trifle in the Polysyllabic Review.

But this sailor had stowed into his mental hold not fact-shadows, but the glowing facts all alive, O. For thirteen years, man and boy, he had beat about the globe, with real eyes, real ears, and real brains ever at work. He had drunk living knowledge like a fish, and at fountainheads.

Yet, to utter intellectual wealth nobly, two things more are indispensable the gift of language and a tunable voice, which last does not always come by talking with tempests.

Well, David Dodd had sucked in a good deal of language from books and tongues; not, indeed, the Norman-French and demi-Latin and jargon of the schools, printed for English in impotent old trimestrials for the further fogification of cliques, but he had laid by a fair store of the best—of the monosyllables—the Saxon—the soul and vestal fire of the great English tongue.

So he was never at a loss for words, simple, clear, strong, like blasts of a horn.

His voice at this period was mellow and flexible. He was a mimic, too; the brighter things he had seen, whether glories of nature or acts of man, had turned to pictures in this man's mind. He flashed these pictures one after another upon the trio; he peopled the soft and cushioned drawing-room with twenty different tribes and varieties of man, barbarous, semi-barbarous, and civilized; their curious customs, their songs and chants, and dances, and struts, and actual postures.

The aspect of famous shores from the sea, glittering coasts, dark straits, volcanic rocks defying sea and sky, and warm, delicious islands clothed with green, that burst on the mariner's sight after rugged places and scowling skies.

The adventures of one unlucky ship, the Connemara, on a single whaling cruise on the coast of Peru. The first slight signs of a gale, seen only by the careful skipper. The hasty preparations for it: all hands to shorten sail; then the moaning of the wind high up in the sky. All hands to reef sail now—the whirl and whoo of the gale as it came down on them. The ship careening as it caught her, the speaking-trumpet—the captain howling his orders through it amid the tumult.

The floating icebergs—the ship among them, picking her way in and out a hundred deaths. Baffled by the unyielding wind off Cape Horn, sailing six weeks on opposite tacks, and ending just where they began, weather-bound in sight of the gloomy Horn. Then the terrors of a land-locked bay, and a lee shore; the ship tacking, writhing, twisting, to weather one jutting promontory; the sea and safety is on the other side of it; land and destruction on this—the attempt, the hope, the failure; then the stout-hearted, skillful captain would try one rare maneuver to save the ship, cargo, and crew. He would club-haul her, "and if that fails, my lads, there is nothing but up mainsail, up helm, run her slap ashore, and lay her bones on the softest bit of rock we can pick."

Long ere this the poor ship had become a live thing to all these four, and they hung breathless on her fate.

Then he showed how a ship is club-hauled, and told how nobly the old Connemara behaved (ships are apt to when well handled—double-barreled guns ditto), and how the wind blew fiercer, and the rocks seemed to open their mouths for her, and how she hung and vibrated between safety and destruction, and at last how she writhed and slipped between Death's lips, yet escaped his teeth, and tossed and tumbled in triumph on the great but fair fighting sea; and how they got at last to the whaling ground, and could not find a whale for many a weary day, and the novices said: "They were all killed before we sailed;" and how, as uncommon ill luck is apt to be balanced by uncommon good luck, one fine evening they fell in with a whole shoal of whales at play, jumping clean into the air sixty feet long, and coming down each with a splash like thunder; even the captain had never seen such a game; and how the crew were for lowering the boats and going at them, but the captain would not let them; a hundred playful mountains of fish, the smallest weighing thirty ton, flopping down happy-go-lucky, he did not like the looks of it.

"The boat will be at the mercy of chance among all those tails, and we are not lucky enough to throw at random. No; since the beggars have taken to dancing, for a change, let them dance all night; to-morrow they shall pay the piper." How, at peep of day, the man at the mast-head saw ten whales about two leagues off on the weather-bow; how the ship tacked and stood toward them; how she weathered on one of monstrous size, and how he and the other youngsters were mad to lower the boat and go after it, and how the captain said: "Ye lubbers, can't ye see that is a right whale, and not worth a button? Look here away over the quarter at this whale. See how low she spouts. She is a sperm whale, and worth seven hundred pounds if she was only dead and towed alongside."

"'That she shall be in about a minute,' cried one; and, indeed, we were all in a flame; the boat was lowered, and didn't I worship the skipper when he told me off to be one of her crew!

"I was that eager to be in at that whale's death, I didn't recollect there might be smaller brutes in danger.

"Just before the oars fell into the water, the skipper looked down over the bulwarks, and says he to one of us that had charge of the rope that is fast to the boat at one end and to the harpoon at the other, 'Now, Jack you are a new hand; mind all I told you last night, or your mother will see me come ashore without you, and that will vex her; and, my lads, remember, if there is a single lubberly hitch in that line, you will none of you come up the ship's side again.'

"'All right, captain,' says Jack, and we pulled off singing,

"'And spring to your oars, and, make your boat fly,

And when you come near her beware of her eye,'

till the coxswain bade us hold our lubberly tongues, and not frighten the whales; however, we soon found we wanted all our breath for our work, and more too." Then David painted the furious race after the whale, and how the boat gradually gained, and how at last, as he was grinding his teeth and pulling like mad, he heard a sound ahead like a hundred elephants wallowing; and now he hoped to see the harpooner leave his oar, and rise and fling his weapon; "but that instant, up flukes, a tower of fish was seen a moment in the air, with a tail-fin at the top of it just about the size of this room we are sitting in, ladies, and down the whale sounded; then it was pull on again in her wake, according as she headed in sounding; pull for the dear life; and after a while the oarsmen saw the steerman's eyes, prying over the sea, turn like hot coals. The men caught fire at this, and put their very backbones into each stroke, and the boat skimmed and flew. Suddenly the steersman cried out fiercely, 'Stand up, harpoon! Up rose the harpooner, his eye like a hot coal now. The men saw nothing; they must pull fiercer than ever. The harpooner balanced his iron, swayed his body lightly, and the harpoon hissed from him. A soft thud—then a heaving of the water all round, a slap that sounded like a church tower falling flat upon an acre of boards, and drenched, and blinded, and half smothered us all in spray, and at the same moment away whirled the boat, dancing and kicking in the whale's foaming, bubbling wake, and we holding on like grim death by the thwarts, not to be spun out into the sea."

"Delightful!" cried Miss Fountain; "the waves bounded beneath you like a steed that knows its rider. Pray continue."

"Yes, Miss Fountain. Now of course you can see that, if the line ran out too easy, the whale would leave us astern altogether, and if it jammed or ran too hard, she would tow us under water."

"Of course we see," said Eve, ironically; "we understand everything by instinct. Hang explanations when I'm excited; go ahead, do!"

"Then I won't explain how it is or why it is, but I'll just let you know that two or three hundred fathom of line are passed round the boat from stem to stern and back, and carried in and out between the oarsmen as they sit. Well, it was all new to me then; but when the boat began jumping and rocking, and the line began whizzing in and out, and screaming and smoking like—there now, fancy a machine, a complicated one, made of poisonous serpents, the steam on, and you sitting in the middle of the works, with not an inch to spare, on the crankest, rockingest, jumpingest, bumpingest, rollingest cradle that ever—"

"David!" said Eve, solemnly.

"Hallo!" sang out David.

"Don't!"

"Oh, yes, do!" cried Lucy, slightly clasping her hands.

"If this little black ugly line was to catch you, it would spin you out of the boat like a shuttlecock; if it held you, it would cut you in two, or hang you to death, or drown you all at one time; and if it got jammed against anything alive or dead that could stand the strain, it would take the boat and crew down to the coral before you could wink twice."

"Oh, dear!" said Lucy; "then I don't think I like it now; it is too terrible. Pray go on, Mr.—Mr.—"

"Well, Miss Fountain, when a novice like me saw this black serpent twisting and twirling, and smoking and hissing in and out among us, I remembered the skipper's words, and I hailed Jack—it was he had laid the line—he was in the bow.

"'Jack,' said I.

"'Hallo!' said he.

"'For God's sake, are there any hitches in the line?' said I.

"'Not as I knows on,' says he, much cooler than you sit there; and that is a sailor all over. Well, she towed us about a mile, and then she was blown, and we hauled up on the line, and came up with her, and drove lances into her, till she spouted blood instead of salt water, and went into her flurry, and rolled suddenly over our way dead, and was within a foot of smashing us to atoms; but if she had it would only have been an accident, for she was past malice, poor thing. Then we took possession, planted our flagstaff in her spouting-hole, you know, and pulled back to the ship, and she came down and anchored to the whale, and then, for the first time, I saw the blubber stripped off a whale and hoisted by tackles into the ship's hold, which is as curious as any part of the business, but a dirtyish job, and not fit for the present company, and I dare say that is enough about whales."

"No! no! no!"

"Well, then, shall I tell you how one old whale knocked our boat clean into the air, bottom uppermost, and how we swam round her and managed to right her?"

"And went back to the ship and had your tea in bed and your clothes dried?"

"No, Eve," replied David, with the utmost simplicity; "we got in and to work again, and killed the whale in less than half an hour, and planted our flag on her, and away after another."

Then he told them how they harpooned one right whale, and by good luck were able to make her fast to the stern of the ship. "And, if you will believe me, Miss Fountain, though there was just a breath on and off right aft, and the foresail, jib and mizzen all set to catch it, she towed the ship astern a good cable's length, and the last thing was she broke the harpoon shaft just below the line, and away she swam right in the wind's eye."

"And there was an end of her and your nasty, cruel, harpoon, and—oh, I'm so pleased!"

"No, there wasn't, Eve; we heard of both fish and harpoon again, but not for a good many years."

"Mr. Dodd!"

"Yes, Miss Fountain. It is curious, like many things that fall out at sea, but not so wonderful as her towing a ship of four hundred tons, with the foresail, mizzen, and jib all aback. Well, sir, did you ever hear of Nantucket? It is a port in the United States; and our harpooner happened to be there full four years after we lost this whale. Some Yankee whalers were treating him to the best of grog, and it was brag Briton, brag Yankee, according to custom whenever these two met. Well, our man had no more invention than a stone; so he was getting the worst of it till he bethought him of this whale; so he up and told how he had struck a right whale in the Pacific, and she had towed the ship with her sails aback, at least her foresail, mizzen, and jib, only he didn't tell it short like me, but as long as the Red Sea, with the day and the hour, the latitude (within four or five degrees, I take it), and what we had done a week before, and what we had not done, all by way of prologue, and for fear of weathering the horn—tic, tic—the point of the story too soon. When he had done there was a general howl of laughter, and they began to cap lies with him, and so they bantered him most cruelly, by all accounts; but at last a long silent chap, weather-beaten to the color of rosewood, put in his word.

"'What was the ship's name, mate?'

"'The Connemara,' says he.

"'And what is your name?' So he told him, 'Jem Green.'

"The other brings a great mutton fist down on the table, and makes all the glasses dance. 'You stay at your moorings till I come back,' says he. 'I have got something belonging to you, Jem Green,' and he sheered off. The others lay to and passed the grog. Presently the long one comes back with a harpoon steel in his hand; there was Connemara stamped on it, and also 'James Green' graved with a knife. 'Is that yours?' 'Is my hand mine?' says Jem; 'but wasn't there a broken shaft to it!"

"'There was,' says the Yankee harpooner; 'I cut it out.'

"'Well!' says Jem, 'that is the harpoon we were fast by to this very whale. Where did you kill her?'

"'In the Greenland seas.' And he whips out his private log. 'Here you are,' says he; 'March 25, 1820, latitude so and so, killed a right whale; lost half the blubber, owing to the carcass sinking; cut an English harpoon out of her.'

"'Avast there, mate!' cried Jem, and he whips, out his log; 'overhaul that.' The other harpooner overhauled it. 'Mates, look, here,' says he; 'I reckon we hain't fathomed the critters yet. The Britisher struck her in the Pacific on the 5th of March, and we killed her off Greenland on the 25th, five thousand miles of water by the lowest reckoning.' By this time there were a dozen heads jammed together, like bees swarming, over the two logs. 'She got a wound in the Pacific! "Hallo!" says she; "this is no sea for a lady to live in;" so she up helm, and right away across the pole into the Atlantic, and met her death.'"

"Your story has an interest you little suspect, young gentleman. If this is true, the northwest passage is proved."

"That has been proved a hundred times, sir, and in a hundred ways; the only riddle is to find it. The man that tells you there is not a northwest passage is no sailor, and the fish that can't find it is not a whale; for there is not a young suckling no bigger than this room that does not know that passage as well as a mid on his first voyage knows the way to the mizzen-top through lubber's hole. How tired you must be of whales, ladies?"

"Oh no."

"Kill us one more, David. I love bloodshed—to hear of."

"Well, now, I don't think that can be Miss Fountain's taste, to look at her."

Then David told them how he had fallen in with a sperm whale, dead of disease, floating as high as a frigate; how, with a very light breeze, the skipper had crept down toward her; how, at half a mile distance the stench of her was severe, but, as they neared her, awful; then so intolerable that the skipper gave the crew leave to go below and close the lee ports. So there were but two men left on the brig's deck, and a ship's company that a hurricane would not have driven from their duty skulked before a foul smell; but such a smell! a smell that struck a chill and a loathing to the heart, and soul, and marrow-bone; a smell like the gases in a foul mine; "it would have suffocated us in a few moments if we had been shut up along with it." Then he told how the skipper and he stuffed their noses and ears with cotton steeped in aromatic vinegar, and their mouths with pig-tail (by which, as it subsequently appeared, Lucy understood pork or bacon in some form unknown to her narrow experience), and lighted short pipes, and breached the brig upon the putrescent monster, and grappled to it, and then the skipper jumped on it, a basket slung to his back, and a rope fast under his shoulders in case of accident, and drove his spade in behind the whale's side-fin."

"His spade, Mr. Dodd?"

"His whale-spade; it is as sharp as a razor;" and how the skipper dug a hole in the whale as big as a well and four feet deep, and, after a long search, gave a shout of triumph, and picked out some stuff that looked like Gloucester cheese; and, when he had nearly filled his basket with this stuff, he slacked the grappling-iron, and David hauled him on board, and the carcass dropped astern, and the captain sang out for rum, and drank a small tumbler neat, and would have fainted away, spite of his precautions, but for the rum, and how a heavenly perfume was now on deck fighting with that horrid odor; and how the crew smelled it, and crept timidly up one by one, and how "the Glo'ster cheese was a great favorite of yours, ladies. It was the king of perfumes— amber-gas; there is some of it in all your richest scents; and the knowing skipper had made a hundred guineas in the turn of the hand. So knowledge is wealth, you see, and the sweet can be got out of the sour by such as study nature."

"Don't preach, David, especially after just telling a fib. A hundred guineas!"

"I am wrong,'" said David.

"Very wrong, indeed."

"There were eight pounds; and he sold it at a guinea the ounce to a wholesale chemist, so that looks to me like 128 pounds."

Then David left the whales, and encouraged by bright eyes and winning smiles, and warm questions, sang higher strains.

Ships in dire distress at sea, yet saved by God's mercy, and the cool, invincible courage of captain and crew—great ships run ashore—the waves breaking them up—the rigging black with the despairing crew, eying the watery death that tumbled and gaped and roared for them below; and then little shore boats, manned by daring hearts, launched into the surf, and going out to the great ship and her peril, risking more life for the chance of saving life. And he did not present the bare skeletons of daring acts; those grand morgues, the journals, do that. There lie the dry bones of giant epics waiting Genius's hand to make them live. He gave them not only the broad outward facts—the bones; but those smaller touches that are the body and soul of a story, true or false, wanting which the deeds of heroes sound an almanac; above all, he gave them glimpses, not only of what men acted, but what they felt: what passed in the hearts of men perishing at sea, in sight of land, houses, fires on the hearth, and outstretched hands, and in the hearts of the heroes that ran their boats into the surf and Death's maw to save them, and of the lookers on, admiring, fearing, shivering, glowing, and of the women that sobbed and prayed ashore with their backs to the sea, just able to risk lover, husband, and son for the honor of manhood and the love of Christ, but not able to look on at their own flesh and blood diving so deep, and lost so long in cockle-shells between the hills of waves.

Such great acts, great feelings, great perils, and the gushes that crowned all of holy triumph when the boats came in with the dripping and saved, and man for a moment looked greater than the sea and the wind and death, this seaman poured hot from his own manly heart into quick and womanly bosoms, that heaved visibly, and glowed with admiring sympathy, and fluttered with gentle fear.

And after a while, though not at first, David's yarns began to contain a double interest to one of the party—Miss Fountain. Those who live to please get to read character at sight, and David, though in these more noble histories he scarcely named himself, was laying a full-length picture of his own mind bare to these keen feminine eyes. As for old Fountain, he was charmed, and saw nothing more than David showed him outright. But the women sat flashing secret intelligence backward and forward from eye to eye after the manner of their sex.

"Do you see?" said one lady's eyes.

"Yes," replied the other. "He was concerned in this feat, though he does not say so."

"Oh, you agree with me? Then we are right," replied the first pair of speakers.

"There again: look; this sailor, whom he describes as a fellow that happened to be ashore at that foreign port with nothing better to do, and who went out with the English smugglers to save the brig when the natives durst not launch a boat?"

"Himself! not a doubt of it."

And so the blue and hazel lightning went dancing to and fro; ay, even when the tale took a sorrowful turn, and dimmed these bright orbs of intelligence, the lightning struggled through the dew, and David was read and discussed by gleams, and glances, and flashes, without a word spoken. And he, all unconscious that he sat between a pair of telegraphs, and heating more and more under his great recollections and his hearers' sympathy, inthralled them with his tuneful voice, his glowing face, his lion eye, and his breathing, burning histories. Heart to dare and do, yet heart to feel, and brain and tongue to tell a deed well, are rare allies, yet here they met.

He mastered his hearers, and played on their breasts as David played the harp, and perhaps Achilles; Bochsa never, nor any of his tribe. He made the old man forget his genealogies, his small ambition, his gout, his years, and be a boy again an hour or two in thought, and blood, and early fire. He made the women's bosoms pant and swell, and seem to aspire to be the nests and cradles of heroes, and their eyes flash and glisten, and their cheeks flush and grow pale by turns; and the four little papered walls that confined them seemed to fall without noise, and they were away in thought out of a carpeted temple of wax, small talk, nonentity, and nonentities, away to sea-breezes that they almost felt in their hair and round their temples as their hearts rose and fell upon a broad swell of passion, perils, waves, male men, realities. The spell was at its height, when the sea-wizard's eye fell on the mantel-piece. Died in a moment his noble ardor: "Why, it is eight bells," said he, servilely; then, doggedly, "time to turn in."

"Hang that clock!" shouted Mr. Fountain; "I'll have it turned out of the room."

Said Lucy, with gentle enthusiasm, "It must be beautiful to be a sailor, and to have seen the real world, and, above all, to be brave and strong like Mr. ——,. must it not, uncle?" and she looked askant at David's square shoulders and lion eye, and for the first time in her life there crossed her an undefined instinct that this gentleman must be the male of her species.

"As for his courage," said Eve, "that we have only his own word for."

David grinned.

"Not even that," replied Lucy, "for I observed he spoke but little of himself."

"I did not notice that," said Eve, pertly; "but as for his strength, he certainly is as strong as a great bear, and as rude. What do you think? my lord carried me all the way from the top of the green lane to your house, and I am no feather."

"No, a skein of silk," put in David.

"I asked the gentleman politely to put me down, and he wouldn't, so then I boxed his ears."

"Oh, how could you?"

"Oh, bless you, he never hits me again; he is too great a coward. And the great mule carried me all the more—carried me to your very door."

"I almost think—I believe I could guess why he carried you, if you will not be offended at my assuming the interpreter," said Lucy, looking at Eve and speaking at David. "You have thin shoes on, Miss Dodd; now I remember the gravel ends at green lane, and the grass begins; so, from what we know of Mr. Dodd, perhaps he carried you that you might not have damp feet."

"Nothing of the kind—yes, it was, though, by his coloring up. La! David, dear boy!"

"What is a man alongside for but to keep a girl out of mischief?" said David, bruskly.

"Pray convert all your sex to that view," laughed Lucy.

So now they were going. Then Mr. Fountain thanked David for the pleasant evening he had given them; then David blushed and stammered. He had a veneration for old age—another of his superstitions.

Her uncle's lead gave Lucy an opportunity she instantly seized. "Mr. Dodd, you have taken us into a new world of knowledge; we never were so interested in our lives." At this pointblank praise David blushed, and was anything but comfortable, and began to back out of it all with a curt bow. Then, as the ladies can advance when a man of merit retreats, Lucy went the length of putting out her hand with a sweet, grateful smile; so he took it, and, in the ardor of encouraging so much spirit and modesty, she unconsciously pressed it. On this delicious pressure, light as it was, he raised his full brown eye, and gave her such a straightforward look of manly admiration and pleasure that she blushed faintly and drew back a little in her turn.

"Well, Davy, dear, how do you like the Fountains?"

"Eve, she is a clipper!"

"And the old gentleman?"

"He was very friendly. What do you think of her?"

"She is an out-and-out woman of the world, and very agreeable, as insincere people generally are. I like her because she was so polite to you."

"Oh, that is your reading of her, is it?"

The rest of the walk passed almost in silence.

"Uncle, I am not sleepy to-night."

"Who is? that young rascal has set me on fire with his yarns. Who would have thought that awkward cub had so much in him?"

"Awkward, but not a cub; say rather a black swan; and you know, uncle, a swan is an awkward thing on land, but when it takes the water it is glorious, and that man was glorious; but—Da—vid Do—dd."

"I don't know whether he was glorious, but I know he amused me, and I'll have him to tea three times a week while he lasts."

"Uncle, do you believe such an unfortunate combination of sounds is his real name?" asked Lucy, gravely.

"Why, who would be mad enough to feign such a name?"

"That is true; but now tell me—if he should ever, think of marrying with such a name?"

"Then there will be two David Dodd's in the world, Mr. and Mrs."

"I don't think so; he will be merciful, and take her name instead of she his; he is so good-natured."

"Ordinary sponsors would have been content with Samuel or Nathan; but no, this one's must, call in 'apt alliteration's artful aid,' and have the two 'd's.'"

Lucy assented with a smile, and so, being no longer under the spell of the enthusiast and the male, the genealogist and the fine lady took the rise out of what Miss Fountain was pleased to call his impossible title,

Da—vid Dodd.

CHAPTER III.

LUCY was not called on to write any more formal invitations to Mr. Talboys. Her uncle used merely to say to her: "Talboys dines with us to-day." She made no remark; she respected her uncle's preference; besides—the pony! Of these trios Mr. Fountain was the true soul. He had to blow the coals of conversation right and left. It is very good of me not to compare him to the Tropic between two frigid zones. At first he took his nap as usual; for he said to himself: "Now I have started them they can go on." Besides, he had seen pictures in the shop windows of an old fellow dozing and then the young ones "popping."

Dozing off with this idea uppermost, he used to wake with his eyes shut and his ears wide open; but it was to hear drowsy monosyllables dropping out at intervals like minute-guns, or to find Lucy gone and Talboys reading the coals. Then the schemer sighed, and took to strong coffee soon after dinner, and gave up his nap, and its loss impaired his temper the rest of the evening.

He indemnified himself for these sleepless dinners by asking David Dodd and his sister to tea thrice a week on the off-nights; this joyous pair amused the old gentleman, and he was not the man to deny himself a pleasure without a powerful motive.

"What, again so soon?" hazarded Lucy, one day that he bade her invite them. "I hardly know how to word my invitation; I have exhausted the forms."

"If you say another word, I'll make them come every night. Am I to have no amusement?" he added, in a deep tone of reproach; "they make me laugh."

"Ah! I forgot; forgive me."

"Little hypocrite; don't they you too, pray? Why, you are as dull as ditchwater the other evenings."

"Me, dear, dull with you?"

"Yes, Miss Crocodile, dull with a pattern uncle and his friend—and your admirer." He watched her to see how she would take this last word. Catch her taking it at all. "I am never dull with you, dear uncle," said she; "but a third person, however estimable, is a certain restraint, and when that person is not very lively—" Here the explanation came quietly to an untimely end, like those old tunes that finish in the middle or thereabouts.

"But that is the very thing; what do I ask them for to-night but to thaw Talboys?"

"To thaw Talboys? he! he!"

Lucy seemed so tickled by this expression that the old gentleman was sorry he had used it.

"I mean, they will make him laugh." Then, to turn it off, he said hastily, "And don't forget the fiddle, Lucy."

"Oh, yes, dear, please let me forget that, and then perhaps they may forget to bring it."

"Why, you pressed him to bring it; I heard you."

"Did I?" said Lucy, ruefully.

"I am sure I thought you were mad after a fiddle, you seconded Eve so warmly; so that was only your extravagant politeness after all. I am glad you are caught. I like a fiddle, so there is no harm done."

Yes, reader, you have hit it. Eve, who openly quizzed her brother, but secretly adored him, and loved to display all his accomplishments, had egged on Mr. Fountain to ask David to bring his violin next time. Lucy had shivered internally. "Now, of all the screeching, whining things that I dislike, a violin!"—and thus thinking, gushed out, "Oh, pray do, Mr. Dodd," with a gentle warmth that settled the matter and imposed on all around.

This evening, then, the Dodds came to tea.

They found Lucy alone in the drawing-room, and Eve engaged her directly in sprightly conversation, into which they soon drew David, and, interchanging a secret signal, plied him with a few artful questions, and—launched him. But the one sketch I gave of his manner and matter must serve again and again. Were I to retail to the reader all the droll, the spirited, the exciting things he told his hearers, there would be no room for my own little story; and we are all so egotistical! Suffice it to say, the living book of travels was inexhaustible; his observation and memory were really marvelous, and his enthusiasm, coupled with his accuracy of detail, had still the power to inthrall his hearers.

"Mr. Dodd," said Lucy, "now I see why Eastern kings have a story-teller always about them—a live story-teller. Would not you have one, Miss Dodd, if you were Queen of Persia?"

"Me? I'd have a couple—one to make me laugh; one miserable."

"One would be enough if his resources were equal to your brother's. Pray go on, Mr. Dodd. It was madness to interrupt you with small talk."

David hung his head for a moment, then lifted it with a smile, and sailed in the spirit into the China seas, and there told them how the Chinamen used to slip on board his ship and steal with supernatural dexterity, and the sailors catch them by the tails, which they observing, came ever with their tails soaped like pigs at a village feast; and how some foolhardy sailors would venture into the town at the risk of their lives; and how one day they had to run for it, and when they got to the shore their boat was stolen, and they had to 'bout ship and fight it out, and one fellow who knew the natives had loaded the sailors' guns with currant jelly. Make ready—present—fire! In a moment the troops of the Celestial Empire smarted, and were spattered with seeming gore, and fled yelling.

Then he told how a poor comrade of his was nabbed and clapped in prison, and his hands and feet were to be cut off at sunrise; himself at noon. It was midnight, and strict orders from the quarterdeck had been issued that no man should leave the ship: what was to be done? It was a moonlight night. They met, silent as death, between decks—daren't speak above a whisper, for fear the officers should hear them. His messmate was crying like a child. One proposed one thing, one another; but it was all nonsense, and we knew it was, and at sunrise poor Tom must die.

At last up jumps one fellow, and cries, "Messmates, I've got it; Tom isn't dead yet."

This was the moment Mr. Fountain and Mr. Talboys chose for coming into the drawing-room, of course. Mr. Fountain, with a shade of hesitation and awkwardness, introduced the Dodds to Mr. Talboys: he bowed a little stiffly, and there was a pause. Eve could not repress a little movement of nervous impatience. "David is telling us one of his nonsensical stories, sir," said she to Mr. Fountain, "and it is so interesting; go on, David."

"Well, but," said David, modestly, "it isn't everybody that likes these sea-yarns as you do, Eve. No, I'll belay, and let my betters get a word in now."

"You are more merciful than most story-tellers, sir," said Talboys.

Eve tossed her head and looked at Lucy, who with a word could have the story go on again. That young lady's face expressed general complacency, politeness, and tout m'est egal. Eve could have beat her for not taking David's part. "Doubleface!" thought she. She then devoted herself with the sly determination of her sex to trotting David out and making him the principal figure in spite of the new-corner.

But, as fast as she heated him, Talboys cooled him. We are all great at something or other, small or great. Talboys was a first-rate freezer. He was one of those men who cannot shine, but can eclipse. They darken all but a vain man by casting a dark shadow of trite sentences on each luminary. The vain man insults them directly, and so gets rid of them.

Talboys kept coming across honest enthusiastic David with little remarks, each skillfully discordant with the rising sentiment. Was he droll, Talboys did a bit of polite gravity on him; was he warm in praise of some gallant action, chill irony trickled on him from T.

His flashes of romance were extinguished by neat little dicta, embodying sordid and false, but current views of life. The gauze wings of eloquence, unsteeled by vanity, will not bear this repeated dabbing with prose glue, so David collapsed and Talboys conquered—"spell" benumbed "charm." The sea-wizard yielded to the petrifier, and "could no more," as the poets say. Talboys smiled superior. But, as his art was a purely destructive one, it ended with its victim; not having an idea of his own in his skull, the commentator, in silencing his text, silenced himself and brought the society to a standstill. Eve sat with flashing eyes; Lucy's twinkled with sly fun: this made Eve angrier. She tried another tack.

"You asked David to bring his fiddle," said she, sharply, "but I suppose now —"

"Has he brought it?" asked Mr. Fountain, eagerly.

"Yes, he has; I made him" (with a glance of defiance at Talboys).

Mr. Fountain rang the bell directly and sent for the fiddle. It came. David took it and tuned it, and made it discourse. Lucy leaned a little back in her chair, wore her "tout m'est egal face," and Eve watched her like a cat. First her eyes opened with a mild astonishment, then her lips parted in a smile; after a while a faint color came and went, and her eyes deepened and deepened in color, and glistened with the dewy light of sensibility.

A fiddle wrought this, or rather genius, in whose hand a jews-harp is the lyre of Orpheus, a fiddle the harp of David, a chisel a hewer of heroic forms, a brush or a pen the scepter of souls, and, alas! a nail a picklock.

Inside every fiddle is a soul, but a coy one. The nine hundred and ninety-nine never win it. They play rapid tunes, but the soul of beautiful gayety is not there; slow tunes, very slow ones, wherein the spirit of whining is mighty, but the sweet soul of pathos is absent; doleful, not nice and tearful. Then comes the Heaven-born fiddler,* who can make himself cry with his own fiddle. David had a touch of this witchcraft. Though a sound musician and reasonably master of his instrument, he could not fly in a second up and down it, tickling the fingerboard and scratching the strings without an atom of tone, as the mechanical monkeys do that boobies call fine players.

    * This is a definition of the Heaven-born fiddler by Pate

Bailey, a gypsy tinker and celestial violinist. Being asked for a test of proficiency on that instrument, he replied that no man is a fiddler "till he can gar himsel greet wi a feddle."

"Great Orpheus played so well he moved Old Nick,
 But these move nothing but their fiddlestick."*

* See how unjust satire is! Don't they move their finger-nails?

But he could make you laugh and crow with his fiddle, and could make you jump up, aetat. 60, and snap your fingers at old age and propriety, and propose a jig to two bishops and one master of the rolls, and, they declining, pity them without a shade of anger, and substitute three chairs; then sit unabashed and smiling at the past; and the next minute he could make you cry, or near it. In a word he could evoke the soul of that wonderful wooden shell, and bid it discourse with the souls and hearts of his hearers.

Meantime Lucy Fountain's face would have interested a subtle student of her sex.

Her sensibility to music was great, and the feeling strains stole into her nature, and stirred the treasures of the deep to the surface. Eve, a keen if not a profound observer, was struck by the rising beauty of this countenance, over which so many moods chased one another. She said to herself: "Well, David is right, after all; she is a lovely girl. Her features are nothing out of the way. Her nose is neither one thing nor the other, but her expression is beautiful. None of your wooden faces for me. And, dear heart, how her neck rises! La! how her color comes and goes! Well, I do love the fiddle myself dearly; and now, if her eyes are not brimming; I could kiss her! La! David," cried she, bursting the bounds of silence, "that is enough of the tune the old cow died of; take and play something to keep our hearts up—do."

Eve's good-humor and mirth were restored by David's success, and now nothing would serve her turn but a duet, pianoforte and violin. Miss Fountain objected, "Why spoil the violin?" David objected too, "I had hoped to hear the piano-forte, and how can I with a fiddle sounding under my chin?" Eve overruled both peremptorily.

"Well, Miss Dodd, what shall we select? But it does not matter; I feel sure Mr. Dodd can play a livre ouvert."

"Not he," said Eve, hypocritically, being secretly convinced he could. "Can you play 'a leevre ouvert,' David?"

"Who is it by, Miss Fountain?" Lucy never moved a muscle.

After a rummage a duet was found that looked promising, and the performance began. In the middle David stopped.

"Ha! ha! David's broke down," shrieked Eve, concealing her uneasiness under fictitious gayety. "I thought he would."

"I beg your pardon," explained David to Miss Fountain, "but you are out of time."

"Am I?" said Lucy, composedly.

"And have been, more or less, all through."

"David, you forget yourself."

"No, no; set me right, by all means, Mr. Dodd. I am not a hardened offender."

"Is it not just possible the violin may be the instrument that is out of time?" suggested Talboys, insidiously.

"No," said David, simply, "I was right enough."

"Let us try again, Mr. Dodd. Play me a few bars first in exact time. Thank you. Now."

"All went merry as a marriage bell" for a page and a half; then David, fiddling away, cried out, "You are getting too fast; 'ri tum tiddy, iddy ri tum ti;" then, by stamping and accenting very strongly, he kept the piano from overflowing its bounds. The piece ended. Eve rubbed her hands. "Now you'll catch it, Mr. David!"

"I am afraid I gave you a great deal of trouble, Mr. Dodd."

"En revanche, you gave us a great deal of pleasure," put in Mr. Talboys.

Lucy turned her head and smiled graciously. "But piano-forte players play so much by themselves, they really forget the awful importance of time."

"I profit by your confession that they do sometimes play by themselves," said Mr. Talboys. "Be merciful, and let us hear you by yourself."' Eve turned as red as fire.

David backed the request sincerely.

Lucy played a piece composed expressly for the piano by a pianist of the day. David sat on her left hand and watched intently how she did it.

When it was over, Talboys did a bit of rapture; Eve another.

"That is playing."

"I would not have believed it if I had not seen it done," said David. "Eve, you should have seen her beautiful fingers thread in and out among the keys; it was like white fire dancing; and as for her hand, it is not troubled with joints like ours, I should say."

"The music, Mr. Dodd," said Lucy, severely.

"Oh, the music! Well, I could hardly take on me to say. You see I heard it by the eye, and that was all in its favor; but I should say the music wasn't worth a button."

"David!"

"How you run off with one's words, Eve! I mean, played by anybody but her. Why, what was it, when you come to think? Up and down the gamut, and then down and up. No more sense in it than a b c—a scramble to the main-masthead for nothing, and back to no good. I'd as lief see you play on the table, Miss Fountain."

"Poor Moscheles!" said Lucy, dryly.

"Revenge is in your power," said Talboys; "play no more; punish us all for this one heretic."

Lucy reflected a moment; she then took from the canterbury a thick old book. "This was my mother's. Her taste was pure in music, as in everything. I shall be sorry if you do not all like this," added she, softly.

It was an old mass; full, magnificent chords in long succession, strung together on a clear but delicate melody. She played it to perfection: her lovely hands seemed to grasp the chords. No fumbling in the base; no gelatinizing in the treble. Her touch, firm and masterly, yet feminine, evoked the soul of her instrument, as David had of his, and she thought of her mother as she played. These were those golden strains from which all mortal dross seems purged. Hearing them so played, you could not realize that he who writ them had ever eaten, drunk, smoked, snuffed, and hated the composer next door. She who played them felt their majesty and purity. She lifted her beaming eye to heaven as she played, and the color receded from her cheek; and when her enchantment ended she was silent, and all were silent, and their ears ached for the departed charm.

Then she looked round a mute inquiry.

Talboys applauded loudly.

But the tear stood in David's eye, and he said nothing.

"Well, David," said Eve, reproachfully, "I'm sure if that does not please you—"

"Please me," cried David, a little fretfully; "more shame for me if it does not. Please is not the word. It is angel music, I call it—ah!"

"Well, you need not break your heart for that: he is going to cry—ha! ha!"

"I'm no such thing," cried David, indignantly, and blew his nose—promptly, with a vague air of explanation and defiance.

But why the male of my species blows its nose to hide its sensibility a deeper than I must decide.

Mr. Talboys for some time had not been at his ease. He had been playing too, and an instrument he hated—second fiddle. He rose and joined Mr. Fountain, who was sitting half awake on a distant sofa.

"Aha!" thought Eve, exulting, "we have driven him away."

Judge her mortification when Lucy, after shutting the piano, joined her uncle and Mr. Talboys. Eve whispered David: "Gone to smooth him down: the high and mighty gentleman wasn't made enough of."

"Every one in their turn," said David, calmly; "that is manners. Look! it is the old gentleman she is being kind to. She could not be unkind to anyone, however."

Eve put her lips to David's ear: "She will be unkind to you if you are ever mad enough to let her see what I see," said she, in a cutting whisper.

"What do you see? More than there is to see, I'll wager," said David, looking down.

"Ah! that is the way with young men, the moment they take a fancy; their sister is nothing to them, their best friend loses their confidence."

"Don't ye say that, Eve—now don't say that!"

"No, no, David, never mind me. I am cross. And if you saw a sore heart in store for anyone you had a regard for, wouldn't you be cross? Young men are so stupid, they can't read a girl no more than Hebrew. If she is civil and affable to them, oh, they are the man directly, when, instead of that, if it was so, she would more likely be shy and half afraid to come near them. David, you are in a fool's paradise. In company, and even in flirtation, all sorts meet and part again; but it isn't so with marriage. There 'it is beasts of a kind that in one are joined, and birds of a feather that came together.' Like to like, David. She is a fine lady and she will marry a fine gentleman, and nothing else, with a large income. If she knew what has been in your head this month past, she would open her eyes and ask if the man was mad."

"She has a right to look down on me, I know," murmured David, humbly; "but" (his eye glowing with sudden rapture) "she doesn't—she doesn't."

"Look down on you! You are better company than she is, or anyone she can get in this-out-of-the-way place; it is her interest to be civil to you. I am too hard upon her. She is a lady—a perfect lady—and that is why she is above giving herself airs. No, David, she is not the one to treat us with disrespect, if we don't forget ourselves. But if ever you let her see that you are in love with her, you will get an affront that will make your cheek burn and my heart smart—so I tell you."

"Hush! I never told you I was in love with her."

"Never told me? Never told me? Who asked you to tell me? I have eyes, if you have none."

"Eve," said David imploringly, "I don't hear of any lover that she has. Do you?"

"No," said Eve carelessly. "But who knows? She passes half the year a hundred miles from this, and there are young men everywhere. If she was a milkmaid, they'd turn to look at her with such a face and figure as that, much more a young lady with every grace and every charm. She has more than one after her that we never see, take my word."

Eve had no sooner said this than she regretted it, for David's face quivered, and he sighed like one trying to recover his breath after a terrible blow.

What made this and the succeeding conversation the more trying and peculiar was, that the presence of other persons in the room, though at a considerable distance, compelled both brother and sister, though anything but calm, to speak sotto voce. But in the history of mankind more strange and incongruous matter has been dealt with in an undertone, and with artificial and forced calmness.

"My poor David!" said Eve sorrowfully; "you who used to be so proud, so high-spirited, be a man! Don't throw away such a treasure as your affection. For my sake, dear David, your sister's sake, who does love you so very, very dearly!"

"And I love you, Eve. Thank you. It was hard lines. Ah! But it is wholesome, no doubt, like most bitters. Yes. Thank you, Eve. I do admire her v-very much," and his voice faltered a little. "But I am a man for all that, and I'll stand to my own words. I'll never be any woman's slave."

"That is right, David."

"I will not give hot for cold, nor my heart for a smile or two. I can't help admiring her, and I do hope she will be—happy—ah!—whoever she fancies. But, if I am never to command her, I won't carry a willow at my mast-head, and drift away from reason and manhood, and my duty to you, and mother, and myself."

"Ah! David, if you could see how noble you look now. Is it a promise, David? for I know you will keep your word if once you pass it."

"There is my hand on it, Eve."

The brother and sister grasped hands, and when David was about to withdraw his, Eve's soft but vigorous little hand closed tighter and kept it firmer, and so they sat in silence.

"Eve."

"My dear!"

"Now don't you be cross."

"No, dear. Eve is sad, not cross; what is it?

"Well, Eve—dear Eve."

"Don't be afraid to speak your mind to me—why should you?"

"Well, then, Eve, now, if she had not some little kindness for me, would she be so pleased with these thundering yarns I keep spinning her, as old as Adam, and as stale as bilge-water? You that are so keen, how comes it you don't notice her eyes at these times? I feel them shine on me like a couple of suns. They would make a statue pay the yarn out. Who ever fancied my chat as she does?"

"David," said Eve, quietly, "I have thought of all this; but I am convinced now there is nothing in it. You see, David, mother and I are used to your yarns, and so we take them as a matter of course; but the real fact is, they are very interesting and very enticing, and you tell them like a book. You came all fresh to this lady, and, as she is very quick, she had the wit to see the merit of your descriptions directly. I can see it myself now. All young women like to be amused, David, and, above all, excited; and your stories are very exciting; that is the charm; that is what makes her eyes fire; but if that puppy there, or that book-shelf yonder, could tell her your stories, she would look at either the puppy or the book-stand with just the same eyes she looks on you with, my poor David."

"Don't say so, Eve. Let me think there is some little feeling for me inside those sweet eyes, that look so kind on me—"

"And on me, and on everybody. It is her manner. I tell you she is so to all the world. She isn't the first I've met. Trust me to read a woman, David; what can you know?"

"I know nothing; but they tell me you can fathom one another better than any man ever could," said David, sorrowfully.

"'David, just now you were telling as interesting a story as ever was. You had just got to the thrilling part."

"Oh, had I? What was I saying?"

"I can't tell you to the very word; I am not your sweetheart any more than she is; but one of the sailors was in danger of his life, and so on. You never told me the story before; I was not worth it. Well, just then does not that affected puppy choose his time to come meandering in?"

"Puppy! I call him a fine gentleman."

"Well, there isn't so much odds. In he comes; your story is broken off directly. Does she care? No, she has got one of her own set; he is not a very bright one; he is next door to a fool. No matter; before he came, to judge by her crocodile eyes, she was hot after your story; the moment he did come, she didn't care a pin for you nor your story. I gave her more than one opening to bring it on again; not she. I tell you, you are nothing but a pass time;* you suit her turn so long as none of her own set are to be had. If she would leave you for such a jackanapes as that, what would she do for a real gentleman? such a man as she is a woman, for instance, and as if there weren't plenty such in her own set— oh, you goose!"

* I write this word as the lady thought proper to pronounce

it.

David interrupted her. "I have been a vain fool, and it is lucky no one has seen it but you," and he hid his face in his hands a moment; then, suddenly remembering where he was, and that this was an attitude to attract attention, he tried to laugh—a piteous effort; then he ground his teeth and said: "Let us go home. All I want now is to get out of the house. It would have been better for me if I had never set foot in it."

"Hush! be calm, David, for Heaven's sake. I am only waiting to catch her eye, and then we'll bid them good-evening."

"Very well, I'll wait"; and David fixed his eyes sadly and doggedly on the ground. "I won't look at her if I can help it," said he, resolutely, but very sadly, and turned his head away.

"Now, David," whispered Eve.

David rose mechanically and moved with his sister toward the other group. Miss Fountain turned at their approach. Somewhat to David's surprise, Eve retreated as quickly as she had advanced.

"We are to stay."

"What for?"

"She made me a signal."

"Not that I saw," said David, incredulously.

"What! didn't you see her give me a look?"

"Yes, I did. But what has that to do with it?"

"That look was as much as to say, Please stay a little longer; I have something to say to you."

"Good Heavens!"

"I think it is about a bonnet, David. I asked her to put me in the way of getting one made like hers. She does wear heavenly bonnets."

"Ay. I did well to listen to you, Eve; you see I can't even read her face, much less her heart. I saw her look up, but that was all. How is a poor fellow to make out such craft as these, that can signal one another a whole page with a flash of the eye? Ah!"

"There, David, he is going. Was I right?"

Mr. Talboys was, in fact, taking leave of Miss Fountain. The old gentleman convoyed his friend. As the door closed on them Miss Fountain's face seemed to catch fire. Her sweet complacency gave way to a half-joyous, half-irritated small energy. She came gliding swiftly, though not hurriedly, up to Eve. "Thank you for seeing." Then she settled softly and gradually on an ottoman, saying, "Now, Mr. Dodd."

David looked puzzled. "What is it?" and he turned to his interpreter, Eve.

But it was Lucy who replied: "'His messmate was crying like a child. At sunrise poor Tom must die. Then up rose one fellow' (we have not any idea who one fellow means in these narratives—have we, Miss Dodd?) 'and cried, "I have it, messmates. Tom isn't dead yet."' Now, Mr. Dodd, between that sentence and the one that is to follow all that has happened in this room was a hideous dream. On that understanding we have put up with it. It is now happily dispersed, and we—go ahead again."

"I see, Eve, she thinks she would like some more of that China yarn."

"Her sentiments are not so tame. She longs for it, thirsts for it, and must and will have it—if you will be so very obliging, Mr. Dodd." The contrast between all this singular vivacity of Miss Fountain and the sudden return to her native character and manner in the last sentence struck the sister as very droll— seemed to the brother so winning, that, scarcely master of himself, he burst out: "You shan't ask me twice for that, or anything I can give you;" and it was with burning cheeks and happy eyes he resumed his tale of bold adventure and skill on one side, of numbers, danger and difficulty on the other. He told it now like one inspired, and both the young ladies hung panting and glowing on his words.

David and Eve went home together.

David was in a triumphant state, but waited for Eve to congratulate him. Eve was silent.

At last David could refrain no longer. "Why, you say nothing."

"No. Common sense is too good to be wasted; don't go so fast."

"No. There—I heave to for convoy to close up. Would it be wasted on me? ha! ha!"

"To-night. There you go pelting on again."

"Eve, I can't help it. I feel all canvas, with a cargo of angels' feathers and sunshine for ballast."

"Moonshine."

"Sun, moon, and stars, and all that is bright by night or day. I'll tell you what to do; you keep your head free, and come on under easy sail; I'll stand across your bows with every rag set and drawing, so then I shall be always within hail."

This sober-minded maneuver was actually carried out. The little corvette sailed steadily down the middle of the lane; the great merchantman went pitching and rolling across her bows; thus they kept together, though their rates of sailing were so different.

Merry Eve never laughed once, but she smiled, and then sighed.

David did not heed her. All of a moment his heart vented itself in a sea-ditty so loud, and clear, and mellow, that windows opened, and out came nightcapped heads to hear him carol the lusty stave, making night jolly.

Meantime, the weather being balmy, Mr. Fountain had walked slowly with Mr. Talboys in another direction. Mr. Talboys inquired, "Who were these people?"

"Oh, only two humble neighbors," was the reply.

"I never met them anywhere. They are received in the neighborhood?"

"Not in society, of course."

"I don't understand you. Have not I just met them here?"

"That is not the way to put it," said the old gentleman, a little confused. "You did not meet them; you did me and my niece the honor to dine with us, and the Dodds dropped in to tea—quite another matter."

"Oh, is it?"

"Is it not? I see you have been so long out of England you have forgotten these little distinctions; society would go to the deuce without them. We ask our friends, and persons of our own class, to dinner, but we ask who we like to tea in this county. Don't you like her? She is the prettiest girl in the village."

"Pretty and pert."

"Ha! ha! that is true. She is saucy enough, and amusing in proportion."

"It is the man I alluded to."

"What, David? ay, a very worthy lad. He is a downright modest, well-informed young man."

"I don't doubt his general merits, but let me ask you a serious question: his evident admiration of Miss Fountain?"

"His ad-mi-ration of Miss Fountain?"

"Is it agreeable to you?"

"It is a matter of consummate indifference to me."

"But not, I think, to her. She showed a submission to the cub's impertinence, and a desire to please instead of putting him down, that made me suspect. Do you often ask Mr. Dodd—what a name!—to tea?"

"My dear friend, I see that, with all your accomplishments, you have something to learn. You want insight into female character. Now I, who must go to school to you on most points, can be of use to you here." Then, seeing that Talboys was mortified at being told thus gently there was a department of learning he had not fathomed, he added: "At all events, I can interpret my own niece to you. I have known her much longer than you have."

Mr. Talboys requested the interpreter to explain the pleasure his niece took in Mr. Dodd's fiddle.

"Part politeness, part sham. Why, she wanted not to ask them this evening, the fiddle especially. I'll give you the clue to Lucy; she is a female Chesterfield, and the droll thing is she is polite at heart as well. Takes it from her mother: she was something between an angel and a duchess."

"Politeness does not account for the sort of partiality she showed for these Dodds while I was in the room."

"Pure imagination, my dear friend. I was there; and had so monstrous a phenomenon occurred I must have seen it. If you think she could really prefer their society to yours, you are as unjust to her as yourself. She may have concealed her real preference out of finesse, or perhaps she has observed that our inferiors are touchy, and ready to fancy we slight them for those of our own rank."

Talboys shrugged his shoulders; he was but half convinced. "Her enthusiasm when the cub scraped the fiddle went beyond mere politeness."

"Beyond other people's, you mean. Nothing on earth ever went beyond hers—ha! ha! ha! To-morrow night, if you like, we will have my gardener, Jack Absolom, in to tea."

"No, I thank you. I have no wish to go beyond Mr. and Miss Dodd."

"Oh, only for an experiment. The first minute Jack will be wretched, and want to sink through the floor; but in five minutes you will fancy Lucy will have made Jack Absolom at home in my drawing-room. He will be laying down the law about Jonquilles, and she all sweetness, curiosity, and enthusiasm outside —ennui in."

"Can her eyes glisten out of politeness?" inquired Talboys, with a subdued sneer.

"Why not?"

"They could shed tears, perhaps, for the same motive?" said Talboys, with crushing irony.

"Well! Hum! I'd back them at four to seven."

Mr. Talboys was silent, and his manner showed that he was a little mortified at a subject turning to joke which he had commenced seriously. He must stop this annoyance. He said severely, "It is time to come to an understanding with you."

At these words, and, above all, at their solemn tone, the senior pricked his ears and prepared his social diplomacy.

"I have visited very frequently at your house, Mr. Fountain."

"Never without being welcome, my dear sir."

"You have, I think, divined one reason of my very frequent visits here."

"I have not been vain enough to attribute them entirely to my own attractions."

"You approve the homage I render to that other attraction?"

"Unfeignedly."

"Am I so fortunate as to have her suffrage, too?"

"I have no better means of knowing than you have."

"Indeed! I was in hopes you might have sounded her inclinations."

"I have scrupulously avoided it," replied the veteran. "I had no right to compromise you upon mere conjecture, however reasonable. I awaited your authority to take any move in so delicate a matter. Can you blame me? On one side my friend's dignity, on the other a young lady's peace of mind, and that young lady my brother's daughter."

"You were right, my dear sir; I see and appreciate your reserve, your delicacy, though I am about to remove its cause. I declare myself to you your niece's admirer; have I your permission to address her?"

"You have, and my warmest wishes for your success."

"Thank you. I think I may hope to succeed, provided I have a fair chance afforded me."

"I will take care you shall have that."

"I should prefer not to have others buzzing about the lady whose affection I am just beginning to gain."

"You pay this poor sailor an amazing compliment," said Mr. Fountain, a little testily; "if he admires Lucy it can only be as a puppy is struck with the moon above. The moon does not respond to all this wonder by descending into the whelp's jaws—no more will my niece. But that is neither here nor there; you are now her declared suitor, and you have a right to stipulate; in short, you have only to say the word, and 'exeunt Dodds,' as the play-books say."

"Dodds? I have no objection to the lady. Would it not be possible to invite her to tea alone?"

"Quite possible, but useless. She would not stir out without her brother."

"She seems a little person likely to give herself airs. Well, then, in that case, though as you say I am no doubt raising Mr. Dodd to a false importance, still —"

"Say no more; we should indulge the whims of our friends, not attack them with reasons. You will see the Dodds no more in my house."

"Oh, as to that, just as you please. Perhaps they would be as well out of it," said Talboys, with a sudden affectation of carelessness. "I must not take you too far. Good-night."

"Go-o-d night!"

Poor David. He was to learn how little real hold upon society has the man who can only instruct and delight it.

Mr. Fountain bustled home, rubbing his hands with delight. "Aha!" thought he; "jealous! actually jealous! absurdly jealous! That is a good sign. Who would have thought so proud a man could be jealous of a sailor? I have found out your vulnerable point, my friend. I'll tell Lucy; how she will laugh. David Dodd! Now we know how to manage him, Lucy and I. If he freezes back again, we have but to send for David Dodd and his fiddle." He bustled home, and up into the drawing-room to tell Lucy Mr. Talboys had at last declared himself. His heart felt warm. He would settle six thousand pounds on Mrs. Talboys during his life and his whole fortune after his death.

He found the drawing-room empty. He rang the bell. "Where is Miss Fountain?" John didn't know, but supposed she had gone to her room.

"You don't know? You never know anything. Send her maid to me."

The maid came and courtesied demurely at the door.

"Tell your mistress I want to speak to her directly—before she undresses."

The maid went out, and soon returned to say that her mistress had retired to rest; but that, if he pleased, she would rise, and just make a demi-toilet, and come to him. This smooth and fair-sounding proposal was not, I grieve to say, so graciously received as offered. "Much obliged," snapped old Fountain. "Her demi-toilette will keep me another hour out of my bed, and I get no sleep after dinner now among you. Tell her to-morrow at breakfast time will do."

CHAPTER IV.

DAVID DODD was so radiant and happy for a day or two that Eve had not the heart to throw cold water on him again.

Three days elapsed, and no invitation to Font Abbey; on this his happiness cooled of itself. But when day after day rolled by, and no Font Abbey, he was dashed, uneasy, and, above all, perplexed. What could be the reason? Had he, with his rough ways, offended her? Had she been too dignified to resent it at the time? Was he never to go to Font Abbey again? Eve's first feeling was unmixed satisfaction. We have seen already that she expected no good from this rash attachment. For a single moment her influence and reasons had seemed to wean David from it; but his violent agitation and joy at two words of kindly curiosity from Miss Fountain, and the instant unreasonable revival of love and hope, showed the strange power she had acquired over him. It made Eve tremble.

But now the Fountains were aiding her to cure this folly. She had read them right, had described them to David aright. A wind of caprice had carried him and her into Font Abbey; another such wind was carrying them out. No event had happened. Mr. and Miss Fountain had been seen more than once in the village of late. "They have dropped us, and thank Heaven!" said Eve, in her idiomatic way.

She pitied David deeply, and was kinder and kinder to him now, to show him she felt for him; but she never mentioned the Font Abbey people to him either to praise or blame them, though it was all she could do to suppress her satisfaction at the turn their insolent caprice had taken.

That satisfaction was soon clouded. This time, instead of rousing himself and his pride, David sank into a moody despondency; varied by occasional fretfulness. His appetite went, and his bright color, and his elastic step. This silent sadness was so new in him, such a contrast to his natural temperature, large, genial, and ever cheerful, that Eve could not bear it. "I must shake him out of this, at all hazards," thought she: yet she put off the experiment, and put it off, partly in hopes that David would speak first, partly because she saw the wound she would probe was deep, and she winced beforehand for her patient.

Meantime, prolonged doubt and suspense now goaded with their intolerable stings the active spirit that chill misgivings had at first benumbed. Spurred into action by these torments, David had already watched several days in the neighborhood of Font Abbey, determined to speak to Miss Fountain, and find out whether he had given her offense; for this was still his uppermost idea. Having failed in this attempt at an interview with her, he was now meditating a more resolute course, and he paced the little gravel-walk at home debating in himself the pros and cons. Raising his head suddenly, he saw his sister walking slowly at the other end of the path. She was coming toward him, but her eyes were bent thoughtfully on the ground. David slipped behind some bushes, not to have his unhappiness and his meditations interrupted. The lover and the lunatic have points in common.

He had been there some time when a grave little voice spoke quietly to him from the lawn. "David, I want to speak to you." David came out.

"Here am I."

"Oh, I knew where you were. Don't do that again, sir, please, or you'll catch it."

"Oh, I didn't think you saw me," said David, somewhat confusedly.

"What has that to do with it, stupid? David," continued she, assuming a benevolent, cheerful, and somewhat magnificent nonchalance, "I sometimes wonder you don't come to me with your troubles. I might advise you as well as here and there one. But perhaps you think now, because I am naturally gay, I am not sensible. You mustn't go by that altogether. Manner is very deceiving. The most foolishly conducted men and women ever I met were as grave as judges, and as demure as cats after cream. Bless you, there is folly in every heart. Your slow ones bottle it up for use against the day wisdom shall be most needed. My sort let it fizz out at their mouths in their daily talk, and keep their good sense for great occasions, like the present."

"Have we drifted among the proverbs of Solomon?" inquired David, dryly. "No need to make so many tacks, Eve. Haven't I seen your sense and profited by it—I and one or two more? Who but you has steered the house this ten years, and commanded the lubberly crew?"*

> * The reader must not be misled by the familiar phraseology
>
> of these two speakers to suppose that anything the least
>
> droll or humorous was intended by either of them at any part
>
> of this singular dialogue. Their hearts were sad and their
>
> faces grave.

"And then again, David, where the heart is concerned, young women are naturally in advance of young men."

"God knows. He made them both. I don't."

"Why, all the world knows it. And then, besides, I am five years older than you.

"So mother says; but I don't know how to believe it. No one would say so to look at you."

"I'll tell you, David. Folk that have small features look a deal younger than their years; and you know poor father used to say my face was the pattern of a flat-iron. So nobody gives me my age; but I am five good years older than you, only you needn't go and tell the town crier."

"Well, Eve?"

"Well, then, put all these together, and now, why not come to me for friendly advice and the voice of reason?"

"Reason! reason! there are other lights besides reason."

"Jack-o'-lantern, eh? and Will-o'-the-wisp."

"Eve, nobody can advise me that can't feel for me. Nobody can feel for me that doesn't know my pain; and you don't know that, because you were never in love."

"Oh, then, if I had ever been in love, you would listen."

"As I would to an angel from Heaven."

"And be advised by me."

"Why not? for then you'd be competent to advise; but now you haven't an idea what you are talking about."

"What a pity! Don't you think it would be as well if you were not to speak to me so sulky?"

"I ask your pardon; Eve. I did not mean to offend you."

"Davy, dear—for God's sake what is this chill that has come between you and me? You are a man. Speak out like a man."

David turned his great calm, sorrowful eye full upon her.

"Well, then, Eve, if the truth must be told, I am disappointed in you."

"Oh, David."

"A little. You are not the girl I took you for. You know which way my fancy lies, yet you keep steering me in the teeth of it; then you see how down-hearted I am this while, but not a word of comfort or hope comes from you, and me almost dried up for want of one."

"Make one word of it, David—I am not a sister to you."

"I don't say that, but you might be kinder; you are against me just when I want you with me the most."

"Now this is what I like," said Eve, cheerfully; "this is plain speaking. So now it is my turn, my lad. Do you remember Balaam and his ass?"

"Sure," said David; but, used as he was to Eve's transitions, he couldn't help staring a little at being carried eastward ho so suddenly.

"Then what did the ass say when she broke silence at last?"

"Well, you know, Eve; I take shame to say I don't remember her very words, but the tune of them I do. Why, she sang out, 'Avast there! it is first fault, so you needn't be so hasty with your thundering rope's end.'"

"There! You'd make a nice commentator. You haven't taken it up one bit; you are as much in the dark as our parson. He preached on her the very Sunday you came home, and it was all I could do to help whipping up into the pulpit, and snatching away his book, and letting daylight in on them."

David was scandalized at the very idea of such a breach of discipline. "That is ridiculous," said he; "one can't have two skippers in a church any more than in a ship, brig, or bark. But you can let daylight in on me."

"I mean. To begin: the ass was in the right and Balaam in the wrong; so what becomes of your 'first fault?' She was frugal of her words, but every syllable was a needle; the worst is, some skins are so thick our needles won't enter 'em. Says she, 'This seven years you have known me; always true to the bridle and true to you. Did ever I disobey you before? Then why go and fancy I do it without some great cause that you can't see?' Then the man's eyes were open, and he saw it was destruction his old friend had run back from, and galled his foot to save his life; so of course he thanked her, and blessed her then. Not he. He was too much of a man."

"Ay, ay, I see; but what is the moral? for I have no heart to expound riddles."

"Oh, I'll tell you the moral sooner than you'll like, perhaps. The ass is a type, David. In Holy Writ you know almost everything is a type. When a thing means one thing and stands for another, that's a type."

"Ducks can swim—at least I've heard so. Now if you could tell me what she is a type of?"

"What, the ass? Don't you know? Why, of women, to be sure—of us poor creatures of burden, underrated and misunderstood all the world over. And Balaam he stands for men, and for you at the head of them," cried she, turning round with flashing eyes on David; "you have known me and my true affection more than seven years, or seventeen. I carried you in my arms when you were a year old and I was six. You were my little curly-headed darling, and have been from that day to this. Did ever I cross you, or be cold or unkind to you, till the other day?"

"No, Eve, no, no, no! Come sit beside me.

"Then shouldn't you have said, 'Don't slobber me; I won't have it; you and I are bad friends.' Oughtn't you to have said, 'Eve could never give herself the pain of crossing me' (no, there isn't a man in the world with gumption enough to say that—that is a woman's thought); but at least you might have said, 'She sees rocks ahead that I can't.' (Balaam couldn't see the drawn sword ahead, but there it was.) it was for you to say, 'My sister Eve would not change from gay to grave all at once, and from indulging me in everything to thwarting me and vexing me, unless she saw some great danger threatening your peace of mind, your career in life, your very reason, perhaps.'"

"I have been to blame, Eve; but speak out and let me know the worst. You have heard something against her character? Speak plain out, for Heaven's sake!"

"It is all very well of you to say speak plain out, but there are things girls don't like to speak about to any man. But after what you said, that you would listen to me if I—so it is my duty. You will see my face red enough in about a minute. Two years ago I couldn't have done this even for you. It is hard I must expose my own folly—my own crime."

"Why, Eve, lass, how you tremble! Drop it now! drop it!"

"Hold your tongue!" said Eve, sharply, but in considerable agitation. "It is too late now, after something you have said to me. If I didn't speak out now, I should be like that bad man you told us of, who let out the beacon light when the wind was blowing hard on shore. Listen, David, and take my words to heart. The road you are on now I have been upon, only I went much farther on it than you shall go." She resumed after a short pause: "You remember Henry Dyke?"

"What, the young clergyman, who used to be always alongside you at our last anchorage?"

"Yes. He was just such a man as Miss Fountain is a woman. He was but a dish of skim-milk, yet he could poison my life."

Then Eve told the story of her heart. She described her lover as he appeared to her in the early days of courtship, young, handsome, good, noble in sentiment, and warm and tender in manner. Halcyon days—not a speck to be seen on love's horizon.

Then she delineated the fine gradations by which the illusion faded, too slowly and too late for her to withdraw the love she had conceived for his person at that time when person and mind seemed alike superior. She painted with the delicate touch of her sex the portrait of a man and a scholar born to please all the world, and incapable of condensing his affections; a pious flirt, no longer stimulated to genuine ardor by doubts of success, but too kind-hearted to pain her beyond measure when a little factitious warmth from time to time would give her hours of happiness, keep her, on the whole, content, and, above all, retain her his. Then she shifted the mirror to herself, the fiery and faithful one, and showed David what centuries of torture a good little creature like this Dyke, with its charming exterior, could make a quick, and ardent, and devoted nature suffer in a year or two. Came out in her narrative, link by link, the gentle delicious complacency of the first period, the chill airs that soon ruffled it, the glowing hopes, the misgivings that dashed them; then the diminution of confidence, more complexing and exasperating than its utter loss; the alternations of joy and doubt, the fever and the ague of the wounded spirit; then the gusts of hatred followed by deeper love; later still, the periodical irritation at hopes long deferred, and still gleams of bliss between the paroxysms, so that now, as the vulgar say in their tremendous Saxon, she "spent her time between heaven and hell"; last of all, the sickness and recklessness of the wornout and wearied heart over which melancholy or fury impended.

It was at this crisis when, as she could now see on a calm retrospect, her mind was distempered, a new and terrible passion stepped upon the scene—jealousy. A friend came and whispered her, "Mr. Dyke was courting another woman at the same time, and that other woman was rich."

"David, at that word a flash of lightning seemed to go through me, and show me the man as he really was."

"The mean scoundrel, to sell himself for money!!"

"No, David, he would not have sold himself, with his eyes open, any more than perhaps your Miss Fountain would; but what little heart he had he could give to any girl that was not a fright. He was a self-deceiver and a general lover, and such characters and their affections sink by nature to where their interest lies. Iron is not conscious, yet it creeps toward the loadstone. Well, while she was with me I held up and managed to question her as coldly as I speak to you now, but as soon as she left me I went off in violent hysterics."

"Poor Eve!"

"She had not been gone an hour when doesn't the Devil put it into his head to send me a long, affectionate letter, and in the postscript he invited himself to supper the same afternoon. Then I got up and dried my eyes, and I seemed to turn into stone with resolution. 'Come!' I said, 'but don't think you shall ever go back to her. Your troubles and mine shall end to-night.'"

"Why, Eve, you turn pale with thinking of it. I fear you have had worse thoughts pass through your mind than any man is worth."

"David, your blood was in my veins, and mine is in yours.

"If I didn't think so! The Lord deliver us from temptation! We don't know ourselves nor those we love."

"He had driven me mad."

"Mad, indeed. What! had you the heart to see the man bleed to death—the man you had loved—you, my little gentle Eve?"

"Oh no, no; no blood!" said Eve, with a shudder. "Laudanum!"

"Good God!"

"Oh, I see your thought. No, I was not like the men in the newspapers, that kill the poor woman with a sure hand, and then give themselves a scratch. It was to be one spoonful for him, but two for me. I can't dwell on it" (and she hid her face in her hands); "it is too terrible to remember how far I was misled. Who, think you, saved us both?" David could not guess.

"A little angel—my good angel, that came home from sea that very afternoon. When I saw your curly head, and your sweet, sunburned face come in at the door, guess if I thought of putting death in the pot after that? Ah! the love of our own flesh and blood, that is the love—God and good angels can smile on it."

"Yes; but go on," said David, impatiently.

"It is ended, David. They say a woman's heart is a riddle, and perhaps you will think so when I tell you that when he had brought me down to this, and hadn't died for it, I turned as cold as ice to him that minute, once and forever. I looked back at the precipice, and I hated him. Ay, from that evening he was like the black dog to my eye. I used to slip anywhere to hide out of his way— just as you did out of mine but now."

"Can't you forget that? Well, to be sure. Well?"

"So then (now you may learn what these skim-milk cheeses are made of), when he found he was my aversion, he fell in love with me again as hot as ever; tried all he could think of to win me back; wrote a letter every day; came to me every other day; and when he saw it was all over for good between us he cried and bellowed till my hate all went, and scorn came in its place. Next time we met he played quite another part—the calm, heart-broken Christian; gave me his blessing; went down on his knees, and prayed a beautiful prayer, that took me off my guard and made me almost respect him; then went away, and quietly married the girl with money; and six months after wrote to me he was miserable, dated from the vicarage her parents had got him."

"Now, you know, if he wasn't a parson, d—n me if I'd turn in to-night till I'd rope's-ended that lubber!"

"As if I'd let you dirty your hands with such rubbish! I sent the note back to him with just one line, 'Such a fool as you are has no right to be a villain.' There, David, there is your poor sister's life. Oh, what I went through for that man! Often I said, is Heaven just, to let a poor, faithful, loving girl, who has done no harm, be played with on the hook, and tortured hot and cold, day after day, month after month, year after year, as I was? But now I see why it was permitted; it was for your sake, that you might profit by my sharp experience, and not fling your heart away on frozen mud, as I did;" and, happy in this feminine theory of Divine justice, Eve rested on her brother a look that would have adorned a seraph, then took him gently round the neck and laid her little cheek flat to his.

She felt as if she had just saved a beloved life.

Who can estimate the value of a happiness so momentary, yet so holy?

Presently looking up, she saw David's face illuminated. "What is it?" she asked joyously; "you look pleased."

David was "pleased because now he was sure she could feel for him, and would side with him."

"That I do; but, David, as it is all over between you and her—"

"All over? Am I dead then?"

Eve gasped with astonishment: "Why, what have I been telling you all this for?"

"Who should you tell your trouble to but your own brother? Why, Eve—ha! ha!—you don't really see any likeness between your case and mine, do you? You are not so blind as to compare her with that thundering muff?"

"They are brother and sister, as we are," was the reply. "Ever since I saw you looked her way, my eye has hardly been off her, and she is Henry Dyke in petticoats."

"I don't thank you for saying that. Well, and if she is, what has that to do with it? I am not a woman. I am not forced to lie to waiting for a wind, as the girls are. I am a man. I can work for the wish of my heart, and, if it does not come to meet me, I can overhaul it." Eve was a little staggered by this thrust, but she was not one to show an antagonist any advantage he had obtained. "David," said she, coldly, "it must come to one of two things; either she will send you about your business in form, which is a needless affront for you and me both, or she will hold you in hand, and play with you and drive you mad. Take warning; remember what is in our blood. Father was as well as you are, but agitation and vexation robbed him of his reason for a while; and you and I are his children. Milk of roses creeps along in that young lady's veins, but fire gallops in ours. Give her up, David, as she has you. She has let you escape;

don't fly back like a moth to the candle! You shan't, however; I won't let you."

"Eve," said David, quietly, "you argue well, but you can't argue light into dark, nor night into day. She is the sun to me. I have seen her light; and now I can't live without it."

He added, more calmly: "It is her or none. I never saw a girl but this that I wanted to see twice, and I never shall."

"But it is that which frightens me for you, David. Often I have wished I could see you flirt a bit and harden your heart."

"And break some poor girl's."

"Oh, hang them! they always contrive to pass it on. What do I care for girls! they are not my brother. But no, David, I can't believe you will go against me and my judgment after the insult she has put on you. No more about it, but just you choose between my respect and this wild-goose chase."

"I choose both," said David, quietly. "Both you shan't have"; and, with this, up bounced Eve, and stood before him bristling like a cat-o'mountain. David tried to soothe her—to coax her—in vain; her cheek was on fire, and her eyes like basilisks'. It was a picture to see the pretty little fury stand so erect and threatening, great David so humble and deprecating, yet so dogged. At last he took out his knife; it was not one of your stabbing-knives, but the sort of pruning-knife that no sailor went without in those days. "Now," said he, sadly, "take and cut my head off—cut me to pieces, if you will—I won't wince or complain; and then you will get your way; but while I do live I shall love her, and I can't afford to lose her by sitting twiddling my thumbs, waiting for luck. I'll try all I know to win her, and if I lose her I won't blame her, but myself for not finding out how to please her; and with that I'll live a bachelor all my days for her, or else die, just as God wills—I shan't much care which."

"Oh, I know you, you obstinate toad," said Eve, clinching her teeth and her little hand. Then she burst out furiously: "Are you quite resolved?"

"Quite, dear Eve," said David, sadly—but somehow it was like a rock speaking.

"Then there is my hand," said Eve, with an instant transition to amiable cheerfulness that dazzled a body like a dark lantern flying open. Used as David was to her, it stupefied him; he stared at her, and was all abroad. "Well, what is the wonder now?" inquired Eve; "there are but two of us. We must be together somehow or another must we not? You won't be wise with me; well, then, I'll be a fool with you. I'll help you with this girl."

"Oh, my dear Eve!"

"You won't gain much. Without me you hadn't the shadow of a chance, and with me you haven't a chance, that is all the odds."

"I have! I have! you have taken away my breath with joy;" and David was quite overcome with the turn Eve had taken in his favor.

"Oh, you need not thank me," said Eve, tossing her head with a hypocrisy all her own. "It is not out of affection for you I do it, you may be very sure of that; but it looks so ridiculous to see my brother slipping out of my way behind a tree as soon as he sees me coming—oh! oh! oh! oh!" And a violent burst of sobs and tears revealed how that incident had rankled in this stoical little heart.

David, with the tear in his own eye, clasped her in his arms, and kissed her and coaxed her and begged her again and again to forgive him. This she did internally at the first word; but externally no; pouted and sobbed till she had exacted her full tribute, then cleared up with sudden alacrity and inquired his plans.

"I am going to call at Font Abbey, and find out whether I have offended her."

Eve demurred, "That would never do. You would betray yourself and there would be an end of you. How good I am not to let you go. No, I'll call there. I shall quietly find out whether it is her doing that we have not been invited so long, or whose it is. You stay where you are. I won't be a minute."

When the minute was thirty-five, David came under her window and called her. She popped her head out: "Well?"

"What are you doing?"

"Putting on my bonnet."

"Why, you have been an hour."

"You wouldn't have me go there a fright, would you?"

At last she came down and started for Font Abbey, and David was left to count the minutes till her return. He paced the gravel sailor-wise, taking six steps and then turning, instead of going in each direction as far as he could. He longed and feared his sister's return. One hour—two hours elapsed; still he walked a supposed deck on the little lawn—six steps and then turn. At last he saw her coming in the distance; he ran to meet her; but when he came up with her he did not speak, but looked wistfully in her face, and tried hard to read it and his fate.

"Now, David, don't make a fool of yourself, or I won't tell you."

"No, no. I'll be calm, I will—be—calm."

"Well, then, for one thing, she is to drink tea with us this evening."

"She? Who? What? Where? Oh!"

"Here."

CHAPTER V.

MR. FOUNTAIN sat at breakfast opposite his niece with a twinkle set in his eye like a cherry-clack in a tree, relishing beforehand her smiles, and blushes, and gratitude to him for having hooked and played his friend, so that now she had but to land him. "I'll just finish this delicious cup of coffee," thought he, "and then I'll tell you, my lady." While he was slowly sipping said cup, Lucy looked up and said graciously to him, "How silly Mr. Talboys was last night—was he not, dear?"

"Talboys? silly? what? do you know? Why, what on earth do you mean?"

"Silly is a harsh word—injudicious, then—praising me a tort et a travers, and was downright ill-bred—was discourteous to another of our guests, Mr. Dodd."

"Confound Mr. Dodd! I wish I had never invited him."

"So do I. If you remember, I dissuaded you."

"I do remember now. What! you don't like him, either?"

"There you are mistaken, dear. I esteem Mr. Dodd highly, and Miss Dodd, too, in spite of her manifest defects; but in making up parties, however small, we should choose our guests with reference to each other, not merely to ourselves. Now, forgive me, it was clear beforehand that Mr. Talboys and the Dodds, especially Miss Dodd, would never coalesce; hence my objection in inviting them; but you overruled me—with a rod of iron, dear."

"Yes; but why? Because you gave me such a bad reason; you never said a word about this incongruity."

"But it was in my mind all the time."

"Then why didn't it come out?"

"Because—because something else would come out instead. As if one gave one's real reasons for things!! Now, uncle dear, you allow me great liberties, but would it have been quite the thing for me to lecture you upon the selection of your own convives?"

"Why, you have ended by doing it."

Lucy colored. "Not till the event proves—not till—"

"Not till your advice is no longer any use."

Lucy, driven into a corner, replied by an imploring look, which had just the opposite effect of argument. It instantly disarmed the old boy; he grinned superior, and spared his supple antagonist three sarcasms that were all on the tip of his tongue. He was rewarded for his clemency by a little piece of advice, delivered by his niece with a sort of hesitating and penitent air he did not understand one bit, eyes down upon the cloth all the time.

It came to this. He was to listen to her suggestions with a prejudice in their favor if he could, and give them credit for being backed by good reasons; at all events, he was never to do them the injustice to suppose they rested on those puny considerations she might put forward in connection with them.

"Silly" is a term carrying with it a certain promptness and decision; above all, it was a very remarkable word for Lucy to use. "The girl is a martinet in these things," thought he; "she can't forgive the least bit of impoliteness. I suppose he snubbed Jack Tar. What a crime! But I had better let this blow over before I go any farther." So he postponed his disclosure till to-morrow.

But, before to-morrow came, he had thought it over again, and convinced himself it would be the wiser course not to interfere at all for the present, except by throwing the young people constantly together. He had lived long enough to see that, in nine cases out of ten, husband and wife might be defined "a man and a woman that were thrown a good deal together—generally in the country." A marries B, and C D; but, under similar circumstances, i.e., thrown together, A would have married D, and C B. This applies to puppy dogs, male and female, as well as to boys and girls.

Perhaps a personal feeling had some little share, too, in bringing him to the above conclusion. He was a bit of a schemer—liked to play puppets. At present, his niece and friend were the largest and finest puppets he had on hand; the day he should bring them to a mutual, rational understanding, the puppet-strings would fall from his hands and the puppets turn independent agents. He represented to Talboys that Lucy was young and very innocent in some respects; that marriage did not seem to run in her head as in most girls'; that a precipitate avowal might startle her, and raise unnecessary difficulties by putting her on her guard too early in their acquaintance. "You have no rival," he concluded; "best win her quietly by degrees. Undermine the coy jade! she is worth it." Cool Talboys acquiesced. David had spurred him out of his pace one night; but David was put out of the way; the course was clear; and, as he could walk over it now, why gallop?

Childish as his friend's jealousy of this poor sailor had seemed to Mr. Fountain, still, the idea once started, he could not help inspecting Lucy to see how she would take his sudden exclusion from these parties. Now Lucy missed the Dodds very much, and was surprised to see them invited no more. But it was not in her character to satisfy a curiosity of this sort by putting a point-blank question to the person who could tell her in two words. She was one of those thorough women whose instinct it is to find out little things, not to ask about them. When day after day passed by, and the Dodds were not invited, it flashed through her mind, first, that there must be some reason for this; secondly, that she had only to take no notice, and the reason, if any, would be sure to pop out. She half suspected Talboys, but gave him no sign of suspicion. With unruffled demeanor and tranquil patience, she watched demurely for disclosures from her uncle or from him like the prettiest little velvet panther conceivable lying flat in a blind path, deranging nobody, but waiting with amiable tranquillity for her friends to come her way.

Thus, under the smooth surface of the little society at Font Abbey finesse was cannily at work. But the surface of every society is like the skin of a man—hides a deal of secret machinery.

Here were two undermining a "coy jade" (perhaps, on the whole, Uncle Fountain, it might be more prudent in you not to call her that name again; you see she is my heroine, and I am a man that could cut you out of this story, and nobody miss you), and the coy jade watching for the miners like a sweet little velvet panther, and, to fling away metaphor, an honest heart set aching sore, hard by, for having come among such a lot.

CHAPTER VI.

A FABLE tells us a fowler one day saw sitting in tree a wood-pigeon. This is a very shy bird, so he had to creep and maneuver to get within gunshot unseen, unheard. He stole from tree to tree, and muffled his footsteps in the long grass so adroitly that, just as he was going to pull the trigger, he stepped light as a feather on a venomous snake. It bit; he died.

This is instructive and pointed, but a trifle severe.

What befell Uncle Fountain, busy enmeshing his cock and hen pheasant, netting a niece and a friend, went to the same tune, but in a lower key, as befitted a domestic tale.*

> * "Domestic," you are aware, is Latin for "tame." Ex.,
>
> "domestic fowl," "domestic drama," "story of domestic
>
> intereet," "or chronicle of small beer,"

Among his letters at breakfast-time came one which he had no sooner read than he flung on the table and went into a fury. Lucy sat aghast; then inquired in tender anxiety what was the matter.

Angry explanations are apt to be dark ones. "It is a confounded shame—it is a trick, child—it is a do."

"Ah! what is that, uncle? 'a do'?—'a do'?"

"Yes, 'a do.' He knew I hated figures; can't bear the sight of them, and the cursed responsibility of adding them up right."

"But who knew all this?"

"He came over here bursting with health, and asked me to be one of his executors—mind, one. I consented on a distinct understanding I was never to be called upon to act. He was twenty years my junior, and like so much mahogany. It was just a form; I did it to soothe a man who called himself my friend, and set his mind at rest."

"But, uncle dear, I don't understand even now. Can it be possible that a friend has abused your good nature?"

"A little," with an angry sneer.

"Has he betrayed your confidence?"

"Hasn't he?"

"Oh dear! What has he done?"

"Died, that is all," snarled the victim.

"Oh, uncle! Poor man!"

"Poor man, no doubt. But how about poor me? Why, it turns out I am sole executor."

"But, dear uncle, how could the poor soul help dying?"

"That is not candid, Lucy," said Mr. Fountain, severely. "Did ever I say he could help dying? But he could help coming here under false colors, a mahogany face, and trapping his friend."

"Uncle, what is the use—your trying to play the misanthrope with me, who know how good you are, in spite of your pretenses to the contrary? To hide your emotion from your poor niece, you go into a feigned fury, and all the time you know how sorry you are your poor friend is gone."

"Of course I am. He has secured one mourner. He might have died to all eternity if he hadn't nailed me first. See how selfish men are, and bad-hearted into the bargain. I believe that young fellow had been to a doctor, and found out he was booked in spite of his mahogany cheeks; so then he rides out here and wheedles an unguarded friend—I'm wired—I'm trapped—I'm snared."

Lucy set herself to soothe her injured relative. "You must say to yourself, 'C'est un petit matheur.'"

"Tell myself a falsehood? What shall I gain by that? Let me tell you, it is these minor troubles that send a man to Bedlam. One breeds another, till they swarm and buzz you distracted, and sting you dead. 'Petit maiheur!' it is a greater one than you have ever encountered since you have been under mywing."

"It is, dear, it is; but I hope to encounter much greater ones before I am your age."

"The deuce you do!"

"Or else I shall die without ever having lived—a vegetable, not a human being."

"Bombast! a 'flower' your lovers will call you."

"And men of sense a 'weed.' But don't let us discuss me. What I wish to know is the nature of your annoyance, dear." He explained to her with a groan that he should have to wind up all the affairs of an estate of 8,000 pounds a year, pay the annual and other encumbrances, etc., etc.

"Well, but, dear, you will be quite at home in this, you have such a turn for business."

"For my own," shrieked the old bachelor, angrily, "not for other people's. Why, Lucy, there will be half a dozen separate accounts, all of four figures. It is not as if executors were paid. And why are they not paid? There ought to be a law compelling the estates they administer to pay them, and handsomely. It never occurred to me before, but now I see the monstrous iniquity of amateur executors, amateur trustees, amateur guardians. They take business out of the hands of those who live by business. I sincerely regret my share in this injustice. If a snob works, he always expects to be paid! how much more a gentleman. He ought to be paid double—once for the work, and once for giving up his natural ease. Here am I, guardian gratis to a cub of sixteen—the worst age—done school, and not begun Oxford and governesses."

"Tutors, you mean."

"Do I? Is it the tutors the whelps fall in love with, little goose? Stop; I'll describe my 'interesting charge,' as the books call it. He has hair you could not tell from tow. He has no eyebrows—a little unfledged slippery horror. He used to come in to dessert, and turn all our stomachs except his silly father's."

"Poor orphan!"

"When you speak to him he never answers—blushes instead."

"Poor child!"

"He has read of eloquent blushes, and thinks there is no need to reply in words—blushing must be such an interesting and effective substitute."

"Poor boy, he wants a little judicious kindness. We will have him here."

"Here!" cried the old gentleman, with horror. "What! make Font Abbey a kennel!!! No, Lucy, no, this house is sacred; no nuisances admitted here. Here, on this single spot of earth, reigns comfort, and shall reign unruffled while I live. This is the temple of peace. If I must be worried, I must, but not beneath this hallowed roof."

This eloquence, delivered as it was with a sudden solemnity, told upon the mind.

"Dear Font Abbey," murmured Lucy, half closing her eyes, "how well you describe it! Societies of the cosey; the walls seem padded, the carpets velvet, and the whole structure care-proof; all is quiet gayety and sweet punctuality. Here comfort and good humor move by clock-work; that is Font Abbey. Yet you are right; if you were to be seen in it no more, it would lose the life of its charm, dear Uncle Fountain."

"Thank you, my dear—thank you. I do like to see my friends about me comfortable, and, above all, to be comfortable myself. The place is well enough, and I am bitterly sorry I must leave it, and sorry to leave you, my dear."

"Leave us? not immediately?"

"This very day. Why, the funeral is to be this week—a grand funeral—and I have to order it all. Then there are relatives to be invited—thirty letters—others to be asked to the reading of the will. It will be one hurry-scurry till we get the house clear of the corpse and the vultures; then at it I must go, head-foremost, into fathomless addition—subtraction—multiplication, and vexation. 'Oh, now forever farewell, something or other—farewell content!' You talk of misanthropy. I shall end there. Lucy."

"Yes, dear uncle."

"I never—do—a good-natured thing—but—I—bitterly—repent it. By Jupiter! the coffee is cold; the first time that has befallen me since I turned off seven servants that battled that point of comfort with me."

Lucy suggested that the coffee might have cooled a little while he was being so kind as to answer her question at unusual length. Then she came round to him bringing a fresh supply of fragrant slow poison, and sat beside him and soothed him till his ire went down, and came the calm depression of a man who, accustomed for many years to do just what he liked, found himself suddenly obliged to do something he did not like—a thing out of the groove of his habits too.

Sure enough, he left Font Abbey the same day, with a promise, exacted by Lucy, that he should make her the partner of all his vexations by writing to her every day.

"And, Lucy," said the old Parthian, as he stepped into his traveling-carriage, "my friend Talboys will miss me; pray be kind to him while I am away. He is a particular friend of mine. I may be wrong, but I do like men of known origin —of old family."

"And you are right. I will be kind to him for your sake, dear."

A slight cold confined Lucy to the house for three or four days after her uncle's departure (by the by, I think this must have been the reason of David's ill success in his endeavors to get an interview with her out of doors).

Thus circumstanced, ladies rummage.

Lucy found in a garret a chest containing a quantity of papers and parchments, and the beautifulest dust. No such dust is made in these degenerate days. Some of these MSS. bore recent dates, and were easily legible, though not so easily intelligible, being written as Gratiano spake.* The writers had omitted to put the idea'd words into red ink, so they had to be picked out with infinite difficulty from the multitude of unidea'd ones.

> * "Gratiano speaks an infinite deal of nothing . . . . his
>
> reasons are as three grains of wheat in two bushels of
>
> chaff."

Other of the MSS., more ancient, wore a double veil. They hid their sense in verbiage, and also in narrow Germanifled letters, farther deformed by contractions and ornamental flourishes, whose joint effect made a word look like a black daddy-long-legs, all sprawling fantastic limbs and the body a dot.

The perusal of these pieces was slow and painful; it was like walking or slipping about among broken ruins overgrown with nettles. But then Uncle Fountain was so anxious to hook on to the Flunkeys—oh, Ciel! what am I saying?—the Funteyns, and his direct genealogical evidence had so completely broken down. She said to herself, "Oh dear! if I could find something among these old writings, and show it him on his return." She had them all dusted and brought down, and a table-cloth laid on a long table in the drawing-room, and spelled them with a good-humored patience that belonged partly to her character, partly to her sex. A female who undertakes this sort of work does not skip as we should; the habit of needle-work in all its branches reconciles that portion of mankind to invisible progress in other matters.

Besides this, they are naturally careful, and, above all, born to endure, they carry patience into nearly all they do.*

> * At about the third rehearsal of a new play our actresses
>
> bring the author's words into their heads, our actors are
>
> still all abroad, and at the first performance the breaks-
>
> down are sure to be among the males; the female jumenta

carry their burden (be it of pig-lead) safe from wing to

wing.

Lucy made her way manfully through all the well-written circumlocution, and in a very short time considering; but the antique [Greek] tried her eyes too much at night, so she gave nearly her whole day to it, for she was anxious to finish all before her uncle's return. It was a curious picture—Venus immersed in musty records.

One day she had studied and spelled four mortal hours, when a visitor was suddenly announced—Miss Dodd. That young lady came briskly in at the heels of the servant and caught Lucy at her work. After the first greeting, her eye rested with such undisguised curiosity on the "mouldy records" that Lucy told her in general terms what she was trying to do for her uncle. "La!" said Eve, "you will ruin your eye-sight; why not send them over to us? I will make David read them."

"And his eyesight?"

"Oh, bless you, he has a knack at reading old writing. He has made a study of it."

"If I thought I was not presuming too far on Mr. Dodd's good nature, I would send one or two of them."

"Do; and I will make him draw up a paper of the contents; I have seen him at this sort of work before now. But there, la! I suppose you know it is all vanity."

"I do it to please my poor uncle."

"And very good you are. But what the better will the poor old gentleman be? We are here to act our own part well; we can't ride up to heaven on our great-grandfather."

These maxims were somewhat coldly received, so Eve shifted her ground. "After all, I don't know why I should be the one to say that, for my own name is older than your uncle's a pretty deal."

Lucy looked puzzled; then suddenly fancying she had caught Eve's meaning, she said: "That is true. Hail mother of mankind!!" and bowed her head with graceful reverence.

Eve stared and colored, not knowing what on earth her companion meant. I am afraid it must be owned that Eve steadily eschewed books and always had. What little book-learning she had came to her filtered through David, and by this channel she accepted it willingly, even sought it at odd times, when there was no bread, pudding, dress, theology, scandal, or fun going on. She turned it off by a sudden inquiry where Mr. Fountain was; "they told me in the village he was away." Now several circumstances combined to make Lucy more communicative than usual. First, she had been studying hard; and, after long study, when a lively person comes to us, it is a great incitement to talk. Pitiful by nature, I spare you the "bent bow." Secondly, she was a little anxious lest her uncle's sudden neglect should have mortified Miss Dodd, and a neutral topic handled at length tends to replace friendly feeling without direct and unpleasant explanations. She therefore answered every question in full; told her that her uncle had lost a dear friend; that he was executor and guardian to the poor boy, now entirely an orphan. Her uncle, with his usual zeal on behalf of his friends; had gone off at once, and doubtless would not return till he had fulfilled in every respect the wishes of the deceased.

To this general sketch she added many details, suppressing the misanthropy Mr. Fountain had exhibited or affected at the first receipt of the intelligence.

In short, angelic gossip. Earthly gossip always backbites, you know. Eve missed something somehow, no doubt the human or backbiting element; still, it was gossip, sacred gossip, far dearer than Shakespeare to the female heart, and Eve's eyes glowed with pleasure and her tongue plied eager questions.

With all this, such instinctive artists are these delicate creatures, both these ladies were secretly in ambush, Lucy to learn whether Eve and David were hurt or surprised at not being invited of late, and why she and he had not called since; Eve to find out what was the cause David and she had been so suddenly dropped: was it Lucy's doing or whose?

Each lady being bent on receiving, not on making revelations, nothing transpired on either side. Seeing this, Eve became impatient and made a bold move.

"Miss Fountain," said she, "you are all alone. I wish you would come over to us this evening and have tea."

Lucy did not immediately reply. Eve saw her hesitation. "It is but a poor place," said she, "to ask you to."

"I will come," said the lady, directly. "I will come with great pleasure."

"Will seven be too early for you?"

"Oh, no, I don't dine now my uncle is away. I call luncheon dinner."

"Perhaps, six, then?"

"Pray let me come at your usual hour. Why derange your family for one person?" Six o'clock was settled.

"I must take some of this rubbish with me," said Eve; "come along, my dears"; and with an ample and mock enthusiastic gesture she caught up an armful of manuscripts.

"The servant shall take them over for you."

"Oh, bother the servant; I am my own servant—if you will lend me a pin or two."

Lucy drew six pins out from different parts of her dress. Eve noticed this, but said nothing. She pinned up her apron so as to make an enormous pocket, and went gayly off with the "spoils of time."

CHAPTER VII.

"Is that what you call being calm, David? Let me alone—don't slobber me. I am sure I wish she had said, 'No.' If I had thought she would come I would never have asked her."

"You would, Eve; you would, for love of me."

"Who knows? Perhaps I might. I am more indulgent than kind."

"Eve, do tell me all. Is she well? does she come of her own good will? Dear Eve!"

"Well, I'll tell you: first we had a bit of a talk for a blind like; and her uncle is away; so then I asked her plump to come to tea. Well, David, first she looked 'No'—only for a single moment, though; she soon altered her mind, and so then, the moment it was to be 'Yes,' she cleared up, and you would have thought she had been asked to the king's banquet. Ah! David, my lad, you have fallen into good hands—you have launched your heart on a deeper ocean than ever your ship sailed on."

David took no notice. He was in a state of exaltation for one thing, and, besides, Eve's simile was sent to the wrong address; we terrestrials fear water in proportion to its depth, but these mariners dread their native element only when it is shallow.

David now kept asking in an excited way what they could do for her. "What could they get to do her honor? Wouldn't she miss the luxuries of her fine place?"

"Now you be quiet, David; we need not put ourselves about, for she will be the easiest girl to please you have ever seen here; or, if she isn't, she'll act it so that you'll be none the wiser. However, you can go and buy some flowers for me."

"That I will; we have none good enough for her here."

"And, David, tea under the catalpa, as we always do on fine nights."

"You don't mean that."

"Ah! but I do. These fine ladies are all for novelties. Now I'm much mistaken if this one has ever had her tea out of doors in all her born days. What! do you think our little stuffy room would be any treat to her, after the drawing-room at Font Abbey? Come, you be off till half-past five; you'll fidget yourself and fidget me else."

David recognized her superiority, obeyed and vanished.

Eve, having got rid of him, showed none of the insouciance she had recommended. She darted into the kitchen, bared her arms, and made wheaten cakes with unequaled rapidity, the servant looking on with demure admiration all the while. These put into the oven, she got her keys and put out the silver teapot, cream jug and sugar basin, things not used every day, I can tell you; item, the best old china tea service; item, some rare tea, of which David had brought home a small quantity from China. At six o'clock Miss Fountain came; a footman marched twenty yards behind her. She dismissed him at the door, and Eve invited her at once into the garden. There David joined them, his heart beating violently. She put out her hand kindly and calmly, and shook hands with him in the most unembarrassed way imaginable. At the touch of her soft hand every fiber in him thrilled and the color rushed into his face. At this a faint blush tinged her own, but no more than the warm welcome she was receiving might account for.

They seated her in a comfortable chair under the catalpa. Presently out came a nice, clean maid, her white neck half hidden, half revealed, by plain, unfigured muslin worn where the frock ended. She put the tea things on the table, and courtesied to Lucy, who returned her salute by a benignant smile. Out came another stouter one with the kettle, hung it from a hoop between two stout sticks, and lighted a fire she had laid underneath, retiring with a parting look at the kettle as soon as it hissed. Then returned maid one with bread, and wheaten cakes, and fruit, butter nice and hard from the cellar, and yellow cream, and went off smiling.

A gentle zeal seemed to animate these domestics, as if they, also, in relative proportions, gave the fete, or at least contributed good will. Lucy's quick eye caught this. It was new to her.

The tea was soon made, and its Oriental fragrance mingled with the other odors that filled the balmy air. Gay golden broken lights flickered in patches on the table, the china cups, the ladies' dresses, and the grass, all but in one place, where the cool deep shadow lay undisturbed around the foot of the tree-stem. Looking up to see whence the flickering gold came that sprinkled her white hand, Lucy saw one of the loveliest and commonest things in nature. The sky was blue—the sun fiery—the air potable gold outside the tree, so that, as she looked up, the mellow green leaves of the catalpa, coming between her and the bright sky and glowing air, shone like transparent gold—staircase upon staircase of great exotic translucent leaves, with specks of lovely blue sky that seemed to come down and perch among the top branches. Charming as these sights were, contrast doubled their beauties; for all these dimples of bright blue and flakes of translucent gold were eyed from the cool and from the deep shade.

The light, it is true, came down and danced on the turf here and there, but it left its heat behind through running the gauntlet of the myriad leaves. Over Lucy's head hung by a silk line from one of the branches a huge globe of humble but fragrant flowers; they were, in point of fact, fastened with marvelous skill all round a damp sponge, but she did not know that. Thus these simple hosts honored their lovely guest. And while these sights and smells stole into her deep eyes and her delicate nostrils, "Fiddle, David," said Eve, loftily, and straightway a simple mellow tune rang sweetly on the cheerful chords—a rustic, dulcet, and immortal ditty, in tune with summer and afternoon, with gold-checkered grass, and leaves that slumbered, yet vibrated, in the glowing air.

A bright, dreamy hour; the soul and senses floated gently in color, fragrance, melody, and great calm. "Each sound seemed but an echo of tranquillity."

Lucy looked up and absorbed the scene, then closed her eyes and listened; and presently her lips parted gradually in so ravishing a smile, her eyes remaining closed, that even Eve, who saw her in her true light, a terrible girl come there to burn and destroy David, remaining cool as a cucumber, could hardly forbear seizing and mumbling her.

In certain companies you shall see a boisterous cordiality, which at bottom is as hollow as diplomacy; but there is a modest geniality which is to society what the bloom is to the plum.

And this charm Lucy found in her hosts of the catalpa. For this very reason that they were her hosts, their manner to her changed a little, and becomingly; they made no secret that it was a downright pleasure to them to have her there. They petted her, and showed her so much simple kindness, that what with the scene, the music, and her companions' goodness, the coy bud opened—timidly at first—but in a way it never had expanded at Font Abbey.

She even developed a feeble sense of fun, followed suit demurely when Eve came out sprightly, laughed like a brook gurgling to Eve's peal of bells, and lo and behold, when the two girls got together, and faced the man, strong in numbers, a favorite trick, backed her ally as cowards back the brave, and set her on to sauce David. They cast doubts upon his skill in navigation. They perplexed him with treacherous questions in geography, put with an innocent affectation of a humble desire for information. In short, they played upon him lightly as they touch the piano. And Eve carolled a song, and David accompanied her on the fiddle; and at the third verse Lucy chimed in spontaneously with a second, and the next verse David struck in with a base, and the tepid air rang with harmony, and poor David thrilled with happiness. His heart felt his voice mingle and blend with hers, and even this contact was delicious to his imagination. And they were happy. But all must end; the shades of evening came down, and the pleasant little party broke up, and, as John had not come, David asked leave to escort her home. Oh no, she could not think of giving him that trouble; so saying, she went home with him. When they were alone, his deep love made him timid and confused. He walked by her side, and did not speak to her. She waited with some surprise at this silence, and then, as he was shy, she talked to him, uttered many airy nothings, and then put questions to him. "Did he always drink tea out of doors?"

"On fine nights in summer. Eve settled all such matters."

"Have you not a voice?"

"I have a voice, but no vote. She is skipper ashore."

"Oh, is she? Who taught her how delicious it is to drink tea out of doors?"

David did not know—fancied it was her own idea. "Did you really like it, Miss Fountain?"

"Like it, Mr. Dodd! It was Elysium. I never passed a sweeter evening in my life."

David colored all over. "I wish I could believe that."

"Was it the tulip-tree, or the violin, or was it your conversation, Mr. Dodd, I wonder?" asked she demurely, looking mock-innocent in his face.

"It was your goodness to be so easily pleased," said Dodd, with a gush that made her color. She smiled, however. "Well, that is one way of looking at things," said she. "Entre nous, I think Miss Dodd was the enchantress."

"Eve is capital company, for that matter."

"Indeed she is; you must be very happy together. Your mutual affection is very charming, Mr. Dodd, but sometimes it almost makes me sad. Forgive me! I have no brother."

"You will never want one to love you a thousand times better than a brother can love."

"Oh, shan't I?" said the lady, and opened her eyes.

"No; and there is more than one that worships the ground you tread on at this moment; but you know that."

"Oh, do I?" She opened her eyes still wider.

David longed to tell how he loved her, but dared not. He looked wistfully at her face. It was quite calm and had suddenly became a little reserved. He felt he was on new and dangerous ground; he sighed and was silent. He turned away his face. When this involuntary sigh broke from him she turned her head a little and looked at him. He felt her eye dwell on him, and his cheeks burned under it.

The next moment they were at Font Hill, and Lucy seemed to David to hesitate whether to give him her hand at parting or not.

She did give him her hand, though not so freely, David thought, as she had done on his own little lawn three hours before, and this dashed his spirits. It seemed to him a step lost, and he had hoped to gain a step somehow by walking home with her. He felt like one who has undertaken to catch some skittish timorous thing, that, if you stand still, will come within a certain small but safe distance, but you must not move a step toward it, or, whir, away it is. He went slowly home, his heart warm and cold by turns; warm when he remembered the sweet hours he had just spent, and her sweet looks and heavenly tones, every one of which he saw and heard again; cold when he thought of the social distance that separated them, and the hundred chances to one against his love. Then he said to himself: "Time was I thought I could never bring a yard down from the foretop to the deck, but I mastered that. Time was I thought I could never work out a logarithm without a formula, but I mastered that. Time was the fiddle beat me so I was ready to cry over it, but at last I learned to make it sing, and now I can make her smile with it (God bless her!) instead of stopping her ears. I can hardly mind the thing that didn't beat me dead for a long while, but I persevered and got the upper hand. Ay, but this is higher and harder than them all—a hundred times harder and higher.

"I'll hold my course, let the wind blow high or low, and if I can't overhaul the wish of my heart, well, I'll carry her flag to the last. I'll die a bachelor for her sake, as sure as you are the moon, my lass, and you the polar star, and from this hour I'll never look at you, but I'll make believe it is her I am looking up at; for she is as high above me, and as bright as you are. God bless her! and to think I never even said good-night to her! I stood there like a mummy." And David reproached himself for his unkindness.

Lucy, on entering the drawing-room, was surprised to find it blazing with candles, but she was more surprised at what she saw seated calmly in an armchair—Mrs. Bazalgette. Lucy stood transfixed; the audacious intruder laughed at her astonishment; the next moment they intertwined, and fell to kissing one another with tender violence.

"Well, love, the fact is, I was passing here on my way home from Devonshire, and I wanted particularly to speak to you, so I thought I would venture just to pop in for a passing call, and lo! I find the old ogre is absent, and not expected back for ever so long, so I have installed myself at his Font Abbey, partly out of love for you, dear, partly, I confess it, out of hate to him. You will write and tell me his face when he comes home and hears I have been living and enjoying myself in his den. I ordered my imperial into his bedroom. I took it for granted that would be the only comfortable one in his house."

"Aunt Bazalgette!" cried Lucy, turning pale; "oh, aunt, what will become of us?"

"Don't be frightened; the gray-haired monster that dyes his whiskers, and gets him up to look only sixty, interposed and forbade the consecration."

"I am glad of it. You shall sleep in mine, dear, and I will go into the east room. It is a sweet little room."

"Is it? then why not put me there?" Lucy colored a little. "I think mine would suit you better, dear, because it is larger and airier, and—"

"I see. As you please; you know I never make difficulties."

"And how long have you been here, aunt?"

"About three hours."

"Three hours, and not send for me! I was only in the village. Did no one tell you?"

"Yes; but you know it is not my way to make a fuss and put people out. How could I tell? You might be agreeably employed, and I was sure of you before bedtime."

Mighty-fine! but the truth is, she came to Font Abbey to pry. She had heard a vague report about Lucy and a gentleman.

She was very glad to find Lucy was out; it gave her an opportunity. She sent for Lucy's maid to help her unpack a dress or two—thirteen. This girl was paid out of Lucy's estate, but did not know that. Mrs. Bazalgette handed her her wages, and that gives an influence. The wily matron did not trust to that alone. In unpacking she gave the girl a dress and several smaller presents, and, this done, slowly and cautiously pumped her. Jane, to fulfill her share of a bargain, which, though never once alluded to, was perfectly understood between both the parties, told her all she knew and all she conjectured; told her, in particular, how constantly Mr. Talboys was in the house, and how, one night, the old gentleman had walked part of the way home with him, "which Mr. Thomas says he didn't think his master would do it for the king, mum!" and had come in all of a flurry, and sent up for miss, and swore* awful when she couldn't come because she was abed. "So you may depend, mum, it is so; leastways, the gentlemen they are willing. We talk it over mostly every day in the servants' hall, mum, and we are all of a mind so fur; but whether it will come to a wedding, that we haven't a settled yet. It's miss beats us; she is like no other young lady ever I came anigh. A man or woman—it is all the same to her—a kind word for everybody, and pass on. But I do really think she likes her own side of the house a trifle the best."

*The ladies of the bedchamber will embellish. After all, it

is their business.

"And there you don't agree with her, Jane?"

"Well, mum—being as we are alone—now is it natural? But Mr. Thomas he says, 'The cold ones take the first offer that comes when there is money ahind it. It isn't us they wants,' says he. I told him I should think not the likes of him —'but our house and land,' says he, 'and hopera box and cetera.' 'But I don't think that of our one,' says I; 'bless you, she is too high-minded.' But what I think, mum, is, she wouldn't say 'no' to her uncle; her mouth don't seem made for saying no, especially to him; and he is bent on Talboys, mum, you take my word."

To return to the drawing-room: Mrs. Bazalgette, after the above delicate discussion, sat there in ambush, knowing more of Lucy's affairs than Lucy knew. Her next point was to learn Lucy's sentiments, and to find whether she was deliberately playing false and breaking her promise, vide.

"Well, Lucy, any lovers yet?"

"No, aunt."

"Take care, Lucy, a little bird whispers in my ear."

"Then it is a humming-bird," and Lucy pouted. "Now, aunt, did you really come to Font Abbey to tease me about such nonsense as—as—gentlemen?" and Lucy looked hurt.

"Here's an actress for you," thought Mrs. Bazalgette; but she calmly dropped the subject, and never recurred to it openly all the evening, but lay secretly in watch, and put many subtle but seeming innocent questions to her niece about her habits, her uncle's guest, whether her uncle kept a horse for her, whether he bought it for her, etc., etc.

The next morning Mrs. Bazalgette breakfasted in bed, during which process she rang her bell seven times. Lucy received at the breakfast-table a letter from her uncle.

"MY DEAR NIECE—The funeral was yesterday, and, I flatter myself, well performed: there were five-and-twenty carriages. After that a luncheon, in the right style, and then to the reading of the will. And here I shall surprise you, but not more than I was myself: I am left 5,000 pounds consols. My worthy friend, whose loss we are called on so suddenly to deplore, accompanied this bequest in his will with many friendly expressions of esteem, which I have always studied and shall study to deserve. He bequeathed to me also, during minority, the care of his boy, the heir to this fine property, which far exceeds the value I had imagined. There is a letter attached to the will; in compliance with it Arthur is to go to Cambridge, but not until he has been well prepared. He will therefore accompany me to Font Abbey to-morrow, and I must contrive somehow or other to find him a mathematical tutor in the neighborhood. There is a handsome allowance made out of the estate for his board, etc., etc.

"He is an interesting boy, and has none of the rudeness and mischievousness they generally have—blue eyes, soft, silky, flaxen hair, and as modest as a girl. His orphaned state merits kindness, and his prospects entitle him to consideration. I mention this because I fancy, when we last discussed this matter, I saw a little disposition on your part to be satirical at the poor boy's expense. I am sure, however, that you will restrain this feeling at my request, and treat him like a younger brother. I only wish he was three or four years older—you understand me, miss.

"To-morrow afternoon, then, we shall be at Font Abbey. Let him have the east room, and tell Brown to light a blazing fire in my bedroom. and warm and air every mortal thing, on pain of death.

"Your affectionate uncle,

"JOHN FOUNTAIN."

On reading this letter Lucy formed an innocent scheme. It had long been matter of regret to her that Aunt Bazalgette could not see the good qualities of Uncle Fountain, and Uncle Fountain of Aunt Bazalgette. "It must be mere prejudice," said she, "or why do I love them both?" She had often wished she could bring them together, and make them know one another better; they would find out one another's good qualities then, and be friends. But how? As Shakespeare says, "Oxen and wain-ropes would not haul them, together."

At last chance aided her—Mrs. Bazalgette was at Font Abbey actually. Lucy knew that if she announced Mr. Fountain's expected return the B would fly off that minute, so she suppressed the information, and, giving up to young Arthur as she had to Mrs. B., moved into a still smaller room than the east room.

And now her heart quaked a little. "But, after all, Uncle Fountain is a gentleman," thought she, "and not capable of showing hostility to her under his own roof. Here she is safe, though nowhere else; only I must see him, and explain to him before he sees her." With this view Lucy declined demurely her aunt's proposal for a walk. No, she must be excused; she had work to do in the drawing-room that could not be postponed.

"Work! that alters the case. Let me see it." She took for granted it was some useful work—something that could be worn when done. "What! is this it—

these dirty parchments? Oh! I see; it is for that selfish old man; who but he would set a lady to parchments!"

"A bad guess," cried Lucy, joyously. "I found them myself, and set myself to work on them."

"Don't tell me! He is at the bottom of it. If it was for yourself you would give it up directly. How amusing for me to see you work at that!" Lucy rose and brought her the new novel. Mrs. Bazalgette took it and sat down to it, but she could not fix her attention long on it. Ladies whose hearts are in dress have no taste for books, however frivolous; can't sit them for above a second or two. Mrs. Bazalgette fidgeted and fidgeted, and at last rose and left the room, book in hand. "How unkind I am!" said Lucy to herself.

She was sitting sentinel till the carriage should arrive; then she could run down and prepare her uncle for his innocent and accidental visitor. It would not be prudent to let him receive the information from a servant, or without the accompanying explanation. This it was that made her so unnaturally firm when the little idle B pressed her to waste in play the shining hours.

Mrs. Bazalgette went book in hand to her bedroom, and had not been there long before she found employment. Many of Lucy's things were still in the wardrobes. Mrs. B. rummaged them, inspected them at the window, and ended by ringing for her maid and trying divers of her niece's dresses on. "They make her dresses better than they do mine; they take more pains." At last she found one that was new to her, though Lucy had worn it several times at Font Abbey.

"Where did she get this, Jane?"

"Present from the old gentleman, mum; he had it down from London for her all at one time with this shawl and twelve puragloves."

Lucy looked two inches taller than Mrs. B., but somehow, I can't tell how, this dress of hers fitted the latter like a glove. It embraced her; it held her tenderly, but tight, as gowns and lovers should. The poor dear could not get out of it. "I must wear it an hour or two," said she. "Besides, it will save my own, knocking about in these country lanes." Thus attired she went into the drawing-room to surprise Lucy. Now Lucy was determined not to move; so, not to be enticed, she did not even look up from her work; on this the other took a mild huff and whisked out.

So keen are the feminine senses, that Lucy, on reflection, recognized something brusk, perhaps angry, in the rustle of that retiring dress, and soon after rang the bell and inquired where Mrs. Bazalgette was. John would make henquiries.

"Your haunt is in the back garden, miss."

"Walking, or what?"

John would make henquiries.

"She is reading, miss; and she is sitting on the seat master 'ad made for you, miss.

"Very well: thank you."

"Any more commands, miss?"

"Not at present." John retired with a regretful air, as one capable of executing important commissions, but lost for lack of opportunity. All the servants in this house liked to come into contact with Lucy. She treated them with a dignified kindness and reserved politeness that wins these good creatures more than either arrogance or familiarity. "Jeames is not such a fool as he looks."

Lucy was glad. Her aunt had got her book. It is an interesting story; she will not miss me now, and the carriage will soon be here, and then I will make up for my unkindness. Curiously enough, at this very juncture, the fair student found something in her parchment which gave her some little hopes of a favorable result.

She was following this clue eagerly, when all of a sudden she started. Her ear had caught the rattle of a carriage over the stones of the stable yard. She rang the bell, and inquired if that was not the carriage.

"Yes, miss.

"My uncle has sent it back, then? He is not coming to-day?"

John would inquire of the coachman.

"Oh yes, miss, master is come, but he got out at the foot of the hill, and walked up through the shrubbery with the young gentleman to show him the grounds." On this news Lucy rose hastily, snatched up a garden hat, and, without any other preparation, went out to intercept her uncle. As she stepped into the garden she heard a loud scream, followed by angry voices; she threw her hands up to heaven in dismay and ran toward the sounds. They came from the back garden. She went like lightning round the corner of the house, and came plump upon an agitated group, of whom she made one directly, spellbound. Here stood Aunt Bazalgette, her head turned haughtily, her cheeks scarlet. There stood Mr. Fountain on the other side of the rustic seat, red as fire, too, but wearing a hang-dog look, and behind him young Arthur, pale, with two eyes like saucers, gazing awestruck at the first row he had ever seen between a full-grown lady and gentleman.

Our narrative must take a step to the rear, as an excellent writer, Private ——* phrases it, otherwise you might be misled to suppose that Uncle Fountain was quarreling with Mrs. B. for having set her foot in sacred Font Abbey.

*"I had an escape myself. As I opened the door of a house, a black fellow was behind waiting for me, and made a chop. I took a step to the rear, fired through the door, and cooked his goose."—Times.

No, the pudding was richer than that. Mr. Fountain had young Arthur in charge, and, not being an ill-natured old gentleman, he pitied the boy, and did all he could to make him feel he was coming among friends. He sent the carriage on, and showed Arthur the grounds, and covertly praised the place and all about it, Lucy included, for was not she an appendage of his abbey. "You will see my niece—a charming young lady, who will be kind to you, and you must make friends with her. She is very accomplished—paints. She plays like an angel, too. Ah! there she is. She has got the gown on I gave her—a compliment to me—a very pretty attention, Arthur, the day of my return. What is she doing?"

Arthur, with his young eyes, settled this question. "The lady is asleep. See, she has dropped her book." And; in fact, the whole attitude was lax and not ungraceful. Her right hand hung down, and the domestic story, its duty done, reposed beneath.

"Now, Arthur," said the senior, making himself young to please the boy, and to show him that, if he looked old, he was not worn out, "would you like a bit of fun? We will startle her—we'll give her a kiss." Arthur hung back irresolute, and his cheeks were dyed with blushes.

"Not you, you young rogue; you are not her uncle." The old gentleman then stole up at the back of the seat, followed with respectful curiosity by Arthur. She happened to move as the senior got near; so, for fear she was going to wake of herself and baffle the surprise, he made a rush and rubbed his beard a little roughly against Mrs. Bazalgette's cheek. Up starts that lady, who was not fast asleep, but only under the influence of the domestic tale, utters a scream, and, when she sees her ravisher, goes into a passion.

"How dare you? What is the meaning of this insult?"

"How came you here?" was the reply, in an equally angry tone.

"Can't a lady come into your little misery of a garden without being outraged?"

"It isn't the garden—it is only the back garden," cried the proprietor of Font Hill; "(blesse) I'll swear that is my niece's gown; so you've invaded that, too."

"Aunt Bazalgette—Uncle Fountain, it was my fault," sighed a piteous voice. This was Lucy, who had just come on the scene. "Dear uncle, forgive me; it was I who invited her."

Lucy's pathetic tones, which were fast degenerating into sobs, were agreeably interrupted.

At one and the same moment the man and woman of the world took a new view of the situation, looked at one another, and burst out laughing. Both these carried a safety-valve against choler—a trait that takes us into many follies, but keeps us out of others—a sense of humor. The next thing to relieve the situation was the senior's comprehensive vanity. He must recover young Arthur's reverence, which was doubtless dissolving all this time. "Now, Arthur," he whispered, "take a lesson from a gentleman of the old school. I hate this she-devil; but this is at my house, so—observe." He then strutted jauntily and feebly up to Mrs. Bazalgette: "Madam, my niece says you are her guest; but permit me to dispute her title to that honor." Mrs. Bazalgette smiled agreeably. She wanted to stay a day or two at Font Abbey. The senior flourished out his arm. "Let me show you what we call the garden here." She took his arm graciously. "I shall be delighted, sir [pompous old fool!]."

Mrs. Bazalgette steeled her mind to admire the garden, and would have done so with ease if it had been hideous. But, unfortunately, it was pretty—prettier than her own; had grassy slopes, a fountain, a grotto, variegated beds, and beds a blaze of one color (a fashion not common at that time); item, a brook with waterlilies on its bosom. "This brook is not mine, strictly speaking," said her host; "I borrowed it of my neighbor." The lady opened her eyes; so he grinned and revealed a characteristic transaction. A quarter of a century ago he had found the brook flowing through a meadow close to his garden hedge. He applied for a lease of the meadow, and was refused by the proprietor in the following terms: "What is to become of my cows?"

He applied constantly for ten years, and met the same answer. Proprietor died, the cows turned to ox-beef, and were eaten in London along with flour and a little turmeric, and washed down with Spanish licorice-water, salt, gentian and a little burned malt. Widow inherited, made hay, and refused F. the meadow because her husband had always refused him. But in the tenth year of her siege she assented, for the following reasons: primo, she had said "no" so often the word gave her a sense of fatigue; secundo, she liked variety, and thought a change for the worse must be better than no change at all.

Her tenant instantly cut a channel from the upper part of the stream into his garden, and brought the brook into the lawn, made it write an S upon his turf, then handed it but again upon the meadow "none the worse," his own comment. These things could be done in the country—jadis.

It cost Mrs. Bazalgette a struggle to admire the garden and borrowed stream—they were so pretty. She made the struggle and praised all. Lucy, walking behind the pair, watched them with innocent satisfaction. "How fast they are making friends," thought she, mistaking an armistice for an alliance.

"Since the place is so fortunate as to please you, you will stay a week with me, madam, at least."

"A week! No, Mr. Fountain; I really admire your courtesy too much to abuse it."

"Not at all; you will oblige me."

"I cannot bring myself to think so."

"You may believe me. I have a selfish motive."

"Oh, if you are in earnest."

"I will explain. If you are my guest for a week, that will give me a claim to be yours in turn." And he bent a keen look upon the lady, as much as to say, "Now I shall see whether you dare let me spy on you as you are doing on me."

"I propose an amendment," said Mrs. Bazalgette, with a merry air of defiance: "for every day I enjoy here you must spend two beneath my roof. On this condition, I will stay a week at Font Abbey."

"I consent," said Mr. Fountain, a little sharply. He liked the bargain. "I must leave you to Lucy for a minute; I have some orders to give. I like my guests to be comfortable." With this he retired to his study and pondered. "What is she here for? it is not affection for Lucy; that is all my eye, a selfish toad like her. (How agreeable she can make herself, though.) She heard I was out, and came here to spy directly. That was sharp practice. Better not give her a chance of seeing my game. I disarmed her suspicion by asking her to stay a week, aha! Well, during that week Talboys must not come, that is all; aha! my lady, I won't give those cunning eyes of yours a chance of looking over my hand." He then wrote a note to Talboys, telling him there was a guest at Font Abbey, a disagreeable woman, "who makes mischief whenever she can. She would be sure to divine our intentions, and use all her influence with Lucy to spite me. You had better stay away till she is gone." He sent this off by a servant, then pondered again.

"She suspects something; then that is a sign she has her own designs on Lucy. Hum! no. If she had, she would not have invited me to her house. She invited me directly and cheerfully—!"

Mrs. Bazalgette walked and sat with an arm round Lucy's waist, and told her seven times before dinner how happy she was at the prospect of a quiet week with her. In the evening she yawned eleven times. Next day she asked Lucy who was coming to dinner.

"Nobody, dear."

"Nobody at all?"

"I thought you would perhaps not care to have our tete-a-tete interrupted yet."

"Oh, but I should like to explore the natives too."

"I will give uncle a hint, dear." The hint was given very delicately, but the malicious senior had a perverse construction ready immediately.

"So this is her mighty affection for you. Can't get through two days without strangers."

"Uncle," said Lucy, imploringly, "she is so used to society, and she has me all day; we ought to give her some little amusement at night."

"Well, I can't make up parties now; my friends are all in London. She only wants something to flirt with. Send for David Dodd."

"What, for her to flirt with?"

"Yes; he is a handsome fellow; he will serve her turn."

"For shame, uncle; what would Mr. Bazalgette say? Poor aunt, she is a coquette now."

"And has been this twenty years."

"Now I was thinking—Mr. Talboys?"

"Talboys is not at home; she must be content with lower game. She shall bring down David."

Lucy hesitated. "I don't think she will like Mr. Dodd, and I am sure he will not like her."

"How can you know that?"

"He is so honest. He will not understand a woman of the world and her little in —sin—No, I don't mean that."

"Well, if he does not understand her he may like her."

"Aunt, he has made me ask the Dodds to tea, and I am afraid you will not like them."

"Well, if I don't we must try some more natives to-morrow. Who are they?" Lucy told her. "Pretty people to ask to meet me," said she, loftily. This scorn dissolved in course of the evening. Lucy, anxious her guests should be pleased with one another, drew the Dodds out, especially David—made him spin a yarn. With this and his good looks he so pleased Mrs. Bazalgette that it was the last yarn he ever span during her stay. She took a fancy to him, and set herself to captivate him with sprightly ardor.

David received her advances politely, but a little coldly. The lady was very agreeable, but she kept him from Lucy; he hardly got three words with her all the evening. As they went home together, Eve sneered: "Well, you managed nicely; it was your business to make friends with that lady."

"With all my heart."

"Then why didn't you do what she bid you?"

"She gave me no orders that I heard," said the literal first mate.

"She gave you a plain hint, though."

"To do what?"

"To do what? stupid! Why, to make love to her, to be sure."

"Why, she is a married woman?"

"If she chooses to forget that, is it your business to remember it?"

"And if she was single, and the loveliest in the world, how could I court her when my heart is full of an angel?"

"If your heart is full, your head is empty. Why, you see nothing."

"I can't see why I should belie my heart."

"Can't you? Then I can. David, in less than a month Miss Fountain goes to this lady and stays a quarter of a year: she told me so herself. Oh, my ears are always open in your service ever since I did agree to be as great a fool as you are. Now don't you see that if you can't get Mrs. Bazalgette to invite you to her house, you must take leave of the other here forever?"

"I see what you mean, Eve; how wise you are! It is wonderful. But what is to be done? I am bad at feigning. I can't make love to her."

"But you can let her make love to you: is that an effort you feel equal to? and I must do the rest. Oh, we have a nice undertaking before us. But, if boys will cry for fruit that is out of their reach, and their silly sisters will indulge them— don't slobber me."

"You are such a dear girl to fight for me so a little against your judgment."

"A little, eh? Dead against it, you mean. Don't look so blank, David; you are all right as far as me. When my heart is on your side you can snap your fingers at my judgment."

David was cheered by this gracious revelation.

Eve was a tormenting little imp. She could not help reminding him every now and then that all her maneuvers and all his love were to end in disappointment. These discouraging comments had dashed poor David's spirits more than once; but he was beginning to discover that they were invariably accompanied or followed by an access of cheerful zeal in the desperate cause—a pleasing phenomenon, though somewhat unintelligible to this honest fellow, who had never microscoped the enigmatical sex.

Mrs. Bazalgette reproached Lucy: "You never told me how handsome Mr.

Dodd was."

"Didn't I?

"No. He is the handsomest man I ever saw."

"I have not observed that, but I think he is one of the worthiest."

"I should not wonder," said the other lady, carelessly. "It is clear you don't appreciate him here. You half apologized to me for inviting him."

"That was because you are such a fashionable lady, and the Dodds have no such pretensions."

"All the better; my taste is not for sophisticated people. I only put up with them because I am obliged. Why, Lucy, you ought to know how my heart yearns for nature and truth; I am sure I have told you so often enough. An hour spent with a simple, natural creature like Captain Dodd refreshes me as a cooling breeze after the heat and odors of a crowded room."

"Miss Dodd is very natural too—is she not?"

"Very. Pertness and vulgarity are natural enough—to some people."

"My uncle likes her the best of the two."

"Then your uncle is mad. But the fact is, men are no judges in such cases; they are always unjust to their own sex, and as blind to the faults of ours as beetles."

"But surely, aunt, she is very arch and lively."

"Pert and fussy, you mean."

"Pretty, at all events? Rather?"

"What, with that snub nose!!?"

Lucy offered to invite other neighbors; Mrs. Bazalgette replied she didn't want to be bothered with rurality. "You can ask Captain Dodd, if you like; there is no need to invite the sister."

"Oh yes, I must; my uncle likes her the best."

"But I don't; and I am only here for a day or two."

"Miss Dodd would be hurt. It would be unkind—discourteous."

"No, no. She watches him all the time like a little dragon."

"Apres? We have no sinister designs on Mr. Dodd, have we?" and something unusually keen flashed upon Aunt Bazalgette out of the tail of the quiet Lucy's eye.

Mrs. Bazalgette looked cross. "Nonsense, Lucy; so tiresome! Can't we have an agreeable person without tacking on a disagreeable one?"

"Aunt," said Lucy, pathetically, "ask me anything else in the world, but don't ask me to be rude, for I can't."

"Well, then, you are bound to entertain her, since she is your choice, and leave me mine."

Lucy acquiesced softly.

David, tutored by his sister, now tried to seem interested in her who came between him and Lucy, and a miserable hand he made of this his first piece of acting. Luckily for him, Mrs. Bazalgette liked the sound of her own voice; and his good looks, too, went a long way with the mature woman. Lucy and Eve sat together at the tea-table; Mr. Fountain slumbered below; Arthur was in the study, nailed to a novel; Eve, under a careless exterior, watched intently to find out if Lucy, under a calm surface, cared for David at all or not, and also watched for a chance to serve him. She observed a certain languor about the young lady, but no attempt to take David from the coquette. At last, however, Lucy did say demurely, "Mr. Dodd seems to appreciate my aunt."

"Don't you think it is rather the other way?"

"That is an insidious question, Miss Dodd. I shall make no admissions; but I warn you she is a very fascinating woman."

"My brother is greatly admired by the ladies, too."

"Oh, since I praised my champion, you have a right to praise yours. But he will get the worst in that little encounter."

"Why so?

"Because my sprightly aunt forgets the very names of her conquests when once she has thoroughly made them."

"She will never make this one; my brother carries an armor against coquettes."

"Ay, indeed; and pray what may that be?" inquired Lucy, a little quizzingly.

"A true and deep attachment."

"Ah!"

"And if you will look at him a little closer you will see that he would be glad to get away from that old flirt; but David is very polite to ladies."

Lucy stole a look from under her silken lashes, and it so happened that at that very moment she encountered a sorrowful glance from David that said plainly enough, I am obliged to be here, but I long to be there. She received his glance full in her eyes, absorbed it blandly, then lowered her lashes a moment, then turned her head with a sweet smile toward Eve. "I think you said your brother was engaged."

"No."

"I misunderstood you, then."

"Yes." Eve uttered this monosyllable so dryly that Lucy drew back, and immediately turned the conversation into chit-chat.

It had not trickled above ten minutes when an exclamation from David interrupted it. The young ladies turned instinctively, and there was David flushing all over, and speaking to Mrs. Bazalgette with a tremulous warmth, that, addressed as it was to a pretty woman, sounded marvelously like love-making.

Lucy turned her crest round a little haughtily, and shot such a glance on Eve. Eve read in it a compound of triumph and pique.

David came to Eve one morning with parchments in his hand and a merry smile. "Eureka!"

"You're another," said Eve, as quick as lightning, and upon speculation.

"I have made Mr. Fountain's pedigree out," explained David.

"You don't say so! won't he be pleased?"

"Yes. Do you think she will be pleased?"

"Why not? She will look pleased, anyway. I say, don't you go and tell them the whole county was owned by the Dodds before Fountain, or Funteyn, or Font, was ever heard of."

"Hardly. I have my own weaknesses, my lass; I've no need to adopt another man's."

"Bless my soul, how wise you are got! So sudden, too! You shouldn't surprise a body like that. Lucky I'm not hysterical. Now let me think, David—Solomon, I mean—no, you shall keep this discovery back awhile; it may be wanted." She then reminded him that the Fountains were capricious; that they had dropped him for a week, and eight again; if so, this might be useful to unlock their street door to him at need.

"Good heavens, Eve, what cunning!"

"David, when I have a bad cause in hand, I do one of two things: I drop it, or I go into it heart and soul. If my zeal offends you, I can retire from the contest with great pleasure."

"No! no! no! no! no! If you leave the helm I shall go ashore directly"—dismay of David; grim satisfaction of his imp.

This matter settled, David asked Eve if she did not think Master Nelson (Mr. Fountain's new ward) was a very nice boy.

"Yes; and I see he has taken a wonderful fancy to you."

"And so have I to him; we have had one or two walks together. He is to come here at twelve o'clock to-day."

"Now why couldn't you have asked me first, David? The painters are coming into the house to-day; and the paperers, and all, and we can't be bothered with mathematics. You must do them at Font Abbey." Eve was a little cross. David only laughed at her; but he hesitated about making a school-house of Font Abbey—it would look like intruding.

"Pooh! nonsense," said Eve; "they will only be too glad to take advantage of your good-nature."

"He is an orphan," said David, doggedly.

However, the lesson was given at Font Abbey, and after it Master Nelson came bounding into the drawing-room to the ladies.

"Oh, Lucy, Mr. Dodd is such a beautiful geometrician! He has been giving me a lesson; he is going to give me one every day. He knows a great deal more than my last tutor." On this Master Nelson was questioned, and revealed that a friendship existed between him and Mr. Dodd such as girls are incapable of (this was leveled at Lucy); being cross-examined as to the date of this friendship, he was obliged to confess that it had only existed four days, but was to last to death.

"But, Arthur," said Lucy, "will not this take up too much of Mr. Dodd's time? I think you had better consult Uncle Fountain before you make a positive arrangement of the kind."

"Oh, I have spoken to my guardian about it, and he was so pleased. He said that would save him a mathematical tutor."

"Oh, then," said Mrs. Bazalgette, "Mr. Dodd is to teach mathematics gratis."

"My friend is a gentleman," was the timid reply. (Juveniles have a pomposity all their own, and exquisitely delicious.*) "We read together because we like one another, and that is why we walk together and play together; if we were to offer him money he would throw it at our heads." Mr. Arthur then relaxed his severity, and, condescending once more to the familiar, added: "And he has made me a kite on mathematical principles—such a whacker—those in the shops are no use; and he has sent his mother's Bath chair on to the downs, and he is going to show me the kite draw him ten knots an hour in it—a knot means a mile, Lucy—so I can't stay wasting my time here; only, if you want to see some fun for once in your lives, come on the downs in about an hour—will you? Oh yes! do come!"

    * Read the Oxford Essays.

"Certainly not," said Mrs. Bazalgette, sharply.

"Excuse us, dear," said Lucy in the same breath.

"Well, Lucy," said Mrs. Bazalgette, "am I wrong about your uncle's selfishness! I have tried in vain ever since I came here to make you see it whereyou were the only sufferer."

"Not quite in vain, aunt," said Lucy sadly; "you have shown me defects in my poor uncle that I should never have discovered."

Mrs. Bazalgette smiled grimly.

"Only, as you hate him, and I love him, and always mean to love him, permit me to call his defects 'thought-lessness.' You can apply the harsh term 'selfish-ness' to the most good-natured, kind, indulgent—oh!"

"Ha! ha! Don't cry, you silly girl. Thoughtless? a calculating old goose, who is eternally aiming to be a fox—never says or does anything without meaning something a mile off. Luckily, his veil is so thin that everybody sees through it but you. What do you think of his thought-less-ness in getting a tutor gratis? Poor Mr. Dodd!"

"I will answer for it, it is a pleasure to Mr. Dodd to be of service to his little friend," said Lucy, warmly.

"How do you know a bore is a pleasure to Mr. Dodd?"

"Mr. Dodd is a new acquaintance of yours, aunt, but I have had opportunities of observing his character, and I assure you all this pity is wasted."

"Why, Lucy, what did you say to Arthur just now. You are contradicting yourself."

"What a love of opposition I must have. Are you not tired of in-doors? Shall we go into the village?"

"No; I exhausted the village yesterday."

"The garden?"

"No."

"Well, then, suppose we sketch the church together. There is a good light."

"No. Let us go on the downs, Lucy."

"Why, aunt, it—it is a long walk."

"All the better."

"But we said 'No.'"

"What has that to do with it?"

Arthur was right; the kites that are sold by shops of prey are not proportioned nor balanced; this is probably in some way connected with the circumstance that they are made to sell, not fly. The monster kite, constructed by the light of Euclid, rose steadily into the air like a balloon, and eventually, being attached to the chair, drew Mr. Arthur at a reasonable pace about half a mile over a narrow but level piece of turf that was on the top of the downs. Q.E.D. This done, these two patient creatures had to wind the struggling monster in, and go back again to the starting point. Before they had quite achieved this, two petticoats mounted the hill and moved toward them across the plateau. At sight of them David thrilled from head to foot, and Arthur cried, "Oh, bother!" an unjust ejaculation, since it was by his invitation they came. His alarms were verified. The ladies made themselves No. 1 directly, and the poor kite became a shield for flirtation. Arthur was so cross.

At last the B's desire to occupy attention brought her to the verge of trouble. Seeing David saying a word to Lucy, she got into the chair, and went gayly off, drawn by the kite, which Arthur, with a mighty struggle, succeeded in hooking to the car for her. Now, the plateau was narrow, and the chair wanted guiding. It was easy to guide it, but Mrs. Bazalgette did not know how; so it sidled in a pertinacious and horrid way toward a long and steepish slope on the left side. She began to scream, Arthur to laugh—the young are cruel, and, I am afraid, though he stood perfectly neutral to all appearance, his heart within nourished black designs. But David came flying up at her screams—just in time. He caught the lady's shoulders as she glided over the brow of the slope, and lifted her by his great strength up out of the chair, which went the next moment bounding and jumping athwart the hill, and soon rolled over and groveled in rather an ugly way.

Mrs. Bazalgette sobbed and cried so prettily on David's shoulder, and had to be petted and soothed by all hands. Inward composure soon returned, though not outward, and in due course histrionics commenced. First the sprain business. None of you do it better, ladies, whatever you may think. David had to carry her a bit. But she was too wise to be a bore. Next, the heroic business: would be put down, would walk, possible or not; would not be a trouble to her kind friends. Then the martyr smiling through pain. David was very attentive to her; for while he was carrying her in his arms she had won his affection, all he could spare from Lucy. Which of you can tell all the consequences if you go and carry a pretty woman, with her little insinuating mouth close to your ears?

Lucy and Arthur walked behind. Arthur sighed. Lucy was reveuse. Arthur broke silence first. "Lucy!"

"Yes, dear."

"When is she going?"

"Arthur, for shame! I won't tell you. To-morrow."

"Lucy," said Arthur, with a depth of feeling, "she spoils everything!!!"

Next morning —— come back? What for? I will have the goodness to tell you what she said in his ear? Why, nothing.

You are a female reader? Oh! that alters the case. To attempt to deceive you would be cowardly, immoral; it would fail. She sighed, "My preserver!" at which David had much ado not to laugh in her face. Then she murmured still more softly, "You must come and see me at my home before you sail—will you not? I insist" (in the tone of a supplicant), "come, promise me."

"That I will—with pleasure," said David, flushing.

"Mind, it is a promise. Put me down. Lucy, come here and make him put me down. I will not be a burden to my friends."

CHAPTER VIII.

THAT same evening, Mrs. Bazalgette, being alone with Lucy in the drawing-room, put her arm round that young lady's waist, and lovingly, not seriously, as a man might have been apt to do, reminded her of her honorable promise—not to be caught in the net of matrimony at Font Abbey. Lucy answered, without embarrassment, that she claimed no merit for keeping her word. No one had had the ill taste to invite her to break it.

"You are either very sly or very blind," replied Mrs. Bazalgette, quietly.

"Aunt!" said Lucy, piteously.

Mrs. Bazalgette, who, by many a subtle question and observation during the last week, had satisfied herself of Lucy's innocence, now set to work and laid Uncle Fountain bare.

"I do not speak in a hurry, Lucy; a hint came round to me a fortnight ago that you had an admirer here, and it turns out to be this Mr. Talboys."

"Mr. Talboys?"

"Yes. Does that surprise you? Do you think a young gentleman would come to Font Abbey three nights in a week without a motive?"

Lucy reflected.

"It is all over the place that you two are engaged."

Lucy colored, and her eyes flashed with something very like anger, but she held her peace.

"Ask Jane else."

"What! take my servant into my confidence?"

"Oh, there is a way of setting that sort of people chattering without seeming to take any notice. To tell the truth, I have done it for you. It is all over the village, and all over the house."

"The proper person to ask must have been Uncle Fountain himself."

"As if he would have told me the truth."

"He is a gentleman, aunt, and would not have uttered a falsehood."

"Doctrine of chivalry! He would have uttered half a dozen in one minute. Besides, why should I question a person I can read without. Your uncle, with his babyish cunning that everybody sees through, has given me the only proof I wanted. He has not had Mr. Talboys here once since I came."

"Cunning little aunt! Mr. Talboys happens not to be at home; uncle told me so himself."

"Simple little niece, uncle told you a fib; Mr. Talboys is at home. And observe! until I came to Font Abbey, he was here three times a week. You admit that. I come; your uncle knows I am not so unobservant as you, and Mr. Talboys is kept out of sight."

"The proof that my uncle has deceived me," said Lucy, coldly, and with lofty incredulity.

"Read that note from Miss Dodd!"

"What! you in correspondence with Miss Dodd?"

"That is to say, she has thrust herself into correspondence with me—just like her assurance."

The letter ran thus:

"DEAR MADAM—My brother requests me to say that, in compliance with your request, he called at the lodge of Talboys Park, and the people informed him Mr. Talboys had not left Talboys Park at all since Easter. I remain yours, etc."

Lucy was dumfounded.

"I suspected something, Lucy, so I asked Mr. Dodd to inquire."

"It was a singular commission to send him on."

"Oh, he takes long walks—cruises, he calls them—and he is so good-natured. Well, what do you think of your uncle's veracity now?"

Lucy was troubled and distressed, but she mastered her countenance: "I think he has sacrificed it for once to his affection for me. I fear you are right; my eyes are opened to many circumstances. But do—oh, pray do!—see his goodness in all this."

"The goodness of a story-teller."

"He admires Mr. Talboys—he reveres him. No doubt he wished to secure his poor niece what he thinks a great match, and now you assign ill motives to him. Yes, I confess he has deviated from truth. Cruel! cruel! what can you give me in exchange if you rob me of my esteem for those I love!"

This innocent distress, with its cause, were too deep for a lady whose bright little intelligence leaned toward cunning rather than wisdom. In spite of her niece's trouble, and the brimming eyes that implored forbearance, she drove the sting, merrily in again and again, till at last Lucy, who was not defending herself, but an absent friend, turned a little suddenly on her and said:

"And do you think he says nothing against you?"

"Oh, he is a backbiter, too, is he? I didn't know he had that vice. Ah! and, pray, what can he find to say against me?"

"Oh, people that hate one another can always find something ill-natured to say," retorted Lucy, with a world of meaning.

Mrs. Bazalgette turned red, and her little nose went up into the air at an angle of forty-five. She said, with majestic disdain: "I don't hate the man—I don't condescend to hate him."

"Then don't condescend to backbite him, dear."

This home-thrust, coming from such a quarter, took away my Lady Disdain's very breath. She sat transfixed; then, upon reflection, got up a tear, and had to be petted.

This sweet lady departed, flinging down her firebrand on those hospitable boards.

Lucy, though she had defended her uncle, was not a little vexed that he had managed matters so as to get her talked of with Mr. Talboys. Her natural modesty and reserve prevented her from remonstrating; nor was there any positive necessity. She was one of those young ladies who seem born mistresses of the art of self-defense. Deriving the art not from experience, but from instinct, they are as adroit at seventeen as they are at twenty-seven; so a last year's bird constructs her first nest as cunningly as can a veteran feathered architect.

Therefore, without a grain of discourtesy or tangible ill-temper, she quietly froze, and a small family with her, they could not tell how or why, for they had never even suspected this girl's power. You would have seemed to them as one that mocketh had you told them they owed their gayety, their good-humor, their happiness, and their conversational powers to her.

Of these Talboys suffered the most. She brought him to a stand-still by a very simple process. She no longer patted or spurred him. To vary the metaphor, a man that has no current must be stirred or stagnate; Lucy's light hand stirred Talboys no more; Talboys stagnated. Mr. Fountain suffered next in proportion.

He began to find that something was the matter, but what he had no idea. He did not observe that, though Lucy answered him as kindly as ever, she did not draw him out as heretofore, far less that she was vexed with him, and on her guard against him and everybody, like a maitresse d'armes. No. "The days were drawing in. The air was heavy; no carbon in it. Wind in the east again!!!" etc. So subtle is the influence of these silly little creatures upon creation's lords.

Mr. Talboys did not take delicate hints. He continued his visits three times a week, and the coast was kept clear for him. On this Miss Fountain proceeded to overt acts of war. She brought a champion on the scene—a terrible champion—a champion so irresistible that I set any woman down as a coward who lets him loose upon a sex already so unequal to the contest as ours. What that champion's real name is I have in vain endeavored to discover, but he is called "Headache." When this terrible ally mingled in the game—on the Talboys nights—dismay fell upon the wretched males that abode in and visited the once cheerful, cozy Font Abbey. Messrs. Fountain and Talboys put their heads together in grave, anxious consultations, and Arthur vented a yell of remonstrance. He found the lady one afternoon preparing indisposition. She was leaning languidly back, and the fire was dying out of her eye, and the color out of her cheek, and the blinds were drawn down. The poor boy burst in upon this prologue. "Oh, Lucy," he cried, in piteous, foreboding tones, "don't go and have a headache to-night. It was so jolly till you took to these stupid headaches."

"I am so sorry, Arthur," said Lucy, apologetically, but at bottom she was inexorable. The disease reached its climax just before dinner. All remedies failed, and there was nothing for it but to return to her own room, and read the last new tale of domestic interest—and principle—until sleep came to her relief.

After dinner Arthur shot out with the retiring servants, and interred himself in the study, where he sought out with care such wild romances as give entirely false views of life, and found them, "and so shut up in measureless content."— Macbeth.

The seniors consulted at their ease. They both appreciated the painful phenomenon, but they differed toto coelo as to the cause. Mr. Fountain ascribed it to the somber influence of Mrs. Bazalgette, and miscalled her, till Jane's hair stood on end: she happened to be the one at the keyhole that night. Mr. Talboys laid all the blame on David Dodd. The discussion was vigorous, and occupied more than two hours, and each party brought forward good and plausible reasons; and, if neither made any progress toward converting the other, they gained this, at least, that each corroborated himself. Now Mrs. Bazalgette was gone no direct reprisals on her were possible. Registering a vow that one day or other he would be even with her, the senior consented, though not very willingly, to co-operate with his friend against an imaginary danger. In answer to his remark that the Dodds were never invited to tea now, Mr. Talboys had replied: "But I find from Mr. Arthur he visits the house every day on the pretense of teaching him mathematics—a barefaced pretense—a sailor teach mathematics!" Mr. Fountain had much ado to keep his temper at this pertinacity in a jealous dream. He gulped his ire down, however, and said, somewhat sullenly: "I really cannot consent to send my poor friend's son to the University a dunce, and there is no other mathematician near."

"If I find you one," said Talboys, hastily, "will you relieve Mr. Dodd of his labors, and me of his presence?"

"Certainly," said the other. Poor David!

"Then there is my friend Bramby. He is a second wrangler. He shall take Arthur, and keep him till Miss Fountain leaves us. Bramby will refuse me nothing. I have a living in my gift, and the incumbent is eighty-eight."

The senior consented with a pitying smile.

"Bramby will take him next week," said Talboys, severely.

Mr. Fountain nodded his head. It was all the assent he could effect: and at that moment there passed through him the sacrilegious thought that the Conqueror must have imported an ass or two among his other forces, and that one of these, intermarrying with Saxon blood, had produced a mule, and that mule was his friend.

The same uneasy jealousy, which next week was to expel David from Font Abbey, impelled Mr. Talboys to call the very next day at one o'clock to see what was being done under cover of trigonometry. He found Mr. and Miss Fountain just sitting down to luncheon. David and Arthur were actually together somewhere, perhaps going through the farce of geometry. He was half vexed at finding no food for his suspicions. Presently, so spiteful is chance, the door opened, and in marched Arthur and David.

"I have made him stay to luncheon for once," said Arthur; "he couldn't refuse me; we are to part so soon." Arthur got next to Lucy, and had David on his left. Mr. Talboys gave Mr. Fountain a look, and very soon began to play his battery upon David.

"How do you naval officers find time to learn geometry?"

"What? don't you know it is a part of our education, sir?"

"I never heard that before."

"That is odd; but perhaps you have spent all your life ashore" (this in commiserating accents). David then politely explained to Mr. Talboys that a man who looked one day to command a ship must not only practice seamanship, but learn navigation, and that navigation was a noble art founded on the exact sciences as well as on practical experiences; that there did still linger upon the ocean a few of the old captains, who, born at a period when a ship, in making a voyage, used to run down her longitude first, and then begin to make her latitude, could handle a ship well, and keep her off a lee shore if they saw it in time, but were, in truth, hardly to be trusted to take her from port to port. "We get a word with these old salts now and then when we are becalmed alongside, and the questions they put make us quite feel for them. Then they trust entirely to their instruments. They can take an observation, but they can't verify one. They can tack her and wear her (I have seen them do one when they should have done the other), and they can read the sky and the water better than we young ones; and while she floats they stick to her, and the greater the danger the louder the oaths—but that is all." He then assured them with modest fervor that much more than that was expected of the modern commander, particularly in the two capital articles of exact science and gentlemanly behavior. He concluded with considerable grace by apologizing for his enthusiastic view of a profession that had been too often confounded with the faults of its professors—faults that were curable, and that they would all, he hoped, live long enough to see cured. Then, turning to Miss Fountain, he said: "And if I began by despising my business, and taking a small view of it, how should I ever hold sticks with my able competitors, who study it with zeal and admiration?"

Lucy. "I don't quite understand all you have said, Mr. Dodd, but that last I think is unanswerable."

Fountain. "I am sure of it. As the Duke of Wellington said the other day in the House of Lords, 'That is a position I defy any noble lord to assault with success'—haw! ho!"

Mr. Talboys averted his attack. "Pray, sir," said he, with a sneer, "may I ask, have nautical commanders a particular taste for education as well as science?"

"Not that I know of. If you mean me, I am hungry to learn, and I find few but what can teach me something, and what little I know I am willing to impart, sir; give and take."

"It is the direction of your teaching that seems to me so singular. Mathematics are horrible enough, and greatly to be avoided."

"That is news to me."

"On terra firma, I mean."

At this opening of the case Talboys versus Newton, Arthur shrugged his shoulders to Lucy and David, and went swiftly out as from the presence of an idiot. It was abominably rude. But, besides being ill-natured and a little shallow, Mr. Talboys was drawling out his words, and Arthur was sixteen—

candid epoch, at which affectation in man or woman is intolerable to us; we get a little hardened to it long before sixty. Mr. Talboys bit his lip at this boyish impertinence, but he was too proud a man to notice it otherwise than by quietly incorporating the offender into his satire. "But the enigma is why you read them with a stripling, of whose breeding we have just had a specimen—mathematics with a hob-ba-de-hoy? Grand Dieu! Do pray tell us, Mr. Dodd, why you come to Font Abbey every day; is it really to teach Master Orson mathematics and manners?"

David did not sink into the earth as he was intended to.

"I come to teach him algebra and geometry, what little I know."

"But your motive, Mr. Dodd?"

David looked puzzled, Lucy uneasy at seeing her guest badgered.

"Ask Miss Fountain why she thinks I do my best for Arthur," said David, lowering his eyes.

Talboys colored and looked at Fountain.

"I think it must be out of pure goodness," said Lucy, sweetly.

Mr. Talboys ignored her calmly. "Pray enlighten us, Mr. Dodd. Now what is the real reason you walk a mile every day to do mathematics with that interesting and well-behaved juvenile?"

"You are very curious, sir," said David, grimly, his ire rising unseen.

"I am—on this point."

"Well, since you must be told what most men could see without help, it is—because he is an orphan; and because an orphan finds a brother in every man that is worth the shoe-leather he stands in. Can ye read the riddle now, ye lubber?" and David started up haughtily, and, with contempt and wrath on his face, marched through the open window and joined his little friend on the lawn, leaving Fountain red with anger and Talboys white.

The next thing was, Lucy rose and went quietly out of the room by the door.

"It is the last time he shall set his foot within my door. Provoking cub!"

"You are convinced at last that he is a dangerous rival?"

"A rival? Nonsense and stuff!!"

"Then why was she so agitated? She went out with tears in her eyes: I saw them."

"The poor girl was frightened, no doubt. We don't have fracases at Font Abbey. On this one spot of earth comfort reigns, and balmy peace, and shall reign unruffled while I live. The passions are not admitted here, sir. Gracious Heaven forbid! I'd as soon see a bonfire in the middle of my dining-room as

Jealousy & Co."

"In that case you had better exclude the cause."

"The cause is your imagination, my good friend; but I will give it no handle. I will exclude David Dodd until she has accepted you in form."

With this understanding the friends parted.

After dinner that same day Arthur sat in the drawing-room with Lucy. He was reading, she working placidly. She looked off her work demurely at him several times. He was absorbed in a flighty romance. "I have dropped my worsted, Arthur. It is by you."

Arthur picked the ball up and brought it to her; then back to his romance, heart and soul. Another sidelong glance at him; then, after a long silence, "Your book seems very interesting."

"I'll fling it against the wall if it does not mind," was the infuriated reply. "Here are two fools quarreling, page after page, and can't see, or won't see, what everybody else can see, that it is an absurd misunderstanding. One word of common sense would put it all right."

"Then why not put the book down and talk to me?"

"I can't. It won't let me. I must see how long the two fools will go on not seeing what everybody else sees."

"Will not the number of volumes tell you that?"

"Signorina, don't you try to be satirical!" said the sprightly youth; "you'll only make a mess of it. What is the use dropping one drop of vinegar into such a great big honey pot?"

"You are a saucy boy," retorted Lucy, in tones of gentle approbation.

A long silence.

"Arthur, will you hold this skein for me?"

Arthur groaned.

"Never mind, dear. I will try and manage with a chair."

"No you won't, now; there."

The victim was caught by the hands. But with fatal instinctive perverseness he sat in silent amazement watching Lucy's supple white hand disentangling impossibilities instead of chattering as he was intended to. Lucy gave a little sigh. Here was a dreadful business—obliged to elicit the information she had resolved should be forced upon her.

"By the by, Arthur," said she, carelessly, "did Mr. Dodd say anything to you on the lawn?"

"What about?"

"About what was said after you went out so ru—so suddenly."

"No; why? what was said? Something about me? Tell me."

"Oh, no, dear; as Mr. Dodd did not mention it, it is not worth while. You must not move your hands, please."

"Now, Lucy, that is too bad. It is not fair to excite one's curiosity and then stop directly."

"But it is nothing. Mr. Talboys teased Mr. Dodd a little, that is all, and Mr. Dodd was not so patient as I have seen him on like occasions. There, youare disentangled at last."

"Now, signorina, let us talk sense. Tell me, which do you like best of all the gentlemen that come here?"

"You, dear; only keep your hands still."

"None of your chaff, Lucy."

"Chaff! what is that?"

"Flattery, then. I hope it isn't that affected fool Talboys, for I hate hun."

"I cannot undertake to share your prejudices, Mr. Arthur."

"Then you actually like him."

"I don't dislike him."

"Then I pity your taste, that is all."

"Mr. Talboys has many good qualities; and if he was what you describe him, Uncle Fountain would not prize him as he does."

"There is something in that, Lucy; but I think my guardian and you are mad upon just that one point. Talboys is a fool and a snob."

"Arthur," said Lucy, severely, "if you speak so of my uncle's friends, you and I shall quarrel."

"You won't quarrel just now, if you can help it."

"Won't I, though? Why not, pray?"

"Because your skein is not wound yet."

"Oh, you little black-hearted thing!"

"I know human nature, miss," said the urchin, pompously; "I have read Miss Edgeworth!!!"

He then made an appeal to her candor and good sense. "Now don't you see my friend Mr. Dodd is worth them all put together?"

"I can't quite see that."

"He is so noble, so kind, so clever."

"You must own he is a trifle brusk."

"Never. And, if he is, that is not like hurting people's feelings on purpose, and saying nasty, ill-natured things wrapped up in politeness that you daren't say out like a man, or you'd get kicked. He is a gentleman inside; that Talboys is only one outside; but you girls can't look below the surface."

"We have not read Miss Edgeworth. His hands are not so white as Mr. Talboys'."

"Nor his liver, either—oh, you goose! Which has the finest eyes? Why, you don't see such eyes as Mr. Dodd's every day. They are as large as yours, only his are dark."

"Don't be angry, dear. You must admit his voice is very loud."

"He can make it loud, but it is always low and gentle whenever he speaks to you. I have noticed that; so that is monstrous ungrateful of you."

"There, the skein is wound. Arthur!"

"Well?"

"I have a great mind to tell you something your friend Mr. Dodd said while you were out of the room—but no, you shall finish your story first."

"No, no; hang the story!"

"Ah! you only say that out of politeness. I have taken you from it so long already."

The impetuous boy jumped up, seized the volumes, dashed out, and presently came running back, crying: "There, I have thrown them behind the bookcase for ever and ever. Now will you tell me what he said?"

Lucy smiled triumphantly. She could relish a bloodless victory over an inanimate rival. Then she said softly, "Arthur, what I am going to tell you is in confidence."

"I will be torn in pieces before I betray it," said the young chevalier.

Lucy smiled at his extravagance, then began again very gravely: "Mr. Talboys, who, with many good qualities, has—what shall I say?—narrow and artificial views compared with your friend—"

"Ah! now you are talking sense."

"Then why interrupt me, dear?—began teasing him, and wanting to know the real reason he comes here."

"The real reason? What did the fool mean?"

"How can I tell, Arthur, any more than you? Mr. Dodd evidently thought that some slur was meant on the purity of his friendship for you."

"Shame! shame! oh!"

"I saw his anger rising; for Mr. Dodd, though not irritable, is passionate—at least I think so. I tried to smooth matters. But no; Mr. Talboys persisted in putting this ungenerous question, when all of a sudden Mr. Dodd burst out, 'You wish to know why I love Arthur? Because he is an orphan; and because an orphan finds a brother in every man who is worth the shoe-leather he stands in. That is all the riddle, you lubber!!' It was terribly rude; but oh! Arthur, I must tell you your friend looked noble; he seemed to swell and rise to a giant as he spoke, and we all felt such little shrimps around him; and his lip trembled, and fire flashed from his eyes. How you would have admired him then; and he swept out of the room, and left us for his little friend, who is worthy of it all, since he stands up for him against us all. Arthur! why, he is crying! poor child! and do you think those words did not go to my heart as well? I am an orphan, too. Arthur, don't cry, love! oh! oh! oh!"

Oh, magic of a word from a great heart! Such a word, uncouth and simple, but hot from a manly bosom, pierced silk and broadcloth as if they had been calico and fustian, and made a fashionable young lady and a bold school-boy take hands and cry together. But such sweet tears dry quickly; they dry almost as they flow.

"Hallo!" cried the mercurial prince; "a sudden thought strikes me. You kept running him down a minute ago."

"Me?" said Lucy, with a look of amazement.

"Why, you know you did. Now tell me what was that for."

"To give you the pleasure of defending him."

"Oh. Hum? Lucy, you are not quite so simple as the others think; sometimes I can't make you out myself."

"Is it possible? Well, you know what to do, dear."

"No, I don't."

"Why, read Miss Edgeworth over again."

CHAPTER IX.

ARTHUR was bundled off to a private tutor, and the Dodds invited to Font Abbey no more, and Talboys dined there three days a week. So far, David Dodd was in a poor and miserable position compared with Talboys, who visited Lucy at pleasure, and could close the very street door against a rival, real or imaginary. But the street door is not the door of the heart, and David had one little advantage over his powerful antagonist; it was a slender one, and he owed it to a subtle source—female tact. His sister had long been aware of Talboys. The gossip of the village had enlightened her as to his visits and supposed pretensions. She had deliberately withheld this information from her brother, for she said to herself: "Men always make such fools of themselves when they are jealous. No. David shan't even know he has got a rival; if he did he would be wretched and live on thorns, and then he would get into passions, and either make a fool of himself in her eyes, or do something rash and be shown to the door."

Thus far Eve, defending her brother. And with this piece of shrewdness she did a little more for him than she intended or was conscious of; for Talboys, either by feeble calculation or instinct of petty rivalry, constantly sneered at David before Lucy; David never mentioned Talboys' name to her. Now superior ignores, inferior detracts. Thus Talboys lowered himself and rather elevated David; moreover, he counteracted his own strongest weapon, the street door. After putting David out of sight, this judicious rival could not let him fade out of mind too; he found means to stimulate the lady's memory, and, as far as in him lay, made the absent present. May all my foes unweave their webs as cleverly! David knew nothing of this. He saw himself shut out from Paradise, and he was sad. He felt the loss of Arthur too. The orphan had been medicine to him. When a man is absorbed in a hopeless passion, to be employed every day in a good action has a magical soothing influence on the racked heart. Try this instead of suicide, despairing lover. It is a quack remedy; no M. D. prescribes it. Never you mind; in desperate ills a little cure is worth a deal of etiquette. Poor David had lost this innocent comfort—lost, too, the pleasure of going every day to the house she lived in. To be sure, when he used to go he seldom caught a glimpse of her, but he did now and then, and always enjoyed the hope.

"I see how it is," said he to Eve one day; "I am not welcome to the master of the house. Well, he is the master; I shall not force my way where I am not welcome"; but after these spirited words he hung his head.

"Oh, nonsense," said Eve. "It isn't him. There are mischief-makers behind."

"Ay? just you tell me who they are. I'll teach them to come across my hawse"; and David's eyes flashed.

"Don't you be silly," said Eve, and turned it off; "and don't be so downhearted. Why, you are not half a man."

"No more I am, Eve. What has come to me?"

"What, indeed? just when everything goes swimmingly."

"Eve, how can you say so?"

"Why, David, she leaves this in a few days for Mrs. Bazalgette's house. You tell me you have got a warm invitation there. Then make the play there, and, if you can't win her, say you don't deserve her, twiddle your thumb, and see a bolder lover carry her off. You foolish boy, she is only a woman; she is to be won. If you don't mind, some man will show you it was as easy as you think it is hard. Timid wooers make a mountain of a mole-hill."

"Why, it is you who have kept me backing and filling all this time, Eve."

"Of course. Prudence at first starting, but that isn't to say courage is never to come in. First creep within the fortification wall; but, once inside, if you don't storm the city that minute, woe be unto you. Come, cheer up! it is only for a few days, and then she goes where you will have her all to yourself; besides, you shall have one sweet delicious evening with her all alone before she goes. What! have you forgotten the pedigree? Wasn't I right to keep that back? and now march and take a good long walk."

Her tongue was a spur. It made David's drooping manhood rear and prance—a trumpet, and pealed victory to come. David kissed her warmly and strode away radiant. She looked sadly after him.

She had never spoken so hopefully, so encouragingly. The reason will startle such of my readers as have not taken the trouble to comprehend her. It was that she had never so thoroughly desponded. Such was Eve. When matters went smoothly, she itched to torment and take the gloss off David; but now the affair looked really desperate, so it would have been unkind not to sustain him with all her soul. The cause of her despondency and consequent cheerfulness shall now be briefly related. Scarce an hour ago she had met Miss Fountain in the village and accompanied her home. For David's sake she had diverted the conversation by easy degrees to the subject of marriage, in order to sound Miss Fountain. "You would never give your hand without your heart, I am sure."

"Heaven forbid," was the reply.

"Not even to a coronet?"

"Not even to a crown."

So far so good; but Miss Fountain went on to say that the heart was not the only thing to be consulted in a matter so important as marriage.

"It is the only thing I would ever consult," said Eve. As Lucy did not reply, Eve asked her next what she would do if she loved a poor man. Lucy replied coldly that it was not her present intention to love anybody but her relations; that she should never love any gentleman until she had been married to him, or, correcting herself, at all events, been some time engaged to him, and she should certainly never engage herself to anyone who would not rather improve her position in society than deteriorate it. Eve met these pretty phrases with a look of contempt, as much as to say, "While you speak I am putting all that into plain vulgar English." The other did not seem to notice it. "To leave this interesting topic for a while," said she, languidly, "let me consult you, Miss Dodd. I have not, as you may have noticed, great abilities, but I have received an excellent education. To say nothing of those soi-disantaccomplishments with which we adorn and sometimes weary society, my dear mother had me well grounded in languages and history. Without being eloquent, I have a certain fluency, in which, they tell me, even members of Parliament are deficient, smoothly as their speeches read made into English by the newspapers. Like yourself, Miss Dodd, and all our sex, I am not destitute of tact, and tact, you know, is 'the talent of talents.' I feel," here she bit her lip, "myself fit for public life. I am ambitious."

"Oh, you are, are you?"

"Very; and perhaps you will kindly tell me how I had best direct that ambition. The army? No; marching against daisies, and dancing and flirting in garrison towns, is frivolous and monotonous too. It isn't as if war was raging, trumpets ringing, and squadrons charging. Your brother's profession? Not for the world; I am a coward" [consistent]. "Shall I lower my pretensions to the learned professions?"

"I don't doubt your cleverness, but the learned professions?"

"A woman has a tongue, you know, and that is their grand requisite. I interrupted you, Miss Dodd; pray forgive me."

"Well, then, let us go through them. To be a clergyman, what is required? To preach, and visit the sick, and feel for them, and understand what passes in the sorrowful hearts of the afflicted. Is that beyond our sex?"

"That last is far more beyond a man at most times; and oh, the discourses one has to sit out in church!"

"Portia made a very passable barrister, Miss Dodd."

"Oh, did she?"

"Why, you know she did; and as for medicine, the great successes there are achieved by honeyed words, with a long word thrown in here and there. I've heard my own mamma say so. Now which shall I be?"

"I suppose you are making fun of me," said Eve; "but there is many a true word spoken in jest. You could be a better, parson, lawyer or doctor than nine out of ten, but they won't let us. They know we could beat them into fits at anything but brute strength and wickedness, so they have shut all those doors in us poor girls' faces."

"There; you see," said Lucy archly, "but two lines are open to our honorable ambition, marriage and—water-colors. I think marriage the more honorable of the two; above all, it is the more fashionable. Can you blame me, then, if my ambition chooses the altar and not the easel?"

"So that is what you have been bringing me to."

"You came of your own accord," was the sly retort. "Let me offer you some luncheon."

"No, thank you; I could not eat a morsel just now."

Eve went away, her bright little face visibly cast down. It was not Miss Fountain's words only, and that new trait of hard satire, which she had so suddenly produced from her secret recesses. Her very tones were cynical and worldly to Eve's delicate sense of hearing.

"Poor, poor David!" she thought, and when she got to the door of the room she sighed; and as she went home she said more than once to herself, "No more heart than a marble statue. Oh, how true our first thought is! I come back to mine—"

Lucy (sola). "Then what right had she to come here and try to turn me inside out?"

CHAPTER X.

As the hour of Lucy's departure drew near, Mr. Fountain became anxious to see her betrothed to his friend, for fear of accidents. "You had better propose to her in form, or authorize me to do so, before she goes to that Mrs. Bazalgette." This time it was Talboys that hung back. He objected that the time was not opportune. "I make no advance," said he; "on the contrary, I seem of late to have lost ground with your niece."

"Oh, I've seen the sort of distance she has put on; all superficial, my dear sir. I read it in your favor. I know the sex; they can't elude me. Pique, sir—nothing on earth but female pique. She is bitter against us for shilly-shallying. These girls hate shilly-shally in a man. They are monopolists—severe monopolists; shilly-shally is one of their monopolies. Throw yourself at her feet, and press her with ardor; she will clear up directly." The proposed attitude did not tempt the stiff Talboys. His pride took the alarm.

"Thank you. It is a position in which I should not care to place myself unless I was quite sure of not being refused. No, I will not risk my proposal while she is under the influence of this Dodd; he is, somehow or other, the cause of her coldness to me."

"Good heavens! why, she has been hermetically sealed against him ever so long," cried Fountain, almost angrily.

"I saw his sister come out of your gate only the other day. Sisters are emissaries—dangerous ones, too. Who knows? her very coldness may be vexation that this man is excluded. Perhaps she suspects me as the cause."

"These are chimeras—wild chimeras. My niece cares nothing for such people as the Dodds."

"I beg your pardon; these low attachments are the strongest. It is a notorious fact."

"There is no attachment; there is nothing but civility, and the affability of a well-bred superior to an inferior. Attachment! why, there is not a girl in Europe less capable of marrying beneath her; and she is too cold to flirt—-but with a view to matrimonial position. The worst of it is, that, while you fear an imaginary danger, you are running into a real one. If we are defeated it will not be by Dodd, but by that Mrs. Bazalgette. Why, now I think of it, whence does Lucy's coldness date? From that viper's visit to my house. Rely on it, if we are suffering from any rival influence, it is that woman's. She is a dangerous woman—she is a character I detest—she is a schemer."

"Am I to understand that Mrs. Bazalgette has views of her own for Miss Fountain?" inquired Talboys, his jealousy half inclined to follow the new lead.

"In all probability."

"Oh, then it is mere surmise."

"No, it is not mere surmise; it is the reasonable conjecture of a man who knows her sex, and human nature, and life. Since I have my views, what more likely than that she has hers, if only to spite me? Add to this her strange visit to Font Abbey, and the somber influence she has left behind. And to this woman Lucy is going unprotected by any positive pledge to you. Here is the true cause for anxiety. And if you do not share it with me, it must be that you do not care about our alliance."

Mr. Talboys was hurt. "Not care for the alliance? It was dear to him—all the dearer for the difficulties. He was attached to Miss Fountain—warmly attached; would do anything for her except run the risk of an affront—a refusal." Then followed a long discussion, the result of which was that he would not propose in form now, but would give proofs of his attachment such as no lady could mistake; inter alia, he would be sure to spend the last evening with her, and would ride the first stage with her next day, squeeze her hand at parting, and look unutterable. And as for the formal proposal, that was only postponed a week or two. Mr. Fountain was to pay his visit to Mrs. Bazalgette, and secretly prepare Miss Fountain; then Talboys would suddenly pounce—

and pop. The grandeur and boldness of this strategy staggered, rather than displeased, Mr. Fountain.

"What! under her own roof?" and he could not help rubbing his hands with glee and spite—"under her own eye, and malgre her personal influence? Why, you are Nap. I."

"She will be quite out of the way of the Dodds there," said Talboys, slyly.

The senior groaned. ("'Mule I.' I should have said.")

And so they cut and dried it all.

The last evening came, and with it, just before dinner, a line by special messenger from Mr. Talboys. "He could not come that evening. His brother had just arrived from India; they had not met for seven years. He could not set him to dine alone."

After dinner, in the middle of her uncle's nap, in came Lucy, and, unheard-of occurrence—deed of dreadful note—woke him. She was radiant, and held a note from Eve. "Good news, uncle; those good, kind Dodds! they are coming to tea."

"What?" and he wore a look of consternation. Recollecting, however, that Talboys was not to be there, he was indifferent again. But when he read the note he longed for his self-invited visitors. It ran thus:

"DEAR MISS FOUNTAIN—David has found out the genealogy. He says there is no doubt you came from the Fountains of Melton, and he can prove it. He has proved it to me, and I am none the wiser. So, as David is obliged to go away to-morrow, I think the best way is for me to bring him over with the papers to-night. We will come at eight, unless you have company."

"He is a worthy young man," shouted Mr. Fountain. "What o'clock is it?"

"Very nearly eight. Oh, uncle, I am so glad. How pleased you will be!"

The Dodds arrived soon after, and while tea was going on David spread his parchments on the table and submitted his proofs. He had eked out the other evidence by means of a series of leases. The three fields that went with Font Abbey had been let a great many times, and the landlord's name, Fountain in the latter leases, was Fontaine in those of remoter date. David even showed his host the exact date at which the change of orthography took place. "You are a shrewd young gentleman," cried Mr. Fountain, gleefully.

David then asked him what were the names of his three meadows. The names of them? He didn't know they had any.

"No names? Why, there isn't a field in England that hasn't its own name, sir. I noticed that before I went to sea." He then told Mr. Fountain the names of his three meadows, and curious names they were. Two of them were a good deal older than William the Conqueror. David wrote them on a slip of paper. He then produced a chart. "What is that, Mr. David?"

"A map of the Melton estate, sir."

"Why, how on earth did you get that?"

"An old shipmate of mine lives in that quarter—got him to make it for me. Overhaul it, sir; you will find the Melton estate has got all your three names within a furlong of the mansion house."

"From this you infer—"

"That one of that house came here, and brought the E along with him that has got dropped somehow since, and, being so far from his birthplace, he thought he would have one or two of the old names about him. What will you bet me he hasn't shot more than one brace of partridges on those fields about Melton when he was a boy? So he christened your three fields afresh, and the new names took; likely he made a point of it with the people in the village. For all that, I have found one old fellow who stands out against them to this day. His name is Newel. He will persist in calling the field next to your house Snap Witcheloe. 'That is what my grandfather allus named it,' says he, 'and that is the name it went by afore there was ever a Fountain in this ere parish.' I have looked in the Parish Register, and I see Newel's grandfather was born in 1690. Now, sir, all this is not mathematical proof; but, when you come to add it to your own direct proofs, that carry you within a cable's length of Port Fontaine, it is very convincing; and, not to pay out too much yarn, I'll bet—my head—to a China orange—"

"David, don't be vulgar."

"Never mind, Mr. Dodd—be yourself."

"Well, then, to serve Eve out, I'll bet her head (and that is a better one than mine) to a China orange that Fontaine and Fountain are one, and that the first Fontaine came over here from Melton more than one hundred and thirty years ago, and less than one hundred and forty, when Newel's grandfather was a young man."

"Probatum est," shouted old Fountain, his eyes sparkling, his voice trembling with emotion. "Miss Fontaine," said he, turning to Lucy, throwing a sort of pompous respect into his voice and manner, "you shall never marry any man that cannot give you as good a home as Melton, and quarter as good a coat of arms with you as your own, the Founteyns'." David's heart took a chill as if an ice-arrow had gone through it. "So join me to thank our young friend here."

Mr. Fountain held out his hand. David gave his mechanically in return, scarcely knowing what he did. "You are a worthy and most intelligent young man, and you have made an old man as happy as a lord," said the old gentleman, shaking him warmly.

"And there is my hand, too," said Lucy, putting out hers with a blush, "to show you I bear you no malice for being more unselfish and more sagacious than us all." Instantly David's cold chill fled unreasonably. His cheeks burned with blushes, his eyes glowed, his heart thumped, and the delicate white, supple, warm, velvet hand that nestled in his shot electric tremors through his whole frame, when glided, with well-bred noiselessness, through the open door, Mr. Talboys, and stood looking yellow at that ardent group, and the massive yet graceful bare arm stretched across the table, and the white hand melting into the brown one.

While he stood staring, David looked up, and caught that strange, that yellow look. Instantly a light broke in on him. "So I should look," felt David, "if I saw her hand in his." He held Lucy's hand tight (she was just beginning to withdraw it), and glared from his seat on the newcomer like a lion ready to spring. Eve read and turned pale; she knew what was in the man's blood.

Lucy now quietly withdrew her hand, and turned with smiling composure toward the newcomer, and Mr. Fountain thrust a minor anxiety between the passions of the rivals. He rose hastily, and went to Talboys, and, under cover of a warm welcome, took care to let him know Miss Dodd had been kind enough to invite herself and David. He then explained with uneasy animation what David had done for him.

Talboys received all this with marked coldness; but it gave him time to recover his self-possession. He shook hands with Lucy, all but ignored David and Eve, and quietly assumed the part of principal personage. He then spoke to Lucy in a voice tuned for the occasion, to give the impression that confidential communication was not unusual between him and her. He apologized, scarce above a whisper, for not having come to dinner on her last day.

"But after dinner," said he, "my brother seemed fatigued. I treacherously recommended bed. You forgive me? The nabob instantly acted on my selfish hint. I mounted my horse, and me voila." In short, in two minutes he had retaliated tenfold on David. As for Lucy, she was a good deal amused at this sudden public assumption of a tenderness the gentleman had never exhibited in private, but a little mortified at his parade of mysterious familiarity; still, for a certain female reason, she allowed neither to appear, but wore an air of calm cordiality, and gave Talboys his full swing.

David, seated sore against his will at another table, whither Mr. Fountain removed him and parchments on pretense of inspecting the leases, listened with hearing preternaturally keen—listened and writhed.

His back was toward them. At last he heard Talboys propose in murmuring accents to accompany her the first stage of her journey. She did not answer directly, and that second was an age of anguish to poor David.

When she did answer, as if to compensate for her hesitation, she said, with alacrity: "I shall be delighted; it will vary the journey most agreeably; I will ride the pony you were so kind as to give me."

The letters swam before David's eyes.

Lucy came to the table, and, standing close behind David—so close that he felt her pure cool breath mingle with his hair, said to her uncle: "Mr. Talboys proposes to me to ride the first stage to-morrow; if I do, you must be of the party."

"Oh, must I? Well, I'll roll after you in my phaeton."

At this moment Eve could bear no longer the anguish on David's beloved face. It made her hysterical. She could hardly command herself. She rose hastily, and saying, "We must not keep you up the night before a journey," took leave with David. As he shook hands with Lucy, his imploring eye turned full on hers, and sought to dive into her heart. But that soft sapphire eye was unfathomable. It was like those dark blue southern waters that seem to reveal all, yet hide all, so deep they are, though clear.

Eve. "Thank Heaven, we are safe out of the house."

David. "I have got a rival."

Eve. "A pretty rival; she doesn't care a button for him."

David. "He rides the first stage with her."

Eve. "Well, what of that?"

David. "I have got a rival."

David was none of your lie-a-beds. He rose at five in summer, six in winter, and studied hard till breakfast time; after that he was at every fool's service. This morning he did not appear at the breakfast table, and the servant had not seen him about. Eve ran upstairs full of anxiety. He was not in his room. The bed had not been slept in; the impress of his body outside showed, however, that he had flung himself down on it to snatch an uneasy slumber.

Eve sent the girl into the village to see if she could find him or hear tidings of him. The girl ran out without her bonnet, partaking her mistress's anxiety, but did not return for nearly half an hour, that seemed an age to Eve. The girl had lost some time by going to Josh Grace for information. Grace's house stood in an orchard; so he was the unlikeliest man in the village to have seen David. She set against this trivial circumstance the weighty one that he was her sweetheart, and went to him first.

"I hain't a-sin him, Sue; thee hadst better ask at the blacksmith's shop," said Joshua Grace.

Susan profited by this hint, and learned at the blacksmith's shop that David had gone by up the road about six in the morning, walking very fast. She brought the news to Eve.

"Toward Royston?"

"Yes, miss; but, la! he won't ever think to go all the way to Royston—without his breakfast."

"That will do, Susan. I think I know what he is gone for."

On the servant retiring, her assumed firmness left her.

"On the road she is to travel! and his rival with her. What mad act is he going to do? Heaven have mercy on him, and me, and her!"

Eve knew what was in the man's blood. She sat trembling at home till she could bear it no longer. She put on her bonnet, and sallied out on the road to Royston, determined to stop the carriage, profess to have business at Royston, and take a seat beside Mr. Fountain. She felt that the very sight of her might prevent David from committing any great rashness or folly. On reaching the high road, she observed a fresh track of narrow wheels, that her rustic experience told her could only be those of a four-wheeled carriage, and, making inquiries, she found she was too late; carriage and riders had gone on before.

Her heart sank. Too late by a few minutes; but somehow she could not turn back. She walked as fast as she could after the gay cavalcade, a prey to one of those female anxieties we have all laughed at as extravagant, proved unreasonable, and sometimes found prophetic.

Meantime Lucy and Mr. Talboys cantered gayly along; Mr. Fountain rolled after in a phaeton; the traveling carriage came last. Lucy was in spirits; motion enlivens us all, but especially such of us as are women. She had also another cause for cheerfulness, that may perhaps transpire. Her two companions and unconscious dependents were governed by her mood. She made them larks to-day, as she had owls for some weeks past, last night excepted. She would fall back every now and then, and let Uncle Fountain pass her; then come dashing up to him, and either pull up short with a piece of solemn information like an aid-de-camp from headquarters, or pass him shooting a shaft of raillery back into his chariot, whereat he would rise with mock fury and yell a repartee after her. Fountain found himself good company—Talboys himself. It was not the lady; oh dear no! it never is.

At last all seemed so bright, and Mr. Talboys found himself so agreeable, that he suddenly recalled his high resolve not to pop in a county desecrated by Dodds. "I'll risk it now," said he; and he rode back to Fountain and imparted his intention, and the senior nearly bounded off his seat. He sounded the charge in a stage whisper, because of the coachman, "At her at once!"

"Secret conference? hum!" said Lucy, twisting her pony, and looking slyly back.

Mr. Talboys rejoined her, and, after a while, began in strange, melodious accents, "You will leave a blank—"

"Shall we canter?" said Lucy, gayly, and off went the pony. Talboys followed, and at the next hill resumed the sentimental cadence.

"You will leave a sad blank here, Miss Fountain."

"No greater than I found," replied the lady, innocently (?). "Oh, dear!" she cried, with sudden interest, "I am afraid I have dropped my comb." She felt under her hat. [No, viper, you have not dropped your comb, but you are feeling for a large black pin with a head to it. There, you have found it, and taken it out of your hair, and got it hid in your hand. What is that for?]

"Ten times greater," moaned the honeyed Talboys; "for then we had not seen you. Ah! my dear Miss Fountain—The devil! wo-ho, Goliah!"

For the pony spilled the treacle. He lashed out both heels with a squeak of amazement within an inch of Mr. Talboys' horse, which instantly began to rear, and plunge, and snort. While Talboys, an excellent horseman, was calming his steed, Lucy was condoling with hers. "Dear little naughty fellow!" said she, patting him ["I did it too hard"].

"As I was saying, the blessing we have never enjoyed we do not miss; but, now that you have shone upon us, what can reconcile us to lose you, unless it be the hope that—Hallo!"

Lucy. "Ah!"

The pony was off with a bound like a buck. She had found out the right depth of pin this time. "Ah! where is my whip? I have dropped it; how careless!" Then they had to ride back for the whip, and by this means joined Mr. Fountain. Lucy rode by his side, and got the carriage between her and her beau. By this plan she not only evaded sentiment, but matured by a series of secret trials her skill with her weapon. Armed with this new science, she issued forth, and, whenever Mr. Talboys left off indifferent remarks and sounded her affections, she probed the pony, and he kicked or bolted as the case might require.

"Confound that pony!" cried Talboys; "he used to be quiet enough."

"Oh, don't scold him, dear, playful little love. He carries me like a wave."

At this simple sentence Talboys' dormant jealousy contrived to revive. He turned sulky, and would not waste any more tenderness, and presently they rattled over the stones of Royston. Lucy commended her pony with peculiar earnestness to the ostler. "Pray groom him well, and feed him well, sir; he is a love." The ostler swore he would not wrong her ladyship's nag for the world.

Lucy then expressed her desire to go forward without delay: "Aunt will expect me." She took her seat in the carriage, bade a kind farewell to both the gentlemen now that no tender answer was possible, and was whirled away.

Thus the coy virgin eluded the pair.

Now her manner in taking leave of Talboys was so kind, so smiling (in the sweet consciousness of having baffled him), that Fountain felt sure it all had gone smoothly. They were engaged.

"Well?" he cried, with great animation.

"No," was the despondent reply.

"Refused?" screeched the other; "impossible!"

"No, thank you," was the haughty reply.

"What then? Did you change your mind? Didn't you propose after all?"

"I couldn't. That d—d pony wouldn't keep still."

Fountain groaned.

Lucy, left to herself, gave a little sigh of relief. She had been playing a part for the last twenty-four hours. Her cordiality with Mr. Talboys naturally misled Eve and David, and perhaps a male reader or two. Shall I give the clue? It may be useful to you, young gentlemen. Well, then, her sex are compounders. Accustomed from childhood never to have anything entirely their own way, they are content to give and take; and, these terms once accepted, it is a point of honor and tact with them not to let a creature see the irksome part of the bargain is not as delicious as the other. One coat of their own varnish goes over the smooth and the rough, the bitter and the sweet.

Now Lucy, besides being singularly polite and kind, was femme jusqu' au bout des ongles. If her instincts had been reasons, and her vague thoughts could have been represented by anything so definite as words, the result might have appeared thus:

"A few hours, and you can bore me no more, Mr. Talboys. Now what must I do for you in return? Seem not to be bored to-day? Mais c'est la moindre des choses. Seem to be pleased with your society? Why not? it is only for an hour or two, and my seeming to like it will not prolong it. My heart swells with happiness at the thought of escaping from you, good bore; you shall share my happiness, good bore. It is so kind of you not to bore me to all eternity."

This was why the last night she sat like Patience on an ottoman smiling on Talboys and racking David's heart; and this was why she made the ride so pleasant to those she was at heart glad to leave, till they tried sentiment on, and then she was an eel directly, pony and all.

Lucy (sola). "That is over. Poor Mr. Talboys! Does he fancy he has an attachment? No; I please and I am courted wherever I go, but I have never been loved. If a man loved me I should see it in his face, I should feel it without a word spoken. Once or twice I fancied I saw it in one man's eyes: they seemed like a lion's that turned to a dove's as they looked at me." Lucy closed her own eyes and recalled her impression: "It must have been fancy. Ought I to wish to inspire such a passion as others have inspired? No, for I could never return it. The very language of passion in romances seems so extravagant to me, yet so beautiful. It is hard I should not be loved, merely because I cannot love. Many such natures have been adored. I could not bear to die and not be loved as deeply as ever woman was loved. I must be loved, adored and worshiped: it would be so sweet—sweet!" She slowly closed her eyes, and the long lovely lashes drooped, and a celestial smile parted her lips as she fell into a vague, delicious reverie. Suddenly the carriage stopped at the foot of a hill. She opened her eyes, and there stood David Dodd at the carriage window.

Lucy put her head out. "Why, it is Mr. Dodd! Oh, Mr. Dodd, is there anything the matter?"

"No."

"You look so pale."

"Do I?" and he flushed faintly.

"Which way are you going?"

"I am going home again now," said David, sorrowfully.

"You came all this way to bid me good-by," and she arched her eyebrows and laughed—a little uneasily.

"It didn't seem a step. It will seem longer going back."

"No, no, you shall ride back. My pony is at the White Horse; will you not ride my pony back for me? then I shall know he will be kindly used; a stranger would whip him."

"I should think my arm would wither if I ill-used him."

"You are very good. I suppose it is because you are so brave."

"Me brave? I don't feel so. Am I to tell him to drive on?" and he looked at her with haggard and imploring eyes.

Her eyes fell before his.

"Good-by, then," said she.

He cried with a choking voice to the postilion, "Go ahead."

The carriage went on and left him standing in the road, his head upon his breast.

At the steepest part of the hill a trace broke, and the driver drew the carriage across the hill and shouted to David. He came running up, and put a large stone behind each wheel.

Lucy was alarmed. "Mr. Dodd! let me out."

He handed her out. The postboy was at a nonplus; but David whipped a piece of cord and a knife out of his pocket, and began, with great rapidity and dexterity, to splice the trace.

"Ah! now you are pleased, Mr. Dodd; our misfortune will elicit your skill in emergencies."

"Oh, no, it isn't that; it is—I never hoped to see you again so soon."

Lucy colored, and her eyes sought the ground; the splice was soon made.

"There!" said David; "I could have spent an hour over it; but you would have been vexed, and the bitter moment must have come at last."

"God bless you, Miss Fountain—oh! mayn't I say Miss Lucy to-day?" he cried, imploringly.

"Of course you may," said Lucy, the tears rising in her eyes at his sad face and beseeching look. "Oh, Mr. Dodd, parting with those we esteem is always sad enough; I got away from the door without crying—for once; don't you make me cry."

"Make you cry?" cried David, as it he had been suspected of sacrilege; "God forbid!" He muttered in a choking voice, "You give the word of command, for I can't."

"You can go on," said her soft, clear voice; but first she gave David her hand with a gentle look—"Good-by."

But David could not speak to her. He held her hand tight in both his powerful hands. They seemed iron to her—shaking, trembling, grasping iron. The carriage went slowly on, and drew her hand away. She shrank into a corner of the carriage; he frightened her.

He followed the carriage to the brow of the hill, then sat down upon a heap of stones, and looked despairingly after it.

Meantime Lucy put her head in her hands and blushed, though she was all alone. "How dare he forget the distance between us? Poor fellow! have not I at times forgotten it? I am worse than he. I lost my self-possession; I should have checked his folly; he knows nothing of les convenances. He has hurt my hand, he is so rough; I feel his clutch now; there, I thought so, it is all red—poor fellow! Nonsense! he is a sailor; he knows nothing of the world and its customs. Parting with a pleasant acquaintance forever made him a little sad.

"He is all nature; he is like nobody else; he shows every feeling instead of concealing it, that is all. He has gone home, I hope." She glanced hastily back. He was sitting on the stones, his arms drooping, his head bowed, a picture of despondency. She put her face in her hands again and pondered, blushing higher and higher. Then the pale face that had always been ruddy before, the simple grief and agitation, the manly eye that did not know how to weep, but was so clouded and troubled, and wildly sad; the shaking hands, that had clutched hers like a drowning man's (she felt them still), the quivering features, choked voice, and trembling lip, all these recoiled with double force upon her mind: they touched her far more than sobs and tears would have done, her sex's ready signs of shallow grief.

Two tears stole down her cheeks.

"If he would but go home and forget me!" She glanced hastily back. David was climbing up a tree, active as a cat. "He is like nobody else—he! he! Stay! is that to see the last of me—the very last? Poor soul! Madman, how will this end? What can come of it but misery to him, remorse to me?

"This is love." She half closed her eyes and smiled, repeating, "This is love.

"Oh how I despise all the others and their feeble flatteries!"

"Heaven forgive me my mad, my wicked wish!

"I am beloved.

"I am adored.

"I am miserable!"

As soon as the carriage was out of sight, David came down and hurried from the place. He found the pony at the inn. The ostler had not even removed his saddle.

"Methought that ostler did protest too much."

David kissed the saddle and the pommels, and the bridle her hand had held, and led the pony out. After walking a mile or two he mounted the pony, to sit in her seat, not for ease. Walking thirty miles was nothing to this athlete; sticking on and holding on with his chin on his knee was rather fatiguing.

Meantime, Eve walked on till she was four miles from home. No David. She sat down and cried a little space, then on again. She had just reached an angle in the road, when—clatter, clatter—David came cantering around with his knee in his mouth. Eve gave a joyful scream, and up went both her hands with sudden delight. At the double shock to his senses the pony thought his end was come, and perhaps the world's. He shied slap into the hedge and stuck there— alone; for, his rider swaying violently the reverse way, the girths burst, the saddle peeled off the pony's back, and David sat griping the pommel of the saddle in the middle of the road at Eve's feet, looking up in her face with an uneasy grin, while dust rose around him in a little column. Eve screeched, and screeched, and screeched; then fell to, with a face as red as a turkey-cock's, and beat David furiously, and hurt—her little hands.

David laughed. This incident did him good—shook him up a bit. The pony groveled out of the ditch and cantered home, squeaking at intervals and throwing his heels.

David got up, hoisted the side saddle on to his square shoulders, and, keeping it there by holding the girths, walked with Eve toward Font Abbey. She was now a little ashamed of her apprehensions; and, besides, when she leathered David, she was, in her own mind, serving him out for both frights. At all events, she did not scold him, but kindly inquired his adventures, and he told her what he had done and said, and what Miss Fountain had said.

The account disappointed Eve. "All this is just a pack of nothing," said she. "It is two lovers parting, or it is two common friendly acquaintances; all depends on how it was done, and that you don't tell me." Then she put several subtle questions as to the looks, and tones and manner of the young lady. David could not answer them. On this she informed him he was a fool.

"So I begin to think," said he.

"There! be quiet," said she, "and let me think it over."

"Ay! ay!" said he.

While he was being quiet and letting her think a carriage came rapidly up behind them, with a horseman riding beside it; and, as the pedestrians drew aside, an ironical voice fell upon them, and the carriage and horseman stopped, and floured, them with dust.

Messrs. Talboys and Fountain took a stroll to look at the new jail that was building in Royston, and, as they returned, Talboys, whose wounded pride had now fermented, told Mr. Fountain plainly that he saw nothing for it but to withdraw his pretensions to Miss Fountain.

"My own feelings are not sufficiently engaged for me to play the up-hill game of overcoming her disinclination."

"Disinclination? The mere shyness of a modest girl. If she was to be 'won unsought,' she would not be worthy to be Mrs. Talboys."

"Her worth is indisputable," said Mr. Talboys, "but that is no reason why I should force upon her my humble claims."

The moment his friend's pride began to ape humility, Fountain saw the wound it had received was incurable. He sighed and was silent. Opposition would only have set fire to opposition.

They went home together in silence. On the road Talboys caught sight of a tall gentleman carrying a side-saddle, and a little lady walking beside him. He recognized his bete noir with a grim smile. Here at least was one he had defeated and banished from the fair. What on earth was the man doing? Oh, he had been giving his sister a ride on a donkey, and they had met with an accident. Mr. Talboys was in a humor for revenge, so he pulled up, and in a somewhat bantering voice inquired where was the steed.

"Oh, he is in port by now," said David.

"Do you usually ease the animal of that part of his burden, sir?"

"No," said David, sullenly.

Eve, who hated Mr. Talboys, and saw through his sneers, bit her lip and colored, but kept silence.

But Mr. Talboys, unwarned by her flashing eye, proceeded with his ironical interrogatory, and then it was that Eve, reflecting that both these gentlemen had done their worst against David, and that henceforth the battlefield could never again be Font Abbey, decided for revenge. She stepped forward like an airy sylph, between David and his persecutor, and said, with a charming smile, "I will explain, sir."

Mr. Talboys bowed and smiled.

"The reason my brother carries this side-saddle is that it belongs to a charming young lady—you have some little acquaintance with her—Miss Fountain."

"Miss Fountain!" cried Talboys, in a tone from which all the irony was driven out by Eve's coup.

"She begged David to ride her pony home; she would not trust him to anybody else."

"Oh!" said Talboys, stupefied.

"Well, sir, owing to—to—an accident, the saddle came off, and the pony ran home; so then David had only her saddle to take care of for her."

"Why, we escorted Miss Fountain to Royston, and we never saw Mr. Dodd."

"Ay, but you did not go beyond Royston," said Eve, with a cunning air.

"Beyond Royston? where? and what was he doing there? Did he go all that way to take her orders about her pony?" said Talboys, bitterly.

"Oh, as to that you must excuse me, sir," cried Eve, with a scornful laugh; "that is being too inquisitive. Good-morning"; and she carried David off in triumph.

The next moment Mr. Talboys spurred on, followed by the phaeton. Talboys' face was yellow.

"La langue d'une femme est son epee."

"Sheer off and repair damages, you lubber," said David, dryly, "and don't come under our guns again, or we shall blow you out of the water. Hum! Eve, wasn't your tongue a little too long for your teeth just now?"

"Not an inch."

"She might be vexed; it is not for me to boast of her kindness."

"Temper won't let a body see everything. I'll tell you what I have done, too— I've declared war."

"Have you? Then run the Jack up to the mizzen-top, and let us fight it out."

"That is the way to look at it, David. Now don't you speak to me till we get home; let me think."

At the gate of Font Abbey, they parted, and Eve went home. David came to the stable yard and hailed, "Stable ahoy!" Out ran a little bandy-legged groom. "The craft has gone adrift," cried David, "but I've got the gear safe. Stow it away"; and as he spoke he chucked the saddle a distance of some six yards on to the bandy-legged groom, who instantly staggered back and sank on a little dunghill, and there sat, saddled, with two eyes like saucers, looking stupefied surprise between the pommels.

"It is you for capsizing in a calm," remarked David, with some surprise, and went his way.

"Well, Eve, have you thought?"

"Yes, David, I was a little hasty; that puppy would provoke a saint. After all there is no harm done; they can't hurt us much now. It is not here the game will be played out. Now tell me, when does your ship sail?"

"It wants just five weeks to a day."

"Does she take up her passengers at —— as usual?"

"Yes, Eve, yes."

"And Mrs. Bazalgette lives within a mile or two of ——. You have a good excuse for accepting her invitation. Stay your last week in her house. There will be no Talboys to come between you. Do all a man can do to win her in that week."

"I will."

"And if she says 'No,' be man enough to tear her out of your heart."

"I can't tear her out of my heart, but I will win her. I must win her. I can't live without her. A month to wait!"

Mr. Talboys. "Well, sir, what do you say now?"

Mr. Fountain (hypocritically). "I say that your sagacity was superior to mine; forgive me if I have brought you into a mortifying collision. To be defeated by a merchant sailor!" He paused to see the effect of his poisoned shaft.

Talboys. "But I am not defeated. I will not be defeated. It is no longer a personal question. For your sake, for her sake, I must save her from a degrading connection. I will accompany you to Mrs. Bazalgette's. When shall we go?"

"Well, not immediately; it would look so odd. The old one would smell a rat directly. Suppose we say in a month's time."

"Very well; I shall have a clear stage."

"Yes, and I shall then use all my influence with her. Hitherto I have used none."

"Thank you. Mr. Dodd cannot penetrate there, I conclude."

"Of course not."

"Then she will be Mrs. Talboys."

"Of course she will."

Lucy sighed a little over David's ardent, despairing passion, and his pale and drawn face. Her woman's instinct enabled her to comprehend in part a passion she was at this period of her life incapable of feeling, and she pitied him. He was the first of her admirers she had ever pitied. She sighed a little, then fretted a little, then reproached herself vaguely. "I must have been guilty of some imprudence—given some encouragement. Have I failed in womanly reserve, or is it all his fault? He is a sailor. Sailors are like nobody else. He is so simple-minded. He sees, no doubt, that he is my superior in all sterling qualities, and that makes him forget the social distance between him and me. And yet why suspect him of audacity? Poor fellow, he had not the courage tosay anything to me, after all. No; he will go to sea, and forget his folly before he comes back." Then she had a gust of egotism. It was nice to be loved ardently and by a hero, even though that hero was not a gentleman of distinction, scarcely a gentleman at all. The next moment she blushed at her own vanity. Next she was seized with a sense of the great indelicacy and unpardonable impropriety of letting her mind run at all upon a person of the other sex; and shaking her lovely shoulders, as much as to say, "Away idle thoughts," she nestled and fitted with marvelous suppleness into a corner of the carriage, and sank into a sweet sleep, with a red cheek, two wet eyelashes, and a half-smile of the most heavenly character imaginable. And so she glided along till, at five in the afternoon, the carriage turned in at Mr. Bazalgette's gates. Lucy lifted her eyes, and there was quite a little group standing on the steps to receive her, and waving welcome to the universal pet. There was Mr. Bazalgette, Mrs. Bazalgette, and two servants, and a little in the rear a tall stranger of gentleman-like appearance.

The two ladies embraced one another so rapidly yet so smoothly, and so dovetailed and blended, that they might be said to flow together, and make one in all but color, like the Saone and the Rhone. After half a dozen kisses given and returned with a spirit and rapidity from which, if we male spectators of these ardent encounters were wise, we might slyly learn a lesson, Aunt Bazalgette suddenly darted her mouth at Lucy's ear, and whispered a few words with an animation that struck everybody present. Lucy smiled in reply. After "the meeting of the muslins," Mr. Bazalgette shook hands warmly, and at last Lucy was introduced to his friend Mr. Hardie, who expressed in courteous terms his hopes that her journey had been a pleasant one.

The animated words Mrs. Bazalgette whispered into Lucy's ear at that moment of burning affection were as follows:

"You have had it washed!"

Lucy (unpacking her things in her bedroom). "Who is Mr. Hardie, dear?"

"What! don't you know? Mr. Hardie is the great banker."

"Only a banker? I should have taken him for something far more distinguished. His manner is good. There is a suavity without feebleness or smallness."

Mrs. Bazalgette's eye flashed, but she answered with apparent nonchalance: "I am glad you like him; you will take him off my hands now and then. He must not be neglected; Bazalgette would murder us. Apropos, remind me to ask him to tell you Mr. Hardie's story, and how he comes to be looked up to like a prince in this part of the world, though he is only a banker, with only ten thousand a year."

"You make me quite curious, aunt. Cannot you tell me?"

"Me? Oh, dear, no! Paper currency, foreign loans, government securities, gold mines, ten per cents, Mr. Peel, and why one breaks and another doesn't! all that is quite beyond me. Bazalgette is your man. I had no idea your mousseline-delame would have washed so well. Why, it looks just out of the shop; it—" Come away, reader, for Heaven's sake!

CHAPTER XI.

THE man whom Mr. Bazalgette introduced so smoothly and off-hand to Lucy Fountain exercised a terrible influence over her life, as you will see by and by.

This alone would make it proper to lay his antecedents before the reader. But he has independent claims to this notice, for he is a principal figure in my work. The history of this remarkable man's fortune is a study. The progress of his mind is another, and its past as well as its future are the very corner-stone of that capacious story which I am now building brick by brick, after my fashion where the theme is large. I invite my reader, therefore, to resist the natural repugnance which delicate minds feel to the ring of the precious metals, and for the sake of the coming story to accompany me into AN OLD BANK.

The Hardies were goldsmiths in the seventeenth century; and when that business split, and the deposit and bill-of-exchange business went one way, and the plate and jewels another, they became bankers from father to son. A peculiarity attended them; they never broke, nor even cracked. Jew James Hardie conducted for many years a smooth, unostentatious and lucrative business. It professed to be a bank of deposit only, and not of discount. This was not strictly true. There never was a bank in creation that did not discount under the rose, when the paper represented commercial effects, and the indorsers were customers and favorites. But Mr. Hardie's main business was in deposits bearing no interest. It was of that nature known as "the legitimate banking business," a title not, I think, invented by the customers, since it is a system destitute of that reciprocity which is the soul of all just and legitimate commercial relations.

You shall lend me your money gratis, and I will lend it out at interest: such is legitimate banking—in the opinion of bankers.

This system, whose decay we have seen, and whose death my young readers are like to see, flourished under old Hardie, green—as the public in whose pockets its roots were buried.

Country gentlemen and noblemen, and tradesmen well-to-do, left floating balances varying from seven, five, three thousand pounds, down to a hundred or two, in his hands. His art consisted in keeping his countenance, receiving them with the air of a person conferring a favor, and investing the bulk of them in government securities, which in that day returned four and five per cent. As he did not pay one shilling for the use of the capital, he pocketed the whole interest. A small part of the aggregate balance was not invested, but remained in the bank coffers as a reserve to meet any accidental drain. It was a point of honor with the squires and rectors, who shared their incomes with him in a grateful spirit, never to draw their balances down too low; and more than once in this banker's career a gentleman has actually borrowed money for a month or two of the bank at four per cent, rather than exhaust his deposit, or, in other words, paid his debtor interest for the temporary use of his own everlasting property. Such capitalists are not to be found in our day; they may reappear at the Millennium.

The banker had three clerks; one a youth and very subordinate, the other two steady old men, at good salaries, who knew the affairs of the bank, but did not chatter them out of doors, because they were allowed to talk about them to their employer; and this was a vent. The tongue must have a regular vent or random explosions—choose! Besides the above compliment paid to years of probity and experience, the ancient regime bound these men to the interest and person of their chief by other simple customs now no more.

At each of the four great festivals of the Church they dined with Mr. and Mrs. Hardie, and were feasted and cordially addressed as equals, though they could not be got to reply in quite the same tone. They were never scorned, but a peculiar warmth of esteem and friendship was shown them on these occasions. One reason was, the old-fangled banker himself aspired to no higher character than that of a man of business, and were not these clerks men of business good and true? his staff, not his menials?

And since I sneered just now at a vital simplicity, let me hasten to own that here, at least, it was wise, as well as just and worthy. Where men are forever handling heaps of money, it is prudent to fortify them doubly against temptation—with self-respect, and a sufficient salary.

It is one thing not to be led into temptation (accident on which half the virtue in the world depends), another to live in it and overcome it; and in a bank it is not the conscience only that is tempted, but the senses. Piles of glittering gold, amiable as Hesperian fruit; heaps of silver paper, that seem to whisper as they rustle, "Think how great we are, yet see how little; we are fifteen thousand pounds, yet we can go into your pocket; whip us up, and westward ho! If you have not the courage for that, at all events wet your finger; a dozen of us will stick to it. That pen in your hand has but to scratch that book there, and who will know? Besides, you can always put us back, you know."

Hundreds and thousands of men take a share in the country's public morality, legislate, build churches, and live and die respectable, who would be jail-birds sooner or later if their sole income was the pay of a banker's clerk, and their eyes, and hands, and souls rubbed daily against hundred-pound notes as his do. I tell you it is a temptation of forty-devil power.

Not without reason, then, did this ancient banker bestow some respect and friendship on those who, tempted daily, brought their hands pure, Christmas after Christmas, to their master's table. Not without reason did Mrs. Hardie pet them like princes at the great festivals, and always send them home in the carriage as persons their entertainers delighted to honor. Herein I suspect she looked also, woman-like, to their security; for they were always expected to be solemnly, not improperly, intoxicated by the end of supper; no wise fuddled, but muddled; for the graceful superstition of the day suspected severe sobriety at solemnities as churlish and ungracious.

The bank itself was small and grave, and a trifle dingy, and bustle there was none in it; but if the stream of business looked sluggish and narrow, it was deep and quietly incessant, and tended all one way—to enrich the proprietor without a farthing risked.

Old Hardie had sat there forty years with other people's money overflowing into his lap as it rolled deep and steady through that little counting-house, when there occurred, or rather recurred, a certain phenomenon, which comes, with some little change of features, in a certain cycle of commercial changes as regularly as the month of March in the year, or the neap-tides, or the harvest moon, but, strange to say, at each visit takes the country by surprise.

CHAPTER XII.

THE nation had passed through the years of exhaustion and depression that follow a long war; its health had returned, and its elastic vigor was already reviving, when two remarkable harvests in succession, and an increased trade with the American continent, raised it to prosperity. One sign of vigor, the roll of capital, was wanting; speculation was fast asleep. The government of the day seems to have observed this with regret. A writer of authority on the subject says that, to stir stagnant enterprise, they directed "the Bank of England to issue about four millions in advances to the state and in enlarged discounts." I give you the man's words; they doubtless carry a signification to you, though they are jargon in a fog to me. Some months later the government took a step upon very different motives, which incidentally had a powerful effect in loosening capital and setting it in agitation. They reduced to four per cent the Navy Five per Cents, a favorite national investment, which represented a capital of two hundred millions. Now, when men have got used to five per cent from a certain quarter, they cannot be content with four, particularly the small holders; so this reduction of the Navy Five per Cents unsettled several thousand capitalists, and disposed them to search for an investment. A flattering one offered itself in the nick of time. Considerable attention had been drawn of late to the mineral wealth of South America, and one or two mining companies existed, but languished in the hands of professed speculators. The public now broke like a sudden flood into these hitherto sluggish channels of enterprise, and up went the shares to a high premium.

Almost contemporaneously, numerous joint-stock companies were formed, and directed toward schemes of internal industry. The small capitalists that had sold out of the Navy Five per Cents threw themselves into them all, and being bona fide speculators, drew hundreds in their train. Adventure, however, was at first restrained in some degree by the state of the currency. It was low, and rested on a singularly sound basis. Mr. Peel's Currency Bill had been some months in operation; by its principal provision the Bank of England was compelled on and after a certain date to pay gold for its notes on demand. The bank, anticipating a consequent rush for gold, had collected vast quantities of sovereigns, the new coin; but the rush never came, for a mighty simple reason. Gold is convenient in small sums, but a burden and a nuisance in large ones. It betrays its presence and invites robbers; it is a bore to lug it about, and a fearful waste of golden time to count it. Men run upon gold only when they have reason to distrust paper. But Mr. Peel's Bill, instead of damaging Bank of England paper, solidified it, and gave the nation a just and novel confidence in it. Thus, then, the large hoard of gold, fourteen to twenty millions, that the caution of the bank directors had accumulated in their coffers, remained uncalled for. But so large an abstraction from the specie of the realm contracted the provincial circulation. The small business of the country moved in fetters, so low was the metal currency. The country bankers petitioned government for relief, and government, listening to representations that were no doubt supported by facts, and backed by other interests, tampered with the principle of Mr. Peel's Bill, and allowed the country bankers to issue 1 pound and 2 pound notes for eleven years to come.

To this step there were but six dissentients in the House of Commons, so little was its importance seen or its consequences foreseen. This piece of inconsistent legislation removed one restraint, irksome but salutary, from commercial enterprise at a moment when capital was showing some signs of a feverish agitation. Its immediate consequences were very encouraging to the legislator; the country bankers sowed the land broadcast with their small paper, and this, for the cause above adverted to, took pro tem. the place of gold, and was seldom cashed at all except where silver was wanted. On this enlargement of the currency the arms of the nation seemed freed, enterprise shot ahead unshackled, and unwonted energy and activity thrilled in the veins of the kingdom. The rise in the prices of all commodities which followed, inevitable consequence of every increase in the currency, whether real or fictitious, was in itself adverse to the working classes; but the vast and numerous enterprises that were undertaken, some in the country itself, some in foreign parts, to which English workmen were conveyed, raised the price of labor higher still in proportion; so no class was out of the sun.

Men's faces shone with excitement and hope. The dormant hordes of misers crept out of their napkins and sepulchral strong-boxes into the warm air of the golden time. The mason's chisel chirped all over the kingdom, and the shipbuilders'* hammers rang all round the coast; corn was plenty, money became a drug, labor wealth, and poverty and discontent vanished from the face of the land. Adventure seemed all wings, and no lumbering carcass to clog it. New joint-stock companies were started in crowds as larks rise and darken the air in winter;** hundreds came to nothing, but hundreds stood, and of these nearly all reached a premium, small in some cases, high in most, fabulous in some; and the ease with which the first calls for cash on the multitudinous shares were met argued the vast resources that had hitherto slumbered in the nation for want of promising investments suited to the variety of human likings and judgments. The mind can hardly conceive any species of earthly enterprise that was not fitted with a company, oftener with a dozen, and with fifty or sixty where the proposed road to metal was direct. Of these the mines of Mexico still kept the front rank, but not to the exclusion of European, Australian and African ore.

* Two hundred new vessels are said to have been laid on the

stocks in one year.

** In two years 624 new companies were projected.

That masterpiece of fiction, "the Prospectus,"* diffused its gorgeous light far and near, lit up the dark mine, and showed the minerals shining and the jewels peeping; shone broad over the smiling fields, soon to be plowed, reaped, and mowed by machinery; and even illumined the depths of the sea, whence the buried treasures of ancient and modern times were about to be recovered by the Diving-bell Company.

* There is a little unlicked anonymuncule going scribbling

about, whose creed seems to be that a little camel, to be

known, must be examined and compared with other quadrupeds,

but that the great arts can be judged out of the depths of a

penny-a-liner's inner consciousness, and to be rated and

ranked need not be compared inter se. Applying the

microscope to the method of the novelist, but diverting the

glass from the learned judge's method in Biography, the

learned historian's method in History, and the daily

chronicler's method in dressing res gestoe for a journal,

this little addle-pate has jumped to a comparative estimate,

not based on comparison, so that all his blindfold

vituperation of a noble art is chimera, not reasoning; it

is, in fact, a retrograde step in science and logic. This is to evade the Baconian method, humble and wise, and crawl back to the lazy and self-confident system of the ancients, that kept the world dark so many centuries. It is [Greek] versus Induction. "[Greek]," ladies, is "divination by means of an ass's skull." A pettifogger's skull, however, will serve the turn, provided that pettifogger has been bitten with an insane itch for scribbling about things so infinitely above his capacity as the fine arts. Avoid this sordid dreamer, and follow, in letters as in science, the Baconian method! Then you will find that all uninspired narratives are more or less inexact, and that one, and one only, Fiction proper, has the honesty to antidote its errors by professing inexactitude. You will find that the Historian, Biographer, Novelist, and Chronicler are all obliged to paint upon their data with colors the imagination alone can supply, and all do it—alive or dead. You will find that Fiction, as distinguished from neat mendacity, has not one form upon earth, but a dozen. You will find the most habitually, willfully, and inexcusably inaccurate, with the means of accuracy under its nose, that form of fiction called "anonymous criticism," political and literary; the most equivocating, perhaps, is the "imaginavit," better known at Lincoln's Inn as the "affidavit." In the article of exaggeration, the mildest and tamest are perhaps History and the Novel, the boldest and most sparkling is the Advertisement, but the grandest, ablest, most gorgeous and plausibly exaggerating is surely the grave commercial prospectus, drawn up and signed by potent, grave and reverend seniors, who fear God, worship Mammon, revere big wigs right or wrong, and never read romances.

One mine was announced with a "vein of ore as pure and solid as a tin flagon."

In another the prospectus offered mixed advantages. The ore lay in so romantic a situation, and so thick, that the eye could be regaled with a heavenly landscape, while the foot struck against neglected lumps of gold weighing from two pounds to fifty.

This put the Bolanos mine on its mettle, and it announced, "not mines, but mountains of silver." Here, then, men might chip metal instead of painfully digging it. With this, up went the shares till they reached 500 premium.

Tialpuxahua was done at 199 premium.

Anglo Mexican 10 pounds paid, went to 158 pounds premium.

United Mexican 10 "   ",   " 155 pounds "

Columbian   10 " ", " 82 pounds "

But the Real del Monte, a mine of longer standing, on which 70 pounds was paid up, went to 550 premium, and at a later period, for I am not following the actual sequence of events, reached the enormous height of 1350 premium.

The Prospectus of the Equitable Loan Company lamented in paragraph one the imposition practiced on the poor, and denounced the pawnbrokers' 15 per cent. In paragraph four it promised 40 per cent to its shareholders.

Philanthropy smiled in the heading, and Avarice stung in the tail. No wonder a royal duke and other good names figured in this concern. Another eloquent sheet appealed to the national dignity. Should a nation that was just now being intersected by forty canal companies, and lighted by thirty gas companies, and every life in it worth a button insured by a score of insurance companies, dwell in hovels? Here was a country that, after long ruling the sea, was now mining the earth, and employing her spoils nobly, lending money to every nation and tribe that would fight for constitutional liberty. Should the principal city of so sovereign a nation be a collection of dingy dwellings made with burned clay? No; let these perishable and ignoble, materials give way, and London be granite, or at least wear a granite front—with which up went the Red Granite Company.

A railway was projected from Dover to Calais, but the shares never came into the market.

The Rhine Navigation shares were snapped up directly. The original holders, having no faith in their own paper, sold large quantities directly for the account. But they had underrated the ardor of the public. At settling day the shares were at 28 premium, and the sellers found they had made a most original hedge; for "the hedge" is not a daring operation that grasps at large gains; it is a timid and cautious maneuver, whose humble aim is to lower the figures of possible loss or gain. To be ruined by a stroke of caution so shocked the directors' sense of justice that they forged new coupons in imitation of the old, and tried to pass them off. The fraud was discovered; a committee sat on it. Respectables quaked. Finally, a scapegoat was put forward and expelled the Stock Exchange, and with that the inquiry was hushed. It would have let too much daylight in on a host of "good names" in the City and on 'Change.

At the same time, the country threw itself with ardor into Transatlantic loans. This, however, was an existing speculation vastly dilated at the period we are treating, but created about five years earlier. Its antecedent history can be dispatched in a few words.

England is said to be governed by a limited monarchy; but in case of a struggle between the two, her heart goes more with unlimited republic than with genuine monarchy. The Spanish colonies in South America found this out, and in their long battle for independence came to us for sympathy and cash. They often obtained both, and in one case something more; we lent Chili a million at six per cent, but we lent her ships, bayonets, and Cochrane gratis. This last, a gallant and amphibious dragoon, went to work in a style the slow Spaniard was unprepared for; blockaded the coast, overawed the Royalist party, and wrenched the state from the mother country, and settled it a republic. One of the first public acts of this Chilian republic was to borrow a million of us to go on with. Peru took only half a million at this period. Colombia, during the protracted struggle her independence cost her, obtained a sort of carte blanche loan from us at ten per cent. We were to deliver the stock in munitions of war, as called for, which, you will 'observe, was selling our loan; for at the bottom of all our romance lies business, business, business. Her freedom secured, the new state accommodated us by taking two millions of 5 per cent stock at 84. In all, about ten millions nominal capital, eight millions cash, crossed the Atlantic while we were cool; but now that we were heated by three hundred joint-stock companies, and the fire fanned by seven hundred prospectuses, fresh loans were effected with a wider range of territory and on a more important scale.

> Brazil now got . . . 3,200,000 l. in two loans;
>
> Colombia . . . . . . 4,750,000 l.;
>
> Peru . . . . 1,366,000 l. in two loans;
>
> Mexico . . . . 6,400,000 l. in two loans;
>
> Buenos Ayres . . . . 1,000,000 l.;

and Guatemala, a state we never heard of till she wanted money, took a million and a half. Besides these there were smaller loans, lent, not to nations, but to tribes. So hot was our money in our pockets that we tried 200,000 pounds on Patagonia. But the savages could not be got to nail us, which was the more to be regretted, as we might have done a good stroke with them; could have sent the stock out in fisherman's boots, cocked hats, beads, Bibles, and army misfits.

Europe found out there existed an island overflowing with faith and overburdened with money; she ran at us for a slice of the latter. We lent Naples two millions and a half at 5 per cent stock 92 1/2. Portugal a million and a half at 87. Austria three millions and a half at 82 1/2. Denmark three millions and a half at 3 per cent stock 75 1/2. Then came a bonne bouche. The subtle Greek had gathered from his western visitors a notion of the contents of Thucydides, and he came to us for sympathy and money to help him shake off the barbarians and their yoke, and save the wreck of the ancient temples. The appeal was shrewdly planned. England reads Thucydides, and skims Demosthenes, though Greece, it is presumed, does not. The impressions of our boyhood fasten upon our hearts, and our mature reason judges them like a father, not like a judge. To sweep the Tartar out of the Peloponnese, and put in his place a free press that should recall from the tomb that soul of freedom, and revive by degrees that tongue of music—who can play Solomon when such a proposal comes up for judgment?

"Give yourself no further concern about the matter," said the lofty Burdett, with a gentlemanlike wave of the hand; "your country shall be saved."

"In a few weeks," said another statesman, "Cochrane will be at Constantinople, and burn the port and its vessels. Having thus disarmed invasion, he will land in the Morea and clear it of the Turks."

Greece borrowed in two loans 2,800,000 pounds at 5 per cent. Russia (droll juxtaposition!) drew up the rear. She borrowed three millions and a half, but upon far more favorable terms than, with all our romance, we accorded to "Graeculus esuriens." The Greek stock ruled * from 56 1/2 to 59.

 * A corruption from the French verb "rouler."

Into these loans, and the multitudinous mines and miscellaneous enterprises, gas, railroad, canal, steam, dock, provision, insurance, milk, water, building, washing, money-lending, fishing, lottery, annuities, herring-curing, poppy-oil, cattle, weaving, bog draining, street-cleaning, house-roofing, old clothes exporting, steel-making, starch, silk-worm, etc., etc., etc., companies, all classes of the community threw themselves, either for investment or temporary speculation, on the fluctuations of the share-market. One venture was ennobled by a prince of the blood figuring as a director; another was sanctified by an archbishop; hundreds were solidified by the best mercantile names in the cities of London, Liverpool, and Manchester. Princes, dukes, duchesses, stags, footmen, poets, philosophers, divines, lawyers, physicians, maids, wives, widows, tore into the market, and choked the Exchange up so tight that the brokers could not get in nor out, and a bare passage had to be cleared by force and fines through a mass of velvet, fustian, plush, silk, rags, lace, and broadcloth, that jostled and squeezed each other in the struggle for gain. The shop-keeper flung down his scales and off to the share-market; the merchant embarked his funds and his credit; the clerk risked his place and his humble respectability. High and low, rich and poor, all hurried round the Exchange, like midges round a flaring gas-light, and all were to be rich in a day.

And, strange to say, all seemed to win and none to lose; for nothing was at a discount except toil and self-denial, and the patient industry that makes men rich, but not in a day.

One cold misgiving fell. The vast quantities of gold and silver that Mexico, mined by English capital and machinery, was about to pour into our ports, would so lower the price of those metals that a heavy loss must fall on all who held them on a considerable scale at their present values in relation to corn, land, labor and other properties and commodities.

"We must convert our gold," was the cry. Others more rash said: "This is premature caution—timidity. There is no gold come over yet; wait till you learn the actual bulk of the first metallic imports." "No, thank you," replied the prudent ones, "it will be too late then; when once they have touched our shores, the fall will be rapid." So they turned their gold, whose value was so precarious, into that unfluctuating material, paper. This solitary fear was soon swallowed up in the general confidence. The king congratulated Parliament, and Parliament the king. Both houses rang with trumpet notes of triumph, a few of which still linger in the memories of living men.

1. "The cotton trade and iron trade were never so flourishing."

2. "The exports surpassed by millions the highest figure recorded in' history."

3. "The hum of industry was heard throughout the fields."

4. "Joy beamed in every face."

5. "The country now reaped in honor and repose all it had sown in courage, constancy and wisdom."

6. "Our prosperity extended to all ranks of men, enhanced by those arts which minister to human comfort, and those inventions by which man seems to have obtained a mastery over Nature through the application of her own powers."

But one honorable gentleman informed the Commons that "distress had vanished from the land,"* and in addressing the throne acknowledged a novel embarrassment: "Such," said he, "is the general prosperity of the country, that I feel at a loss how to proceed; whether to give precedence to our agriculture, which is the main support of the country, to our manufactures, which have increased to an unexampled extent, or to our commerce, which distributes them to the ends of the earth, finds daily new outlets for their distribution, and new sources of national wealth and prosperity."

* "The poor ye shall have always with you."—Chimerical Evangelist.

Our old bank did not profit by the golden shower. Mr. Hardie was old, too, and the cautious and steady habits of forty years were not to be shaken readily. He declined shares, refused innumerable discounts, and loans upon scrip and invoices, and, in short, was behind the time. His bank came to be denounced as a clog on commerce. Two new banks were set up in the town to oil the wheels of adventure, on which he was a drag, and Hardie fell out of the game.

He was not so old or cold as to be beyond the reach of mortification, and these things stung him. One day he said fretfully to old Skinner, "It is hardly worth our while to take down the shutters now, for anything we do."

One afternoon two of his best customers, who were now up to their chins in shares, came and solicited a heavy loan on their joint personal security. Hardie declined. The gentlemen went out. Young Skinner watched them, and told his father they went into the new bank, stayed there a considerable time, and came out looking joyous. Old Skinner told Mr. Hardie. The old gentleman began at last to doubt himself and his system.

"The bank would last my time," said he, "but I must think of my son. I have seen many a good business die out because the merchant could not keep up with the times; and here they are inviting me to be director in two of their companies—good mercantile names below me. It is very flattering. I'll write to Dick. It is just he should have a voice; but, dear heart! at his age we know beforehand he will be for galloping faster than the rest. Well, his old father is alive to curb him."

It was always the ambition of Mr. Richard Hardie to be an accomplished financier. For some years past he had studied money at home and abroad— scientifically. His father's connection had gained him a footing in several large establishments abroad, and there he sat and worked en amateur as hard as a clerk. This zeal and diligence in a young man of independent means soon established him in the confidence of the chiefs, who told him many a secret. He was now in a great London bank, pursuing similar studies, practical and theoretical.

He received his father's letters sketching the rapid decline of the bank, and finally a short missive inviting him down to consider an enlarged plan of business. During the four days that preceded the young man's visit, more than one application came to Hardie senior for advances on scrip, cargoes coming from Mexico, and joint personal securities of good merchants that were in the current ventures. Old Hardie now, instead of refusing, detained the proposals for consideration. Meantime, he ordered five journals daily instead of one, sought information from every quarter, and looked into passing events with a favorable eye. The result was that he blamed himself, and called his past caution timidity. Mr. Richard Hardie arrived and was ushered into the bank parlor. After the first affectionate greetings old Skinner was called in, and, in a little pompous, good-hearted speech, invited to make one in a solemn conference. The compliment brought the tears into the old man's eyes. Mr. Hardie senior opened, showed by the books the rapid decline of business, pointed to the rise of two new banks owing to the tight hand he had held unseasonably, then invited the other two to say whether an enlarged system was not necessary to meet the times, and submitted the last, proposals for loans and discounts. "Now, sir, let me have your judgment."

"After my betters, sir," was old Skinner's reply.

"Well, Dick, have you formed any opinion on this matter?"

"I have, sir."

"I am extremely glad of it," said the old gentleman, very sincerely, but with a shade of surprise; "out with it, Dick."

The young man thus addressed by his father would not have conveyed to us the idea of "Dick." His hair was brown; there were no wrinkles under his eyes or lines in his cheek, but in his manner there was no youth whatever. He was tall, commanding, grave, quiet, cold, and even at that age almost majestic. His first sentence, slow and firm, removed the paternal notion that a cipher or a juvenile had come to the council-table.

"First, sir, let me return to you my filial thanks for that caution which you seem to think has been excessive. There I beg respectfully to differ with you."

"I am glad of it, Dick; but now you see it is time to relax, eh?"

"No, sir."

The two old men stared at one another. The senile youth proceeded: "That some day or other our system will have to be relaxed is probable, but just now all it wants is—tightening."

"Why, Dick? Skinner, the boy is mad. You can't have watched the signs of the times."

"I have, sir; and looked below the varnish."

"To the point, then, Dick. There is a general proposal 'to relax our system.' The boy uses good words, Skinner, don't he? and here are six particulars over which you can cast your eye. Hand them to him, Skinner."

"I will take things in that order," said Richard, quietly running his eye over the papers. There was a moment's silence. "It is proposed to connect the bank with the speculations of the day."

"That is not fairly stated, Dick; it is too broad. We shall make a selection; we won't go in the stream above ankle deep."

"That is a resolution, sir, that has been often made but never kept—for this reason: you can't sit on dry land and calculate the force of the stream. It carries those who paddle in it off their feet, and then they must swim with it or—sink."

"Dick, for Heaven's sake, no poetry here."

"Nay, sir," said old Skinner, "remember, 'twas you brought the stream in."

"More fool I. 'Flow on, thou shining Dick'; only the more figures of arithmetic, and the fewer figures of speech, you can give old Skinner and me, the more weight you will carry with us."

The young man colored a moment, but never lost his ponderous calmness.

"I will give you figures in their turn, But we were to begin with the general view. Half-measures, then, are no measures; they imply a vacillating judgment; they are a vain attempt to make a pound of rashness and a pound of timidity into two pounds of prudence. You permit me that figure, sir; it comes from the summing-book. The able man of business fidgets. He keeps quiet, or carries something out."

Old Skinner rubbed his hands. "These are wise words, sir."

"No, only clever ones. This is book-learning. It is the sort of wisdom you and I have outgrown these forty years. Why, at his age I was choke-full of maxims. They are good things to read; but act proverbs, and into the Gazette you go. My faith in any general position has melted away with the snow of my seventy winters."

"What, then, if it was established that all adders bite, would you refuse to believe his adder would bite you, sir?"

"Dick, if a single adder bit me, it would go farther to convince me that the next adder would bite me too than if fifty young Buffons told me all adders bite."

The senile youth was disconcerted for a single moment. He hesitated. The keys that the old man had himself said would unlock his judgment lay beside him on the table. He could not help glancing slyly at them, but he would not use them before their turn. His mind was methodical. His will was strong in all things. He put his hand in his side-pocket, and drew out a quantity of papers neatly arranged, tied, and indorsed.

The old men instantly bestowed a more watchful sort of attention on him.

"This, gentlemen, is a list of the joint-stock companies created last year. What do you suppose is their number?"

"Fifty, I'll be bound, Mr. Richard."

"More than that, Skinner. Say eighty."

"Two hundred and forty-three, gentlemen. Of these some were stillborn, but the majority hold the market. The capital proposed to be subscribed on the sum total is two hundred and forty-eight millions."

"Pheugh! Skinner!"

"The amount actually paid at present (chiefly in bank-notes) is stated at 43,062,608 pounds, and the balance due at the end of the year on this set of ventures will be 204,937,392 pounds or thereabouts. The projects of this year have not been collected, but they are on a similar scale. Full a third of the general sum total is destined to foreign countries, either in loans or to work mines, etc., the return for which is uncertain and future. All these must come to nothing, and ruin the shareholders that way, or else must sooner or later be paid in specie, since no foreign nation can use our paper, but must sell it to the Bank of England. We stand, then, pledged to burst like a bladder, or to export in a few months thrice as much specie as we possess. To sum up, if the country could be sold to-morrow, with every brick that stands upon it, the proceeds would not meet the engagements into which these joint-stock companies have inveigled her in the course of twenty months. Viewed then, in gross, under the test, not of poetry and prospectus, but of arithmetic, the whole thing is a bubble."

"A bubble?" uttered both the seniors in one breath, and almost in a scream.

"But I am ready to test it in detail. Let us take three main features—the share-market, the foreign loans, and the inflated circulation caused by the provincial banks. Why do the public run after shares? Is it in the exercise of a healthy judgment? No; a cunning bait has been laid for human weakness. Transferable shares valued at 100 pounds can be secured and paid for by small instalments of 5 pounds or less. If, then, his 100 pound shares rise to 130 pounds each, the adventurer can sell at a nominal profit of 30 per cent, but a real profit of 600 per cent on his actual investment. This intoxicates rich and poor alike. It enables the small capitalist to operate on the scale that belongs, in healthy times, to the large capitalist; a beggar can now gamble like a prince; his farthings are accepted as counters for sovereigns; but this is a distinct feature of all the more gigantic bubbles recorded. Here, too, you see, is illusory credit on a vast scale, with its sure consequence, inflated and fictitious values; another bit of soap that goes to every bubble in history. Now for the Transatlantic loans. I submit them to a simple test. Judge nations like individuals. If you knew nothing of a man but that he had set up a new shop, would you lend him money? Then why lend money to new republics of whom you know nothing but that, born yesterday, they may die to-morrow, and that they are exhausted by recent wars, and that, where responsibility is divided, conscience is always subdivided?"

"Well said, Richard, well said."

"If a stranger offered you thirty per cent, would you lend him your money?"

"No; for I should know he didn't mean to pay."

"Well, these foreign negotiators offer nominally five per cent, but, looking at the price of the stock, thirty, forty, and even fifty per cent. Yet they are not so liberal as they appear; they could afford ninety per cent. You understand me, gentlemen. Would you lend to a man that came to you under an alias like a Newgate thief? Cast your eye over this prospectus. It is the Poyais loan. There is no such place as Poyais."

"Good heavens!"

"It is a loan to an anonymous swamp by the Mosquito River. But Mosquito suggests a bite. So the vagabonds that brought the proposal over put their heads together as they crossed the Atlantic, and christened the place Poyais; and now fools that are not fools enough to lend sixpence to Zahara, are going to lend 200,000 pounds to rushes and reeds."

"Why, Richard, what are you talking about? 'The air is soft and balmy; the climate fructifying; the soil is spontaneous'—what does that mean? mum! mum! 'The water runs over sands of gold.' Why, it is a description of Paradise. And, now I think of it, is not all this taken from John Milton?"

"Very likely. It is written by thieves."

"It seems there are tortoise-shell, diamonds, pearls—"

"In the prospectus, but not in the morass. It is a good, straightforward morass, with no pretensions but to great damp. But don't be alarmed, gentlemen, our countrymen's money will not be swamped there. It will all be sponged up in Threadneedle Street by the poetic swindlers whose names, or aliases, you hold in your hand. The Greek, Mexican, and Brazilian loans may be translated from Prospectish into English thus: At a date when every sovereign will be worth five to us in sustaining shriveling paper and collapsing credit, we are going to chuck a million sovereigns into the Hellespont, five million sovereigns into the Gulf of Mexico, and two millions into the Pacific Ocean. Against the loans to the old monarchies there is only this objection, that they are unreasonable; will drain out gold when gold will be life-blood; which brings me, by connection, to my third item—the provincial circulation. Pray, gentlemen, do you remember the year 1793?"

For some minutes past a dead silence and a deep, absorbed attention had received the young man's words; but that quiet question was like a great stone descending suddenly on a silent stream. Such a noise, agitation, and flutter.

The old banker and his clerk both began to speak at once.

"Don't we?"

"Oh, Lord, Mr. Richard, don't talk of 1793."

"What do you know about 1793? You weren't born."

"Oh, Mr. Richard, such a to-do, sir! 1800 firms in the Gazette. Seventy banks stopped."

"Nearer a hundred, Mr. Skinner. Seventy-one stopped in the provinces, and a score in London."

"Why, sir, Mr. Richard knows everything, whether he was born or not."

"No, he doesn't, you old goose; he doesn't know how you and I sat looking at one another, and pretending to fumble, and counting out slowly, waiting sick at heart for the sack of guineas that was to come down by coach. If it had not come we should not have broken, but we should have suspended payment for twenty-four hours, and I was young enough then to have cut my throat in the interval."

"But it came, sir—it came, and you cried, 'Keep the bank open till midnight!' and when the blackguards heard that, and saw the sackful of gold, they crept away; they were afraid of offending us. Nobody came anigh us next day. Banks smashed all round us like glass bottles, but Hardie & Co. stood, and shall stand for ever and ever. Amen."

"Who showed the white feather, Mr. Skinner? Who came creeping and sniveling, and took my hand under the counter, and pressed it to give me courage, and then was absurd enough to make apologies, as if sympathy was as common as dirt? Give me your hand directly, you old—Hallo!"

"God bless you, sir! God bless you! It is all right, sir. The bank is safe for another fifty years. We have got Master Richard, and he has got a head. O Gemini, what a head he has got, and the other day playing marbles!"

"Yes, and we are interrupting him with our nonsense. Go on, Richard."

Richard had secretly but fully appreciated the folly of the interruption. His was a great mind, and moved in a sort of pecuniary ether high above the little weaknesses my reader has observed in Hardie senior and old Skinner. Being, however, equally above the other little infirmities of fretfulness and fussiness, he waited calmly and proceeded coolly.

"What was the cause of the distress in 1793?"

"Ah! that was the puzzle—wasn't it, Skinner? We were never so prosperous as that year. The distress came over us like a thunder-storm all in a moment. Nobody knows the exact cause."

"I beg your pardon, sir, it is as well known as any point of history whatever. Some years of prosperity had created a spawn of country banks, most of them resting on no basis; these had inflated the circulation with their paper. A panic and a collapse of this fictitious currency was as inevitable as the fall of a stone forced against nature into the air."

"There were a great many petty banks, Richard, and, of course, plenty of bad paper. I believe you are right. The causes of things were not studied in those days as they are now."

"All that we know now, sir, is to be found in books written long before 1793."

"Books! books!"

"Yes, sir; a book is not dead paper except to sleepy minds. A book is a man giving you his best thoughts in his very best words. It is only the shallow reader that can't learn life from genuine books. I'll back him who studies them against the man who skims his fellow-creatures, and vice versa. A single page of Adam Smith, studied, understood, and acted on by the statesmen of your day, would have averted the panic of 1793. I have the paragraph in my note-book. He was a great man, sir; oblige me, Mr. Skinner."

"Certainly, sir, certainly. 'Should the circulation of paper exceed the value of the gold and silver of which it supplies the place, many people would immediately perceive they had more of this paper than was necessary for transacting their business at home; and, as they could not send it abroad, bank paper only passing current where it is issued, there would be a run upon the banks to the extent of this superfluous paper.'"

Richard Hardie resumed. "We were never so overrun with rotten banks as now. Shoemakers, cheesemongers, grocers, write up 'Bank' over one of their windows, and deal their rotten paper by the foolscap ream. The issue of their larger notes is colossal, and renders a panic inevitable soon or late; but, to make it doubly sure, they have been allowed to utter 1 pound and 2 pound notes. They have done it, and on a frightful scale. Then, to make it trebly sure, the just balance between paper and specie is disturbed in the other scale as well as by foreign loans to be paid in gold. In 1793 the candle was left unsnufled, but we have lighted it at both ends and put it down to roast. Before the year ends, every sovereign in the banks of this country may be called on to cash 30 pounds of paper—bank-paper, share-paper, foolscap-paper, waste-paper. In 1793, a small excess of paper over specie had the power to cause a panic and break some ninety banks; but our excess of paper is far larger, and with that fatal error we have combined foreign loans and three hundred bubble companies. Here, then, meet three bubbles, each of which, unaided, secures a panic. Events revolve, gentlemen, and reappear at intervals. The great French bubble of 1719 is here to-day with the addition of two English tom-fooleries, foreign loans and 1 pound notes. Mr. Law was a great financier. Mr. Law was the first banker and the greatest. All mortal bankers are his pupils, though they don't know it. Mr. Law was not a fool; his critics are. Mr. Law did not commit one error out of six that are attributed to him by those who judge him without reading, far less studying, his written works. He was too sound and sober a banker to admit small notes. They were excluded from his system. He found France on the eve of bankruptcy; in fact, the state had committed acts of virtual bankruptcy. He saved her with his bank.

"Then came his two errors, one remedial, the other fatal. No. 1, he created a paper company and blew it up to a bubble. When the shares had reached the skies, they began to come down, like stones, by an inevitable law. No. 2, to save them from their coming fate, he propped them with his bank. Overrating the power of governments, and underrating Nature's, he married the Mississippi shares (at forty times their value) to his banknotes by edict. What was the consequence? The bank paper, sound in itself, became rotten by marriage. Nothing could save the share-paper. The bank paper, making common cause with it, shared its fate. Had John Law let his two tubs each stand on its own bottom, the shares would have gone back to what they came from—nothing; the bank, based as it was on specie, backed stoutly by the government, and respected by the people for great national services, would have weathered the storm and lasted to this day. But he tied his rickety child to his healthy child, and flung them into a stormy sea, and told them to swim together: they sank together. Now observe, sir, the fatal error that ruined the great financier in 1720 is this day proposed to us. We are to connect our bank with bubble companies by the double tie of loans and liability. John Law was sore tempted. The Mississippi Company was his own child as well as the bank. Love of that popularity he had drunk so deeply, egotism, and parental partiality, combined to obscure that great man's judgment. But, with us, folly stands naked on one side, bubbles in hand—common sense and printed experience on the other. These six specimen bubbles here are not our children. Let me see whose they are, aliases excepted."

"Very good, young gentleman, very good. Now it is my turn. I have got a word or two to say on the other side. The journals, which are so seldom agreed, are all of one mind about these glorious times. Account for that!"

"How can you know their minds, sir?"

"By their leading columns."

"Those are no clue."

"What! Do they think one thing and print another? Why should the independent press do that? Nonsense."

"Why, sir? Because they are bribed to print it, but they are not bribed to think it."

"Bribed? The English press bribed?"

"Oh, not directly, like the English freeman. Oblige me with a journal or two, no matter which; they are all tarred with the same stick in time of bubble. Here, sir, are 50 pounds worth of bubble advertisements, yielding a profit of say 25 pounds on this single issue. In this one are nearer 100 pounds worth of such advertisements. Now is it in nature that a newspaper, which is a trade speculation, should say the word that would blight its own harvest? This is the oblique road by which the English press is bribed. These leaders are mere echoes of to-day's advertisement sheet, and bidders for to-morrow's."

"The world gets worse every day, Skinner."

"It gets no better," replied Richard, philosophically.

"But, Richard, here is our county member, and ——, staid, sober men both, and both have pledged their honor on the floor of the House of Commons to the sound character of some of these companies."

"They have, sir; but they will never redeem the said honor, for they are known to be bribed, and not obliquely, by those very companies." (The price current of M. P. honor, in time of bubble, ought to be added to the works of arithmetic.) "Those two Brutuses get 500 pounds apiece per annum for touting those companies down at Stephen's. —— goes cheaper and more oblique. He touts, in the same place, for a gas company, and his house in the square flares from cellar to garret, gratis."

"Good gracious! and he talked of the light of conscience in his very last speech. But this cannot apply to all. There is the archbishop; he can't have sold his name to that company."

"Who knows? He is over head and ears in debt."

"But the duke, he can't have."

"Why not? He is over head and ears in debt. Princes deep in debt by misconduct, and bishops deep in ditto by ditto, are half-honest, needy men; and half-honest, needy men are all to be bought and sold like hogs in Smithfield, especially in time of bubble."

"What is the world come to!"

"What it was a hundred years ago."

"I have got one pill left for him, Skinner. Here is the Chancellor of the Exchequer, a man whose name stands for caution, has pronounced a panegyric on our situation. Here are his words quoted in this leader; now listen: 'We may safely venture to contemplate with instructive admiration the harmony of its proportions and the solidity of its basis.' What do you say to that?"

"I say it is one man's opinion versus the experience of a century. Besides, that is a quotation, and may be a fraudulent one."

"No, no. The speech was only delivered last Wednesday: we will refer to it. Mum! mum! Ah, here it is. 'The Chancellor of the Exchequer rose and—' mum! mum! ah—'I am of—o-pinion that—if, upon a fair review of our situation, there shall appear to be nothing hollow in its foundation, artificial in its superstructure, or flimsy in its general results, we may safely venture to contemplate with instructive admiration the harmony of its proportions and the solidity of its basis.'"

"Ha! ha! ha! I quite agree with cautious Bobby. If it is not hollow, it may be solid; if it is not a gigantic paper balloon, it may be a very fine globe, and vice versa, which vice versa he in his heart suspects to be the truth. You see, sir, the mangled quotation was a swindle, like the flimsy superstructures it was intended to prop. The genuine paragraph is a fair sample of Robinson, and of the art of withholding opinion by means of expression. But as quoted, by a fraudulent suppression of one half, the unbalanced half is palmed off as a whole, and an indecision perverted into a decision. I might just as fairly cite him as describing our situation to be 'hollow in its basis, artificial in its superstructure, flimsy in its general result.' Since you value names, I will cite you one man that has commented on the situation; not, like Mr. Robinson, by misty sentences, each neutralizing the other, but by consistent acts: a man, gentlemen, whose operations have always been numerous and courageous in less prosperous times, yet now he is out of everything but a single insurance company."

"Who is the gentleman?"

"It is not a gentleman; it is a blackguard," said the exact youth.

"You excite my curiosity. Who is the capitalist, then, that stands aloof?"

"Nathan Meyer Rothschild."

"The devil."

Old Skinner started sitting. "Rothschild hanging back. Oh, master, for Heavens sake don't let us try to be wiser than those devils of Jews. Mr. Richard, I bore up pretty well against your book-learning, but now you've hit me with a thunderbolt. Let us get in gold, and keep as snug as mice, and not lend one of them a farthing to save them from the gallows. Those Jews smell farther than a Christian can see. Don't let's have any more 1793's, sir, for Heaven's sake. Listen to Mr. Richard; he has been abroad, and come back with a head."

"Be quiet, Skinner. You seem to possess private information, Richard."

"I employ three myrmidons to hunt it; it will be useful by and by."

"It may be now. Remark on these proposals."

"Well, sir, two of them are based on gold mines, shares at a fabulous premium. Now no gold mine can be worked to a profit by a company. Primo:Gold is not found in veins like other metals. It is an abundant metal made scarce to man by distribution over a wide surface. The very phrase gold mine is delusive. Secundo: Gold is a metal that cannot be worked to a profit by a company for this reason: workmen will hunt it for others so long as the daily wages average higher than the amount of metal they find per diem; but, that Rubicon once passed, away they run to find gold for themselves in some spot with similar signs; if they stay, it is to murder your overseers and seize your mine. Gold digging is essentially an individual speculation. These shares sell at 700 pounds apiece; a dozen of them are not worth one Dutch tulip-root. Ah! here is a company of another class, in which you have been invited to be director; they would have given you shares and made you liable." Mr. Richard consulted his note-book. "This company, which 'commands the wealth of both Indies'—in perspective—dissolved yesterday afternoon for want of eight guineas. They had rented offices at eight guineas a week, and could not pay the first week. 'Turn out or pay,' said the landlord, a brute absorbed in the present, and with no faith in the glorious future. They offered him 1,500 pounds worth of shares instead of his paltry eight guineas cash. On this he swept his premises of them. What a godsend you would have been to these Jeremy Diddlers, you and the ten thousand they would have bled you of."

The old banker turned pale.

"Oh, that is nothing new, sir. 'To-morrow the first lord of the treasury calls at my house, and brings me 11,261 pounds 14s. 11 3/4d., which is due to me from the nation at twelve of the clock on that day; you couldn't lend me a shilling till then, could ye?' Now for the loans. Baynes upon Haggart want 2,000 pounds at 5 per cent."

"Good names, Richard, surely," said old Hardie, faintly.

"They were; but there are no good names in time of bubble. The operations are so enormous that in a few weeks a man is hollowed out and his frame left standing. In such times capitalists are like filberts; they look all nut, but half of them are dust inside the shell, and only known by breaking. Baynes upon Haggart, and Haggart upon Baynes, the city is full of their paper. I have brought some down to show it to you. A discounter, who is a friend of mine, did it for them on a considerable scale at thirty per cent discount (cast your eye over these bills, Haggart on Baynes). But he has burned his fingers even at that, and knows it. So I am authorized to offer all these to you at fifty per cent discount."

"Good heavens! Richard!"

"If, therefore, you think of doing rotten apple upon rotten pear, otherwise

Haggart upon Baynes, why do it at five per cent when it is to be had by the quire at fifty?"

"Take them out of my sight," said old Hardie, starting up—"take them all out of my sight. Thank God I sent for you. No more discussion, no more doubt. Give me your hand, my son; you have saved the bank!"

The conference broke up with these eager words, and young Skinner retired swiftly from the keyhole.

The next day Mr. Hardie senior came to a resolution which saddened poor old Skinner. He called the clerks in and introduced them to Mr. Richard as his managing partner.

"Every dog has his day," said the old gentleman. "Mine has been a long one. Richard has saved the bank from a fatal error; Richard shall conduct it as Hardie & Son. Don't be disconsolate, Skinner; I'll look in on you now and then."

Hardie junior sent back all the proposals with a polite negative. He then proceeded on a two-headed plan. Not to lose a shilling when the panic he expected should come, and to make 20,000 pounds upon its subsiding. Hardie & Son held Exchequer bills on rather a large scale. They were at half a crown premium. He sold every one and put gold in his coffers. He converted in the same way all his other securities except consols. These were low, and he calculated they would rise in any general depreciation of more pretentious investments. He drew out his balance, a large one, from his London correspondent, and put his gold in his coffers. He drew a large deposit from the Bank of England. Whenever his own notes came into the bank, he withdrew them from circulation. "They may hop upon Hardie & Son," said he, "but they shan't run upon us, for I'll cut off their legs and keep them in my safe."

One day he invited several large tradesmen in the town to dine with him at the bank. They came full of curiosity. He gave them a luxurious dinner, which pleased them. After dinner he exposed the real state of the nation, as he understood it. They listened politely, and sneered silently, but visibly. He then produced six large packets of his banknotes; each packet contained 3,000 pounds. Skinner, then present, enveloped these packets in cartridge-paper, and the guests were requested to seal them up. This was soon done. In those days a bunch of gigantic seals dangled and danced on the pit of every man's stomach. The sealed packets went back into the safe.

"Show us a sparkle o' gold, Mr. Richard," said Meredith, linen-draper and wag.

"Mr. Skinner, oblige me by showing Mr. Meredith a little of your specie—a few anti-bubble pills, eh! Mr. Meredith."

Omnes. "Ha! ha! ha!"

Presently a shout from Meredith: "Boys, he has got it here by the bushel. All new sovereigns. Don't any of ye be a linen-draper, if you have got a chance to be a banker. How much is there here, Mr. Richard?"

"We must consult the books to ascertain that, sir."

"Must you? Then just turn your head away, Mr. Richard, and I'll put in a claw."

Omnes. "Haw! haw! ho!"

Richard Hardie resumed. "My precautions seem extravagant to you now, but in a few months you will remember this conversation, and it will lead to business." The rest of the evening he talked of anything, everything, except banking. He was not the man to dilute an impression.

Hardie junior was so confident in his reading and his reasonings that he looked every day into the journals for the signs of a general collapse of paper and credit; instead of which, public confidence seemed to increase, not diminish, and the paper balloon, as he called it, dilated, not shrank; and this went on for months. His gold lay a dead and useless stock, while paper was breeding paper on every side of him. He suffered his share of those mortifications which every man must look to endure who takes a course of his own, and stems a human current. He sat somber and perplexed in his bank parlor, doing nothing; his clerks mended pens in the office. The national calamity so confidently predicted, and now so eagerly sighed for, came not.

In other words, Richard Hardie was a sagacious calculator, but not a prophet; no man is till afterward, and then nine out of ten are. At last he despaired of the national calamity ever coming at all. So then, one dark November day, an event happened that proved him a shrewd calculator of probabilities in the gross, and showed that the records, of the past, "studied" instead of "skimmed," may in some degree counterbalance youth and its narrow experience. Owing to the foreign loans, there were a great many bills out against this country. Some heavy ones were presented, and seven millions in gold taken out of the Bank of England and sent abroad. This would have trickled back by degrees; but the suddenness and magnitude of the drain alarmed the bank directors for the safety of the bank, subject as it was by Mr. Peel's bill to a vast demand for gold.

Up to this period, though they had amassed specie themselves, they had rather fed the paper fever in the country at large, but now they began to take a wide and serious view of the grave contingencies around them. They contracted their money operations, refused in two cases to discount corn, and, in a word, put the screw on as judiciously as they could. But time was up. Public confidence had reached its culminating point. The sudden caution of the bank could not be hidden; it awoke prudence, and prudence after imprudence drew terror at its heels. There was a tremendous run upon the country banks. The smaller ones "smashed all around like glass bottles," as in 1793; the larger ones made gigantic and prolonged efforts to stand, and generally fell at last.

Many, whose books showed assets 40s. in the pound, suspended payment; for in a violent panic the bank creditors can all draw their balances in a few hours or days, but the poor bank cannot put a similar screw on its debtors. Thus no establishment was safe. Honor and solvency bent before the storm, and were ranked with rottenness; and, as at the same time the market price of securities sank with frightful rapidity, scarcely any amount of invested capital was safe in the unequal conflict.

Exchequer bills went down to 60s. discount, and the funds rose and fell like waves in a storm.

London bankers were called out of church to answer dispatches from their country correspondents.

The Mint worked day and night, and coined a hundred and fifty thousand sovereigns per diem for the Bank of England; but this large supply went but a little way, since that firm had in reality to cash nearly all the country notes that were cashed.

Post-chaises and four stood like hackney-coaches in Lombard Street, and every now and then went rattling off at a gallop into the country with their golden freight. In London, at the end of a single week, not an old sovereign was to be seen, so fiercely was the old coinage swept into the provinces, so active were the Mint and the smashers; these last drove a roaring trade; for paper now was all suspected, and anything that looked like gold was taken recklessly in exchange.

Soon the storm burst on the London banks. A firm known to possess half a million in undeniable securities could not cash them fast enough to meet the checks drawn on their counter, and fell. Next day, a house whose very name was a rock suspended for four days. An hour or two later two more went hopelessly to destruction. The panic rose to madness. Confidence had no longer a clue, nor names a distinction. A man's enemies collected three or four vagabonds round his door, and in another hour there was a run upon him, that never ceased till he was emptied or broken. At last, as, in the ancient battles, armies rested on their arms to watch a duel in which both sides were represented, the whole town watched a run upon the great house of Pole, Thornton & Co. The Bank of England, from public motives, spiced of course with private interest, had determined to support Pole, Thornton & Co., and so perhaps stem the general fury, for all things have their turning-point. Three hundred thousand pounds were advanced to Pole & Co., who with this aid and their own resources battled through the week, but on Saturday night were drained so low that their fate once more depended on the Bank of England. Another large sum was advanced them. They went on; but, ere the next week ended, they succumbed, and universal panic gained the day.

Climax of all, the Bank of England notes lost the confidence of the public, and a frightful run was made on it. The struggle had been prepared for, and was gigantic on both sides. Here the great hall of the bank, full of panic-stricken citizens jostling one another to get gold for the notes of the bank; there, foreign nations sending over ingots and coin to the bank, and the Mint working night and day, Sunday and week-day, to turn them into sovereigns to meet the run. Sovereigns or else half-sovereigns were promptly delivered on demand. No hesitation or sign of weakness peeped out; but under this bold and prudent surface, dismay, sickness of heart, and the dread of a great humiliation. At last, one dismal evening, this establishment, which at the beginning of the panic had twenty millions specie, left off with about five hundred thousand pounds in coin, and a similar amount in bullion. A large freight of gold was on the seas, coming to their aid, and due, but not arrived; the wind was high; and in a few hours the people would be howling round their doors again. They sent a hasty message to the government, and implored them to suspend, by order in council, the operation of Mr. Peel's bill for a few days. A plump negative from Mr. Canning.

Then, being driven to expedients, they bethought them of a chest of 1 pound notes that they had luckily omitted to burn.

Another message to the government, "May we use these?"

"As a temporary expedient, yes."

The one-pound notes were whirling all over the country before daybreak, and, marvelous anomaly, which took Richard Hardie by surprise, they oiled the waves, the panic abated from that hour. The holders of country notes took the 1 pound B. E. notes as cash with avidity. The very sight of them piled on a counter stopped a run in more than one city.

The demand for gold at the Bank of England continued, but less fiercely; and as the ingots still came tumbling in, and the Mint hailed sovereigns on them, their stock of specie rose as the demand declined, and they came out of their fiercest battle with honor. But, ere the tide turned, things in general came to a pass scarcely known in the history of civilized nations. Ladies and gentlemen took heirlooms to the pawnbrokers', and swept their tills of the last coin. Not only was wild speculation, hitherto so universal and ardent, snuffed out like a candle, but investment ceased and commerce came to a stand-still. Bank stock, East India stock, and, some days, consols themselves, did not go down; they went out, were blotted from the book of business. No man would give them gratis; no man would take them on any other terms. The brokers closed their books; there were no buyers nor sellers. Trade was coming to the same pass, except the retail business in eatables; and an observant statesman and economist, that watched the phenomenon, pronounced that in forty-eight hours more all dealings would have ceased between man and man, or returned to the rude and primitive form of barter, or direct exchange of men's several commodities, labor included.

Finally, things crept into their places; shades of distinction were drawn between good securities and bad. Shares were forfeited, companies dissolved, bladders punctured, balloons flattened, bubbles burst, and thousands of families ruined—thousands of people beggared—and the nation itself, its paper fever reduced by a severe bleeding, lay sick, panting, exhausted, and discouraged for a year or two to await the eternal cycle—torpor, prudence, health, plethora, blood-letting; torpor, prudence, health, plethora, bloodletting, etc., etc., etc., etc., in secula seculorum.

The journals pitched into "speculation."

Three banks lay in the dust in the town of ——, and Hardie & Son stood looking calmly down upon the ruins.

Richard Hardie had carried out his double-headed plan.

There was no run upon him—could not be one in the course of nature, his balances were so low, and his notes were all at home. He created artificially a run of a very different kind. He dined the same party of tradesmen—all but one, who could not come, being at supper after Polonius his fashion. After dinner he showed the packets still sealed, and six more unsealed. "Here, gentlemen, is our whole issue." There was a huge wood fire in the old-fashioned room. He threw a packet of notes into it. A most respectable grocer yelled and lost color: victim of his senses, he thought sacred money was here destroyed, and his host a well-bred, and oh! how plausible, maniac. The others derided him, and packet after packet fed the flames. When two only were left, containing about five thousand pounds between them, Hardie junior made a proposal that they should advertise in their shop windows to receive Hardie's five-pound notes as five guineas in payment for their goods. Observing a natural hesitation, he explained that they would by this means, crush their competitors, and could easily clap a price on their goods to cover the odd shillings. The bargain was soon struck. Mr. Richard was a great man. All his guests felt in their secret souls and pockets—excuse the tautology—that some day or other they should want to borrow money of him. Besides, "crush their competitors!"

Next day Mr. Richard loosed his hand and let a flock of his own bank-notes fly (they were asked for earnestly every day). Some soon found their way to the shops in question. The next day still more took wing and buzzed about the shops. Presently other tradesmen, finding people rushed to the shops in question, began to bid against them for Hardie's notes, a result the long-headed youth had expected; and said notes went up to ten shillings premium. Too calm and cold to be betrayed into deserting his principles, he confined the issue within the bounds he had prescribed, and when they were all out seldom saw one of them again. By this means he actually lowered the Bank of England notes in public estimation, and set his own high above them in the town of ——. Deposits came in. Confidence unparalleled took the place of fear so far as he was concerned, and he was left free to work the other part of his plan.

To the amazement and mystification of old Skinner, he laid out ten thousand pounds in Exchequer bills, and followed this up by other large purchases of paper, paper, nothing but paper.

Hardie senior was nervous.

"Are you true to your own theory, Richard?"

The youth explained to him that blind confidence always ends in blind distrust, and then all paper becomes depreciated alike, but good paper is sure to recover. "Sixty-two shillings discount, sir, is a ridiculous decline of Exchequer bills. We are at peace, and elastic, and the government is strong. My other purchases all rest upon certain information, carefully and laboriously amassed while the world was so busy blowing bubbles. I am now buying paper that is unjustly depreciated in Panic, i.e., in the second act of that mania of which Bubble is the first act." He added: "When the herd buy, the price rises; when they sell, it falls. To buy with them and sell with them is therefore to buy dear and sell cheap. My game—and it is a game that reduces speculation to a certainty—is threefold:

"First, never, at any price or under any temptation, buy anything that is not as good as gold.

"Secondly, buy that sound article when the herd sells it.

"Thirdly, sell it when the herd buys it."

"Richard," said the old man, "I see what it is—you are a genius."

"No."

"It is no use your denying it, Richard."

"Common sense, sir, common sense."

"Yes, but common sense carried to such a height as you do is genius."

"Well, sir, then I own to the genius of common sense."

"I admire you, Richard—I am proud of you; but the bank has stood one hundred and forty years, and never a genius in it;" the old man sighed.

Hardie senior, having relieved his mind of this vague misgiving, never returned to it—probably never felt it again. It was one of those strange flashes that cross a mind as a meteor the sky.

The old gentleman, having little to do, talked more than heretofore, and, like fathers, talked about his son, and, unlike sons, cried him up at his own expense. The world is not very incredulous; above all, it never disbelieves a man who calls himself a fool. Having then gained the public ear by the artifice of self-depreciation, he poured into it the praises of Hardie junior. He went about telling how he, an old man, was all but bubbled till this young Daniel came down and foretold all. Thus paternal garrulity combined for once with a man's own ability to place Richard Hardie on the pinnacle of provincial grandeur.

A few years more and Hardie senior died. (His old clerk, Skinner, followed him a month later.)

Richard Hardie, now sole partner and proprietor, assumed a mode of living unknown to his predecessors. He built a large, commodious house, and entertained in the first style. The best families in the neighborhood visited a man whose manner was quiet and stately, his income larger than their own, and his house and table luxurious without vulgar pretensions, and the red-hot gilding and glare with which the injudicious parvenu brands himself and furniture.

The bank itself put on a new face. Twice as much glass fronted the street, and a skylight was let into the ceiling: there were five clerks instead of three; the new ones at much smaller salaries than the pair that had come down from antiquity.

CHAPTER XIII.

SUCH was Mr. Hardie at twenty-five, and his townspeople said: "If he is so wise now he is a boy, what in Heaven's name will he be at forty?" To sixty the provincial imagination did not attempt to follow his wisdom. He was now past thirty, and behind the scenes of his bank was still the able financier I have sketched. But in society he seemed another man. There his characteristics were quiet courtesy, imperturbability, a suave but impressive manner, vast information on current events, and no flavor whatever of the shop.

He had learned the happy art, which might be called "the barrister's art," hoc agendi, of throwing the whole man into a thing at one time, and out of it at another. In the bank and in his own study he was a devout worshiper of Mammon; in society, a courteous, polished, intelligent gentleman, always ready to sift and discuss any worthy topic you could start except finance. There was some affectation in the cold and immovable determination with which he declined to say three words about money. But these great men act habitually on a preconceived system: this gives them their force.

If Lucy Fountain had been one of those empty girls that were so rife at the time, the sterling value of his conversation would have disgusted her, and his calm silence where there was nothing to be said (sure proof of intelligence) would have passed for stupidity with her. But she was intelligent, well used to bungling, straightforward flattery, and to smile with arch contempt at it, and very capable of appreciating the more subtle but less satirical compliment a man pays a pretty girl by talking sense to her; and, as it happened, her foible favored him no less than did her strong points. She attached too solid a value to manner; and Mr. Hardie's manner was, to her fancy, male perfection. It added to him in her estimation as much as David Dodd's defects in that kind detracted from the value of his mind and heart.

To this favorable opinion Mr. Hardie responded in full.

He had never seen so graceful a creature, nor so young a woman so courteous and high-bred.

He observed at once, what less keen persons failed to discover, that she was seldom spontaneous or off her guard. He admired her the more. He had no sympathy with the infantine in man or woman. "She thinks before she speaks," said he, with a note of admiration. On the other hand, he missed a trait or two the young lady possessed, for they happened to be virtues he had no eye for; but the sum total was most favorable; in short, it was esteem at first sight.

As a cobweb to a cabbage-net, so fine was Mrs. Bazalgette's reticulation compared with Uncle Fountain's. She invited Mr. Hardie to stay a fortnight with her, commencing just one day before Lucy's return. She arranged a round of gayety to celebrate the double event. What could be more simple? Yet there was policy below. The whirl of pleasure was to make Lucy forget everybody at Font Abbey; to empty her heart, and pave Mrs. B.'s candidate's way to the vacancy. Then, she never threw Mr. Hardie at Lucy's head, contenting herself with speaking of him with veneration when Lucy herself or others introduced his name. She was always contriving to throw the pair together, but no mortal could see her hand at work in it. Bref, a she-spider. The first day or two she watched her niece on the sly, just to see whether she regretted Font Abbey, or, in other words, Mr. Talboys. Well acquainted with all the subtle signs by which women read one another, she observed with some uneasiness that Lucy appeared somewhat listless and pensive at times, when left quite to herself. Once she found her with her cheek in her hand, and, by the way the young lady averted her head and slid suddenly into distinct cheerfulness, suspected there must have been tears in her eyes, but could not be positive. Next, she noticed with satisfaction that the round of gayety, including, as it did, morning rides as well as evening dances, dissipated these little reveries and languors. She inferred that either there was nothing in them but a sort of sediment of ennui, the natural remains of a visit to Font Abbey, or that, if there was anything more, it had yielded to the active pleasures she had provided, and to the lady's easy temper, and love of society, "the only thing she loves, or ever will," said Mrs. B., assuming prophecy.

"Aunt, how superior Mr. Hardie's conversation is. He interests one in topics that are unbearable generally; politics now. I thought I abhorred them, but I find it was only those little paltry Whig and Tory squabbles that wearied me. Mr. Hardie's views are neither Whig nor Tory; they are patriotic, and sober, and large-minded. He thinks of the country. I can take some interest in what he calls politics."

"And, pray, what is that?"

"Well, aunt, the liberation of commerce from its fetters for one thing. I can contrive to be interested in that, because I know England can be great only by commerce. Then the education of all classes, because without that England cannot be enlightened or good."

"He never says a word to me about such things," said Mrs. Bazalgette; "I suppose he thinks they are above poor me." She delivered this with so admirable an imitation of pique, that the courtier was deceived, and applied butter to "a fox's wound."

"Oh no, aunt. Consider; if that was it, he would not waste them on me, who am so inferior to you in sagacity. More likely he says, 'This young lady has not yet completed her education; I will sprinkle a little good sense among her frivolous accomplishments.' Whatever the motive, I am very much obliged to Mr. Hardie. A man of sense is so refreshing after—(full stop). What do you think of his voice?"

"His voice? I don't remember anything about it."

"Yes, you do—you must; it is a very remarkable one; so mellow, so quiet, yet so modulated."

"Well, I do remember now; it is rather a pleasant voice—for a man."

"Rather a pleasant voice!" repeated Lucy, opening her eyes; "why, it is a voice to charm serpents."

"Ha! ha! It has not charmed him one yet, you see."

This speech was not in itself pellucid; but these sweet ladies among themselves have so few topics compared with men, and consequently beat their little manor so often, that they seize a familiar idea, under any disguise, with the rapidity of lightning.

"Oh, charmers are charm-proof," replied Lucy; "that is the only reason why. I am sure of that." Then she reflected awhile. "It is his natural voice, is it not? Did you ever hear him speak in any other? Think."

"Never."

"Then he must be a good man. Apropos, is Mr. Hardie a good man, aunt?"

"Why, of course he is."

"How do you know?"

"I never heard of any scandal against him."

"Oh, I don't mean your negative goodness. You never heard anything against me out of doors."

"Well, and are you not a good girl?"

"Me, aunt? Why, you know I am not."

"Bless me, what have you done?"

"I have done nothing, aunt," exclaimed Lucy, "and the good are never nullities. Then I am not open, which is a great fault in a character. But I can't help it! I can't! I can't!"

"Well, you need not break your heart for that. You will get over it before you have been married a year. Look at me; I was as shy as any of you at first going off, but now I can speak my mind; and a good thing too, or what would become of me among the selfish set?"

"Meaning me, dear?"

"No. Divide it among you. Come, this is idle talk. Men's voices, and whether they are good, bad, or indifferent, as if that mattered a pin, provided their incomes are good and their manners endurable. I want a little serious conversation with you."

"Do you?" and Lucy colored faintly; "with all my heart."

"We go to the Hunts' ball the day after to-morrow, Lucy; I suppose you know that? Now what on earth am I to wear? that is the question. There is no time to get a new dress made, and I have not got one—"

"That you have not worn at least once."

"Some of them twice and three times;" and the B looked aghast at the state of nudity to which she was reduced. Lucy sidled toward the door.

"Since you consult me, dear, I advise you to wear what I mean to wear myself."

"Ah! what a capital idea! then we shall pass for sisters. I dare say I have got some old thing or other that will match yours; but you had better tell me at once what you do mean to wear."

"A gown, a pair of gloves, and a smirk"; and with this heartless expression of nonchalance Lucy glided away and escaped the impending shower.

"Oh, the selfishness of these girls!" cried the deserted one. "I have got her a husband to her taste, so now she runs away from me to think of him."

The next moment she looked at the enormity from another point of view, and then with this burst of injured virtue gave way to a steady complacency.

"She is caught at last. She notices his very voice. She fancies she cares for politics—ha! ha! She is gone to meditate on him—could not bear any other topic—would not even talk about dress, a thing her whole soul was wrapped up in till now. I have known her to go on for hours at a stretch about it."

There are people with memories so constructed that what they said, and another did not contradict or even answer, seems to them, upon retrospect, to have been delivered by that other person, and received in dead silence by themselves.

Meantime Lucy was in her own room and the door bolted.

So she was the next day; and uneasy Mrs. Bazalgette came hunting her, and tapped at the door after first trying the handle, which in Lucy's creed was not a discreet and polished act.

"Nobody admitted here till three o'clock."

"It is me, Lucy."

"So I conclude," said Lucy gayly. "'Me' must call again at three, whoever it is."

"Not I," said Aunt Bazalgette, and flounced off in a pet.

At three Dignity dissolved in curiosity, and Mrs. Bazalgette entered her niece's room in an ill-temper; it vanished like smoke at the sight of two new dresses, peach-colored and glacees, just finished, lying on the bed. An eager fire of questions. "Where did you get them? which is mine? who made them?"

"A new dressmaker."

"Ah! what a godsend to poor us! Who is she?"

"Let me see how you like her work before I tell you. Try this one on."

Mrs. Bazalgette tried on her dress, and was charmed with it. Lucy would not try on hers. She said she had done so, and it fitted well enough for her.

"Everything fits you, you witch," replied the B. "I must have this woman's address; she is an angel."

Lucy looked pleased. "She is only a beginner, but desirous to please you; and 'zeal goes farther than talent,' says Mr. Dodd."

"Mr. Dodd! Ah! by-the-by, that reminds me—I am so glad you mentioned his name. Where does the woman live?"

"The woman, or, as some consider her, the girl, lives at present with a charming person called by the world Mrs. Bazalgette, but by the dressmaker her sweet little aunt—" (kiss) (kiss) (kiss); and Lucy, whose natural affection for this lady was by a certain law of nature heated higher by working day and night for her in secret, felt a need of expansion, and curled, round her like a serpent with a dove's heart.

Mrs. Bazalgette did what you and I, manly reader, should have been apt to omit. She extricated herself, not roughly, yet a little hastily—like a water-snake gliding out of the other sweet serpent's folds.* Sacred dress being present, she deemed caresses frivolous—and ill-timed. "There, there, let me alone, child, and tell me all about it directly. 'What put it into your head? Who taught you? Is this your first attempt? Have you paid for the silk, or am I to? Do tell me quick; don't keep me on thorns!"

   * Here flashes on the cultivated mind the sprightly couplet,

    "Oh, that I had my mistress at this bay,

     To kiss and clip me—till I run away."

       SHAKESPEARE.—Venus and Adonis.

Lucy answered this fusillade in detail. "You know, aunt, dressmakers bring us their failures, and we, by our hints, get them made into successes."

"So we do."

"So I said to myself, 'Now why not bring a little intelligence to bear at the beginning, and make these things right at once?' Well, I bought several books, and studied them, and practiced cutting out, in large sheets of brown paper first; next I ventured a small flight—I made Jane a gown."

"What! your servant?"

"Yes. I had a double motive; first attempts are seldom brilliant, and it was better to fail in merino, and on Jane, than on you, madam, and in silk. In the next place, Jane had been giving herself airs, and objecting to do some work of that kind for me, so I thought it a good opportunity to teach her that dignity does not consist in being disobliging. The poor girl is so ashamed now: she comes to me in her merino frock, and pesters me all day to let her do things for me. I am at my wit's end sometimes to invent unreal distresses, like the writers of fiction, you know; and, aunty, dear, you will not have to pay for the stuff: to tell you the real truth, I overheard Mr. Bazalgette say something about the length of your last dressmaker's bill, and, as I have been very economical at

Font Abbey, I found I had eighteen pounds to spare, so I said nothing, but I thought we will have a dress apiece that nobody shall have to pay for."

"Eighteen pounds? These two lovely dresses, lace, trimmings, and all, for eighteen pounds!"

"Yes, aunt. So you see those good souls that make our dresses have imposed upon us without ceremony: they would have been twenty-five pounds apiece; now would they not?"

"At least. Well, you are a clever girl. I might as well try on yours, as you won't."

"Do, dear."

She tried on Lucy's gown, and, as before, got two looking-glasses into a line, twisted and twirled, and inspected herself north, south, east and west, and in an hour and a half resigned herself to take the dress off. Lucy observed with a sly smile that her gayety declined, and she became silent and pensive.

"In the dead of the night, when with labor oppressed, All mortals enjoy the sweet blessing of rest," a phantom stood at Lucy's bedside and fingered her. She awoke with a violent scream, the first note of which pierced the night's dull ear, but the second sounded like a wail from a well, being uttered a long way under the bedclothes. "Hush! don't be a fool," cried the affectionate phantom; and kneaded the uncertain form through the bedclothes; "fancy screeching so at sight of me!" Then gradually a single eye peeped timidly between two white hands that held the sheets ready for defense like a shield.

"B—b—but you are all in white," gulped Lucy, trembling all over; for her delicate fibers were set quivering, and could not be stilled by a word, fingered at midnight all in a moment by a shape.

"Why, what color should I be—in my nightgown?" snapped the specter. "What color is yours?" and she gave Lucy a little angry pull—"and everybody else's?"

"But at the dead of night, aunt, and without any warning—it's terrible. Oh dear!" (another little gulp in the throat, exceeding pretty).

"Lucy, be yourself," said the specter, severely; "you used not to be so selfish as to turn hysterical when your aunt came to you for advice."

Lucy had to do a little. "Forgive, blessed shade!" She apologized, crushed down her obtrusive, egotistical tremors, and vibrated to herself.

Placable Aunt Bazalgette accepted her excuses, and opened the business that brought her there.

"I didn't leave my bed at this hour for nothing, you may be sure."

"N—no, aunt."

"Lucy," continued Mrs. Bazalgette, deepening, "there is a weight on my mind."

Up sat Lucy in the bed, and two sapphire eyes opened wide and made terror lovely.

"Oh, aunt, what have you been doing? It is remorse, then, that will not let you sleep. Ah! I see! your flirtations—your flirtations—this is the end of them."

"My flirtations!" cried the other, in great surprise. "I never flirt. I only amuse myself with them."*

> *In strict grammar this "them" ought to refer to
>
> "flirtations;" but Lucy's aunt did not talk strict grammar.
>
> Does yours?

"You—never—flirt? Oh! oh! oh! Mr. Christopher, Mr. Horne, Sir George Healey, Mr. M'Donnell, Mr. Wolfenton, Mr. Vaughan—there! oh, and Mr. Dodd!"

"Well, at all events, it's not for any of those fools I get out of my bed at this time of night. I have a weight on my mind; so do be serious, if you can. Lucy, I tried all yesterday to hide it from myself, but I cannot succeed."

"What, dear aunt?"

"That your gown fits me ever so much better than my own." She sighed deeply.

Lucy smiled slyly; but she replied, "Is not that fancy?"

"No, Lucy, no," was the solemn reply; "I have tried to shut my eyes to it, but I can't."

"So it seems. Ha! ha!"

"Now do be serious; it is no laughing matter. How unfortunate I am!"

"Not at all. Take my gown; I can easily alter yours to fit me, if necessary."

"Oh, you good girl, how clever you are! I should never have thought of that." N. B—She had been thinking of nothing else these six hours.

"Go to bed, dear, and sleep in peace," said Lucy, soothingly. "Leave all to me."

"No, I can't leave all to you. Now I am to have yours, I must try it on." It was hers now, so her confidence in its fitting was shaken.

Mrs. Bazalgette then lighted all the candles in the sconces, and opened Lucy's drawers, and took out linen, and put on the dress with Lucy's aid, and showed Lucy how it fitted, and was charmed, like a child with a new toy.

Presently Lucy interrupted her raptures by an exclamation. Mrs. Bazalgette looked round, and there was her niece inspecting the ghostly robe which had caused her such a fright.

"Here are oceans of yards of lace on her very nightgrown!" cried Lucy.

"Well, does not every lady wear lace on her nightgown?" was the tranquil reply. "What is that on yours, pray?"

"A little misery of Valenciennes an inch broad; but this is Mechlin—superb! delicious! Well, aunt, you are a sincere votary of the graces; you put on fine things because they are fine things, not with the hollow motive of dazzling society; you wear Mechlin, not for eclat, but for Mechlin. Alas! how few, like you, pursue quite the same course in the dark that they do in the world's eye."

"Don't moralize, dear; unhook me!"

After breakfast Mrs. Bazalgette asked Lucy how long she could give her to choose which of the two gowns to take, after all.

"Till eight o'clock."

Mrs. Bazalgette breathed again. She had thought herself committed to No. 2, and No. 1 was beginning to look lovely in consequence. At eight, the choice being offered her with impenetrable nonchalance by Lucy, she took Lucy's without a moment's hesitation, and sailed off gayly to her own room to put it on, in which progress the ample peach-colored silk held out in both hands showed like Cleopatra's foresail, and seemed to draw the dame along.

Lucy, too, was happy—demurely; for in all this business the female novice, "la ruse sans le savoir," had outwitted the veteran. Lucy had measured her whole aunt. So she made dress A for her, but told her she was to have dress B. This at once gave her desires a perverse bent toward her own property, the last direction they could have been warped into by any other means; and so she was deluded to her good, and fitted to a hair, soul and body.

Going to the ball, one cloud darkened for an instant the matron's mind.

"I am so afraid they will see it only cost nine pounds."

"Enfant!" replied Lucy, "aetat. 20." At the ball Mr. Hardie and Lucy danced together, and were the most admired couple.

The next day Mr. Hardie announced that he was obliged to curtail his visit and go up to London. Mrs. Bazalgette remonstrated. Mr. Hardie apologized, and asked permission to make out the rest of his visit on his return. Mrs. B. accorded joyfully, but Lucy objected: "Aunt, don't you be deluded into any such arrangement; Mr. Hardie is liable to another fortnight. We have nothing to do with his mismanagement. He comes to spend a fortnight with us: he tries, but fails. I am sorry for Mr. Hardie, but the engagement remains in full force. I appeal to you, Mr. Bazalgette, you are so exact."

"I don't see myself how he can get out of it with credit," said Bazalgette, solemnly.

"I am happy to find that my duty is on the side of my inclination," said Mr. Hardie. He smiled, well pleased, and looked handsomer than ever.

They all missed him more or less, but nobody more than Lucy. His conversation had a peculiar charm for her. His knowledge of current events was unparalleled; then there was a quiet potency in him she thought very becoming in a man; and then his manner. He was the first of our unfortunate sex who had reached beau ideal. One was harsh, another finicking; a third loud; a fourth enthusiastic; a fifth timid; and all failed in tact except Mr. Hardie. Then, other male voices were imperfect; they were too insignificant or too startling, too bass or too treble, too something or too other. Mr. Hardie's was a mellow tenor, always modulated to the exact tone of good society. Like herself, too, he never laughed loud, seldom out; and even his smiles, like her own, did not come in unmeaning profusion, so they told when they did come.

The Bazalgettes led a very quiet life for the next fortnight, for Mrs. Bazalgette was husbanding invitations for Mr. Hardie's return.

Mrs. Bazalgette yawned many times during this barren period, but with considerate benevolence she shielded Lucy from ennui. Lucy was a dressmaker, gifted, but inexperienced; well, then, she would supply the latter deficiency by giving her an infinite variety of alterations to make in a multitude of garments. There are egotists who charge for tuition, but she would teach her dear niece gratis. A mountain of dresses rose in the drawing-room, a dozen metamorphoses were put in hand, and a score more projected.

"She pulled down, she built up, she rounded the angular, and squared the round." And here Mr. Bazalgette took perverse views and misbehaved. He was a very honest man, but not a refined courtier. He seldom interfered with these ladies, one way or other, except to provide funds, which interference was never snubbed; for was he not master of the house in that sense? But, having observed what was going on day after day in the drawing-room or workshop, he walked in and behaved himself like a brute.

"How much a week does she give you, Lucy?" said he, looking a little red.

Lucy opened her eyes in utter astonishment, and said nothing; her very needle and breath were suspended.

Mrs. Bazalgette shrugged her shoulders to Lucy, but disdained words. Mr. Bazalgette turned to his wife.

"I have often recommended economy to you, Jane, I need not say with what success; but this sort of economy is not for your credit or mine. If you want to add a dressmaker to your staff—with all my heart. Send for one when you like, and keep her to all eternity. But this young lady is our ward, and I will not have her made a servant of for your convenience."

"Put your work down, dear," said Mrs. Bazalgette resignedly. "He does not understand our affection, nor anything else except pounds, shillings and pence."

"Oh, yes I do. I can see through varnished selfishness for one thing."

"You certainly ought to be a judge of the unvarnished article," retorted the lady.

"Having had it constantly under my eyes these twenty years," rejoined the gentleman.

"Oh, aunt! Oh, Mr. Bazalgette!" cried Lucy, rising and clasping her hands; if you really love me, never let me be the cause of a misunderstanding, or an angry word between those I esteem; it would make me too miserable; and, dear Mr. Bazalgette, you must let people be happy in their own way, or you will be sure to make them unhappy. My aunt and I understand one another better than you do."

"She understands you, my poor girl."

"Not so well as I do her. But she knows I hate to be idle, and love to do these bagatelles for her. It is my doing from the first, not hers; she did not even know I could do it till I produced two dresses for the Hunts' ball. So, you see —"

"That is another matter; all ladies play at work. But you are in for three months' hard labor. Look at that heap of vanity. She is making a lady's-maid of you. It is unjust. It is selfish. It is improper. It is not for my credit, of which I am more jealous than coquettes are of theirs; besides, Lucy, you must not think, because I don't make a parade as she does, that I am not fond of you. I have a great deal more real affection for you than she has, and so you will find if we are ever put to the test."

At this last absurdity Mrs. Bazalgette burst out laughing. But "la rusee sans le savoir" turned toward the speaker, and saw that he spoke with a certain emotion which was not ordinary in him. She instantly went to him with both hands gracefully extended. "I do think you have an affection for me. If you really have, show it me some other way, and not by making me unhappy."

"Well, then, I will, Lucy. Look here; if Solomon was such a fool as to argue with one of you young geese you would shut his mouth in a minute. There, I am going; but you will always be the slave of one selfish person or other; you were born for it."

Thus impotently growling, the merchant prince retired from the field, escorted with amenity by the courtier. In the passage she suddenly dropped forward like a cypress-tree, and gave him her forehead to kiss. He kissed it with some little warmth, and confided to her, in friendly accents, that she was a fool, and off he went, grumbling inarticulately, to his foreign loans and things.

The courtier returned to smooth her aunt in turn, but that lady stopped her with a lofty gesture.

"My plan is to look on these monstrosities as horrid dreams, and go on as if nothing had happened."

Happy philosophy.

Lucy acquiesced with a smile, and in an instant both immortal souls plunged and disappeared in silk, satin, feathers and point lace.

The afternoon post brought letters that furnished some excitement. Mr. Hardie announced his return, and Captain Kenealy accepted an invitation that had been sent to him two days before. But this was not all. Mrs. Bazalgette, with something between a laugh and a crow, handed Lucy a letter from Mr. Fountain, in which that diplomatic gentleman availed himself of her kind invitation, and with elephantine playfulness proposed, as he could not stay a month with her, to be permitted to bring a friend with him for a fortnight. This friend had unfortunately missed her through absence from his country-house at the period of her visit to Font Abbey, and had so constantly regretted his ill fortune that he (Fountain) had been induced to make this attempt to repair the calamity. His friend's name was Talboys; he was a gentleman of lineage, and in his numerous travels had made a collection of foreign costumes which were really worth inspecting, and, if agreeable to Mrs. Bazalgette, he should send them on before by wagon, for no carriage would hold them.

Lucy colored on reading this letter, for it repeated a falsehood that had already made her blush. The next moment, remembering how very keenly her aunt must be eying her, and reading her, she looked straight before her, and said coldly, "Uncle Fountain ought to be welcome here for his courtesy to you at Font Abbey, but I think he takes rather a liberty in proposing a stranger to you."

"Rather a liberty? Say a very great liberty."

"Well, then, aunt, why not write back that any friend of his would be welcome, but that the house is full? You have only room for Uncle Fountain."

"But that is not true, Lucy," said Mrs. Bazalgette, with sudden dignity.

Lucy was staggered and abashed at this novel objection; recovering, she whined humbly, "but it is very nearly true."

It was plain Lucy did not want Mr. Talboys to visit them. This decided Mrs. Bazalgette to let his dresses and him come. He would only be a foil to Mr. Hardie, and perhaps bring him on faster. Her decision once made on the above grounds, she conveyed it in characteristic colors. "No, my love; where I give my affection, there I give my confidence. I have your word not to encourage this gentleman's addresses, so why hurt your uncle's feelings by closing my door to his friend? It would be an ill compliment to you as well as to Mr. Fountain; he shall come."

Her postscript to Mr. Fountain ran thus:

"Your friend would have been welcome independently of the foreign costumes; but as I am a very candid little woman, I may as well tell you that, now you have excited my curiosity, he will be a great deal more welcome with them than without them."

And here I own that I, the simpleminded, should never have known all that was signified in these words but for the comment of John Fountain, Esq.

"It is all right, Talboys," said he. "My bait has taken. You must pack up these gimcracks at once and send them off, or she'll smile like a marble Satan in your face, and stick you full of pins and needles."

The next day Mr. Bazalgette walked into the room, haughtily overlooked the pyramid of dresses, and asked Lucy to come downstairs and see something. She put her work aside, and went down with him, and lo! two ponies—a cream-colored and a bay. "Oh, you loves!" cried the virgin, passionately, and blushed with pleasure. Her heart was very accessible—to quadrupeds.

"Now you are to choose which of these you will have."

"Oh, Mr. Bazalgette!"

"Have you forgotten what you told me? 'Try and make me happy some other way,' says you. Now I remembered hearing you say what a nice pony you had at Font Abbey; so I sent a capable person to collect ponies for you. These have both a reputation. Which will you have?"

"Dear, good, kind Uncle Bazalgette; they are ducks!"

"Let us hope not; a duck's paces won't suit you, if you are as fond of galloping as other young ladies. Come, jump up, and see which is the best brute of the two."

"What, without my habit?"

"Well, get your habit on, then. Let us see how quick you can be."

Off ran Lucy, and soon returned fully equipped. She mounted the ponies in turn, and rode them each a mile or two in short distances. Finally she dismounted, and stood beaming on the steps of the hall. The groom held the ponies for final judgment.

"The bay is rather the best goer, dear," said she, timidly.

"Miss Fountain chooses the bay, Tom."

"No, uncle, I was going to ask you if I might have the cream-colored one. He is so pretty."

"Ha! ha! ha! here's a little goose. Why, they are to ride, not to wear. Come, I see you are in a difficulty. Take them both to the stable, Tom."

"No, no, no," cried Lucy. "Oh, Mr. Bazalgette, don't tempt me to be so wicked." Then she put both her fingers in her ears and screamed, "Take the bay darling out of my sight, and leave the cream-colored love." And as she persisted in this order, with her fingers in her ears, and an inclination to stamp with her little feet, the bay disappeared and color won the day.

Then she dropped suddenly like a cypress toward Mr. Bazalgette, which meant "you can kiss me." This time it was her cheek she proffered, all glowing with exercise and innocent excitement.

Captain Kenealy was the first arrival: a well-appointed soldier; eyes equally bright under calm and excitement, mustache always clean and glossy; power of assent prodigious. He looked so warlike, and was so inoffensive, that he was in great request for miles and miles round the garrison town of ——. The girls, at first introduction to him, admired him, and waited palpitating to be torn from their mammas, and carried half by persuasion, half by force, to their conqueror's tent; but after a bit they always found him out, and talked before, and at, and across this ornament as if it had been a bronze Mars, or a mustache-tipped shadow. This the men viewing from a little distance envied the gallant captain, and they might just as well have been jealous of a hair-dresser's dummy.

One eventful afternoon, Mrs. Bazalgette and Miss Fountain walked out, taking the gallant captain between them as escort. Reginald hovered on the rear. Kenealy was charmingly equipped, and lent the party a luster. If he did not contribute much to the conversation, he did not interrupt it, for the ladies talked through him as if he had been a column of red air. Sing, muse, how often Kenealy said "yaas" that afternoon; on second thoughts, don't. I can weary my readers without celestial aid: Toot! toot! toot! went a cheerful horn, and the mail-coach came into sight round a corner, and rolled rapidly toward them. Lucy looked anxiously round, and warned Master Reginald of the danger now impending over infants. The terrible child went instantly (on the "vitantes stulti vitia" principle) clean off the road altogether into the ditch, and clayed (not pipe) his trousers to the knee. As the coach passed, a gentleman on the box took off his hat to the ladies and made other signs. It was Mr. Hardie.

Mrs. Bazalgette proposed to return home to receive him. They were about a mile from the house. They had not gone far before the rear-guard intermitted blackberrying for an instant, and uttered an eldrich screech; then proclaimed, "Another coach! another coach!" It was a light break coming gently along, with two showy horses in it, and a pony trotting behind.

At one and the same moment Lucy recognized a four-footed darling, and the servant recognized her. He drew up, touched his hat, and inquired respectfully whether he was going right for Mr. Bazalgette's. Mrs. Bazalgette gave him directions while Lucy was patting the pony, and showering on him those ardent terms of endearment some ladies bestow on their lovers, but this one consecrated to her trustees and quadrupeds. In the break were saddles, and a side-saddle, and other caparisons, and a giant box; the ladies looked first at it, and then through Kenealy at one another, and so settled what was inside that box.

They had not walked a furlong before a traveling-carriage and four horses came dashing along, and heads were put out of the window, and the postboys ordered to stop. Mr. Talboys and Mr. Fountain got out, and the carriage was sent on. Introductions took place. Mrs. Bazalgette felt her spirits rise like a veteran's when line of battle is being formed. She was one of those ladies who are agreeable or disagreeable at will. She decided to charm, and she threw her enchantment over Messrs. Fountain and Talboys. Coming with hostile views, and therefore guilty consciences, they had expected a cold welcome. They received a warm, gay, and airy one. After a while she maneuvered so as to get between Mr. Fountain and Captain Kenealy, and leave Lucy to Mr. Talboys. She gave her such a sly look as she did it. It implied, "You will have to tell me all he says to you while we are dressing."

Mr. Talboys inquired who was Captain Kenealy. He learned by her answer that that officer had arrived to-day, and she had no previous acquaintance with him.

Whatever little embarrassment Lucy might feel, remembering her equestrian performance with Mr. Talboys and its cause, she showed none. She began about the pony, and how kind of him it was to bring it. "And yet," said she, "if I had known, I would not have allowed you to take the trouble, for I have a pony here."

Mr. Talboys was sorry for that, but he hoped she would ride his now and then, all the same.

"Oh, of course. My pony here is very pretty. But a new friend is not like an old friend."

Mr. Talboys was gratified on more accounts than one by this speech. It gave him a sense of security. She had no friend about her now she had known as long as she had him, and those three months of constant intimacy placed him above competition. His mind was at ease, and he felt he could pop with a certainty of success, and pop he would, too, without any unnecessary delay.

The party arrived in great content and delectation at the gates that led to the house. "Stay!" said Mrs. Bazalgette; "you must come across the way, all of you. Here is a view that all our guests are expected to admire. Those, that cry out 'Charming! beautiful! Oh, I never!' we take them in and make them comfortable. Those that won't or can't ejaculate—"

"You put them in damp beds," said Mr. Fountain, only half in jest.

"Worse than that, sir—we flirt with them, and disturb the placid current of their hearts forever and ever. Don't we, Lucy?"

"You know best, aunt," said Lucy, half malice, half pout. The others followed the gay lady, and, when the view burst, ejaculated to order.

But Mr. Fountain stood ostentatiously in the middle of the road, with his legs apart, like him of Rhodes. "I choose the alternative," cried he. "Sooner than pretend I admire sixteen plowed fields and a hill as much as I do a lawn and flower-beds, I elect to be flirted, and my what do ye call 'em?—my stagnant current—turned into a whirlpool." Ere the laugh had well subsided, caused by this imitation of Hercules and his choice, he struck up again, "Good news for you, young gentleman; I smell a ball; here is a fiddle-case making for this hospitable mansion."

"No," said Mrs. Bazalgette, "I never ordered any musician to come here."

A tall but active figure came walking light as a feather, with a large carpet-bag on his back, a boy behind carrying a violin-case.

Lucy colored and lowered her eyes, but never said a word.

The young man came up to the gate, and then Mr. Talboys recognized him.

He hesitated a single moment, then turned and came to the group and took off his hat to the ladies. It was David Dodd!

CHAPTER XIV.

THE new guest's manner of presenting himself with his stick over his shoulder, and his carpet-bag on his back, subjected him to a battery of stares from Kenealy, Talboys, Fountain, and abashed him sore.

This lasted but a moment. He had one friend in the group who was too true to her flirtations while they endured, and too strong-willed, to let her flirtee be discouraged by mortal.

"Why, it is Mr. Dodd," cried she, with enthusiasm, and she put forth both hands to him, the palms downward, with a smiling grace. "Surely you know Mr. Dodd," said she, turning round quickly to the gentlemen, with a smile on her lip, but a dangerous devil in her eye.

The mistress of the house is all-powerful on these occasions. Messrs. Talboys and Fountain were forced to do the amiable, raging within; Lucy anticipated them; but her welcome was a cold one. Says Mrs. Bazalgette, tenderly, "And why do you carry that heavy bag, when you have that great stout lad with you? I think it is his business to carry it, not yours"; and her eyes scathed the boy, fiddle and all.

All the time she was saying this David was winking to her, and making faces to her not to go on that tack. His conduct now explained his pantomime. "Here, youngster," said he, "you take these things in-doors, and here is your half-crown."

Lucy averted her head, and smiled unobserved.

As soon as the lad was out of hearing, David continued: "It was not worth while to mortify him. The fact is, I hired him to carry it; but, bless you, the first mile he began to go down by the head, and would have foundered; so we shifted our cargoes." This amused Kenealy, who laughed good-humoredly. On this, David laughed for company.

"There," cried his inamorata, with rapture, "that is Mr. Dodd all over; thinks of everybody, high or low, before himself." There was a grunt somewhere behind her; her quick ear caught it; she turned round like a thing on a pivot, and slapped the nearest face. It happened to be Fountain's; so she continued with such a treacle smile, "Don't you remember, sir, how he used to teach your cub mathematics gratis?" The sweet smile and the keen contemporaneous scratch confounded Mr. Fountain for a second. As soon as he revived he said stiffly, "We can all appreciate Mr. Dodd."

Having thus established her Adonis on a satisfactory footing, she broke out all over graciousness again, and, smiling and chatting, led her guests beneath the hospitable roof.

But one of these guests did not respond to her cheerful strain. The Norman knight was full of bitterness. Mr. Talboys drew his friend aside and proposed to him to go back again. The senior was aghast. "Don't be so precipitate," was all that he could urge this time. "Confound the fellow! Yes, if that is the man she prefers to you, I will go home with you to-morrow, and the vile hussy shall never enter my doors again."

In this mind the pair went devious to their dressing-rooms.

One day a witty woman said of a man that "he played the politician about turnips and cabbages." That might be retorted (by a snob and brute) on her own sex in general, and upon Mrs. Bazalgette in particular. This sweet lady maneuvered on a carpet like Marlborough on the south of France. She was brimful of resources, and they all tended toward one sacred object, getting her own way. She could be imperious at a pinch and knock down opposition; but she liked far better to undermine it, dissolve it, or evade it. She was too much of a woman to run straight to her je-le-veux, so long as she could wind thitherward serpentinely and by detour. She could have said to Mr. Hardie, "You will take down Lucy to dinner," and to Mr. Dodd, "You will sit next me"; but no, she must mold her males—as per sample.

To Mr. Fountain she said, "Your friend, I hear, is of old family."

"Came in with the Conqueror, madam."

"Then he shall take me down: that will be the first step toward conquering me —ha! ha!" Fountain bowed, well pleased.

To Mr. Hardie she said, "Will you take down Lucy to-day? I see she enjoys your conversation. Observe how disinterested I am."

Hardie consented with twinkling composure.

Before dinner she caught Kenealy, drew him aside, and put on a long face. "I am afraid I must lose you to-day at dinner. Mr. Dodd is quite a stranger, and they all tell me I must put him at his ease.

"Yaas."

"Well, then, you had better get next Lucy, as you can't have me."

"Yaas."

"And, Captain Kenealy, you are my aid-de-camp. It is a delightful post, you know, and rather a troublesome one."

"Yaas."

"You must help me be kind to this sailor."

"Yaas. He is a good fellaa. Carried the baeg for the little caed."

"Oh, did he?"

"And didn't maind been laughed at."

"Now, that shows how intelligent you must be," said the wily one; "the others could not comprehend the trait. Well, you and I must patronize him. Merit is always so dreadfully modest."

"Yaas."

This arrangement was admirable, but human; consequently, not without a flaw. Uncle Fountain was left to chance, like the flying atoms of Epicurus, and chance put him at Bazalgette's right hand save one. From this point his inquisitive eye commanded David Dodd and Mrs. Bazalgette, and raked Lucy and her neighbors, who were on the opposite side of the table. People who look, bent on seeing everything, generally see something; item, it is not always what they would like to see.

As they retired to rest for the night, Mr. Fountain invited his friend to his room.

"We shall not have to go home. I have got the key to our antagonist. Young Dodd is her lover." Talboys shook his head with cool contempt. "What I mean is that she has invited him for her own amusement, not her niece's. I never saw a woman throw herself at any man's head as she did at that sailor's all dinner. Her very husband saw it. He is a cool hand, that Bazalgette; he only grinned, and took wine with the sailor. He has seen a good many go the same road— soldiers, sailors, tinkers, tai—"

Talboys interrupted him. "I really must call you to order. You are prejudiced against poor Mrs. Bazalgette, and prejudice blinds everybody. Politeness required that she should show some attention to her neighbor, but her principal attention was certainly not bestowed on Mr. Dodd."

Fountain was surprised. "On whom, then?"

"Well, to tell the truth, on your humble servant."

Fountain stared. "I observed she did not neglect you; but when she turned to Dodd her face puckered itself into smiles like a bag."

"I did not see it, and I was nearer her than you," said Talboys coldly.

"But I was in front of her."

"Yes, a mile off." There being no jurisconsult present to explain to these two magistrates that if fifty people don't see a woman pucker her face like a bag, and one does see her p. h. f. l. a. b., the affirmative evidence preponderates, they were very near coming to a quarrel on this grave point. It was Fountain who made peace. He suddenly remembered that his friend had never been known to change an opinion. "Well," said he, "let us leave that; we shall have other opportunities of watching Dodd and her; meantime I am sorry I cannot convince you of my good news, for I have some bad to balance it. You have a rival, and he did not sit next Mrs. Bazalgette."

"Pray may I ask whom he did sit next?" sneered Talboys.

"He sat—like a man who meant to win—by the girl herself."

"Oh, then it is that sing-song captain you fear, sir?" drawled Talboys.

"No, sir, no more than I dread the epergne. Try the other side."

"What, Mr. Hardie? Why, he is a banker."

"And a rich one."

"She would never marry a banker."

"Perhaps not, if she were uninfluenced; but we are not at Talboys Court or Font Abbey now. We have fallen into a den of parvenues. That Hardie is a great catch, according to their views, and all Mrs. Bazalgette's influence with Lucy will be used in his favor.

"I think not. She spoke quite slightingly of him to me."

"Did she? Then that puts the matter quite beyond doubt. Why should she speak slightingly of him? Bazalgette spoke to me of him with grave veneration. He is handsome, well behaved, and the girl talked to him nineteen to the dozen. Mrs. Bazalgette could not be sincere in underrating him. She undervalued him to throw dust in your eyes."

"It is not so easy to throw dust in my eyes."

"I don't say it is; but this woman will do it; she is as artful as a fox. She hoodwinked even me for a moment. I really did not see through her feigned politeness in letting you take her down to dinner."

"You mistake her character entirely. She is coquettish, and not so well-bred as her niece, but artful she is not. In fact, there is almost a childish frankness about her."

At this stroke of observation Fountain burst out laughing bitterly.

Talboys turned pale with suppressed ire, and went on doggedly: "You are mistaken in every particular. Mrs. Bazalgette has no fixed views for her niece, and I by no means despair of winning her to my side. She is anything but discouraging."

Fountain groaned.

"Mr. Hardie is a new acquaintance, and Miss Fountain told me herself she preferred old friends to new. She looked quite conscious as she said it. In a word, Mr. Dodd is the only rival I have to fear—good-night;" and he went out with a stately wave of the hand, like royalty declining farther conference. Mr. Fountain sank into an armchair, and muttered feebly, "Good-night." There he sat collapsed till his friend's retiring steps were heard no more; then, springing wildly to his feet, he relieved his swelling mind with a long, loud, articulated roar of Anglo-Saxon, "Fool! dolt! coxcomb! noodle! puppy! ass!!!!"

Did ye ever read "Tully 'de Amicitia'?"

David Dodd was saved from misery by want of vanity. His reception at the gate by Miss Fountain was cool and constrained, but it did not wound him. For the last month life had been a blank to him. She was his sun. He saw her once more, and the bare sight filled him with life and joy. His was naturally a sanguine, contented mind. Some lovers equally ardent would have seen more to repine at than to enjoy in the whole situation; not so David. She sat between Kenealy and Hardie, but her presence filled the whole room, and he who loved her better than any other had the best right to be happy in the place that held her. He had only to turn his eyes, and he could see her. What a blessing, after a month of vacancy and darkness. This simple idolatry made him so happy that his heart overflowed on all within reach. He gave Mrs. Bazalgette answers full of kindness and arch gayety combined. He charmed an old married lady on his right. His was the gay, the merry end of the table, and others wished themselves up at it.

After the ladies had retired, his narrative powers, bonhomie and manly frankness soon told upon the men, and peals of genuine laughter echoed up to the very drawing-room, bringing a deputation from the kitchen to the keyhole, and irritating the ladies overhead, who sat trickling faint monosyllables about their three little topics.

Lucy took it philosophically. "Now those are the good creatures that are said to be so unhappy without us. It was a weight off their minds when the door closed on our retiring forms—ha! ha!"

"It was a restraint taken off them, my dear," said Mrs. Mordan, a starched dowager, stiffening to the naked eye as she spoke. "When they laugh like that, they are always saying something improper."

"Oh, the wicked things," replied Lucy, mighty calmly.

"I wish I knew what they are saying," said eagerly another young lady; then added, "Oh!" and blushed, observing her error mirrored in all eyes.

Lucy the Clement instructed her out of the depths of her own experience in impropriety. "They swear. That is what Mrs. Mordan means," and so to the piano with dignity.

Presently in came Messrs. Fountain and Talboys. Mrs. Bazalgette asked the former a little crossly how he could make up his mind to leave the gay party downstairs.

"Oh, it was only that fellow Dodd. The dog is certainly very amusing, but 'there's metal more attractive here.'"

Coffee and tea were fired down at the other gentlemen by way of hints; but Dodd prevailed over all, and it was nearly bedtime when they joined the ladies.

Mr. Talboys had an hour with Lucy, and no rival by to ruffle him.

Next day a riding-party was organized. Mr. Talboys decided in his mind that Kenealy was even less dangerous than Hardie, so lent him the quieter of his two nags, and rode a hot, rampageous brute, whose very name was Lucifer, so that will give you an idea. The grooms had driven him with a kicking-strap and two pair of reins, and even so were reluctant to drive him at all, but his steady companion had balanced him a bit. Lucy was to ride her old pony, and Mrs. Bazalgette the new. The horses came to the door; one of the grooms offered to put Lucy up. Talboys waved him loftily back, and then, strange as it may appear, David, for the first time in his life, saw a gentleman lift a lady into the saddle.

Lucy laid her right hand on the pommel and resigned her left foot; Mr. Talboys put his hand under that foot and heaved her smoothly into the saddle. "That is clever," thought simple David; "that chap has got more pith in his arm than one would think." They cantered away, and left him looking sadly after them. It seemed so hard that another man should have her sweet foot in his hand, should lift her whole glorious person, and smooth her sacred dress, and he stand by helpless; and then the indifference with which that man had done it all. To him it had been no sacred pleasure, no great privilege. A sense of loneliness struck chill on David as the clatter of her pony's hoofs died away. He was in the house; but in that house was a sort of inner circle, of which she was the center, and he was to be outside it altogether.

Liable to great wrath upon great occasions, he had little of that small irritability that goes with an egotistical mind and feminine fiber, so he merely hung his head, blamed nobody, and was sad in a manly way. While he leaned against the portico in this dejected mood, a little hand pulled his coat-tail. It was Master Reginald, who looked up in his face, and said timidly, "Will you play with me?" The fact is, Mr. Reginald's natural audacity had received a momentary check. He had just put this same question to Mr. Hardie in the library, and had been rejected with ignominy, and recommended to go out of doors for his own health and the comfort of such as desired peaceable study of British and foreign intelligence.

"That I will, my little gentleman," said David, "if I know the game."

"Oh, I don't care what it is, so that it is fun. What is your name?"

"David Dodd."

"Oh."

"And what is yours?"

"What, don't—you—know??? Why, Reginald George Bazalgette. I am seven. I am the eldest. I am to have more money than the others when papa dies, Jane says. I wonder when he will die."

"When he does you will lose his love, and that is worth more than his money; so you take my advice and love him dearly while you have got him."

"Oh, I like papa very well. He is good-natured all day long. Mamma is so ill-tempered till dinner, and then they won't let me dine with her; and then, as soon as mamma has begun to be good-tempered upstairs in the drawing-room, my bedtime comes directly; it's abominable!!" The last word rose into a squeak under his sense of wrong.

David smiled kindly: "So it seems we all have our troubles," said he.

"What! have you any troubles?" and Reginald opened his eyes in wonder. He thought size was an armor against care.

"Not so many as most folk, thank God, but I have some," and David sighed.

"Why, if I was as big as you, I'd have no troubles. I'd beat everybody that troubled me, and I would marry Lucy directly"; and at that beloved name my lord falls into a reverie ten seconds long.

David gave a start, and an ejaculation rose to his lips. He looked down with comical horror upon the little chubby imp who had divined his thought.

Mr. Reginald soon undeceived him. "She is to be my wife, you know. Don't you think she will make a capital one?" Before David could decide this point for him, the kaleidoscopic mind of the terrible infant had taken another turn. "Come into the stable-yard; I'll show you Tom," cried young master, enthusiastically. Finally, David had to make the boy a kite. When made it took two hours for the paste to dry; and as every ten minutes spent in waiting seemed an hour to one of Mr. Reginald's kidney, as the English classics phrase it, he was almost in a state of frenzy at last, and flew his new kite with yells. But after a bit he missed a familiar incident; "It doesn't tumble down; my other kites all tumble down."

"More shame for them," said David, with a dash of contempt, and explained to him that tumbling down is a flaw in a kite, just as foundering at sea is a vile habit in a ship, and that each of these descents, however picturesque to childhood's eye, implies a construction originally derective, or some little subsequent mismanagement. It appeared by Reginald's retort that when his kite tumbled he had the tumultuous joy of flying it again, but, by its keeping the air like this, monotony reigned; so he now proposed that his new friend should fasten the string to the pump-handle, and play at ball with him beneath the kite. The good-natured sailor consented, and thus the little voluptuary secured a terrestrial and ever-varying excitement, while occasional glances upward soothed him with the mild consciousness that there was his property still hovering in the empyrean; amid all which, poor love-sick David was seized with a desire to hear the name of her he loved, and her praise, even from these small lips. "So you are very fond of Miss Lucy?" said he.

"Yes," replied Reginald, dryly, and said no more; for it is a characteristic of the awfu' bairn to be mute where fluency is required, voluble where silence.

"I wonder why you love her so much," said David, cunningly. Reginald's face, instead of brightening with the spirit of explanation, became instantly lack-luster and dough-like; for, be it known, to the everlasting discredit of human nature, that his affection and matrimonial intentions, as they were no secret, so they were the butt of satire from grown-up persons of both sexes in the house, and of various social grades; down to the very gardener, all had had a fling at him. But soon his natural cordiality gained the better of that momentary reserve. "Well, I'll tell you," said he, "because you have behaved well all day."

David was all expectation.

"I like her because she has got red cheeks, and does whatever one asks her."

Oh, breadth of statement! Why was not David one of your repeaters? He would have gone and told Lucy. I should have liked her to know in what grand primitive colors peach-bloom and queenly courtesy strike what Mr. Tennyson is pleased to call "the deep mind of dauntless infancy." But David Dodd was not a reporter, and so I don't get my way; and how few of us do! not even Mr. Reginald, whose joyous companionship with David was now blighted by a footman. At sight of the coming plush, "There, now!" cried Reginald. He anticipated evil, for messages from the ruling powers were nearly always adverse to his joys. The footman came to say that his master would feel obliged if Mr. Dodd would step into his study a minute.

David went immediately.

"There, now!" squeaked Reginald, rising an octave. "I'm never happy for two hours together." This was true. He omitted to add, "Nor unhappy for one." The dear child sought comfort in retaliation. He took stones and pelted the footman's retiring calves. His admirers, if any, will be glad to learn that this act of intelligent retribution soothed his deep mind a little.

Mr. Bazalgette had been much interested by David's conversation the last night, and, hearing he was not with the riding-party, had a mind to chat with him. David found him in a magnificent study, lined with books, and hung with beautiful maps that lurked in mahogany cylinders attached to the wall; and you pulled them out by inserting a brass-hooked stick into their rings, and hauling. Mr. Bazalgette began by putting him a question about a distant port to which he had just sent out some goods. David gave him full information. Began, seaman-like, with the entrance to the harbor, and told him what danger his captain should look out for in running in, and how to avoid it; and from that went to the character of the natives, their tricks upon the sailors, their habits, tastes, and fancies, and, entering with intelligence into his companion's business, gave him some very shrewd hints as to the sort of cargo that would tempt them to sell the very rings out of their ears. Succeeding so well in this, Mr. Bazalgette plied him on other points, and found him full of valuable matter, and, by a rare union of qualities, very modest and very frank. "Now I like this," said Mr. Bazalgette, cheerfully. "This is a return to old customs. A century or two ago, you know, the merchant and the captain felt themselves parts of the same stick, and they used to sit and smoke together before a voyage, and sup together after one, and be always putting their heads together; but of late the stick has got so much longer, and so many knots between the handle and the point, that we have quite lost sight of one another. Here we merchants sit at home at ease, and send you fine fellows out among storms and waves, and think more of a bale of cotton spoiled than of a captain drowned."

David. "And we eat your bread, sir, as if it dropped from the clouds, and quite forget whose money and spirit of enterprise causes the ship to be laid on the stocks, and then built, and then rigged, and then launched, and then manned, and then sailed from port to port."

"Well, well, if you eat our bread, we eat your labor, your skill, your courage, and sometimes your lives, I am sorry to say. Merchants and captains ought really to be better acquainted."

"Well, sir," said David, "now you mention it, you are the first merchant of any consequence I ever had the advantage of talking with."

"The advantage is mutual, sir; you have given me one or two hints I could not have got from fifty merchants. I mean to coin you, Captain Dodd."

David laughed and blushed. "I doubt it will be but copper coin if you do. But I am not a captain; I am only first mate."

"You don't say so! Why, how comes that?"

"Well, sir, I went to sea very young, but I wasted a year or two in private ventures. When I say wasted, I picked up a heap of knowledge that I could not have gained on the China voyage, but it has lost me a little in length of standing; but, on the other hand, I have been very lucky; it is not every one that gets to be first mate at my age; and after next voyage, if I can only make a little bit of interest, I think I shall be a captain. No, sir, I wish I was a captain; I never wished it as now;" and David sighed deeply.

"Humph!" said Mr. Bazalgette, and took a note.

He then showed David his maps. David inspected them with almost boyish delight, and showed the merchant the courses of ships on Eastern and Western voyages, and explained the winds and currents that compelled them to go one road and return another, and in both cases to go so wonderfully out of what seems the track as they do. Bref, the two ends of the mercantile stick came nearer.

"My study is always open to you, Mr. Dodd, and I hope you will not let a day pass without obliging me by looking in upon me."

David thanked him, and went out innocently unconscious that he had performed an unparalleled feat. In the hall he met Captain Kenealy, who, having received orders to amuse him, invited him to play at billiards. David consented, out of good-nature, to please Kenealy. Thus the whole day passed, andles facheux would not let him get a word with Lucy.

At dinner he was separated from her, and so hotly and skillfully engaged by Mrs. Bazalgette that he had scarcely time to look at his idol. After dinner he had to contest her with Mr. Talboys and Mr. Hardie, the latter of whom he found a very able and sturdy antagonist. Mr. Hardie had also many advantages over him. First, the young lady was not the least shy of Mr. Hardie, but the parting scene beyond Royston had put her on her guard against David, and her instinct of defense made her reserved with him. Secondly, Mrs. Bazalgette was perpetually making diversions, whose double object was to get David to herself and leave Lucy to Mr. Hardie.

With all this David found, to his sorrow, that, though he now lived under the same roof with her, he was not so near her as at Font Abbey. There was a wall of etiquette and of rivals, and, as he now began to fear, of her own dislike between them. To read through that mighty transparent jewel, a female heart, Nauta had recourse—to what, do you think? To arithmetic. He set to work to count how many times she spoke to each of the party in the drawing-room, and he found that Mr. Hardie was at the head of the list, and he was at the bottom. That might be an accident; perhaps this was his black evening; so he counted her speeches the next evening. The result was the same. Droll statistics, but sad and convincing to the simple David. His spirits failed him; his aching heart turned cold. He withdrew from the gay circle, and sat sadly with a book of prints before him, and turned the leaves listlessly. In a pause of the conversation a sigh was heard in the corner. They all looked round, and saw David all by himself, turning over the leaves, but evidently not inspecting them.

A sort of flash of satirical curiosity went from eye to eye.

But tact abounded at one end of the room, if there was a dearth of it at the other.

La rusee sans le savoir made a sign to them all to take no notice; at the same time she whispered: "Going to sea in a few days for two years; the thought will return now and then." Having said this with a look at her aunt, that, Heaven knows how, gave the others the notion that it was to Mrs. Bazalgette she owed the solution of David's fit of sadness, she glided easily into indifferent topics. So then the others had a momentary feeling of pity for David. Miss Lucy noticed this out of the tail of her eye.

That night David went to bed thoroughly wretched. He could not sleep, so he got up and paced the deck of his room with a heavy heart. At last, in his despair, he said, "I'll fire signals of distress." So he sat down and took a sheet of paper, and fired: "Nothing has turned as I expected. She treats me like a stranger. I seem to drop astern instead of making any way. Here are three of us, I do believe, and all seem preferred to your poor brother; and, indeed, the only thing that gives me any hope is that she seems too kind to be in earnest, for it is not in her angelic nature to be really unkind; and what have I done? Eve, dear, such a change from what she was at Font Abbey, and that happy evening when she came and drank tea with us, and lighted our little garden up, and won your heart, that was always a little set against her. Now it is so different that I sit and ask myself whether all that is not a dream. Can anyone change so in one short month? I could not. But who knows? perhaps I do her wrong. You know I never could read her at home without your help, and, dear Eve, I miss you now from my side most sadly. Without you I seem to be adrift, without rudder or compass."

Then, as he could not sleep, he dressed himself, and went out at four o'clock in the morning. He roamed about with a heavy heart; at last he bethought him of his fiddle. Since Lucy's departure from Font Abbey this had been a great solace to him. It was at once a depository and vent to him; he poured out his heart to it and by it; sometimes he would fancy, while he played, that he was describing the beauties of her mind and person; at others, regretting the sad fate that separated him from her; or, hope reviving, would see her near him, and be telling her how he loved her; and, so great an inspirer is love, he had invented more than one clear melody during the last month, he who up to that time had been content to render the thoughts of others, like most fiddlers and composers.

So he said to himself, "I had better not play in the house, or I shall wake them out of their first sleep."

He brought out his violin, got among some trees near the stable-yard, and tried to soothe his sorrowful heart. He played sadly, sweetly and dreamingly. He bade the wooden shell tell all the world how lonely he was, only the magic shell told it so tenderly and tunefully that he soon ceased to be alone. The first arrival was on four legs: Pepper, a terrier with a taste for sounds. Pepper arrived cautiously, though in a state of profound curiosity, and, being too wise to trust at once to his ears, avenue of sense by which we are all so much oftener deceived than by any other, he first smelled the musician carefully and minutely all round. What he learned by this he and his Creator alone know, but apparently something reassuring; for, as soon as he had thoroughly snuffed his Orpheus, he took up a position exactly opposite him, sat up high on his tail, cocked his nose well into the air, and accompanied the violin with such vocal powers as Nature had bestowed on him. Nor did the sentiment lose anything, in intensity at all events, by the vocalist. If David's strains were plaintive, Pepper's were lugubrious; and what may seem extraordinary, so long as David played softly the Cerberus of the stableyard whined musically, and tolerably in tune; but when he played loud or fast poor Pepper got excited, and in his wild endeavors to equal the violin vented dismal and discordant howls at unpleasantly short intervals. All this attracted David's attention, and he soon found he could play upon Pepper as well as the fiddle, raising him and subduing him by turns; only, like the ocean, Pepper was not to be lulled back to his musical ripple quite so quickly as he could be lashed into howling frenzy.

While David was thus playing, and Pepper showing a fearful broadside of ivory teeth, and flinging up his nose and sympathizing loudly and with a long face, though not perhaps so deeply as he looked, suddenly rang behind David a chorus of human chuckles. David wheeled, and there were six young women's faces set in the foliage and laughing merrily. Though perfectly aware that David would look round, they seemed taken quite by surprise when he did look, and with military precision became instantly two files, for the four impudent ones ran behind the two modest ones, and there, by an innocent instinct, tied their cap-strings, which were previously floating loose, their custom ever in the early morning.

"Play us up something merry, sir," hazarded one of the mock-modest ones in the rear.

"Shan't I be taking you from your work?" objected David dryly.

"Oh, all work and no play is bad for the body," replied the minx, keeping ostentatiously out of sight.

Good-natured David played a merry tune in spite of his heart; and even at that disadvantage it was so spirit-stirring compared with anything the servants had heard, it made them all frisky, of which disposition Tom, the stable boy, who just then came into the yard, took advantage, and, leading out one of the housemaids by the polite process of hauling at her with both hands, proceeded to country dancing, in which the others soon demurely joined.

Now all this was wormwood to poor David; for to play merriment when the heart is too heavy to be cheered by it makes that heart bitter as well as sad. But the good-natured fellow said to himself: "Poor things, I dare say they work from morning till night, and seldom see pleasure but at a distance; why not put on a good face, and give them one merry hour." So he played horn-pipes and reels till all their hearts were on fire, and faces red, and eyes glittering, and legs aching, and he himself felt ready to burst out crying, and then he left off. As for il penseroso Pepper, he took this intrusion of merry music upon his sympathies very ill. He left singing, and barked furiously and incessantly at these ancient English melodies and at the dancers, and kept running from and running at the women's whirling gowns alternately, and lost his mental balance, and at last, having by a happier snap than usual torn off two feet of the under-housemaid's frock, shook and worried the fragment with insane snarls and gleaming eyes, and so zealously that his existence seemed to depend on its annihilation.

David gave those he had brightened a sad smile, and went hastily in-doors. He put his violin into its case, and sealed and directed his letter to Eve. He could not rest in-doors, so he roamed out again, but this time he took care to go on the lawn. Nobody would come there, he thought, to interrupt his melancholy. He was doomed to be disappointed in that respect. As he sat in the little summer-house with his head on the table, he suddenly heard an elastic step on the dry gravel. He started peevishly up and saw a lady walking briskly toward him: it was Miss Fountain.

She saw him at the same instant. She hesitated a single half-moment; then, as escape was impossible, resumed her course. David went bashfully to meet her.

"Good-morning, Mr. Dodd," said she, in the most easy, unembarrassed way imaginable.

He stammered a "good-morning," and flushed with pleasure and confusion.

He walked by her side in silence. She stole a look at him, and saw that, after the first blush at meeting her, he was pale and haggard. On this she dashed into singularly easy and cheerful conversation with him; told him that this morning walk was her custom—"My substitute for rouge, you know. I am always the first up in this languid house; but I must not boast before you, who, I dare say, turn out—is not that the word?—at daybreak. But, now I think of it, no! you would have crossed my hawse before, Mr. Dodd," using naval phrases to flatter him.

"It was my ill-luck; I always cruised a mile off. I had no idea this bit of gravel was your quarter-deck."

"It is, though, because it is always dry. You would not like a quarter-deck with that character, would you?"

"Oh yes, I should. I'd have my bowsprit always wet, and my quarter-deck always dry. But it is no use wishing for what we cannot have."

"That is very true," said Lucy, quietly.

David reflected on his own words, and sighed deeply.

This did not suit Lucy. She plied him with airy nothings, that no man can arrest and impress on paper; but the tone and smile made them pleasing, and then she asked his opinion of the other guests in such a way as implied she took some interest in his opinion of them, but mighty little in the people themselves. In short, she chatted with him like an old friend, and nothing more; but David was not subtle enough in general, nor just now calm enough, to see on what footing all this cordiality was offered him. His color came back, his eye brightened, happiness beamed on his face, and the lady saw it from under her lashes.

"How fortunate I fell in with you here! You are yourself again—on your quarter-deck. I scarce knew you the last few days. I was afraid I had offended you. You seemed to avoid me."

"Nonsense, Mr. Dodd; what is there about you to avoid?"

"Plenty, Miss Fountain; I am so inferior to your other friends."

"I was not aware of it, Mr. Dodd."

"And I have heard your sex has gusts of caprice, and I thought the cold wind was blowing upon me; and that did seem very sad, just when I am going out, and perhaps shall never see your sweet face or hear your lovely voice again."

"Don't say that, Mr. Dodd, or you will make me sad in earnest. Your prudence and courage, and a kind Providence, will carry you safe through this voyage, as they have through so many, and on your return the acquaintance you do me the honor to value so highly will await you—if it depends on me."

All this was said kindly and beautifully, and almost tenderly, but still with a certain majesty that forbade love-making—rendered it scarce possible, except to a fool. But David was not captious. He could not, like the philosopher, sift sunshine. For some days he had been almost separated from her. Now she was by his side. He adored her so that he could no longer realize sorrow or disappointment to come. They were uncertain—future. The light of her eyes, and voice, and face, and noble presence were here; he basked in them.

He told her not to mind a word he had said. "It was all nonsense. I am happier now—happier than ever."

At this Lucy looked grave and became silent.

David, to amuse her, told her there was "a singing dog aboard," and would she like to hear him?

This was a happy diversion for Lucy. She assented gayly. David ran for his fiddle, and then for Pepper. Pepper wagged his tail, but, strong as his musical taste was, would not follow the fiddle. But at this juncture Master Reginald dawned on the stable-yard with a huge slice of bread and butter. Pepper followed him. So the party came on the lawn and joined Lucy. Then David played on the violin, and Pepper performed exactly as hereinbefore related. Lucy laughed merrily, and Reginald shrieked with delight, for the vocal terrier was mortal droll.

"But, setting Pepper aside, that is a very sweet air you are playing now, Mr. Dodd. It is full of soul and feeling."

"Is it?" said David, looking wonderstruck; "you know best."

"Who is the composer?"

David looked confused and said, "No one of any note."

Lucy shot a glance at him, keen as lightning. What with David's simplicity and her own remarkable talent for reading faces, his countenance was a book to her, wide open, Bible print. "The composer's name is Mr. Dodd," said she, quietly.

"I little thought you would be satisfied with it," replied David, obliquely.

"Then you doubted my judgment as well as your own talent."

"My talent! I should never have composed an air that would bear playing but for one thing."

"And what was that?" said Lucy, affecting vast curiosity. She felt herself on safe ground now—the fine arts.

"You remember when you went away from Font Abbey, and left us all so heavy-hearted?"

"I remember leaving Font Abbey," replied Lucy, with saucy emphasis, and an air of lofty disbelief in the other incident.

"Well, I used to get my fiddle, and think of you so far away, and sweet sad airs came to my heart, and from my heart they passed into the fiddle. Now and then one seemed more worthy of you than the rest were, and then I kept that one."

"You mean you took the notes down," said Lucy coldly.

"Oh no, there was no need; I wrote it in my head and in my heart. May I play you another of your tunes? I call them your tunes."

Lucy blushed faintly, and fixed her eyes on the ground. She gave a slight signal of assent, and David played a melody.

"It is very beautiful," said she in a low voice. "Play it again. Can you play it as we walk?"

"Oh yes." He played it again. They drew near the hall door. She looked up a moment, and then demurely down again.

"Now will you be so good as to play the first one twice?" She listened with her eyelashes drooping. "Tweedle dee! tweedle dum! tweedle dee." "Andnow we will go into breakfast," cried Lucy, with sudden airy cheerfulness, and, almost with the word, she darted up the steps, and entered the house without even looking to see whether David followed or what became of him.

He stood gazing through the open door at her as she glided across the hall, swift and elastic, yet serpentine, and graceful and stately as Juno at nineteen.

"Et vera iucessu patuit lady."

These Junones, severe in youthful beauty, fill us Davids with irrational awe; but, the next moment, they are treated like small children by the very first matron they meet; they resign their judgment at once to hers, and bow their wills to her lightest word with a slavish meanness.

Creation's unmarried lords, realize your true position—girls govern you, and wives govern girls.

Mrs. Bazalgette, on Lucy's entrance, ran a critical eye over her, and scolded her like a six-year-old for walking in thin shoes.

"Only on the gravel, aunt," said the divine slave, submissively.

"No matter; it rained last night. I heard it patter. You want to be laid up, I suppose."

"I will put on thicker ones in future, dear aunt," murmured the celestial serf.

Now Mrs. Bazalgette did not really care a button whether the servile angel wore thick soles or thin. She was cross about something a mile off that. As soon as she had vented her ill humor on a sham cause, she could come to its real cause good-temperedly. "And, Lucy, love, do manage better about Mr. Dodd."

Lucy turned scarlet. Luckily, Mrs. Bazalgette was evading her niece's eye, so did not see her telltale cheek.

"He was quite thrown out last night; and really, as he does not ride with us, it is too bad to neglect him in-doors."

"Oh, excuse me, aunt, Mr. Dodd is your protege. You did not even tell me you were going to invite him."

"I beg your pardon, that I certainly did. Poor fellow, he was out of spirits last night."

"Well, but, aunt, surely you can put an admirer in good spirits when you think proper," said Lucy slyly.

"Humph! I don't want to attract too much attention. I see Bazalgette watching me, and I don't wish to be misinterpreted myself, or give my husband pain."

She said this with such dignity that Lucy, who knew her regard for her husband, had much ado not to titter. But courtesy prevailed, and she said gravely: "I will do whatever you wish me, only give me a hint at the time; a look will do, you know."

The ladies separated; they met again at the breakfast-room door. Laughter rang merrily inside, and among the gayest voices was Mr. Dodd's. Lucy gave Mrs. Bazalgette an arch look. "Your patient seems better;" and they entered the room, where, sure enough, they found Mr. Dodd the life and soul of the assembled party.

"A letter from Mrs. Wilson, aunt."

"And, pray, who is Mrs. Wilson?"

"My nurse. She tells me 'it is five years since she has seen me, and she is wearying to see me.' What a droll expression, 'wearying.'"

"Ah!" said David Dodd.

"You have heard the word before, Mr. Dodd?"

"No, I can't say I have; but I know what it must mean."

"Lying becalmed at the equator, eh! Dodd?" said Bazalgette, misunderstanding him.

"Mrs. Wilson tells me she has taken a farm a few miles from this."

"Interesting intelligence," said Mrs. Bazalgette.

"And she says she is coming over to see me one of these days, aunt," said Lucy, with a droll expression, half arch, half rueful. She added timidly, "There is no objection to that, is there?"

"None whatever, if she does not make a practice of it; only mind, these old servants are the greatest pests on earth."

"I remember now," said Lucy thoughtfully, "Mrs. Wilson was always very fond of me. I cannot think why, though."

"No more can I," said Mr. Hardie, dryly; "she must be a thoroughly unreasonable woman."

Mr. Hardie said this with a good deal of grace and humor, and a laugh went round the table.

"I mean she only saw me at intervals of several years."

"Why, Lucy, what an antiquity you are making yourself," said Fountain.

But Lucy was occupied with her puzzle. "She calls me her nursling," said Lucy, sotto voce, to her aunt, but, of course, quite audibly to the rest of the company; "her dear nursling;" and says, "she would walk fifty miles to see me. Nursling? hum! there is another word I never heard, and I do not exactly know —Then she says—"

"Taisez-vous, petite sotte!" said Mrs. Bazalgette, in a sharp whisper, so admirably projected that it was intelligible only to the ear it was meant for.

Lucy caught it and stopped short, and sat looking by main force calm and dignified, but scarlet, and in secret agony. "I have said something amiss," thought Lucy, and was truly wretched.

"We don't believe in Mrs. Wilson's affection on this side the table," said Mr. Hardie; "but her revelations interest us, for they prove that Miss Fountain had a beginning. Now we had thought she rose from the foam like Venus, or sprung from Jove's brow like Minerva, or descended from some ancient pedestal, flawless as the Parian itself."

"What, sir," cried Bazalgette, furiously, "did you think our niece was built in a day? So fair a structure, so accomplished a—"

"Will you be quiet, good people?" said Mrs. Bazalgette. "She was born, she was bred, she was brought up, in which I had a share, and she is a very good girl, if you gentlemen will be so good as not to spoil her for me with your flattery."

"There!" said Lucy, courageously, enforcing her aunt's thunderbolt; and she leaned toward Mrs. Bazalgette, and shot back a glance of defiance, with arching neck, at Mr. Bazalgette.

After breakfast she ran to Mrs. Bazalgette. "What was it?"

"Oh, nothing; only the gentlemen were beginning to grin."

"Oh, dear! did I say anything—ridiculous?"

"No, because I stopped you in time. Mind, Lucy, it is never safe to read letters out from people in that class of life; they talk about everything, and use words that are quite out of date. I stopped you because I know you are a simpleton, and so I could not tell what might pop out next."

"Oh, thank you, aunt—thank you," cried Lucy, warmly. "Then I did not expose myself, after all."

"No, no; you said nothing that might not be proclaimed at St. Paul's Cross—ha! ha!"

"Am I a simpleton, aunt?" inquired Lucy, in the tone of an indifferent person seeking knowledge.

"Not you," replied this oblivious lady. "You know a great deal more than most girls of your age. To be sure, girls that have been at a fashionable school generally manage to learn one or two things you have no idea of."

"Naturally."

"As you say—he! he! But you make up for it, my dear, in other respects. If the gentlemen take you for a pane of glass, why, all the better; meantime, shall I tell you your real character? I have only just discovered it myself."

"Oh, yes, aunt, tell me my character. I should so like to hear it from you."

"Should you?" said the other, a little satirically; "well, then, you are an INNOCENT FOX."

"Aunt!"

"An in-no-cent fox; so run and get your work-box. I want you to run up a tear in my flounce."

Lucy went thoughtfully for her workbox, murmuring ruefully, "I am an innocent fox—I am an in-nocent fox."

She did not like her new character at all; it mortified her, and seemed self-contradictory as well as derogatory.

On her return she could not help remonstrating: "How can that be my character? A fox is cunning, and I despise cunning; and I am sure I am notinnocent," added she, putting up both hands and looking penitent. With all this, a shade of vexation was painted on her lovely cheeks as she appealed against her epigram.

Mrs. Bazalgette (with the calm, inexorable superiority of matron despotism). "You are an in-nocent fox!! Is your needle threaded? Here is the tear; no, not there. I caught against the flowerpot frame, and I'll swear I heard my gown go. Look lower down, dear. Don't give it up."

All which may perhaps remind the learned and sneering reader of another fox —the one that "had a wound, and he could not tell where."

They rode out to-day as usual, and David had the equivocal pleasure of seeing them go from the door.

Lucy was one of the first down, and put her hand on the saddle, and looked carelessly round for somebody to put her up. David stepped hastily forward, his heart beating, seized her foot, never waited for her to spring, but went to work at once, and with a powerful and sustained effort raised her slowly and carefully like a dead weight, and settled her in the saddle. His gripe hurt her foot. She bore it like a Spartan sooner than lose the amusement of his simplicity and enormous strength, so drolly and unnecessarily exerted. It cost her a little struggle not to laugh right out, but she turned her head away from him a moment and was quit for a spasm. Then she came round with a face all candor.

"Thank you, Mr. Dodd," said she, demurely; and her eyes danced in her head. Her foot felt encircled with an iron band, but she bore him not a grain of malice for that, and away she cantered, followed by his longing eyes.

David bore the separation well. "To-morrow morning I shall have her all to myself," said he. He played with Kenealy and Reginald, and chatted with Bazalgette. In the evening she was surrounded as usual, and he obtained only a small share of her attention. But the thought of the morrow consoled him. He alone knew that she walked before breakfast.

The next morning he rose early, and sauntered about till eight o'clock, and then he came on the lawn and waited for her. She did not come. He waited, and waited, and waited. She never came. His heart died within him. "She avoids me," said he; "it is not accident. I have driven her out of her very garden; she always walked here before breakfast (she said so) till I came and spoiled her walk; Heaven forgive me."

David could not flatter himself that this interruption of her acknowledged habit was accidental. On the other hand, how kind and cheerful she had been with him on the same spot yesterday morning. To judge by her manner, his company on her quarter-deck was not unwelcome to her yet she kept her room to-day, from the window of which she could probably see him walking to and fro, longing for her. The bitter disappointment was bad enough, but here tormenting perplexity as to its cause was added, and between the two the pining heart was racked.

This is the cruelest separation; mere distance is the mildest. Where land and sea alone lie between two loving hearts, they pine, but are at rest. A piece of paper, and a few lines traced by the hand that reads like a face, and the two sad hearts exult and embrace one another afresh, in spite of a hemisphere of dirt and salt water, that parts bodies but not minds. But to be close, yet kept aloof by red-hot iron and chilling ice, by rivals, by etiquette and cold indifference— to be near, yet far—this is to be apart—this, this is separation.

A gush of rage and bitterness foreign to his natural temper came over Mr. Dodd. "Since I can't have the girl I love, I will have nobody but my own thoughts. I cannot bear the others and their chat to-day. I will go and think of her, since that is all she will let me do"; and directly after breakfast David walked out on the downs and made by instinct for the sea. The wounded deer shunned the lively herd.

The ladies, as they sat in the drawing-room, received visits of a less flattering character than usual. Reginald kept popping in, inquiring, "Where was Mr. Dodd?" and would not believe they had not hid him somewhere. He was followed by Kenealy, who came in and put them but one question, "Where is Dawd?"

"We don't know," said Mrs. Bazalgette sharply; "we have not been intrusted with the care of Mr. Dodd."

Kenealy sauntered forth disconsolate. Finally Mr. Bazalgette put his head in, and surveyed the room keenly but in silence; so then his wife looked up, and asked him satirically if he did not want Mr. Dodd.

"Of course I do," was the gracious reply; "what else should I come here for?"

"Well, he is lost; you had better put him in the 'Hue and Cry.'"

La Bazalgette was getting jealous of her own flirtee: he attracted too much of that attention she loved so dear.

At last Reginald, despairing of Dodd, went in search of another playmate— Master Christmas, a young gentleman a year older than himself, who lived within half a mile. Before he went he inquired what there was for his dinner, and, being informed "roast mutton," was not enraptured; he then asked with greater solicitude what was the pudding, and, being told "rice," betrayed disgust and anger, as was remembered when too late.

At two o'clock, the day being fine, the ladies went for a long ride, accompanied by Talboys only. Kenealy excused himself: "He must see if he could not find Dawd."

Mrs. Bazalgette started in a pet; but, after the first canter, she set herself to bewitch Mr. Talboys, just to keep her hand in; she flattered him up hill and down dale. Lucy was silent and distraite.

"From that hill you look right down upon the sea," said Mrs. Bazalgette; "what do you say? It is only two miles farther."

On they cantered, and, leaving the high road, dived into a green lane which led them, by a gradual ascent, to Mariner's Folly on the summit of the cliff. Mariner's Folly looked at a distance like an enormous bush in the shape of a lion; but, when you came nearer, you saw it was three remarkably large blackthorn-trees planted together. As they approached it at a walk, Mrs. Bazalgette told Mr. Talboys its legend.

"These trees were planted a hundred and fifty years ago by a retired buccaneer."

"Aunt, now, it was only a lieutenant."

"Be quiet, Lucy, and don't spoil me; I call him a buccaneer. Some say it is named his "Folly," because, you must know, his ghost comes and sits here at times, and that is an absurd practice, shivering in the cold. Others more learned say it comes from a Latin word 'folio,' or some such thing, that means a leaf; the mariner's leafy screen." She then added with reckless levity, "I wonder whether we shall find Buckey on the other side, looking at the ships through a ghostly telescope—ha! ha!—ah! ah! help! mercy! forgive me! Oh, dear, it is only Mr. Dodd in his jacket—you frightened me so. Oh! oh! There— I am ill. Catch me, somebody;" and she dropped her whip, and, seeing David's eye was on her, subsided backward with considerable courage and trustfulness, and for the second time contrived to be in her flirtee's arms.

I wish my friend Aristotle had been there; I think he would have been pleased at her [Greek] (presence of mind) in turning even her terror of the supernatural so quickly to account, and making it subservient to flirtation.

David sat heart-stricken and hopeless, gazing at the sea. The hours passed by his heavy heart unheeded. The leafy screen deadened the light sound of the horses' feet on the turf, and, moreover, his senses were all turned inward. They were upon him, and he did not move, but still held his head in his hands and gazed upon the sea. At Mrs. Bazalgette's cries he started up, and looked confusedly at them all; but, when she did the feinting business, he thought she was going to faint, and caught her in his arms; and, holding her in them a moment as if she had been a child, he deposited her very gently in a sitting posture at the foot of one of the trees, and, taking her hand, slapped it to bring her to.

"Oh, don't! you hurt me," cried the lady in her natural voice.

Lucy, barbarous girl, never came to her aunt's assistance. At the first fright she seemed slightly agitated, but she now sat impassive on her pony, and even wore a satirical smile.

"Now, dear aunt, when you have done, Mr. Dodd will put you on your horse again."

On this hint David lifted her like a child, malgre a little squeak she thought it well to utter, and put her in the saddle again. She thanked him in a low, murmuring voice. She then plied David with a host of questions. "How came he so far from home?" "Why had he deserted them all day?" David hung his head, and did not answer. Lucy came to his relief: "It would be as well if you would make him promise to be at home in time for dinner; and, by the way, I have a favor to ask of you, Mr. Dodd."

"A favor to ask of me?!"

"Oh, you know we all make demands upon your good-nature in turn."

"That is true," said La Bazalgette, tenderly. "I don't know what will become of us all when he goes."

Lucy then explained "that the masked ball suggested by Mr. Talboys' beautiful dresses was to be very soon, and she wanted Mr. Dodd to practice quadrilles and waltzes with her; it will be so much better with the violin and piano than with a piano alone, and you are such an excellent timist—will you, Mr. Dodd?"

"That I will," said David, his eyes sparkling with delight; "thank you."

"Then, as I shall practice before the gentlemen join us, and it is four o'clock now, had you not better turn your back on the sea, and make the best of your way home?"

"I will be there almost as soon as you."

"Indeed! what, on foot, and we on horseback?"

"Ay; but I can steer in the wind's eye."

"Aunt, Mr. Dodd proposes a race home."

"With all my heart. How much start are we to give him?"

"None at all," said David; "are you ready? Then give way," and he started down the hill at a killing pace.

The equestrians were obliged to walk down the hill, and when they reached the bottom David was going as the crow flies across some meadows half a mile ahead. A good canter soon brought them on a line with him, but every now and then the turns of the road and the hills gave him an advantage. Lucy, naturally kind-hearted, would have relaxed her pace to make the race more equal, but Talboys urged her on; and as a horse is, after all, a faster animal than a sailor, they rode in at the front gate while David was still two fields off.

"Come," said Mrs. Bazalgette, regretfully, "we have beat him, poor fellow, but we won't go in till we see what has become of him."

As they loitered on the lawn, Henry the footman came out with a salver, and on it reposed a soiled note. Henry presented it with demure obsequiousness, then retired grinning furtively.

"What is this—a begging-letter? What a vile hand! Look, Lucy; did you ever? Why, it must be some pauper."

"Have a little mercy, aunt," said Lucy, piteously; "that hand has been formed under my care and daily superintendence: it is Reginald's."

"Oh, that alters the case. What can the dear child have to say to me! Ah! the little wretch! Send the servants after him in every direction. Oh, who would be a mother!"

The letter was written in lines with two pernicious defects. 1st. They were like the wooden part of a bow instead of its string. 2d. They yielded to gravity— kept tending down, down, to the righthand corner more and more. In the use of capitals the writer had taken the copyhead as his model. The style, however, was pithy, and in writing that is the first Christian grace—no, I forgot, it is the second; pellucidity is the first.

"Dear mama, me and johnny

Cristmas are gone to the north

Pole his unkle went twise we

Shall be back in siks munths

Please give my love to lucy and

Papa and ask lucy to be kind to

My ginnipigs i shall want them

Wen i come back. too much

Cabiges is not good for ginnipigs.

Wen i come back i hope there

Will be no rise left. it is very

Unjust to give me those nasty

Messy pudens i am not a child

There filthy there abbommanabel.

Johny says it is funy at the north

Pole and there are bares

and they

Are wite.

I remain

"Your duteful son

"Reginald George Bazalgette."

This innocent missive set house and premises in an uproar. Henry was sent east through the dirt, multa reluctantem, in white stockings. Tom galloped north. Mrs. Bazalgette sat in the hall, and did well-bred hysterics for Kenealy and Talboys. Lucy pinned up her habit, and ran to the boundary hedge on the bare chance of seeing the figures of the truants somewhere short of the horizon. Lo, and behold, there was David Dodd crossing the very nearest field and coming toward her, an urchin in each hand.

Lucy ran to meet them. "Oh, you dear naughty children, what a fright you have given us! Oh, Mr. Dodd, how good of you! Where did you find them?"

"Under that hedge, eating apples. They tell me they sailed for the North Pole this morning, but fell in with a pirate close under the land, so 'bout ship and came ashore again."

"A pirate, Mr. Dodd? Oh, I see, a beggar—a tramp."

"A deal worse than that, Miss Lucy. Now, youngster, why don't you spin your own yarn?"

"Yes, tell me, Reggy."

"Well, dear, when I had written to mamma, and Johnny had folded it—because I can write but I can't fold it, and he can fold it but he can't write it—we went to the North Pole, and we got a mile; and then we saw that nasty Newfoundland dog sitting in the road waiting to torment us. It is Farmer Johnson's, and it plays with us, and knocks us down, and licks us, and frightens us, and we hate it; so we came home."

"Ha! ha! good, prudent children. Oh, dear, you have had no dinner."

"Oh, yes we had, Lucy, such a nice one: we bought such a lot of apples of a woman. I never had a dinner all apples before; they always spoil them with mutton and things, and that nasty, nasty rice"

"Hear to that!" shouted David Dodd. "They have been dining upon varjese" (verjuice), "and them growing children. I shall take them into the kitchen, and put some cold beef into their little holds this minute, poor little lambs."

"Oh yes, do; and I will run and tell the good news." She ran across the lawn, and came into the hall red with innocent happiness and agitation. "They are found, aunt, they are found; don't cry. Mr. Dodd found them close by, They have had no dinner, so that good, kind Mr. Dodd is taking them into the kitchen. I will send Master Christmas home with a servant. Shall I bring you Reggy to kiss?"

"No, no; wicked little wretch, to frighten his poor mother! Whip him, somebody, and put him to bed."

In the evening, soon after the ladies had left the dining-room, the pianoforte was heard playing quadrilles in the drawing-room. David fidgeted on his seat a little, and presently rose and went for his violin, and joined Lucy in the drawing-room alone. Mrs. B. was trying on a dress. Between the tunes Lucy chatted with him as freely and kindly as ever. David was in heaven. When the gentlemen came up from the dining-room, his joy was interrupted, but not for long. The two musicians played with so much spirit, and the fiddle, in particular, was so hearty, that Mrs. Bazalgette proposed a little quiet dance on the carpet: and this drew the other men away from the piano, and left David and Lucy to themselves.

She stole a look more than once at his bright eyes and rich ruddy color, and asked herself, "Is that really the same face we found looking wan and haggard on the sea? I think I have put an end to that, at all events." The consciousness of this sort of power is secretly agreeable to all men and all women, whether they mean to abuse it or no. She smiled demurely at her mastery over this great heart, and said to herself, "One would think I was a witch." Later in the evening she eyed him again, and thought to herself, "If my company and a few friendly words can make him so happy, it does seem very hard I should select him to shun for the few days he has to pass in England now; but then, if I let him think—I don't know what to do with him. Poor Mr. Dodd."

Miss Fountain did not torment her bolder aspirants with alternate distance and familiarity. She rode out every fine day with Mr. Talboys, and was all affability. She sat next Mr. Hardie at dinner, and was all affability.

Narrative has its limits and, to relate in some sequence the honest sailor's tortures in love with a tactician, I have necessarily omitted concurrent incidents of a still tamer character; but the reader may, by the help of his own intelligence, gather their general results from the following dialogues, which took place on the afternoon and evening of the terrible infant's escapade.

Mrs. Bazalgette. "'Well, my dear friend, and how does this naughty girl of mine use you?"

Mr. Hardie. "As well as I could expect, and better than I deserve."

Mrs. B. "Then she must be cleverer than any girl that ever breathed. However, she does appreciate your conversation; she makes no secret of it."

Mr. H. "I have so little reason to complain of my reception that I will make my proposal to her this evening if you think proper."

Mrs. Bazalgette started, and glanced admiration on a man of eight thousand a year, who came to the point of points without being either cajoled or spurred thither; but she shook her head. "Prudence, my dear Mr. Hardie, prudence. Not just yet. You are making advances every day; and Lucy is an odd girl; with all her apparent tenderness, she is unimpressionable."

"That is only virgin modesty," said Hardie, dogmatically.

"Fiddlestick," replied Mrs. B., good-humoredly. "The greatest flirts I ever met with were virgins, as you call them. I tell you she is not disposed toward marriage as all other girls are until they have tasted its bitters."

Mr. H. "If I know anything of character, she will make a very loving wife."

Mrs. B. (sharply). "That means a nice little negro. Well, I think she might, when once caught; but she is not caught, and she is slippery, and, if you are in too great a hurry, she may fly off; but, above all, we have a dangerous rival in the house just now."

Mr. H. "What, that Mr. Talboys? I don't fear him. He is next door to a fool."

Mrs. B. "What of that? Fools are dangerous rivals for a lady's favor. We don't object to fools. It depends on the employment. There is one office we are apt to select them for."

Mr. H. "A husband, eh?" The lady nodded.

Mrs. B. "I meant to marry a fool in Bazalgette, but I found my mistake. The wretch had only feigned absurdity. He came out in his true colors directly."

Mr. H. "A man of sense, eh? The sinister hypocrite! He only wore the caps and bells to allure unguarded beauty, and doffed them when he donned the wedding-suit."

Mrs. B. "Yes. But these are reminiscences so sweet that I shall be glad to return from them to your little affair. Seriously, then, Mr. Talboys is not to be overlooked, for this reason: he is well backed."

"By whom?"

"By some one who has influence with Lucy—her nearest relation, Mr. Fountain."

"What! is he nearer to her than you are?"

"Certainly; and she is fond of him to infatuation. One day I did but hint that selfishness entered into his character (he is eaten up with it), and that he told fibs; Mr. Hardie, she turned round on me like a tigress—Oh, how she made me cry!"

The keen hand, Hardie, smiled satirically, and after a pause answered with consummate coolness: "I believe thus much, that she loves her uncle, and that his influence, exerted unscrupulously—"

"Which it will be. He may be strong enough to spoil us, even though he should not be able to carry his own point; now trust me, my dear friend, Lucy's preference is clearly for you, but I know the weakness of my own sex, and, above all, I know Lucy Fountain. A mouse can help a lion in a matter of small threads, too small for his nobler and grander wisdom to see. Let me be your mouse for once." The little woman caught the great man with the everlasting hook, and the discussion ended in "claw me and I will claw thee," and in the mutual self-complacency that follows that arrangement. Vide "Blackwood,"passim.

Mr. H. "I really think she would accept me if I offered to-day; but I have so high an opinion of your sagacity and friendship for me, madam, that I will defer my judgment to yours. I must, however, make one condition, that you will not displace my plan without suggesting a distinct course of action for me to adopt in its place."

This smooth proposal, made quietly but with twinkling eye, would have shut the mouth of nine advisers in ten, but it found the Bazalgette prepared.

"Oh, the pleasure of having a man of ability to deal with!" cried she, with enthusiasm. "This is my advice, then: stay Mr. Fountain out. He must go in a day or two. His time is up, and I will drop a hint of fresh visitors expected. When he is gone, warm by degrees, and offer yourself either in person, or through Bazalgette, or me."

"In person, then, certainly. Of all foibles, employing another pair of eyes, another tongue, another person to make love for one is surely the silliest."

"I am quite of your opinion," cried the lady, with a hearty laugh.

Mr. Fountain. "So you are satisfied with the state of things?"

Mr. Talboys. "Yes, I think I have beaten the sailor out of the field."

"Well, but—this Hardie?"

"Hardie! a shopkeeper. I don't fear him."

"In that case, why not propose? I have been doing the preliminaries—sounding your praises."

Mr. Talboys (tyrannically). "I propose next Saturday."

Mr. Fountain. "Very well."

Talboys. "In the boat."

"In the boat? What boat? There's no boat."

"I have asked her to sail with me from —— in a boat; there is a very nice little lugger-rigged one. I am having the seats padded and stuffed and lined, and an awning put up, and the boat painted white and gold."

"Bravo! Cleopatra's galley."

"I assure you she looks forward to it with pleasure; she guesses why I want to get her into that boat. She hesitated at first, but at last consented with a look—a conscious look; I can hardly describe it."

"There is no need," cried Fountain. "I know it; the jade turned all eyelashes."

"That is rather exaggerated, but still—"

"But still I have described it—to a hair. Ha! ha!"

Talboys (gravely). "Well, yes."

Mr. Talboys, I am bound to own, was accurate. During the last day or two Lucy had taken a turn; she had been bewitching; she had flattered him with tact, but deliciously; had consulted him as to which of his beautiful dresses she should wear at the masked ball, and, when pressed to have a sail in the boat he was fitting for her, she ended by giving a demure assent.

Chorus of male readers, "Oh, les femmes, les femmes!"

David Dodd had by nature a healthy as well as a high mind; but the fever and ague of an absorbing passion were telling on it. Like many a great heart before his day, his heart was tossed like a ship, and went up to heaven, and down again to despair, as a girl's humor shifted, or seemed to shift, for he forgot that there is such a thing as accident, and that her sex are even more under its dominion than ours. No; whatever she did must be spontaneous, voluntary, premeditated even, and her lightest word worth weighing, her lightest action worth anxious scrutiny as to its cause.

Still he had this about him that the peevish and puny lover has not. Her bare presence was joy to him. Even when she was surrounded by other figures, he saw and felt but the one; the rest were nothings. But when she went out of his sight, some bright illusion seemed to fade into cold and dark reality. Then it fell on him like a weighty, icy hammer, that in three days he must go to sea for two years, and that he was no nearer her heart now than he was at Font Abbey.

Was he even as near?

So the next afternoon he thrust in before Talboys, and put Lucy on her horse by brute force, and griped her stout little boot, which she had slyly substituted for a shoe, and touched her glossy habit, and felt a thrill of bliss unspeakable at his momentary contact with her; but she was no sooner out of sight than a hollow ache seized the poor fellow, and he hung his head and sighed.

"I say, capting," said a voice in his ear. He looked up, and there stood Tom, the stable-boy, with both hands in his pockets. Tom was not there by his own proper movement, but was agent of Betsy, the under-housemaid.

Female servants scan the male guests pretty closely too, without seeming to do it, and judge them upon lamentably broad principles—youth, health, size, beauty, and good temper. Oh, the coarse-minded critics! Hence it befell that in their eyes, especially after the fiddle business, David was a king compared with his rivals.

"If I look at him too long, I shall eat him," said the cook-maid.

"He is a darling," said the upper housemaid.

Betsy aforesaid often opened a window to have a sly look at him, and on one of these occasions she inspected him from an upper story at her leisure. His manner drew her attention. She saw him mount Lucy, and eye her departing form sadly and wistfully. Betsy glowered and glowered, and hit the nail on the head, as people will do who are so absurd as to look with their own eyes, and draw their own conclusions instead of other people's. After this she took an opportunity, and said to Tom, with a satirical air, "How are you off for nags, your way?"

"Oh, we have got enough for our corn," replied Tom, on the defensive.

"It seems you can't find one for the captain among you."

"Will you give a kiss if I make you out a liar?"

"Sooner than break my arm. Come, you might, Tom. Now is it reasonable, him never to get a ride with her, and that useless lot prancing about with her all day long?"

"Why don't you ride with 'em, capting?"

"I have no horse."

"I have got a horse for you, sir—master's."

"That would be taking a liberty."

"Liberty, sir! no; master would be so pleased if you would but ride him. He told me so."

"Then saddle him, pray."

"I have a-saddled him. You had better come in the stable-yard, capting; then you can mount and follow; you will catch them before they reach the Downs." In another minute David was mounted.

"Do you ride short or long, capting?" inquired Tom, handling the stirrup-leather.

David wore a puzzled look. "I ride as long as I can stick on;" and he trotted out of the stable-yard. As Tom had predicted, he caught the party just as they went off the turn-pike on to the grass. His heart beat with joy; he cantered in among them. His horse was fresh, squeaked, and bucked at finding himself on grass and in company, and David announced his arrival by rolling in among their horses' feet with the reins tight grasped in his fist. The ladies screamed with terror. David got up laughing; his horse had hoped to canter away without him, and now stood facing him and pulling.

"No, ye don't," said David. "I held on to the tiller-ropes though I did go overboard." Then ensued a battle between David and his horse, the one wanting to mount, the other anxious to be unencumbered with sailors. It was settled by David making a vault and sitting on the animal's neck, on which the ladies screamed again, and Lucy, half whimpering, proposed to go home.

"Don't think of it," cried David. "I won't be beat by such a small craft as this—hallo!" for, the horse backing into Talboys, that gentleman gave him a clandestine cut, and he bolted, and, being a little hard-mouthed, would gallop in spite of the tiller-ropes. On came the other nags after him, all misbehaving more or less, so fine a thing is example. When they had galloped half a mile the ground began to rise, and David's horse relaxed his pace, whereon David whipped him industriously, and made him gallop again in spite of remonstrance.

The others drew the rein, and left him to gallop alone. Accordingly, he made the round of the hill and came back, his horse covered with lather and its tail trembling. "There," said he to Lucy, with an air of radiant self-satisfaction, "he clapped on sail without orders from quarter-deck, so I made him carry it till his bows were under water."

"You will kill my uncle's horse," was the reply, in a chilling tone.

"Heaven forbid!"

"Look at its poor flank beating."

David hung his head like a school-girl rebuked. "But why did he clap on sail if he could not carry it?" inquired he, ruefully, of his monitress.

The others burst out laughing; but Lucy remained grave and silent.

David rode along crestfallen.

Mrs. Bazalgette brought her pony close to him, and whispered, "Never mind that little cross-patch. She does not care a pin about the horse; you interrupted her flirtation, that is all."

This piece of consolation soothed David like a bunch of stinging-nettles.

While Mrs. Bazalgette was consoling David with thorns, Kenealy and Talboys were quizzing his figure on horseback.

He sat bent like a bow and visibly sticking on: item, he had no straps, and his trousers rucked up half-way to his knee.

Lucy's attention being slyly drawn to these phenomena by David's friend Talboys, she smiled politely, though somewhat constrainedly; but the gentlemen found it a source of infinite amusement during the whole ride, which, by the way, was not a very long one, for Miss Fountain soon expressed a wish to turn homeward. David felt guilty, he scarce knew why.

The promised happiness was wormwood. On dismounting, she went to the lawn to tend her flowers. David followed her, and said bitterly, "I am sorry I came to spoil your pleasure."

Miss Fountain made no answer.

"I thought I might have one ride with you, when others have so many."

"Why, of course, Mr. Dodd. If you like to expose yourself to ridicule, it is no affair of mine." The lady's manner was a happy mixture of frigidity and crossness. David stood benumbed, and Lucy, having emptied her flower-pot, glided indoors without taking any farther notice of him.

David stood rooted to the spot. Then he gave a heavy sigh, and went and leaned against one of the pillars of the portico, and everything seemed to swim before his eyes.

Presently he heard a female voice inquire, "Is Miss Lucy at home?" He looked, and there was a tall, strapping woman in conference with Henry. She had on a large bonnet with flaunting ribbons, and a bushy cap infuriated by red flowers. Henry's eye fell upon these embellishments: "Not at home," chanted he, sonorously.

"Eh, dear," said the woman sadly, "I have come a long way to see her."

"Not at home, ma'am," repeated Henry, like a vocal machine.

"My name is Wilson, young man," said she, persuasively, and the Amazon's voice was mellow and womanly, spite of her coal-scuttle full of field poppies. "I am her nurse, and I have not seen her this five years come Martinmas;" and the Amazon gave a gentle sigh of disappointment.

"Not at home, ma'am!" rang the inexorable Plush.

But David's good heart took the woman's part. "She is at home, now," said he, coming forward. "I saw her go into the house scarce a minute ago."

"Oh, thank you, sir," said Mrs. Wilson. But Mr. Plush's face was instantly puckered all over with signals, which David not comprehending, he said, "Can I say a word with you, sir?" and, drawing him on one side, objected, in an injured and piteous tone. "We are not at home to such gallimaufry as that; it is as much as my place is worth to denounce that there bonnet to our ladies."

"Bonnet be d—d," roared David, aloud. "It is her old nurse. Come, heave ahead;" and he pointed up the stairs.

"Anything to oblige you, captain," said Henry, and sauntered into the drawing-room; "Mrs. Wilson, ma'am, for Miss Fountain."

"Very well; my niece will be here directly."

Lucy had just gone to her own room for some working materials.

"You had better come to an anchor on this seat, Mrs. Wilson," said David.

"Thank ye kindly, young gentleman," said Mrs. Wilson; and she settled her stately figure on the seat. "I have walked a many miles to-day, along of our horse being lame, and I am a little tired. You are one of the family, I do suppose?"

"No, I am only a visitor."

"Ain't ye now? Well, thank ye kindly, all the same. I have seen a worse face than yours, I can tell you," added she; for in the midst of it all she had found time to read countenances more mulierurn.

"And I have seen a good many hundred worse than yours, Mrs. Wilson."

Mrs. Wilson laughed. "Twenty years ago, if you had said so, I might have believed you, or even ten; but, bless you, I am an old woman now, and can say what I choose to the men. Forty-two next Candlemas."

In the country they call themselves old at forty-two, because they feel young. In town they call themselves young at forty-two, because they feel old.

David found that he had fallen in with a gossip; and, being in no humor for vague chat, he left Mrs. Wilson to herself, with an assurance that Miss Fountain would be down to her directly.

In leaving her he went into worse company—his own thoughts; they were inexpressibly sad and bitter. "She hates me, then," said he. "Everybody is welcome to her at all hours, except me. That lady said it was because I interrupted her flirtation. Aha! well, I shan't interrupt her flirtation much longer. I shan't be in her way or anybody's long. A few short hours, and this bitter day will be forgotten, and nothing left me but the memory of the kindness she had for me once, or seemed to have, and the angel face I must carry in my heart wherever I go, by land or sea. The sea? would to God I was upon it this minute! I'd rather be at sea than ashore in the dirtiest night that ever blew."

He had been walking to and fro a good half-hour, deeply dejected and turning bitter, when, looking in accidentally at the hall door, he caught sight of Mrs. Wilson sitting all alone where he had left her. "Why, what on earth is the meaning of that?" thought he; and he went into the hall and asked Mrs. Wilson how she came to be there all alone.

"That is what I have been asking myself a while past," was the dry reply.

"Have you not seen her?"

"No, sir, I have not seen her, and, to my mind, it is doubtful whether I am to see her."

"But I say you shall see her."

"No, no, don't put yourself out, sir," said the woman, carelessly; "I dare say I shall have better luck next time, if I should ever come to this house again, which it is not very likely." She added gently, "Young folk are thoughtless; we must not judge them too hardly."

"Thoughtless they may be, but they have no business to be heartless. I have a great mind to go up and fetch her down."

"Don't ye trouble, sir. It is not worth while putting you about for an old woman like me." Then suddenly dropping the mask of nonchalance which women of this class often put on to hide their sensibility, she said, very, very gravely, and with a sad dignity, that one would not have expected from her gossip and her finery, "I begin to fear, sir, that the child I have suckled does not care to know me now she is a woman grown."

David dashed up the stairs with a red streak on his brow. He burst into the drawing-room, and there sat Mrs. Bazalgette overlooking, and Lucy working with a face of beautiful calm. She looked just then so very like a pure, tranquil Madonna making an altar-cloth, or something, that David's intention to give her a scolding was withered in the bud, and he gazed at her surprised and irresolute, and said not a word.

"Anything the matter?" inquired Mrs. Bazalgette, attracted by the bruskness of his entry.

"Yes, there is," said David sternly.

Lucy looked up.

"Miss Fountain's old nurse has been sitting in the hall more than half an hour, and nobody has had the politeness to go near her."

"Oh, is that all? Well, don't look daggers at me. There is Lucy; give her a lesson in good-breeding, Mr. Dodd." This was said a little satirically, and rather nettled David.

"Perhaps it does not become me to set up for a teacher of that. I know my own deficiencies as well as anybody in this house knows them; but this I know, that, if an old friend walked eight miles to see me, it would not be good-breeding in me to refuse to walk eight yards to see her. And, another thing, everybody's time is worth something; if I did not mean to see her, I would have that much consideration to send down and tell her so, and not keep the woman wasting her time as well as her trouble, and vexing her heart into the bargain."

"Where is she, Mr. Dodd?" asked Lucy quickly.

"Where is she?" cried David, getting louder and louder. "Why, she is cooling her heels in the hall this half hour and more. They hadn't the manners to show her into a room."

"I will go to her, Mr. Dodd," said Lucy, turning a little pale. "Don't be angry; I will go directly"; and, having said this with an abject slavishness that formed a miraculous contrast with her late crossness and imperious chilliness, she put down her work hastily and went out; only at the door she curved her throat, and cast back, Parthian-like, a glance of timid reproach, as much as to say, "Need you have been so very harsh with a creature so obedient as this is?"

That deprecating glance did Mr. Dodd's business. It shot him with remorse, and made him feel a brute.

"Ha! ha! That is the way to speak to her, Mr. Dodd; the other gentlemen spoil her."

"It was very unbecoming of me to speak to her harshly like that."

"Pooh! nonsense; these girls like to be ordered about; it saves them the trouble of thinking for themselves; but what is to become of me? You have sent off my workwoman."

"I will do her work for her."

"What! can you sew?"

"Where is the sailor that can't sew?"

"Delightful! Then please to sew these two thick ends together. Here is a large needle."

David whipped out of his pocket a round piece of leather with strings attached, and fastened it to the hollow of his hand.

"What is that?"

"It is a sailor's thimble." He took the work, held it neatly, and shoved the needle from behind through the thick material. He worked slowly and uncouthly, but with the precision that was a part of his character, and made exact and strong stitches. His task-mistress looked on, and, under the pretense of minute inspection, brought a face that was still arch and pretty unnecessarily close to the marine milliner, in which attitude they were surprised by Mr. Bazalgette, who, having come in through the open folding-doors, stood looking mighty sardonic at them both before they were even aware he was in the room.

Omphale colored faintly, but Hercules gave a cool nod to the newcomer, and stitched on with characteristic zeal and strict attention to the matter in hand.

At this Bazalgette uttered a sort of chuckle, at which Mrs. Bazalgette turned red. David stitched on for the bare life.

"I came to offer to invite you to my study, but—"

"I can't come just now," said David, bluntly; "I am doing a lady's work for her."

"So I see," retorted Bazalgette, dryly.

"We all dine with the Hunts but you and Mr. Dodd," said Mrs. Bazalgette, "so you will be en tete-a-tete all the evening."

"All the better for us both." And with this ingratiating remark Mr. Bazalgette retired whistling.

Mrs. Bazalgette heaved a gentle sigh: "Pity me, my friend," said she, softly.

"What is the matter?" inquired David, rather bluntly.

"Mr. Bazalgette is so harsh to me—ah!—to me, who longs so for kindness and gentleness that I feel I could give my very soul in exchange for them."

The bait did not take.

"It is only his manner," said David, good-naturedly. "His heart is all right; I never met a better. What sort of a knot is that you are tying? Why, that is a granny's knot;" and he looked morose, at which she looked amazed; so he softened, and explained to her with benevolence the rationale of a knot. "A knot is a fastening intended to be undone again by fingers, and not to come undone without them. Accordingly, a knot is no knot at all if it jams or if it slips. A granny's knot does both; when you want to untie it you must pick at it like taking a nail out of a board, and, for all that, sooner or later it always comes undone of itself; now you look here;" and he took a piece of string out of his pocket, and tied her a sailor's knot, bidding her observe that she could untie it at once, but it could never come untied of itself. He showed her with this piece of string half a dozen such knots, none of which could either jam or slip.

"Tie me a lover's knot," suggested the lady, in a whisper.

"Ay! ay!" and he tied her a lover's knot as imperturbably as he had the reef knot, bowling-knot, fisherman's bend, etc.

"This is very interesting," said Mrs. Bazalgette, ironically. She thought David might employ a tete-a-tete with a flirt better than this. "What a time Lucy is gone!"

"All the better."

"Why?" and she looked down in mock confusion.

"Because poor Mrs. Wilson will be glad."

Mrs. Bazalgette was piqued at this unexpected answer. "You seem quite captivated with this Mrs. Wilson; it was for her sake you took Lucy to task. Apropos, you need not have scolded her, for she did not know the woman was in the house."

"What do you mean?"

"I mean Lucy was not in the room when Mrs. Wilson was announced. I was, but I did not tell her; the all-important circumstance had escaped my memory. Where are you running to now?"

"Where? why, to ask her pardon, to be sure."

Mrs. B. [Brute!]

David ran down the stairs to look for Lucy, but he found somebody else instead—his sister Eve, whom the servant had that moment admitted into the hall. It was "Oh, Eve!" and "Oh, David!" directly, and an affectionate embrace.

"You got my letter, David?"

"No."

"Well, then you will before long. I wrote to tell you to look out for me; I had better have brought the letter in my pocket. I didn't know I was coming till just an hour before I started. Mother insisted on my going to see the last of you. Cousin Mary had invited me to ——, so I shall see you off, Davy dear, after all. I thought I'd just pop in and let you know I was in the neighborhood. Mary and her husband are outside the gate in their four-wheel. I would not let them drive in, because I want to hear your story, and they would have bothered us."

"Eve, dear, I have no good news for you. Your words have come true. I have been perplexed, up and down, hot and cold, till I feel sometimes like going mad. Eve, I cannot fathom her. She is deeper than the ocean, and more changeable. What am I saying? the sea and the wind; they are to be read; they have their signs and their warnings; but she—"

"There! there! that is the old song. I tell you it is only a girl—a creature as shallow as a puddle, and as easy to fathom, as you call it, only men are so stupid, especially boys. Now just you tell me all she has said, all she has done, and all she has looked, and I will turn her inside out like a glove in a minute."

Cheered by this audacious pledge, David pumped upon Eve all that has trickled on my readers, and some minor details besides, and repeated Lucy's every word, sweet or bitter, and recalled her lightest action—Meminerunt omnia amantes—and every now and then he looked sadly into Eve's keen little face for his doom.

She heard him in silence until the last fatal incident, Lucy's severity on the lawn. Then she put in a question. "Were those her exact words?"

"Do I ever forget a syllable she says to me?"

"Don't be angry. I forgot what a ninny she has made of you. Well, David, it is all as plain as my hand. The girl likes you—that is all."

"The girl likes me? What do you mean? How can you say that? What sign of liking is there?"

"There are two. She avoids you, and she has been rude to you."

"And those are signs of liking, are they?" said David, bitterly.

"Why, of course they are, stupid. Tell me, now, does she shun this Captain Keely?"

"Kenealy. No."

"Does she shun Mr. Harvey?"

"Hardie. No."

"Does she shun Mr. Talboys?"

"Oh Eve, you break my heart—no! no! She shuns no one but poor David."

"Now think a little. Here are three on one sort of footing, and one on a different footing; which is likeliest to be the man, the one or the three? You have gained a point since we were all together. She distinguishes you."

"But what a way to distinguish me. It looks more like hatred than love, or liking either."

"Not to my eye. Why should she shun you? You are handsome, you are good-tempered, and good company. Why should she be shy of you? She is afraid of you, that is why; and why is she afraid of you? because she is afraid of her own heart. That is how I read her. Then, as for her snubbing you, if her character was like mine, that ought to go for nothing, for I snub all the world; but this is a little queen for politeness. I can't think she would go so far out of her way as to affront anybody unless she had an uncommon respect for him."

"Listen to that, now! I am on my beam-ends."

"Now think a minute, David," said Eve, calmly, ignoring his late observation; "did you ever know her snub anybody?"

"Never. Did you?"

"No; and she never would, unless she took an uncommon interest in the person. When a girl likes a man, she thinks she has a right to ill-use him a little bit; he has got her affection to set against a scratch or two; the others have not. So she has not the same right to scratch them. La! listen to me teaching him A B C. Why, David, you know nothing; it's scandalous."

Eve's confidence communicated itself at last to David; but when he asked her whether she thought Lucy would consent to be his wife, her countenance fell in her turn. "That is a very different thing. I am pretty sure she likes you; how could she help it? but I doubt she will never go to the altar with you. Don't be angry with me, Davy, dear. You are in love with her, and to you she is an angel. But I am of her own sex, and see her as she is; no matter who she likes, she will never be content to make a bad match, as they call it. She told me so once with her own lips. But she had no need to tell me; worldliness is written on her. David, David, you don't know these great houses, nor the fair-spoken creatures that live in them, with tongues tuned to sentiment, and mild eyes fixed on the main chance. Their drawing-rooms are carpeted market-places; you may see the stones bulge through the flowery pattern; there the ladies sell their faces, the gentlemen their titles and their money; and much I fear Miss Fountain's hand will go like the rest—to the highest bidder."

"If I thought so, my love, deep as it is, would turn to contempt; I would tear her out of my heart, though I tore my heart out of my body." He added, "I will know what she is before many hours."

"Do, David. Take her off her guard, and make hot love to her; that is your best chance. It is a pity you are so much in love with her; you might win her by a surprise if you only liked her in moderation."

"How so, dear Eve?"

"The battle would be more even. Your adoring her gives her the upper hand of you. She is sure to say 'no' at first, and then I am afraid you will leave off, instead of going on hotter and hotter. The very look she will put on to check you will check you, you are so green. What a pity I can't take your place for half an hour. I would have her against her will. I would take her by storm. If she said 'no' twenty times, she should say 'yes' the twenty-first; but you are afraid of her; fancy being afraid of a woman. Come, David, you must not shilly-shally, but attack her like a man; and, if she is such a fool she can't see your merit, forgive her like a man, and forget her like a man. Come, promise me you will."

"I promise you this, that if I lose her it shall not be for want of trying to win her; and, if she refuses me because I am not her fancy, I shall die a bachelor for her sake." Eve sighed. "But if she is the mercenary thing you take her for —if she owns to liking me, but prefers money to love, then from that moment she is no more to me than a picture or a statue, or any other lovely thing that has no soul."

With these determined words he gave his sister his arm, and walked with her through the grounds to the road where her cousin was waiting for her.

Lucy found Mrs. Wilson in the hall. "Come into the library, Mrs. Wilson," said she; "I have only just heard you were here. Won't you sit down? Are you not well, Mrs. Wilson? You tremble. You are fatigued, I fear. Pray compose yourself. May I ring for a glass of wine for you?"

"No, no, Miss Lucy," said the woman, smiling; "it is only along of you coming to me so sudden, and you so grown. Eh! sure, can this fine young lady be the little girl I held in my lap but t'other day, as it seems?"

There was an agitation and ardor about Mrs. Wilson that, coupled with the flaming bonnet, made Miss Fountain uneasy. She thought Mrs. Wilson must be a little cracked, or at least flighty.

"Pray compose yourself, madam," said she, soothingly, but with that dignity nobody could assume more readily than she could. "I dare say I am much grown since I last had the pleasure of seeing you; but I have not outgrown my memory, and I am happy to receive you, or any of our old servants that knew my dear mother."

"Then I must not look for a welcome," said Mrs. Wilson, with feminine logic, "for I was never your servant, nor your mamma's." Lucy opened her eyes, and her face sought an explanation.

"I never took any money for what I gave you, so how could I be a servant? To see me a dangling of my heels in your hall so long, one would say I was a servant; but I am not a servant, nor like to be, please God, unless I should have the ill luck to bury my two boys, as I have their father. So perhaps the best thing I can do, miss, is to drop you my courtesy and walk back as I came." The Amazon's manner was singularly independent and calm, but the tell-tale tears were in the large gray honest eyes before she ended.

Lucy's natural penetration and habit of attending to faces rather than words came to her aid. "Wait a minute, Mrs. Wilson," said she; "I think there is some misunderstanding here. Perhaps the fault is mine. And yet I remember more than one nursery-maid that was kind enough to me; but I have heard nothing of them since."

"Their blood is not in your veins as mine is, unless the doctors have lanced it out."

"I never was bled in my life, if you mean that, madam. But I must ask you to explain how I can possibly have the—the advantage of possessing yourblood in my veins."

Mrs. Wilson eyed her keenly. "Perhaps I had better tell you the story from first to last, young lady," said she quietly.

"If you please," said the courtier, mastering a sigh; for in Mrs. Wilson there was much that promised fluency.

"Well, miss, when you came into the world, your mamma could not nurse you. I do notice the gentry that eat the fat of the land are none the better for it; for a poor woman can do a mother's part by her child, but high-born and high-fed folk can't always; so you had to be brought up by hand, miss, and it did not agree with you, and that is no great wonder, seeing it is against nature. Well, my little girl, that was born just two days after you, died in my arms of convulsion fits when she was just a month old. She had only just been buried, and me in bitter grief, when doesn't the doctor call and ask me as a great favor, would I nurse Mrs. Fountain's child, that was pining for want of its natural food. I bade him get out of my sight. I felt as if no woman had a right to have a child living when my little darling was gone. But my husband, a just man as ever was, said, 'Take a thought, Mary; the child is really pining, by all accounts.' Well, I would not listen to him. But next Sunday, after afternoon church, my mother, that had not said a word till then, comes to me, and puts her hand on my shoulder with a quiet way she had. 'Mary,' says she, 'I am older than you, and have known more.' She had buried six of us, poor thing. Says she, scarce above a whisper, 'Suckle that failing child. It will be the better for her, and the better for you, Mary, my girl.' Well, miss, my mother was a woman that didn't interfere every minute, and seldom gave her reasons; but, if you scorned her advice, you mostly found them out to your cost; and then she was my mother; and in those days mothers were more thought of, leastways by us that were women and had suffered for our children, and so learned to prize the woman that had suffered for us. 'Well, then,' I said, 'if you say so, mother, I suppose I didn't ought to gainsay you, on the Lord His day.' For you see my mother was one that chose her time for speaking—eh! but she was wise. 'Mother,' says I, 'to oblige you, so be it'; and with that I fell to crying sore on my mother's neck, and she wasn't long behind me, you may be sure. Whiles we sat a crying in one another's arms, in comes John, and goes to speak a word of comfort. 'It is not that,' says my mother; 'she have given her consent to nurse Mrs. Fountain's little girl.' 'It is much to her credit,' says he: says he, 'I will take her up to the house myself.' 'What for?' says I; 'them that grants the favor has no call to run after them that asks it.' You see, Miss Lucy, that was my ignorance; we were small farmers, too independent to be fawning, and not high enough to weed ourselves of upishness. Your mamma, she was a real lady, so she had no need to trouble about her dignity; she thought only of her child; and she didn't send the child, but she came with it herself. Well, she came into our kitchen, and made her obeisance, and we to her, and mother dusted her a seat. She was pale-like, and a mother's care was in her face, and that went to my heart. 'This is very, very kind of you, Mrs. Wilson,' said she. Those were her words. 'Mayhap it is,' says I; and my heart felt like lead. Mother made a sign to your mamma that she should not hurry me. I saw the signal, for I was as quick as she was; but I never let on I saw it. At last I plucked up a bit of courage, and I said, 'Let me see it.' So mother took you from the girl that held you all wrapped up, and mother put you on my knees; and I took a good look at you. You had the sweetest little face that ever came into the world, but all peaked and pining for want of nature. With you being on my knees, my bosom began to yearn over you, it did. 'The child is starved,' said I; 'that is all its grief. And you did right to bring it' here.' Your mother clasps her hands, 'Oh, Mrs. Wilson,' says she, 'God grant it is not too late.' So then I smiled back to her, and I said, 'Don't you fret; in a fortnight you shan't know her.' You see I was beginning to feel proud of what I knew I could do for you. I was a healthy young woman, and could have nursed two children as easy as some can one. To make a long story short, I gave you the breast then and there; and you didn't leave us long in doubt whether cow's milk or mother's milk is God's will for sucklings. Well, your mamma put her hands before her face, and I saw the tears force their way between her fingers. So, when she was gone, I said to my mother, 'What was that for?' 'I shan't tell you,' says she. 'Do, mother,' says I. So she said, 'I wonder at your having to ask; can't you see it was jealousy-like. Do you think she has not her burden to bear in this world as well as you? How would you like to see another woman do a mother's part for a child of yours, and you sit looking on like a toy-mother? Eh! Miss Lucy, but I was vexed for her at that, and my heart softened; and I used to take you up to the great house, and spend nearly the whole day there, not to rob her of her child more than need be."

"Oh, Mrs. Wilson! Oh, you kind, noble-hearted creature, surely Heaven will reward you."

"That is past praying for, my dear. Heaven wasn't going to be long in debt to a farmer's wife, you may be sure; not a day, not an hour. I had hardly laid you to my breast when you seemed to grow to my heart. My milk had been tormenting me for one thing. My good mother had thought of that, I'll go bail; and of course you relieved me. But, above all, you numbed the wound in my heart, and healed it by degrees: a part of my love that lay in the churchyard seemed to come back like, and settle on the little helpless darling that milked me. At whiles I forgot you were not my own; and even when I remembered it, it was—I don't know—somehow—as if it wasn't so. I knew in my head you were none of mine, but what of that? I didn't feel it here. Well, miss, I nursed you a year and two months, and a finer little girl never was seen, and such a weight! And, of course, I was proud of you; and often your dear mother tried to persuade me to take a twenty-pound note, or ten; but I never would. I could not sell my milk to a queen. I'd refuse it, or I'd make a gift of it, and the love that goes with it, which is beyond price. I didn't say so to her in so many words, but I did use to tell her 'I was as much in her little girl's debt as she was in mine,' and so I was. But as for a silk gown, and a shawl, and the like, I didn't say 'No' to them; who ever does?"

"Nurse!"

"My lamb!"

"Can you ever forgive me for confounding you with a servant? I am so inexperienced. I knew nothing of all this."

"Oh, Miss Lucy, 'let that flea stick in the wall,' as the saying is."

"But, dear Mrs. Wilson, now only think that your affection for me should have lasted all these years. You speak as if such tenderness was common. I fear you are mistaken there: most nurses go away and think no more of those to whom they have been as mothers in infancy."

"How do you know that, Miss Lucy? Who can tell what passes inside those poor women that are ground down into slaves, and never dare show their real hearts to a living creature? Certainly hirelings will be hirelings, and a poor creature that is forced to sell her breast, and is bundled off as soon as she has served the grand folks' turn, why, she behooves to steel herself against nature, and she knows that from the first; but whether she always does get to harden herself, I take leave to doubt. Miss Lucy; I knew an unfortunate girl that nursed a young gentleman, leastways a young nobleman it was, and years after that I have known her to stand outside the hedge for an hour to catch a sight of him at play on the lawn among the other children. Ay, and if she had a penny piece to spare she would go and buy him sugar-plums, and lay wait for him, and give them him, and he heir to thousands a year."

"Poor thing! Poor thing!"

"Next to the tie of blood, Miss Lucy, the tie of milk is a binding affection. When you went to live twenty miles from us, I behooved to come in the cart and see you from time to time."

"I remember, nurse, I remember."

"When I came to our new farm hard by, you were away; but as soon as I heard you were come back, it was like a magnet drawing me. I could not keep away from you."

"Heaven forbid you should; and I will come and see you, dear nurse."

"Will ye, now? Do now. I have got a nice little parlor for you. It is a very good house for a farm-house; and there we can set and talk at our ease, and no fine servants, dressed like lords, coming staring in."

Lucy now proffered a timid request that Mrs. Wilson would take off her bonnet. "I want to see your good kind face without any ornament."

"Hear to that, now, the darling;" and off came the bonnet.

"Now your cap."

"Well, I don't know; I hadn't time to do my hair as should be before coming."

"What does that matter with me? I must see you without that cap."

"What! don't you like my new cap? Isn't it a pretty cap? Why, I bought it a purpose to come and see you in."

"Oh, it is a very pretty cap in itself," said the courtier, "but it does not suit the shape of your face. Oh, what a difference! Ah! now I see your heart in your face. Will you let me make you a cap?"

"Will you, now, Miss Lucy? I shall be so proud wearing it our house will scarce hold me."

At this juncture a footman came in with a message from Mrs. Bazalgette to remind Lucy that they dined out.

"I must go and dress, nurse." She then kissed her and promised to ride over and visit her at her farm next week, and spend a long time with her quietly, and so these new old friends parted.

Lucy pondered every word Mrs. Wilson had said to her, and said to herself: "What a child I am still! How little I know! How feebly I must have observed!"

The party at dinner consisted of Mr. Bazalgette, David, and Reginald, who, taking advantage of his mother's absence and Lucy's, had prevailed on the servants to let him dine with the grown-up ones. "Halo? urchin," said Mr. Bazalgette, "to what do we owe this honor?"

"Papa," said Reginald, quaking at heart, "if I don't ever begin to be a man what is to become of me?"

Mr. Reginald did not exhibit his full powers at dinner-time. He was greatest at dessert. Peaches and apricots fell like blackberries. He topped up with the ginger and other preserves; then he uttered a sigh, and his eye dwelt on some candied pineapple he had respited too long. Putting the pineapple's escape and the sigh together, Mr. Bazalgette judged that absolute repletion had been attained. "Come, Reginald," said he, "run away now, and let Mr. Dodd and me have our talk." Before the words were even out of his mouth a howl broke from the terrible infant. He had evidently feared the proposal, and got this dismal howl all ready.

"Oh, papa! Oh! oh!"

"What is the matter?"

"Don't make me go away with the ladies this time. Jane says I am not a man because I go away when the ladies go. And Cousin Lucy won't marry me till I am a man. Oh, papa, do let me be a man this once."

"Let him stay, sir," said David.

"Then he must go and play at the end of the room, and not interrupt our conversation."

Mr. Reginald consented with rapture. He had got a new puzzle. He could play at it in a corner; all he wanted was to be able to stop Jane's mouth, should she ever jeer him again. Reginald thus disposed of, Mr. Bazalgette courted David to replenish his glass and sit round to the fire. The fire was huge and glowing, the cut glass sparkled, and the ruby wine glowed, and even the faces shone, and all invited genial talk. Yet David, on the eve of his departure and of his fate, oppressed with suspense and care, was out of the reach of those genial, superficial influences. He could only just mutter a word of assent here and there, then relapsed into his reverie, and eyed the fire thoughtfully, as if his destiny lay there revealed. Mr. Bazalgette, on the contrary, glowed more and more in manner as well as face, and, like many of his countrymen, seemed to imbibe friendship with each fresh glass of port.

At last, under the double influence of his real liking for David and of the Englishman-thawing Portuguese decoction, he gave his favorite a singular proof of friendship. It came about as follows. Observing that he had all the talk to himself, he fixed his eyes with an expression of paternal benevolence on his companion, and was silent in turn.

David looked up, as we all do when a voice ceases, and saw this mild gaze dwelling on him.

"Dodd, my boy, you don't say a word; what is the matter?"

"I am very bad company, sir, that is the truth."

"Well, fill your glass, then, and I'll talk for you. I have got something to say for you, young gentleman." David filled his glass and forced himself to attend; after a while no effort was needed.

"Dodd," resumed the mature merchant, "I need hardly tell you that I have a particular regard for you; the reason is, you are a young man of uncommon merit."

"Mr. Bazalgette! sir! I don't know which way to look when you praise me like that. It is your goodness; you overrate me."

"No, I don't. I am a judge of men. I have seen thousands, and seen them too close to be taken in by their outside. You are the only one of my wife's friends that ever had the run of my study. What do you think of that, now?"

"I am very proud of it, sir; that is all I can find to say."

"Well, young man, that same good opinion I have of you induces me to do something else, that I have never done for any of your predecessors."

Mr. Bazalgette paused. David's heart beat. Quick as lightning it darted through his mind, "He is going to ask a favor for me. Promotion? Why not? He is a merchant. He has friends in the Company.'"

"I am going to interfere in your concerns, Dodd."

"You are very good, sir."

"Well, perhaps I am. I have to overcome a natural reluctance. But you are worth the struggle. I shall therefore go against the usages of the world, which I don't care a button for, and my own habits, which I care a great deal for, and give you, humph—a piece of friendly advice."

David looked blank.

"Dodd, my boy, you are playing the fool in this house."

David looked blanker.

"It is not your fault; you are led into it by one of those sweet creatures that love to reduce men to the level of their own wisdom. You are in love, or soon will be."

David colored all over like a girl, and his face of distress was painful to see.

"You need not look so frightened; I am your friend, not your enemy. And do you really think others besides me have not seen what is going on? Now, Dodd, my dear fellow, I am an old man, and you are a young one. Moreover, I understand the lady, and you don't."

"That is true, sir; I feel I cannot fathom her."

"Poor fellow! Well, but I have known her longer than you."

"That is true, sir."

"And on closer terms of intimacy."

"No doubt, sir."

"Then listen to me. She is all very charming outside, and full of sensibility outside, but she has no more real feeling than a fish. She will go a certain length with you, or with any agreeable young man, but she can always stop where it suits her. No lady in England values position and luxury more than she does, or is less likely to sacrifice them to love, a passion she is incapable of. Here, then, is a game at which you run all the risk. No! leave her to puppies like Kenealy; they are her natural prey. You must not play such a heart as yours against a marble taw. It is not an even stake."

David groaned audibly. His first thought was, "Eve says the same of her." His second, "All the world is against her, poor thing."

"Is she to bear the blame of my folly?"

"Why not? She is the cause of your folly. It began with her setting her cap at you."

"No, sir, you do her wrong. She is modesty itself."

"Ta! ta! ta! you are a sailor, green as sea-weed."

"Mr. Bazalgette, as I am a gentleman, she never has encouraged me to love her as I do."

"Your statement, sir, is one which becomes a gentleman—under the circumstances. But I happen to have watched her. It is a thing I have taken the trouble to do for some time past. It was my interest in you that made me curious, and apprehensive—on your account."

"Then, if you have watched her, you must have seen her avoid me."

"Pooh! pooh! that was drawing the bait; these old stagers can all do that."

"Old stagers!" and David looked as if blasphemy had been uttered. Bazalgette wore a grin of infinite irony.

"Don't be shocked," said he; "of course, I mean old in flirtation; no lady is old in years."

"She is not, at all events."

"It is agreed. There are legal fictions, and why not social ones?"

"I don't understand you, sir; and, in truth, it is all a puzzle to me. You don't seem angry with me?"

"Why, of course not, my poor fellow; I pity you."

"Yet you discourage me, Mr. Bazalgette."

"But not from any selfish motive. I want to spare you the mortification that is in store for you. Remember, I have seen the end of about a dozen of you."

"Good Heavens! And what is the end of us?"

"The cold shoulder without a day's warning, and another fool set in your place, and the house door slammed in your face, etc., etc. Oh, with her there is but one step from flirtation to detestation. Not one of her flames is her friend at this moment."

David hung his head, and his heart turned sick; there was a silence of some seconds, during which Bazalgette eyed him keenly. "Sir," said David, at last, "your words go through me like a knife."

"Never mind. It is a friendly surgeon's knife, not an assassin's."

"Yet you say it is only out of regard for me you warn me so against her."

"I repeat it."

"Then, sir, if, by Heaven's mercy, you should be mistaken in her character—if, little as I deserve it, I should succeed in winning her regard—I might reckon on your permission—on your kind—support?"

"Hardly," said Mr. Bazalgette, hastily. He then stared at the honest earnest face that was turned toward him. "Well," said he, "you modest gentlemen have a marvelous fund of assurance at bottom. No, sir; with the exception of this piece of friendly advice I shall be strictly neutral. In return for it, if you should succeed, be so good as to take her out of the house, that is the only stipulation I venture to propose."

"I should be sure to do that," cried David, lifting his eyes to Heaven with rapture; "but I shall not have the chance."

"So I keep telling you. You might as well hope to tempt a statue of the Goddess Flirtation. She infinitely prefers wealth and vanity to anything, even to vice."

"Vice, sir! is that a term for us to apply to a lady like her, whom we are all unworthy to approach?" and David turned very red.

"Well, you need not quarrel with me about her, as I don't with you."

"Quarrel with you, dear sir? I hope I feel your kindness, and know my duty better; but, sir, I am agitated, and my heart is troubled; and surely you go beyond reason. She is not old enough to have had so many lovers."

"Humph! she has made good use of her time."

"Even could I believe that she, who seems to me an angel, is a coquette, still she cannot be hard and heartless as you describe her. It is impossible; it does not belong to her years."

"You keep harping on her age, Dodd. Do you know her age? If you do, you have the advantage of me. I have not seen her baptismal register. Have you?"

"No, sir, but I know what she says is her age."

"That is only evidence of what is not her age."

"But there is her face, sir; that is evidence."

"You have never seen her face; it is always got up to deceive the public."

"I have seen it at the dawn, before any of you were up."

"What is that? Halo! the deuce—where?"

"In the garden."

"In the garden? Oh, she does not jump off her down-bed on to a flowerbed. She had been an hour at work on that face before ever the sun or you got leave to look on it."

"I'll stake my head I tell her age within a year, Mr. Bazalgette."

"No you will not, nor within ten years."

"That is soon seen. I call her one-and-twenty."

"One-and-twenty! You are mad! Why, she has had a child that would be fifteen now if it had lived."

"Miss Lucy? A child? Fifteen years? What on earth do you mean?"

"What do you mean? What has Miss Lucy to do with it? You know very well it is MY WIFE I am warning you against, not that innocent girl."

At this David burst out in his turn. "YOUR WIFE! and have you so vile an opinion of me as to think I would eat your bread and tempt your wife under your roof. Oh, Mr. Bazalgette, is this the esteem you profess for me?"

"Go to the Devil!" shouted Bazalgette, in double ire at his own blunder and at being taken to task by his own Telemachus; he added, but in a very different tone, "You are too good for this world."

The best things we say miss fire in conversation; only second-rate shots hit the mind through the ear. This, we will suppose, is why David derived no amusement or delectation from Mr. Bazalgette's inadvertent but admirable bon-mot.

"Go to the Devil! you are too good for this world."

He merely rose, and said gravely, "Heaven forgive you your unjust suspicions, and God bless you for your other kindness. Good-by!"

"Why, where on earth are you going?"

"To stow away my things; to pack up, as they call it."

"Come back! come back! why, what a terrible fellow you are; you make no allowances for metaphors. There, forgive me, and shake hands. Now sit down. I esteem you more than ever. You have come down from another age and a much better one than this. Now let us be calm, quiet, sensible, tranquil. Hallo!" (starting up in agitation), "a sudden light bursts on me. You are in love, and not with my wife; then it is my ward."

"It is too late to deny it, sir."

"That is far more serious than the other," said Bazalgette, very gravely; "the old one would have been sure to cure you of your fancy for her, soon or late, but Lucy! Now, just look at that young buffer's eyes glaring at us like a pair of saucers."

"I am not listening, papa; I haven't heard a word you and Mr. Dodd have said about naughty ladies. I have been such a good boy, minding my puzzle."

"I wish he may not have been minding ours instead," muttered his sire, and rang the bell, and ordered the servant to take away Master Reginald and bring coffee.

The pair sipped their coffee in dead silence. It was broken at last by David saying sadly and a little bitterly, "I fear, sir, your good opinion of me does not go the length of letting me come into your family."

The merchant seemed during the last five minutes to have undergone some starching process, so changed was his whole manner now; so distant, dignified and stiff. "Mr. Dodd," said he, "I am in a difficult position. Insincerity is no part of my character. When I say I have a regard for a man, I mean it. But I am the young lady's guardian, sir. She is a minor, though on the verge of her majority, and I cannot advise her to a match which, in the received sense, would be a very bad one for her. On the other hand, there are so many insuperable obstacles between you and her, that I need not combat my personal sentiments so far as to act against you; it would, indeed, hardly be just, as I have surprised your secret unfairly, though with no unfair intention. My promise not to act hostilely implies that I shall not reveal this conversation to Mrs. Bazalgette; if I did I should launch the deadliest of all enemies— irritated vanity—upon you, for she certainly looks on you as her plaything, not her niece's; and you would instantly be the victim of her spite, and of her influence over Lucy, if she discovered you have the insolence to escape her, and pursue another of her sex. I shall therefore keep silence and neutrality. Meantime, in the character, not of her guardian, but of your friend, I do strongly advise you not to think seriously of her. She will never marry you. She is a good, kind, amiable creature, but still she is a girl of the world—has all its lessons at her finger ends. Bless your heart, these meek beauties are as ambitious as Lucifer, and this one's ambition is fed by constant admiration, by daily matrimonial discussions with the old stager, and I believe by a good offer every now and then, which she refuses, because she is waiting for a better. Come, now, it only wants one good wrench—"

David interrupted him mildly: "Then, sir," said he, thoughtfully; "the upshot is that, if she says 'Yes,' you won't say 'No.'"

The mature merchant stared.

"If," said he, and with this short sentence and a sardonic grin he broke off trying

"To fetter flame with flaxen band."

So nothing more was said or done that evening worth recording.

The next day, being the day of the masquerade, was devoted by the ladies to the making, altering, and trying on of dresses in their bedrooms. This turned the downstairs rooms so dark and unlovely that the gentlemen deserted the house one after the other. Kenealy and Talboys rode to see a cricket match ten miles off. Hardie drove into the town of —— and David paced the gravel walk in hopes that by keeping near the house he might find Lucy alone, for he was determined to know his fate and end his intolerable suspense.

He had paced the walk about an hour when fortune seemed to favor his desires. Lucy came out into the garden. David's heart beat violently. To his great annoyance, Mr. Fountain followed her out of the house and called her. She stopped, and he joined her; and very soon uncle and niece were engaged in a conversation which seemed so earnest that David withdrew to another part of the garden not to interfere with them.

He waited, and waited, and waited till they should separate; but no, they walked more and more slowly, and the conversation seemed to deepen in interest. David chafed. If he had known the nature of that conversation he would have writhed with torture as well as fretted with impatience, for there the hand of her he loved was sought in marriage before his eyes, and within a few steps of him. On such threads hangs human life. Had he been at the hall door instead of in the garden, he might have anticipated Mr. Fountain. As it was, Mr. Fountain stole the march on him.

CHAPTER XV.

TO-MORROW Lucy had agreed to sail, and in the boat Mr. Talboys was to ask and win her band. But from the first Mr. Fountain had never a childlike confidence in the scheme, and his understanding kept rebelling more and more.

"'The man that means to pop, pops," said he; "one needn't go to sea—to pop. Terra firma is poppable on, if it is nothing else. These young fellows are like novices with a gun: the bird must be in a position or they can't shoot it—with their pop-guns. The young sparks in my day could pop them down flying. We popped out walking, popped out riding, popped dancing, popped psalm-singing. Talboys could not pop on horseback, because the lady's pony fidgeted, not his. Well, it will be so to-morrow. The boat will misbehave, or the wind will be easterly, and I shall be told southerly is the popping wind. The truth is, he is faint-hearted. His sires conquered England, and he is afraid of a young girl. I'll end this nonsense. He shall pop by proxy."

In pursuance of this resolve, seeing his niece pass through the hall with her garden hat on, he called to her that he would get his hat and join her. They took one turn together almost in silence. Fountain was thinking how he should best open the subject, and Lucy waiting after her own fashion, for she saw by the old man's manner he had something to say to her.

"Lucy, my dear, I leave you in a day or two."

"So soon, uncle."

"And it depends on you whether I am to go away a happy or a disappointed old man."

At these words, to which she was too cautious to reply in words, Lucy wore a puzzled air; but underneath it a keen observer might have noticed her cheek pale a little, a very little, and a quiver of suppressed agitation pass over her like a current of air in summer over a smooth lake.

Receiving no answer, Mr. Fountain went on to remind her that he was her only kinsman, Mrs. Bazalgette being her relation by half-blood only; and told her that, looking on himself as her father, he had always been anxious to see her position in life secured before his own death.

"I have been ambitious for you, my dear," said he, "but not more so than your beauty and accomplishments, and your family name entitle us to be. Well, my ambition for you and my affection for you are both about to be gratified; at least, it now rests with you to gratify them. Will you be Mrs. Talboys?"

Lucy looked down, and said demurely, "What a question for a third person to put!"

"Should I put it if I had not a right?"

"I don't know.'"

"You ought to know, Lucy."

"Mr. Talboys has authorized you, dear?"

"He has.'"

"Then this is a formal proposal from Mr. Talboy's?"

"Of course it is," said the old gentleman, fearlessly, for Lucy's manner of putting these questions was colorless; nobody would have guessed what she was at.

She now drew her arm round her uncle's neck, and kissed him, which made him exult prematurely.

"Then, dear uncle," said she lovingly, "you must tell Mr. Talboys that I thank him for the honor he does me, and that I decline."

"Accept, you mean?"

"No I don't—ha! ha!"

Her laugh died rapidly away at sight of the effect of her words. Mr. Fountain started, and his face turned red and pale alternately.

"Refuse my friend—refuse Talboys in that way? Thoughtless girl, you don't know what you are doing. His family is all but noble. What am I saying? noble? why, half the House of Peers is sprung from the dregs of the people, and got there either by pettifogging in the courts of law, or selling consciences in the Lower House; and of the other half, that are gentlemen of descent, not two in twenty can show a pedigree like Talboys. And with that name a princely mansion—antiquity stamped on it—stands in its own park, in the middle of its vast estates, with title-deeds in black-letter, girl."

"But, uncle, all this is encumbered—"

"It is false, whoever told you so. There is not a mortgage on any part of it—only a few trifling copyholds and pepper-corn rents."

"You misunderstand me; I was going to say, it is encumbered with a gentleman for whom I could never feel affection, because he does not inspire me with respect."

"Nonsense! he inspires universal respect."

"It must be by his estates, then, not his character. You know, uncle, the world is more apt to ask, 'What has he, then what is he?'"

"He is a polished gentleman."

"But not a well-bred one."

"The best bred I ever saw.

"Then you never looked in a glass, dear. No, dear uncle, I will tell you. Mr. Talboys has seen the world, has kept good society, is at his ease (a great point), and is perfect in externals. But his good manners are—what shall I say?—coat deep. His politeness is not proof against temptation, however petty. The reason is, it is only a spurious politeness. Real politeness is founded and built on the golden rule, however delicate and artificial its superstructure may be. But, leaving out of the question the politeness of the heart, he has not in any sense the true art of good-breeding; he has only the common traditions. Put him in a novel situation, with no rules and examples to guide him, he would be maladroit as a school-boy. He is just the counterpart of Mr. Dodd in that respect. Poor Mr. Dodd is always shocking one by violating the commonest rules of society; but every now and then he bursts out with a flash of natural courtesy so bright, so refined, so original, yet so worthy of imitation, that you say to yourself this is genius—the genius of good-breeding."

Mr. Fountain chafed with impatience during this tirade, in which he justly suspected an attempt to fritter away a serious discussion.

"Come off your hobby, Lucy," cried he, "and speak to me like a woman and like my niece. If this is your objection, overcome it for my sake."

"I would, dear," said Lucy, "but it is only one of my objections, and by no means the most serious."

On being invited to come at once to the latter, Lucy hesitated. "Would not that be unamiable on my part? Mr. Talboys has just paid me the highest compliment a gentleman can pay a lady; it is for me to decline him courteously, not abuse him to his friend and representative."

"No humbug, Lucy, if you please; I am in no humor for it."

"We should all be savages without a little of it."

"I am waiting."

"Then pledge me your word of honor no word of what I now say to the disadvantage of poor Mr. Talboys shall ever reach him."

"You may take your oath of that."

"Then he is a detractor, a character I despise."

"Who does he detract from? I never heard him."

"From all his superiors—in other words, from everybody he meets. Did you ever know him fail to sneer at Mr. Hardie?"

"Oh, that is the offense, is it?"

"No, it is the same with others; there, the other day, Mr. Dodd joined us on horseback. He did not dress for the occasion. He had no straps on. He came in a hurry to have our society, not to cut a dash. But there was Mr. Talboys, who can only do this one thing well, and who, thanks to his servant, had straps on, sneering the whole time at Mr. Dodd, who has mastered a dozen far more difficult and more honorable accomplishments than putting on straps and sitting on horses. But he is always backbiting and sneering; he admires nothing and nobody."

"He has admired you ever since he saw you."

"What! has he never sneered at me?"

"Never! ungrateful girl, never."

"How humiliating! He takes me for his inferior. His superiors he always sneers at. If he had seen anything good or spirited in me, he could not have helped detracting from me. Is not this a serious reason—that I despise the person who now solicits my love, honor and obedience? Well, then, there is another—a stronger still. But perhaps you will call it a woman's reason."

"I know. You don't like him—that is, you fancy you don't, and can't."

"No, uncle, it is not that I don't like him. It is that I HATE HIM."

"You hate him?" and Mr. Fountain looked at her to see if it was his niece Lucy who was uttering words so entirely out of character.

"I am but a poor hater. I have but little practice; but, with all the power of hating I do possess, I hate that Mr. Talboys. Oh, how delicious it is to speak one's mind out nice and rudely. It is a luxury I seldom indulge in. Yes, uncle," said Lucy, clinching her white teeth, "I hate that man, and I did hope his proposal would come from himself; then there would have been nothing to alloy my quiet satisfaction at mortifying one who is so ready to mortify others. But no, he has bewitched you; and you take his part, and you look vexed; so all my pleasure is turned to pain."

"It is all self-deception," gasped Fountain, in considerable agitation; "you girls are always deceiving yourselves: you none of you hate any man—unless you love him. He tells me you have encouraged him of late. You had better tell me that is a lie."

"A lie, uncle; what an expression! Mr. Talboys is a gentleman; he would not tell a falsehood, I presume."

"Aha! it is true, then, you have encouraged him?"

"A little."

"There, you see; the moment we come from the generalities to facts, what a simpleton you are proved to be. Come, now, did you or did you not agree to go in a boat with him?"

"I did, dear."

"That was a pretty strong measure, Lucy."

"Very strong, I think. I can tell you I hesitated."

"Now you see how you have mistaken your own feelings."

Lucy hung her head. "Oh uncle, you call me simple—and look at you! fancy not seeing why I agreed to go—dans cette galere. It was that Mr. Talboys might declare himself, and so I might get rid of him forever. I saw that if I could not bring him to the point, he would dangle about me for years, and perhaps, at last, succeed in irritating me to rudeness. But now, of course, I shall stay on shore with my uncle to-morrow. Qu'irais je faire dana cette galere? you have done it all for me. Oh, my dear, dear uncle, I am so grateful to you!"

She showed symptoms of caressing Mr. Fountain, but he recoiled from her angrily. "Viper! but no, this is not you. There is a deeper hand than you in all this. This is that Mrs. Bazalgette's doings."

"No, indeed, uncle."

"Give me a proof it is not."

"With pleasure; any proof that is in my power."

"Then promise me not to marry Mr. Hardie."

"My dear uncle, Mr. Hardie has never asked me."

"But he will."

"What right have I to say so? What right have I to constitute Mr. Hardie my admirer? I would not for all the world put it into any gentleman's power to say, 'Why say "no," Miss Fountain, before I have asked you to say "yes"?' Oh!"

And, with this, Lucy put her face into her hands, but they were not large enough to hide the deep blush that suffused her whole face at the bare idea of being betrayed into an indelicacy of this sort.

"How could he say that? how could he know?" said Mr. Fountain, pettishly.

"Uncle, I cannot, I dare not. You and my aunt hate one another; so you might be tempted to tell her, and she would be sure to tell him. Besides, I cannot; my very instinct revolts from it. It would not be modest. I love you, uncle. Let me know your wishes, and have some faith in my affection, but pray do not press me further. Oh, what have I done, to be spoken of with so many gentlemen!"

Lucy was in evident agitation, and the blushes glowed more and more round her snowy hands and between her delicate fingers; and there is something so sacred about the modesty alarmed of an intelligent young woman—it is a feeling which, however fantastical, is so genuine in her, and so manifestly intense beyond all we can ourselves feel of the kind, that no man who is not utterly stupid or depraved can see it without a certain awe. Even Mr. Fountain, who looked on Lucy's distress as transcendent folly with a dash of hypocrisy, could not go on making her cheek burn so. "There! there!" cried he, "don't torment yourself, Lucy. I will spare your fanciful delicacy, though you have no pity on me—on your poor old uncle, whose heart you will break if you decline this match."

At these words, and the old man's change from anger to sadness, Lucy looked up in dismay, and the vivid color died, like a retiring wave, out of her cheek.

"You look surprised, Lucy. What! do you think this will not be a heartbreaking disappointment to me? If you knew how I have schemed for it—what I have done and endured to bring it about! To quarter the arms of Fontaine and Talboys! I put by the 5,000 pounds directly, and as much more of my own, that you should not go into that noble family without a proper settlement. It was the dream of my heart; I could have died contented the next hour. More fool I to care for anybody but myself. Your selfish people escape these bitter disappointments. Well, it is a lesson. From this hour I will live for myself and care for nobody, for nobody cares for me."

These words, uttered with great agitation, and, I believe, with perfect sincerity, on his own unselfishness and hard fate, were terrible to Lucy. She wreathed her arms suddenly round him.

"Oh, uncle," she cried, despairingly, "kill me! send me to Heaven! send me to my mother, but don't stab me with such bitter words;" and she trembled with an emotion so much more powerful and convulsing than his, in which temper had a large share, that she once more cowed him.

"There! there!" he muttered, "I don't want to kill you, child, God knows, or to hurt you in any way."

Lucy trembled, and tried to smile. The good nature, which was the upper crust of this man's character, got the better of him.

"There! there! don't distress yourself so. I know who I have to thank for all this."

"She has not the power," said Lucy, in a faint voice, "to make me ungrateful to you."

Mind is more rapid than lightning. At this moment, in the middle of a sentence, it flashed across Lucy that her aunt had convinced her, sore against her will, that there was a strong element of selfishness in Mr. Fountain. "But it is that he deceives himself," thought Lucy. "He would sacrifice my happiness to his hobby, and think he has done it for love of me." Enlightened by this rapid reflection, she did not say to him as one of his own sex would, "Look in your own heart, and you will see that all this is not love of me, but of your own schemes." Oh, dear, no, that would not have been the woman. She took him round the neck, and, fixing her sapphire eyes lovingly on his, she said, "It is for love of me you set your heart on this great match? You wish to see me well settled in the world, and, above all, happy?"

"Of course it is. I told you so. What other object can I have?"

"Then, if you saw me wretched, and degraded in my own eyes, your heart would bleed for your poor niece—too late. Well, uncle, I love you, too, and I save you this day from remorse. Oh, think what it must be to hate and despise a man, and link yourself body and soul to that man for life. Oh, think and shudder with me. I have a quick eye. I have seen your lip curl with contempt when that fool has been talking—ah! you blush. You are too much his superior in everything but fortune not to despise him at heart. See the thing as it is. Speak to me as you would if my mother stood here beside us, uncle, and to speak to me, you must look her in the face. Could you say to me before her, 'I love you; marry a man we both despise!'?"

Mr. Fountain made no answer. He was disconcerted. Nothing is so easy to resist as logic solo. We see it, as a general rule, resisted with great success in public and private every day; but when it comes in good company, a voice of music, an angel face, gentle, persuasive caresses, and imploring eyes, it ceases to revolt the understanding. And so, caught in his own trap, foiled, baffled, soothed, caressed, all in one breath, Mr. Fountain hung his head, and could not immediately reply.

Lucy followed up her advantage. "No," cried she; "say to me, 'I love you, Lucy; marry nobody; stay with your uncle, and find your happiness in contributing to his comfort.'"

"What is the use my saying that, when I have got Mother Bazalgette against me, and her shopkeeper?"

"Never mind, uncle, you say it, and time will show whether your influence is small with me, and my affections small for you"; and she looked in his face with glistening eyes.

"Well, then," said he, "I do say it, and I suppose that means I must urge you no more about poor Talboys."

A shower of kisses descended upon him that moment. Moral: Lose no time in sealing a good bargain.

"Come, now, Lucy, you must do me a favor."

"Oh, thank you! thank you! what is it?"

"Ah! but it is about Talboys too."

"Never mind," faltered Lucy, "if it is anything short of—" (full stop).

"It is a long way short of that. Look here, Lucy, I must tell you the truth. He intends to ask your hand himself: he confided this to me, but he never authorized me to commit him as I have done, so that this conversation cannot be acted on: it must be a secret between you and me."

"Oh, dear! and I thought I had got rid of him so nicely."

"Don't be alarmed," groaned Fountain; "such matches as this can always be dropped; the difficulty is to bring them on. All I ask of you, then, is not to make mischief between me and my friend, the proudest man in England. If you don't value his friendship, I do. You must not let him know I have got him insulted by a refusal. For instance, you had better go out sailing with him to-morrow as if nothing had passed. Will your affection for me carry you as far as that?"

The proposal was wormwood to Lucy. So she smiled and said eagerly: "Is that all? Why, I will do it with pleasure, dear. It is not like being in the same boat with him for life, you know. Can you give me nothing more than that to do for you?"

"No; it does not do to test people's affection too severely. You have shown me that. Go on with your walk, Lucy. I shall go in."

"May I not come with you?"

"No; my head aches with all this; if I don't mind I shall eat no dinner. Agitation and vexation, don't agree with me. I have carefully avoided them all my life. I must go in and lie down for an hour"; and he left her rather abruptly.

She looked after him; her subtle eye noticed directly that he walked a little more feebly than usual. She ascribed this to his disappointment, justly perhaps, for at his age the body has less elastic force to resist a mental blow. The sight of him creeping away disappointed, and leaning heavier than usual on his stick, knocked at her cool but affectionate heart. She began to cry bitterly. When he was quite out of sight, she turned and paced the gravel slowly and sadly. It was new to her to refuse her uncle anything, still more strange to have to refuse him a serious wish. She was prepared, thoroughly prepared, for the proposal, but not to find the old man's heart so deeply set upon it. A wild impulse came over her to call him back and sacrifice herself; but the high spirit and intelligence that lay beneath her tenderness and complaisance stood firm. Yet she felt almost guilty, and very, very unhappy, as we call it at her age. She kept sighing; "Poor uncle!" and paced the gravel very slowly, hanging her sweet head, and crying as she went.

At the end of the walk David Dodd stood suddenly before her. He came flurried on his own account, but stopped thunder-struck at her tears. "What is the matter, Miss Lucy?'" said he, anxiously.

"Oh, nothing, Mr. Dodd;" and they flowed afresh.

"Can I do anything for you, Miss Lucy?"

"No, Mr. Dodd."

"Won't you tell me what is the matter? Are you not friends with me to-day?"

"I was put out by a very foolish circumstance, Mr. Dodd, and it is one with which I shall not trouble you, nor any person of sense. I prefer to retain your sympathy by not revealing the contemptible cause of my babyish—There!" She shook her head proudly, as if tears were to be dispersed like dewdrops. "There!" she repeated; and at this second effort she smiled radiantly.

"It is like the sun coming out after a shower," cried David rapturously.

"That reminds me I must be going in, Mr. Dodd."

"Don't say that, Miss Lucy. What for?"

"To arrange another shower, one of pearls, on a dress I am to wear to-night."

David sighed. "Ah! Miss Lucy, at sight of me you always make for the hall door."

Lucy colored. "Oh, do I? I really was not aware of that. Then I suppose I am afraid of you. Is that what you would insinuate? '"

"No, Miss Lucy, you are not afraid of me; but I sometimes fear—" and he hesitated.

"It must blow very hard that day," said Lucy, with a world of politeness. Her tongue was too quick for him. He found it so, and announced the fact after his fashion. "I can't tack fast enough to follow you," said he despondently.

"But you are not required to follow me," replied this amiable eel, with hypocritical benignity; "I am going to my aunt's room to do what I told you. I leave you in charge of the quarter-deck." So saying, she walked slowly up the steps, and left David standing sorrowfully on the gravel. At the top step Miss Lucy turned and inquired gently when he was to sail. He told her the ship was expected to anchor off the fort to-morrow, but she would not sail till she had got all her passengers on board.

"Oh!" said Lucy, with an air of reflection. She then leaned in an easy posture against the wall, and, whether it was that she relented a little, or that, having secured her retreat, she was now indifferent to flight, certain it is that she did after her own fashion what many a daughter of Eve has done before her, and many a duchess and many a dairymaid will do after La Fountain and I are gone from earth. A minute ago it had been, "She must go directly." The more opposition to her departure, the more inexorable the necessity for her going; opposition withdrawn, and the door open, she stayed no end.

Full twenty minutes did that young lady stand there unsolicited, and chat with David Dodd in the kindest, sweetest, most amicable way imaginable.

She little knew she had an auditor—a female auditor, keen as a lynx.

All this day Reginald George Bazalgette, Esq., might have been defined "a pest in search of a playmate." Tom had got a holiday. Lucy only came out of her workshop to be seized by Mr. Fountain. David, who was waiting in the garden for Lucy, begged Reginald to excuse him for once. The young gentleman had recourse as a pis aller to his mamma. He invaded her bedroom, and besought her piteously to play at battledoor. That lady, sighing deeply at being taken from her dress, consented. Her soul not being in it, she played very badly. Her cub did not fail to tell her so. "Why, I can keep up a hundred with Mr. Dodd," said he.

"Oh, we all know Mr. Dodd is perfection," said the lady with a sneer. She was piqued with David. He had gone and left her in a brutal way, to make his apologies to Lucy.

"No, he is not," said Reginald. "I have found him out. He is as unjust as the rest of them."

"Dear me! and, pray, what has he done?"

"I will tell you, mamma, if you will promise not to tell papa, because he told me not to listen, and I didn't listen, mamma, because, you know, a gentleman always keeps his word; but they talked so loud the words would come into my ear; I could not keep them out. Mamma, are there any naughty ladies here?"

"No, my dear."

"Then what did papa mean, warning Mr. Dodd against one?"

Mrs. Bazalgette began to listen as he wished.

"Oh, he called her all the names. He said she was a statue of flirtation."

"Who? Lucy?"

"Lucy? no! the naughty lady—the one that had twelve husbands. He kept warning him, and warning him, and then Mr. Dodd and papa they began to quarrel almost, because Mr. Dodd said the naughty lady was quite young, and papa said she was ever so old. Mr. Dodd said she was twenty-one. But papa told him she must be more than that, because she had a child that would be fifteen years old; only it died. How old would sister Emily be if she was alive, mamma? La, mamma, how pretty you are: you have got red cheeks like Lucy —redder, oh, ever so much redder—and in general they are so pale before dinner. Let me kiss you, mamma. I do love the ladies when their cheeks are red."

"There! there! now go on, dear; tell me some more."

"It is very interesting, isn't it, dear mamma?"

"It is amusing, at all events."

"No, it is not amusing—at least, what came after, isn't: it is wicked, it is unjust, it is abominable."

"Tell me, dear."

"It turned out it wasn't the naughty lady Mr. Dodd was in love for, and who do you think he is in love of?"

"I have not an idea."

"MY LUCY!!!"

"Nonsense, child."

"No, no, mamma, it is not. He owned it plump."

"Are you quite sure, love?"

"Upon my honor."

"What did they say next?"

"Oh, next papa began to talk his fine words that I don't know what the meaning of them is one bit. But Mr. Dodd, he could make them out, I suppose, for he said, 'So, then, the upshot is—' There, now, what is upshot? I don't know. How stupid grown-up people are; they keep using words that one doesn't know the meaning of."

"Never mind, love! tell me. What came after upshot?" said Mrs. Bazalgette, soothingly, with great apparent calmness and flashing eye.

"How kind you are to-day, mamma! That is twice you have called me love, and three times dear; only think. I should love you if you were always so kind, and your cheeks as red as they are now."

"Never mind my cheeks. What did Mr. Dodd say? Try and remember—come —'The upshot was—'"

"The upshot was—what was the upshot? I forget. No, I remember; the upshot was, if Lucy said 'yes,' papa would not say 'no;' that meant to marry him. Now didn't you promise me her ever so long ago—the day you and I agreed if I went a whole day without being naughty once I should have her for ever and ever? and I did go."

"Go to Lucy's room, and tell her to come to me," said Mrs. Bazalgette, in a stern, thoughtful voice, which startled poor Reginald, coming so soon after the calinerie. However, he told her it was no use his going to Lucy's room, for she was out in the garden; he had seen her there walking with Mr. Fountain. Reginald then ran to the window which commanded the garden, to look for Lucy. He had scarcely reached it when he began to squeak wildly, "Come here! come here! come here!" Mrs. Bazalgette was at the window in a moment, and lo! at the end of the garden, walking slowly side by side, were Lucy and Mr. Dodd.

Ridiculous as it may appear, a pang of jealousy shot through the married flirt's heart that made her almost feel sick. This was followed at the interval of half a second by as pretty a flame of hatred as ever the spretoe injuria formoe lighted up in a coquette's heart. Doubt drove in its smaller sting besides, and at sight of the couple she resolved to have better evidence than Reginald's, especially as to Lucy's sentiments. The plan she hit upon was effective, but vulgar, and must not be witnessed by a boy of inconvenient memory and mistimed fluency. She got rid of him with high-principled dexterity. "Reginald," said she, sadly, "you are a naughty boy, a disobedient boy, to listen when your papa told you not, and to tell me a pack of falsehoods. I must either tell your papa, or I must punish you myself; I prefer to do it myself, he would whip you so"; with this she suddenly opened her dressing-room door, and pushed the terrible infant in, and locked the door. She then told him through the keyhole he had better cease yelling, because, if he kept quiet, his punishment would only last half an hour, and she flew downstairs. There was a large hot-house with two doors, one of which came very near to the house door that opened into the garden. Mrs. Bazalgette entered the hothouse at the other end, and, hidden by the exotic trees and flowers, made rapidly for the door Lucy and David must pass. She found it wide open. She half shut it, and slipped behind it, listening like a hare and spying like a hawk through the hinges. And, strange as it may appear, she had an idea she should make a discovery. As the finished sportsman watches a narrow ride in the wood, not despairing by a snap-shot to bag his hare as she crosses it, though seen but for a moment, so the Bazalgette felt sure that, as the couple passed her ambush, something, either in the two sentences they might utter, or, more probably, in their tones and general manner, would reveal to one of her experience on what footing they were.

A shrewd calculation! But things will be things. They take such turns, I might without exaggeration say twists, that calculation is baffled, and prophecy dissolved into pitch and toss. This thing turned just as not expected. Primo, instead of getting only a snap-shot, Mrs. Bazalgette heard every word of a long conversation; and, secundo, when she had heard it she could not tell for certain on what footing the lady and gentleman were. At first, from their familiarity, she inclined to think they were lovers; but, the more she listened, the more doubtful she seemed. Lucy was the chief speaker, and what she said showed an undisguised interest in her companion; but the subject accounted in great measure for that; she was talking of his approaching voyage, of the dangers and hardships of his profession, and of his return two years hence, his chances of promotion, etc. But here was no proof positive of love; they were acquaintances of some standing. Then Lucy's manner struck her as rather amicable than amorous. She was calm, kind, self-possessed, and almost voluble. As for David, he only got in a word here and there. When he did, there was something so different in his voice from anything he had ever bestowed on her, that she hated him, and longed to stick scissors into him from the rear, unseen. At last Lucy suddenly recollected, or seemed to recollect, she was busy, and retired hastily—so hastily that David saw too late his opportunity lost. But the music of her voice had so charmed him that he did not like to interrupt it even to speak of that which was nearest his heart. David sighed deeply, standing there alone.

Mrs. Bazalgette clinched her little fists and looked round for the means of vengeance. David went down on his knees. La Bazalgette glared through the crack, and wondered what on earth he was at now. Oh! he was praying. "He loves her: he is eccentricity itself; so he is praying for her, and on mydoorsteps" (the householder wounded as well as the flirt). It was lucky she had not "a thunderbolt in her eye"—Shakespeare, or a celestial messenger of the wrong sort would have descended on the devout mariner. It was more than

Mrs. Bazalgette could bear: she had now and then, not often, unladylike impulses. One of them had set her crouching behind the door of an outhouse, and listening through a crack; and now she had another, an irresistible one: it was, to take that empty flower-pot, fling it as hard as ever she could at the devotee, then shut the door quick, fly out at the other door, and leave her faithless swain in the agony of knowing himself detected and exposed by some unknown and undiscoverable enemy.

For a vengeance extemporized in less than half a second this was very respectable. Well, she clawed the flower-pot noiselessly, put her other hand on the door, cast a hasty glance at the means of retreat, and—things took another twist: she heard the rustle of a coming gown, and drew back again, and out came Lucy, and nearly ran over David, who was not on his knees after all, but down on his nose, prostrate Orientally. The fact is, Lucy, among her other qualities, good and bad, was a born housewife, and solicitously careful of certain odds and ends called property. She found she had dropped one of her gloves in the garden, and she came back in a state of disproportionate uneasiness to find it, and nearly ran over David Dodd.

"What are you doing, Mr. Dodd?"

David arose from his Oriental position, and, being a young man whose impulse always was to tell the simple truth, replied, "I was kissing the place where you stood so long."

He did not feel he had done anything extraordinary, so he gave her this information composedly; but her face was scarlet in an instant; and he, seeing that, began to blush too. For once Lucy's tact was baffled; she did not know what on earth to say, and she stood blushing like a girl of fifteen.

Then she tried to turn it off.

"Mr. Dodd, how can you be so ridiculous?" said she, affecting humorous disdain.

But David was not to be put down now; he was launched.

"I am not ridiculous for loving and worshiping you, for you are worthy of even more love than any human heart can hold."

"Oh, hush, Mr. Dodd. I must not hear this."

"Miss Lucy, I can't keep it any longer—you must, you shall hear me. You can despise my love if you will, but you shall know it before you reject it."

"Mr. Dodd, you have every right to be heard, but let me persuade you not to insist. Oh, why did I come back?"

"The first moment I saw you, Miss Lucy, it was a new life to me. I never looked twice at any girl before. It is not your beauty only—oh, no! it is your goodness—goodness such as I never thought was to be found on earth. Don't turn your head from me; I know my defects; could I look on you and not see them? My manners are blunt and rude—oh, how different from yours! but you could soon make me a fine gentleman, I love you so. And I am only the first mate of an Indiaman; but I should be a captain next voyage, Miss Lucy, and a sailor like me has no expenses; all he has is his wife's. The first lady in the land will not be petted as you will, if you will look kindly on me. Listen to me," trying to tempt her. "No, Miss Lucy, I have nothing to offer you worth your acceptance, only my love. No man ever loved woman as I love you; it is not love, it is worship, it is adoration! Ah! she is going to speak to me at last!"

Lucy presented at this moment a strange contrast of calmness and agitation. Her bosom heaved quickly, and she was pale, but her voice was calm, and, though gentle, decided.

"I know you love me, Mr. Dodd, and I feared this. I have tried to save you the mortification of being declined by one who, in many things, is your inferior. I have even been rude and unkind to you. Forgive me for it. I meant it kindly. I regret it now. Mr. Dodd, I thank you for the honor you do me, but I cannot accept your love." There was a pause, but David's tongue seemed glued to the roof of his mouth. He was not surprised, yet he was stupefied when the blow came.

At last he gasped out, "You love some other man?"

Lucy was silent.

"Answer me, for pity's sake; give me something to help me."

"You have no right to ask me such a question, but—I have no attachment, Mr. Dodd."

"Ah! then one word more. Is it because you cannot love me, or because I am poor, and only first mate of an Indiaman?"

"That I will not answer. You have no right to question a lady why she—Stay! you wish to despise me. Well, why not, if that will cure you of this unfortunate —Think what you please of me, Mr. Dodd," murmured Lucy, sadly.

"Ah! you know I can't," cried David, despairingly.

"I know that you esteem me more than I deserve. Well, I esteem you, Mr. Dodd. Why, then, can we not be friends? You have only to promise me you will never return to this subject—come!"

"Me promise not to love you! What is the use? Me be your friend, and nothing more, and stand looking on at the heaven that is to be another's, and never to be mine? It is my turn to decline. Never. Betrothed lovers or strangers, but nothing between! It would drive me mad. Away from you, and out of sight of your sweet face, I may make shift to live, and go through my duty somehow, for my mother's and sister's sake."

"You are wiser than I was, Mr. Dodd. Yes, we must part."

"Of course we must. I have got my answer, and a kinder one than I deserve; and now what is the polite thing for me to do, I wonder?" David said this with terrible bitterness.

"You frighten me," sighed Lucy.

"Don't you be frightened, sweet angel; there! I have been used to obey orders all my life, and I am like a ship tossed in the breakers, and you are calm—calm as death. Give me my orders, for God's sake."

"It is not for me to command you, Mr. Dodd. I have forfeited that right. But listen to her who still asks to be your friend, and she will tell you what will be best for you, and kindest and most generous to her."

"Tell me about that last; the other is a waste of words."

"I will, then. Your sister is somewhere in the neighborhood."

"She is at ——; how did you know?"

"I saw her on your arm. I am glad she is so near—Oh, so glad! Bid my uncle and aunt good-by; make some excuse. Go to your sister at once. She loves you. She is better than I am, if you will but see us as we really are. Go to her at once," faltered Lucy, who disliked Eve, and Eve her.

"I will! I will! I have thought too little of my own flesh and blood. Shall I go now?"

"Yes," murmured Lucy softly, trying to disarm the fatal word. "Forget me—and—forgive me!" and, with this last word scarce audible, she averted her face, and held out her hand with angelic dignity, modesty and pity.

The kind words and the gentle action brought down the stout heart that had looked death in the face so often without flinching. "Forgive you, sweet angel!" he cried; "I pray Heaven to bless you, and to make you as happy as I am desolate for your sake. Oh, you show me more and more what I lose this day. God bless you! God bless—" and David's heart filled to choking, and he burst out sobbing despairingly, and the hot tears ran suddenly from his eyes over her hand as he kissed and kissed it. Then, with an almost savage feeling of shame (for these were not eyes that were wont to weep), he uttered one cry of despair and ran away, leaving her pale and panting heavily.

She looked piteously at her hand, wet with a hero's tears, and for the second time to-day her own began to gush. She felt a need of being alone. She wanted to think on what she had done. She would hide in the garden. She ran down the steps; lo! there was Mr. Hardie coming up the gravel-walk. She uttered a little cry of impatience, and dashed impetuously into the hot-house, driving the half-open door before her with her person as well as her arm.

A scream of terror and pain issued from behind it, with a crash of pottery.

Lucy wheeled round at the sound, and there was her aunt, flattened against the flower-frame.

Lucy stood transfixed.

But soon her look of surprise gave way to a frown; ay! and a somber one.

CHAPTER XVI.

THAT ready-minded lady extricated herself from the pots, and wriggled out of the moral situation. "I was a listener, dear! an unwilling listener; but now I do not regret it. How nobly you behaved!" and with this she came at her with open arms, crying, "My own dear niece."

Her own dear niece recoiled with a shiver, and put up both her hands as a shield.

"Oh, don't touch me, please. I never heard of a lady listening!!!!"

She then turned her back on her aunt in a somewhat uncourtier-like manner, and darted out of the place, every fiber of her frame strung up tight with excitement. She felt she was not the calm, dispassionate being of yesterday, and hurried to her own room and locked herself in.

Mrs. Bazalgette remained behind in a state of bitter mortification, and breathing fury on her small scale. But what could she do? David would be out of her reach in a few minutes, and Lucy was scarce vulnerable.

In the absence of any definite spite, she thought she could not go wrong in thwarting whatever Lucy wished, and her wish had been that David should go. Besides, if she kept him in the house, who knows, she might pique him with Lucy, and even yet turn him her way; so she lay in wait for him in the hall. He soon appeared with his bag in his hand. She inquired, with great simplicity, where he was going. He told her he was going away. She remonstrated, first tenderly, then almost angrily. "We all counted on you to play the violin. We can't dance to the piano alone."

"I am very sorry, but I have got my orders." Then this subtle lady said, carelessly, "Lucy will be au desespoir. She will get no dancing. She said to me just now, 'Aunt, do try and persuade Mr. Dodd to stay over the ball. We shall miss him so.'"

"When did she say that?"

"Just this minute. Standing at the door there."

"Very well; then I'll stay over the ball." And without a word more he carried his bag and violin-case up to his room again. Oh, how La Bazalgette hated him! She now resigned all hope of fighting with him, and contented herself with the pleasure of watching him and Lucy together. One would be wretched, and the other must be uncomfortable.

Lucy did not come down to dinner; she was lying down with headache. She even sent a message to Mrs. Bazalgette to know whether she could be dispensed with at the ball. Answer, "Impossible!" At half-past eight she got up, put on her costume, took it off again, and dressed in white watered silk. Her assumption of a character was confined to wearing a little crown rising to a peak in front. Many of the guests had arrived when she glided into the room looking every inch a queen. David was dazzled at her, and awestruck at her beauty and mien, and at his own presumption.

Her eye fell on him. She gave a little start, but passed on without a word. The carpets had been taken up, and the dancing began.

Mrs. Bazalgette arranged that Lucy and David should play pianoforte and violin until some lady could be found to take her part.

I incline to think Mrs. Bazalgette, spiteful as mortified vanity is apt to be, did not know the depth of anguish her subtle vengeance inflicted on David Dodd.

He was pale and stern with the bitter struggle for composure. He ground his teeth, fixed his eyes on the music-book, and plowed the merry tunes as the fainting ox plows the furrow. He dared not look at Lucy, nor did he speak to her more than was necessary for what they were doing, nor she to him. She was vexed with him for subjecting himself and her to unnecessary pain, and in the eye of society—her divinity.

Another unhappy one was Mr. Fountain. He sat disconsolate on a seat all alone. Mrs. Bazalgette fluttered about like a butterfly, and sparkled like a Chinese firework.

Two young ladies, sisters, went to the piano to give Miss Fountain an opportunity of dancing. She danced quadrilles with four or five gentlemen, including her special admirers. She declined to waltz: "I have a little headache; nothing to speak of."

She then sat down to the piano again. "I can play alone, Mr. Dodd; you have not danced at all."

"I am not in the humor."

"Very well."

This time they played some of the tunes they had rehearsed together that happy evening, and David's lip quivered.

Lucy eyed him unobserved.

"Was this wise—to subject yourself to this?"

"I must obey orders, whatever it costs me—'ri tum ti tum ti tum ti tum.'"

"Who ordered you to neglect my advice?—'ri tum tum tum.'"

"You did—'ri tum ti tum tiddy iddy.'"

A look of silent disdain: "Ri tum, ti tum, tiddy iddy." (Ah! perdona for relating things as they happen, and not as your grand writers pretend they happen.)

Between the quadrilles she asked an explanation.

"Your aunt met me with my bag in my hand, and told me you wanted me to play to the company."

When he said this, David heard a sound like the click of a trigger. He looked up; it was Lucy clinching her teeth convulsively. But time was up: the woman of the world must go on like the prizefighter. The couples were waiting.

"Ri tum ti tum ti tum ti tum tiddy iddy." For all that, she did not finish the tune. In the middle of it she said to David, "'Ri tum ti tum—' can you get through this without me?—'ri tum.'"

"If I can get through life without you, I can surely get through this twaddle: 'ri tum ti tum ti tum ti tum tiddy iddy.'" Lucy started from her seat, leaving David plowing solo. She started from her seat and stood a moment, looking like an angel stung by vipers. Her eye went all round the room in one moment in search of some one to blight. It surprised Mr. Hardie and Mrs. Bazalgette sitting together and casting ironical glances pianoward: "So she has been betraying to Mr. Hardie the secret she gained by listening," thought Lucy. The pair were probably enjoying David's mortification, his misery.

She walked very slowly down the room to this couple. She looked them long and full in the face with that confronting yet overlooking glance which women of the world can command on great occasions. It fell, and pressed on them both like lead, they could not have told you why. They looked at one another ruefully when she had passed them, and then their eyes followed her. They saw her walk straight up to her uncle, and sit down by him, and take his hand. They exchanged another uneasy look.

"Uncle," said Lucy, speaking very quickly, "you are unhappy. I am the cause. I am come to say that I promise you not to marry anyone my aunt shall propose to me."

"My dear girl, then you won't marry that shopkeeper there?"

"What need of names, still less of epithets? I will marry no friend of hers."

"Ah! now you are my brother's daughter again."

"No, I love you no better than I did this morning; but the—"

Celestial happiness diffused itself over old Fountain's face, and Lucy glided back to the piano just as the quadrille ended.

"Give me your arm, Mr. Dodd," said she, authoritatively. She took his arm, and made the tour of the room leaning on him, and chatting gayly.

She introduced him to the best people, and contrived to appear to the whole room joyous and flattered, leaning on David's arm.

The young fellows envied him so.

Every now and then David felt her noble white arm twitch convulsively, and her fingers pinch the cloth of his sleeve where it was loose.

She guided him to the supper-room. It was empty. "Oblige me with a glass of water."

He gave it her. She drank it.

"Mr. Dodd, the advice I gave you with my own lips I never retracted. My aunt imposed upon you. It was done to mortify you. It has failed, as you may have observed. My head aches so, it is intolerable. When they ask you where I am, say I am unwell, and have retired to my room. I shall not be at breakfast; directly after breakfast go to your sister, and tell her your friend Lucy declined you, though she knows your value, and would not let you be mortified by nullities and heartless fools. Good-by, Mr. Dodd; try and believe that none of us you leave in this house are worth remembering, far less regretting."

She vanished haughtily; David crept back to the ball-room. It seemed dark by comparison now she who lent it luster was gone. He stayed a few minutes, then heavy-hearted to bed.

The next morning he shook hands with Mr. Bazalgette, the only one who was up, kissed the terrible infant, who, suddenly remembering his many virtues, formally forgave him his one piece of injustice, and, as he came, so he went away, his bag on his shoulder and his violin-case in his hand.

He went to Cousin Mary and asked for Eve. Cousin Mary's face turned red: "You will find her at No. 80 in this street. She is gone into lodgings." The fact is, the cousins had had a tiff, and Eve had left the house that moment.

Oh! my sweet, my beloved heroines—you young vipers, when will you learn to be faultless, like other people? You have turned my face into a peony, blushing for you at every fourth page.

David came into her apartment. He smiled sweetly, but sadly. "Well, it is all over. I have offered, and been declined."

At seeing him so quiet and resigned, Eve burst out crying.

"Don't you cry, dear," said David. "It is best so. It is almost a relief. Anything before the suspense I was enduring."

Then Eve, recovering her spirits by the help of anger, began to abuse Lucy for a cold-hearted, deceitful girl; but David stopped her sternly.

"Not a word against her—not a word. I should hate anyone that miscalled her. She speaks well of you, Eve; why need you speak ill of her? She and I parted friends, and friends let us be. There is no hate can lie alongside love in a true heart. No, let nobody speak of her at all to me. I shan't; my thoughts, they are my own. 'Go to your sister,' said she, and here I am; and I beg your pardon, Eve, for neglecting you as I have of late."

"Oh, never mind that, David; our affection will outlast this folly many a long year."

"Please God! Your hand in mine, Eve, my lamb, and let us talk of ourselves and mother: the time is short."

They sat hand in hand, and never mentioned Lucy's name again; and, strange to say, it was David who consoled Eve; for, now the battle was lost, her spirit seemed to have all deserted her, and she kept bursting out crying every now and then irrelevantly.

It was three in the afternoon. David was sitting by the window, and Eve packing his chest in the same room, not to be out of his sight a minute, when suddenly he started up and cried, "There she is," and an instinctive unreasonable joy illumined his face; the next moment his countenance fell.

The carriage passed down the street.

"I remember now," muttered David, "I heard she was to go sailing, and Mr. Talboys was to be skipper of the boat. Ah! well."

"Well, let them sail, David. It is not your business."

"That it is not, Eve—nobody's less than mine.

"Eve, there is plenty of wind blowing up from the nor'east."

"Is there? I am afraid that will bring your ship down quick."

"Yes; but it is not that. I am afraid that lubber won't think of looking to windward."

"Nonsense about the wind; it is a beautiful day. Come, David, it is no use lighting against nature. Put on your hat, then, and run down to the beach, and see the last of her; only, for my sake, don't let the others see you, to jeer you."

"No, no."

"And mind and be back to dinner at four. I have got a nice roast fowl for you."

"Ay ay."

A little before four o'clock a sailor brought a note from David, written hastily in pencil. It was sent up to Eve. She read it, and clasped her hands vehemently.

"Oh, David, she was born to be your destruction."

CHAPTER XVII.

MR. FOUNTAIN, Miss Fountain, and Mr. Talboys started to go on the boating expedition. As they were getting into the boat, Mr. Fountain felt a little ill, and begged to be excused. Mr. Talboys offered to return with him. He declined: "Have your little sail. I will wait at the inn for you."

This pantomime had, I blush to say, been arranged beforehand. Miss Fountain, we may be sure, saw through it, but she gave no sign. A lofty impassibility marked her demeanor, and she let them do just what they liked with her.

The boat was launched, the foresail set, and Fountain remained on shore in anything but a calm and happy state.

But friendships like these are not free from dross; and I must confess that among the feelings which crossed his mind was a hope that Talboys would pop, and be refused, as he had been. Why should he, Fountain, monopolize defeat? We should share all things with a friend.

Meantime, by one of those caprices to which her sex are said to be peculiarly subject, Lucy seemed to have given up all intention of carrying out her plan for getting rid of Mr. Talboys. Instead of leading him on to his fate, she interposed a subtle but almost impassable barrier between him and destruction; her manner and deportment were of a nature to freeze declarations of love upon the human lip. She leaned back languidly and imperially on the luxurious cushions, and listlessly eyed the sky and the water, and ignored with perfect impartiality all the living creatures in the boat.

Mr. Talboys endeavored in vain to draw her out of this languid mood. He selected an interesting subject of conversation to—himself; he told her of his feats yachting in the Mediterranean; he did not tell her, though, that his yacht was sailed by the master and not by him, her proprietor. In reply to all this Lucy dropped out languid monosyllables.

At last Talboys got piqued and clapped on sail.

There had not been a breath of air until half an hour before they started; but now a stiff breeze had sprung up; so they had smooth water and yet plenty of wind, and the boat cut swiftly through-the bubbling water.

"She walks well," said the yachtsman.

Lucy smiled a gracious, though still rather too queenly assent. I think the motion was pleasing her. Lively motion is very agreeable to her sex.

"This is a very fast boat," said Mr. Talboys. "I should like to try her speed. What do you say, Miss Fountain?"

"With all my heart," said Lucy, in a tone that expressed her utter indifference.

"Here is this lateen-rigged boat creeping down on our quarter; we will stand east till she runs down to us, and then we will run by her and challenge her." Accordingly Talboys stood east.

But he did not get his race; for, somewhat to his surprise, the lateen-rigged boat, instead of holding her course, which was about south-southwest, bore up directly and stood east, keeping about half a mile to windward of Talboys.

This puzzled Talboys. "They are afraid to try it," said he. "If they are afraid of us sailing on a wind, they would not have much chance with us in beating to windward. A lugger can lie two points nearer the wind than a schooner."

All this science was lost on Lucy. She lay back languid and listless.

Mr. Talboy's crew consisted of a man and a boy. He steered the boat himself. He ordered them to go about and sail due west. It was no sooner done than, lo and behold, the schooner came about and sailed west, keeping always half a mile to windward.

"That boat is following us, Miss Fountain."

"What for?" inquired she; "is it my uncle coming after us?"

"No; I see no one aboard but a couple of fishermen."

"They are not fishermen," put in the boy; "they are sailors—coastguard men, likely."

"Besides," said Mr. Talboys, "your uncle would run down to us at once, but these keep waiting on us and dogging us. Confound their impudence."

"It is all fancy," said Lucy; "run away as fast as you can that way," and she pointed down the wind, "and you will see nobody will take the trouble to run after us."

"Hoist the mainsail," cried Talboys.

They had hitherto been sailing under the foresail only. In another minute they were running furiously before the wind with both sails set. The boat yawed, and Lucy began to be nervous; still, the increased rapidity of motion excited her agreeably. The lateen-schooner, sailing under her fore-sail only, luffed directly and stood on in the lugger's wake. Lucy's cheek burned, but she said nothing.

"There," cried Talboys, "now do you believe me? I think we gain on her, though."

"We are going three knots to her two, sir," said the old man, "but it is by her good will; that is the fastest boat in the town, sailing on a wind; at beating to windward we could tackle her easy enough, but not at running free. Ah! there goes her mainsel up; I thought she would not be long before she gave us that."

"Oh, how beautiful!" cried Lucy; "it is like a falcon or an eagle sailing down on us; it seems all wings. Why don't we spread wings too and fly away?"

"You see, miss," explained the boatman, "that schooner works her sails different from us; going down wind she can carry her mainsel on one side of the craft and her foresel on the other. By that she keeps on an even keel, and, what is more, her mainsel does not take the wind out of her foresel. Bless you, that little schooner would run past the fastest frigate in the king's service with the wind dead aft as we have got it now; she is coming up with us hand over head, and as stiff on her keel as a rock; this is her point of sailing, beating to windward is ours. Why, if they ain't reefing the foresel, to make the race even; and there go three reefs into her mainsel too." The old boatman scratched his head.

"Who is aboard her, Dick? they are strangers to me."

By taking in so many reefs the lateen had lowered her rate of sailing, and she now followed in their wake, keeping a quarter of a mile to windward.

Talboys lost all patience. "Who is it, I wonder, that has the insolence to dog us so?" and he looked keenly at Miss Fountain.

She did not think herself bound to reply, and gazed with a superior air of indifference on the sky and the water.

"I will soon know," said Talboys.

"What does it matter?" inquired Lucy. "Probably somebody who is wasting his time as we are."

"The road we are on is as free to him as to us," suggested the old boatman, with a fine sense of natural justice. He added, "But if you will take my advice, sir, you will shorten sail, and put her about for home. It is blowing half a gale of wind, and the sea will be getting up, and that won't be agreeable for the young lady."

"Gale of wind? Nonsense," said Talboys; "it is a fine breeze."

"Oh, thank you, sir," said Lucy to the old man; "I love the sea, but I should not like to be out in a storm."

The old boatman grinned. "'Storm is a word that an old salt reserves for one of those hurricanes that blow a field of turnips flat, and teeth down your throat. You can turn round and lean your back against it like a post; and a carrion-crow making for the next parish gets fanned into another county. That is a storm."

The old boatman went forward grinning, and he and his boy lowered the mainsail. Then Talboys at the helm brought the boat's head round to the wind. She came down to her bearings directly, which is as much as to say that to Lucy she seemed to be upsetting.

Lucy gave a little scream. The sail, too, made a report like the crack of a pistol.

"Oh, what is that?" cried Lucy.

"Wind, mum," replied the boatman, composedly.

"What is that purple line on the water, sir, out there, a long way beyond the other boat?

"Wind, mum."

"It seems to move. It is coming this way."

"Ay, mum, that is a thing that always makes to leeward," said the old fellow, grinning. "I'll take in a couple of reefs before it comes to us."

Meantime, the moment the lugger lowered her mainsail, the schooner, divining, as it appeared, her intention, did the same, and luffed immediately, and was on the new tack first of the two.

"Ay, my lass," said the old boatman, "you are smartly handled, no doubt, but your square stern and your try-hanglar sail they will take you to leeward of us pretty soon, do what you can."

The event seemed to justify this assertion; the little lugger was on her best point of sailing, and in about ten minutes the distance between the two boats was slightly but sensibly diminished. The lateen, no doubt, observed this, for she began to play the game of short tacks, and hoisted her mainsail, and carried on till she seemed to sail on her beam-ends, to make up, as far as possible, by speed and smartness for what she lost by rig in beating to windward.

"They go about quicker than we do," said Talboys.

"Of course they do; they have not got to dip their sail, as we have, every time we tack."

This was the true solution, but Mr. Talboys did not accept it.

"We are not so smart as we ought to be. Now you go to the helm, and I and the boy will dip the lug."

The old boatman took the helm as requested, and gave the word of command to Mr. Talboys. "Stand by the foretack."

"Yes," said Mr. Talboys, "here I am."

"Let go the fore-tack"; and, contemporaneously with the order, he brought the boat's head round.

Now this operation is always a nice one, particularly in these small luggers, where the lug has to be dipped, that is to say, lowered, and raised again on the opposite side of the mast; for the lug should not be lowered a moment too soon, or the boat, losing her way, would not come round; nor a moment too late, lest the sail, owing to the new position the boat is taking under the influence of the rudder, should receive the wind while between the wind and the mast, and so the craft be taken aback, than which nothing can well happen more disastrous.

Mr. Talboys, though not the accomplished sailor he thought himself, knew this as well as anybody, and with the boy's help he lowered the sail at the right moment; but, getting his head awkwardly in the way, the yard, in coming down, hit him on the nose and nearly knocked him on to his beam-ends. It would have been better if it had done so quite instead of bounding off his nose on to his shoulder and there resting; for, as it was, the descent of the sail being thus arrested half-way at the critical moment, and the boat's head coming round all the same, a gust of wind caught the sail and wrapped it tight round the mast to windward. The boy uttered a cry of terror so significant that Lucy trembled all over, and by an uncontrollable impulse leaned despairingly back and waved her white handkerchief toward the antagonist boat. The old boatman with an oath darted forward with an agility he could not have shown ashore.

The effect on the craft was alarming. If the whole sail had been thus taken aback, she would have gone down like lead; for, as it was, she was driven on her side and at the same time driven back by the stern; the whole sea seemed to rise an inch above her gunwale; the water poured into her at every drive the gusts of wind gave her, and the only wonder seemed why the waves did not run clean over her.

In vain the old boatman, cursing and swearing, tugged at the canvas to free it from the mast. It was wrapped round it like Dejanira's shirt, and with as fatal an effect; the boat was filling; and as this brought her lower in the water, and robbed her of much of her buoyancy, and as the fatal cause continued immovable, her destruction was certain.

Every cheek was blanched with fear but Lucy's, and hers was red as fire ever since she waved her handkerchief; so powerful is modesty with her sex. A true virgin can blush in death's very grasp.

In the midst of this agitation and terror, suddenly the boat was hailed. They all looked up, and there was the lateen coming tearing down on them under all her canvas, both her broad sails spread out to the full, one on each side. She seemed all monstrous wing. The lugger being now nearly head to wind, she came flying down on her weather bow as if to run past her, then, lowering her foresail, made a broad sweep, and brought up suddenly between the lugger and the wind. As her foresail fell, a sailor bounded over it on to the forecastle, and stood there with one foot on the gunwale, active as Mercury, eye glowing, and a rope in his hand.

"Stand by to lower your mast," roared this sailor in a voice of thunder to the boatman of the lugger; and the moment the schooner came up into the wind athwart the lugger's bows he bounded over ten feet of water into her, and with a turn of the hand made the rope fast to her thwart, then hauling upon it, brought her alongside with her head literally under the schooner's wing.

He and the old boatman then instantly unstepped the mast and laid it down in the boat, sail and all. It was not his great strength that enabled them to do this (a dozen of him could not have done it while the wind pressed on the mast); it was his address in taking all the wind out of the lug by means of the schooner's mainsail. The old man never said a word till the work was done; then he remarked, "That was clever of you."

The new-comer took no notice whatever. "Reef that sail, Jack," he cried; "it will be in the lady's face by and by; and heave your bailer in here; their boat is full of water."

"Not so full as it would if you hadn't brought up alongside," said the old boatman.

"Do you want to frighten the lady?" replied the sailor, in his driest and least courtier-like way.

"I am not frightened, Mr. Dodd," said Lucy. "I was, but I am not now."

"Come and help me get the water out of her, Jack. Stay! Miss Fountain had better step into the dry boat, meantime. Now, Jack, look alive; lash her longside aft."

This done, the two sailors, one standing on the lugger's gunwale, one on the schooner's, handed Miss Fountain into the schooner, and gave her the cushions of the lugger to sit upon. They then went to work with a will, and bailed half a ton of water out.

When she was dry David jumped back into his own boat. "Now, Miss Fountain, your boat is dry, but the sea is getting up, and I think, if I were you, I would stay where you are."

"I mean to," said the lady, calmly. "Mr. Talboys, would you mind coming into this boat? We shall be safer here; it—it is larger."

The gentleman thus addressed was embarrassed between two mortifications, one on each side him. If he came into David's boat he would be second fiddle, he who had gone out of port first fiddle. If he stuck to the lugger Lucy would go off with Dodd, and he would look like a fool coming ashore without her. He hesitated.

David got impatient. "Come, sir," he cried, "don't you hear the lady invite you? and every moment is precious." And he held out his hand to him.

Talboys decided on taking it, and he even unbent so far as to jump vigorously —so vigorously that, David pulling him with force at the same moment, he came flying into the schooner like a cannon-ball, and, toppling over on his heels, went down on the seat with his head resting on the weather gunwale, and his legs at a right angle with his back.

"That is one way of boarding a craft," muttered David, a little discontentedly; then to the old boatman: "Here, fling us that tarpaulin. I say, here is more wind coming; are you sure you can work that lugger, you two?"

"We will be ashore before you can, now there's nobody to bother us," was the prompt reply.

"Then cast loose; here we are, drifting out to sea."

The old man cast the rope loose; David hauled it on board, and the schooner shot away from her companion and bore up north-north-west, leaving the luggar rocking from side to side on the rising waves. But the next minute Lucy saw her sail rise, and she bore up and stood northeast.

"Good-by to you, little horror," said Lucy.

"We shall fall in with her a good many times more before we make the land," said David Dodd.

Lucy inquired what he meant; but he had fallen to hauling the sheet aft and making the sail stand flatter, and did not answer her. Indeed, he seemed much more taken up with Jack than with her, and, above all, entirely absorbed in the business of sailing the boat.

She was a little mortified at this behavior, and held her tongue. Talboys was sulky, and held his. It was a curious situation. In the hurry and bustle, none of the parties had realized it; but now, as the boat breasted the waves, and all was silent on board, they had time to review their position.

Talboys grew gloomier and gloomier at the poor figure he cut. Lucy kept blushing at intervals as she reflected on the obligation she had laid herself under to a rejected lover. The rejected lover alone seemed to mind his business and nothing else; and, as he was almost ludicrously unconscious that he was doing a chivalrous action, a misfortune to which those who do these things are singularly liable, he did not gild the transaction with a single graceful speech, and permitted himself to be more occupied with the sails than with rescued beauty.

Succeeding events, however, explained, and in some degree excused, this commonplace behavior.

The next time they tacked some spray came flying in, and wetted all hands. Lucy laughed. The lugger had also tacked, and the two boats were now standing toward each other; when they met the lugger had weathered on them some sixty or seventy yards.

A furious rain now came on almost horizontally, and the sailors arranged the tarpaulin so as to protect Mr. Talboys and Miss Fountain.

"But you will be wet through yourself, Mr. Dodd. Will you not come under shelter too?"

"And who is to sail the boat?" He added, "I am glad to see the rain. I hope it will still the wind; if it doesn't, we shall have to try something else, that is all."

"Pray, when do you undertake to land us, Mr. Dodd?" inquired Mr. Talboys, superciliously.

"Well, sir, if it does not blow any harder, about eight bells."

"Eight bells? Why, that means midnight," exclaimed Talboys.

"Wind and tide both dead against us," replied David, coolly.

"Oh, Mr. Dodd, tell me the truth: is there any danger?"

"Danger? Not that I see; but it is very uncomfortable, and unbecoming, for you to be beating to windward against the tide for so many hours, when you ought to be sitting on the sofa at home. However, next time you run out of port, I hope those that take charge of you will look to the almanac for the tide, and look to windward for the weather: Jack, the lugger lies nearer the wind than we do.

"A little, sir."

"Will you take the helm a minute, Mr. Talboys? and you come forward and unbend this." The two sailors put their heads together amidships, and spoke in an undertone. "The wind is rising with the rain instead of falling."

"'Seems so, sir."

"What do you think yourself?"

"Well, sir, it has been blowing harder and harder ever since we came out, and very steady."

"It will turn out one of those dry nor'easters, Jack."

"I shouldn't wonder, sir. I wish she was cutter-rigged, sir. A boat has no business to be any other rig but cutter; there ought to be a nact o' parliam't against these outlandish rigs."

"I don't know; I have seen wonders done with this lateen rig in the Pacific."

"The lugger forereaches on us, sir."

"A little, but, for all that, I am glad she is on board our craft; we have got more beam, and, if it comes to the worst, we can run. The lugger can't with her sharp stern. I'll go to the helm."

Just as David was stepping aft to take the helm, a wave struck the boat hard on the weather bow, close to the gunwale, and sent a bucket of salt water flying all over him; he never turned his head even—took no more notice of it than a rock does when the sea spits at it. Lucy shrieked and crouched behind the tarpaulin. David took the helm, and, seeing Talboys white, said kindly: "Why don't you go forward, sir, and make yourself snug under the folksel deck? she is sure to wet us abaft before we can make the land."

No. Talboys resisted his inclination and the deadly nausea that was creeping over him.

"Thank you, but I like to see what is going on; and" (with an heroic attempt at sea-slang) "I like a wet boat."

They now fell in with the lugger again lying on the opposite tack, and a hundred yards at least to windward.

Just before they crossed her wake David sang out to Jack:

"Our masts—are they sound?"

"Bran-new, sir; best Norway pine."

"What d'ye think?"

"Think we are wasting time and daylight."

"Then stand by the main sheet."

"Yes, sir."

"Slack the main sheet."

"Ay, ay, sir."

The boat instantly fell off into the wind, and, as she went round, David stood up in the stern-sheets and waved his cap to the men on board the lugger, who were watching him. The old man was seen to shake his head in answer to the signal, and point to his lug-sail standing flat as a board, and the next moment they parted company, and the lateen was running close-reefed before the wind.

Mr. Talboys was sitting collapsed in the lethargy that precedes seasickness. He started up. "What are you doing?" he shrieked.

"Keep quiet, sir, and don't bother," said David, with calm sternness, and in his deepest tones.

"Pray don't interfere with Mr. Dodd," said Lucy; "he must know best."

"You don't see what he is doing, then," cried Talboys, wildly; "the madman is taking us out to sea."

"Are you taking us out to sea, Mr. Dodd?" inquired Lucy, with dismay.

"I am doing according to my judgment of tide and wind, and the abilities of the craft I am sailing," said David, firmly; "and on board my own craft I am skipper, and skipper I will be. Go forward, sir, if you please, and don't speak except to obey orders."

Mr. Talboys, sick, despondent and sulky, went gloomily forward, coiled himself up under the forecastle deck, and was silent and motionless.

"Don't send me," cried Lucy, "for I will not go. Nothing but your eye keeps up my courage. I don't mind the water," added she, hastily and a little timidly, anxious to meet every reason that could be urged for imprisoning her in the forecastle hold.

"You are all right where you are, miss," said Jack, cheerfully; "we shan't have no more spray come aboard us; it won't come in by the can full if it doesn't come by the ton."

"Will you belay your jaw?" roared David, in a fury that Lucy did not comprehend at the time. "What a set of tarnation babblers in one little boat."

"I won't speak any more, Mr. Dodd; I won't speak."

"Bless your heart, it isn't you I meant. 'Twould be hard if a lady might not put her word in. But a man is different. I do love to see a man belay his jaw, and wait for orders, and then do his duty; hoist the mainsel, you!"

"Ay, ay, sir."

"Shake out a couple of reefs."

"Ay, ay, sir."

And the lateen spread both her great wings like an albatross, and leaped and plunged, and flew before the mighty gale.

CHAPTER XVIII.

"THIS is nice. The boat does not upset or tumble as it did. It only courtesies and plunges. I like it."

"The sea has not got up yet, miss," said Jack.

"Hasn't it? the waves seem very large."

"Lord love you, wait till we have had four or five hours more of this."

"Belay your jaw, Jack."

"Ay, ay, sir."

"Why so, Mr. Dodd?" objected Lucy gently. "I am not so weak as you think me. Do not keep the truth from me. I share the danger; let me share the sense of danger, too. You shall not blush for me."

"Danger? There is not a grain of it, unless we make danger by inattention— and babbling."

"You will not do that," said Lucy.

Equivoque missed fire.

"Not while you are on board," replied David, simply.

Lucy felt inclined to give him her hand. She had it out half-way; but he had lately asked her to marry him, so she drew it back, and her eyes rested on the bottom of the boat.

The wind rose higher. The masts bent so that each sail had every possible reef taken in. Her canvas thus reduced she scudded as fast as before, such was now the fury of the gale. The sea rose so that the boat seemed to mount with each wave as high as the second story of a house, and go down again to the cellar at every plunge. Talboys, prostrated by seasickness in the forehold, lay curled but motionless, like a crooked log, and almost as indifferent to life or death. Lucy, pale but firm, put no more questions that she felt would not be answered, but scanned David Dodd's face furtively yet closely. The result was encouraging to her. His cheek was not pale, as she felt her own. On the contrary, it was slightly flushed; his eye bright and watchful, but lion-like. He gave a word or two of command to Jack every now and then very sharply, but without the slightest shade of agitation, and Jack's "ay, ay" came back as sharply, but cheerfully.

The principal feature she discerned in both sailors was a very attentive, business-like manner. The romantic air with which heroes face danger in story was entirely absent; and so, being convinced by his yarns that David was a hero, she inferred that their situation could not be dangerous, but, as David himself had inferred, merely one in which watchfulness was requisite.

The sun went down red and angry. The night came on dark and howling. No moon. A murky sky, like a black bellying curtain above, and huge ebony waves, that in the appalling blackness seemed all crested with devouring fire, hemmed in the tossing boat, and growled, and snarled, and raged above, below, and around her.

Then, in that awful hour, Lucy Fountain felt her littleness and the littleness of man. She cowered and trembled.

The sailors, rough but tender nurses, wrapped shawls round her one above the other, "to make her snug for the night," they said. They seemed to her to be mocking her. "Snug? Who could hope to outlive such a fearful night? and what did it matter whether she was drowned in one shawl or a dozen?"

David being amidships, bailing the boat out, and Jack at the helm, she took the opportunity, and got very close to the latter, and said in his ear—

"Mr. Jack, we are in danger."

"Not exactly in danger, miss; but, of course, we must mind our eye. But I have often been where I have had to mind my eye, and hope to be again."

"Mr. Jack," said Lucy, shivering, "what is our danger? Tell me the nature of it, then I shall not be so cowardly; will the boat break?"

"Lord bless you, no."

"Will it upset?"

"No fear of that."

"Will not the sea swallow us?"

"No, miss. How can the sea swallow us? She rides like a cork, and there is the skipper bailing her out, to make her lighter still. No; I'll tell you, miss; all we have got to mind is two things; we must not let her broach to, and we must not get pooped."

"But why must we not?"

"Why? Because we mustn't."

"But I mean, what would be the consequence of—broaching to?"

Jack opened his eyes in astonishment. "Why, the sea would run over her quarter, and swamp her."

"Oh!! And if we get pooped?"

"We shall go to Davy Jones, like a bullet."

"Who is Davy Jones?"

"The Old One, you know—down below. Leastways you won't go there, miss; you will go aloft, and perhaps the skipper; but Davy will have me; so I won't give him a chance, if I can help it."

Lucy cried.

"Where are we, Mr. Jack?"

"British Channel."

"I know that; but whereabouts?"

"Heaven knows; and no doubt the skipper, he knows; but I don't. I am only a common sailor. Shall I hail the skipper? he will tell you."

"No, no, no. He is so angry if we speak."

"He won't be angry if you speak to him, miss," said Jack, with a sly grin, that brought a faint color into Lucy's cheek; "you should have seen him, how anxious he was about you before we came alongside; and the moment that lubber went forward to dip the lug, says he, 'Jack, there will be mischief; up mainsail and run down to them. I have no confidence in that tall boy.' (He do seem a long, weedy, useless sort of lubber.) Lord bless you, miss, we luffed, and were running down to you long before you made the signal of distress with your little white flag." Lucy's cheeks got redder. "No, miss, if the skipper speaks severe to you, Jack Painter is blind with one eye, and can't see with t'other."

Lucy's cheeks were carnation.

But the next moment they were white, for a terrible event interrupted this chat. Two huge waves rolled one behind the other, an occurrence which luckily is not frequent; the boat, descending into the valley of the sea, had the wind taken out of her sails by the high wave that was coming. Her sails flapped, she lost her speed, and, as she rose again, the second wave was a moment too quick for her, and its combing crest caught her. The first thing Lucy saw was Jack running from the helm with a loud cry of fear, followed by what looked an arch of fire, but sounded like a lion rushing, growling on its prey, and directly her feet and ankles were in a pool of water. David bounded aft, swearing and splashing through it, and it turned into sparks of white fire flying this way and that. He seized the helm, and discharged a loud volley of curses at Jack.

"Fling out ballast, ye d—d cowardly, useless lubber," cried he; and while Jack, who had recoiled into his normal state of nerves with almost ridiculous rapidity, was heaving out ballast, David discharged another rolling volley at him.

"Oh, pray don't!" cried Lucy, trembling like an aspen leaf. "Oh, think! we shall soon be in the presence of our Maker—of Him whose name you—"

"Not we," cried David, with broad, cheerful incredulity; "we have lots more mischief to do—that lubber and I. And if he thinks he is going there, let him end like a man, not like a skulking lubber, running from the helm, and letting the craft come up in the wind."

"No, no, it was the sea he ran from. Who would not?"

"The lubber! If it had been a tiger or a bear I'd say nothing; but what is the use of trying to run from the sea? Should have stuck to his post, and set that thundering back of his up—it's broad enough—and kept the sea out of your boots. The sea, indeed! I have seen the sea come on board me, and clear the deck fore and aft, but it didn't come in the shape of a cupful o' water and a spoonful o' foam." Here David's wrath and contempt were interrupted by Jack singing waggishly at his work,

"Cease—rude Boreas—blustering—railer!!"

At which sly hit David was pleased, and burst into a loud, boisterous laugh.

Lucy put her hands to her ears. "Oh, don't! don't! this is worse than your blasphemies—laughing on the brink of eternity; these are not men—they are devils."

"Do you hear that, Jack? Come, you behave!" roared David.

A faint snarl from Talboys. The water had penetrated him, and roused him from a state of sick torpor; he lay in a tidy little pool some eight inches deep.

The boat was bailed and lightened, but Lucy's fears were not set at rest. What was to hinder the recurrence of the same danger, and with more fatal effect? She timidly asked David's permission to let her keep the sea out. Instead of snubbing her as she expected, David consented with a sort of paternal benevolence tinged with incredulity. She then developed her plan; it was, that David, Jack, and she should sit in a triangle, and hold the tarpaulin out to windward and fence the ocean out. Jack, being summoned aft to council, burst into a hoarse laugh; but David checked him.

"There is more in it than you see, Jack—more than she sees, perhaps. My only doubt is whether it is possible; but you can try."

Lucy and Jack then tried to get the tarpaulin out to windward; instead of which, it carried them to leeward by the force of the wind. The mast brought them up, or Heaven knows where their new invention would have taken them. With infinite difficulty they got it down and kneeled upon it, and even then it struggled. But Lucy would not be defeated; she made Jack gather it up in the middle, and roll it first to the right, then to the left, till it became a solid roll with two narrow open edges. They then carried it abaft, and lowered it vertically over the stern-port; then suddenly turned it round, and sat down. "Crack!" the wind opened it, and wrapped it round the boat and the trio.

"Hallo!" cried David, "it is foul of the rudder;" and, he whipped out his knife and made a slit in the stuff. It now clung like a blister.

"There, Mr. Dodd, will not that keep the sea out?" asked Lucy, triumphantly.

"At any rate, it may help to keep us ahead of the sea. Why, Jack, I seem to feel it lift her; it is as good as a mizzen."

"But, oh, Mr. Dodd, there is another danger. We may broach to."

"How can she broach to when I am at the helm? Here is the arm that won't let her broach to."

"Then I feel safe."

"You are as safe as on your own sofa; it is the discomfort you are put to that worries me."

"Don't think so meanly of me, Mr. Dodd. If it was not for my cowardice, I should enjoy this voyage far more than the luxurious ease you think so dear to me. I despise it."

"Mr. Dodd, now I am no longer afraid. I am, oh, so sleepy."

"No wonder—go to sleep. It is the best thing you can do."

"Thank you, sir. I am aware my conversation is not very interesting." Having administered this sudden bloodless scratch, to show that, at sea or ashore, in fair weather or foul, she retained her sex, Lucy disposed herself to sleep.

David, steering the boat with his left hand, arranged the cushion with his right. She settled herself to sleep, for an irresistible drowsiness had followed the many hours of excitement she had gone through. Twice the heavy plunging sea brought her into light contact with David. She instantly awoke, and apologized to him with gentle dismay for taking so audacious a liberty with that great man, commander of the vessel; the third time she said nothing, a sure sign she was unconscious.

Then David, for fear she might hurt herself, curled his arm around her, and let her head decline upon his shoulder. Her bonnet fell off; he put it reverently on the other side the helm. The air now cleared, but the gale increased rather than diminished. And now the moon rose large and bright. The boat and masts stood out like white stone-work against the flint-colored sky, and the silver light played on Lucy's face. There she lay, all unconscious of her posture, on the man's shoulder who loved her, and whom she had refused; her head thrown back in sweet helplessness, her rich hair streaming over David's shoulder, her eyes closed, but the long, lovely lashes meeting so that the double fringe was as speaking as most eyes, and her lips half open in an innocent smile. The storm was no storm to her now. She slept the sleep of childhood, of innocence and peace; and David gazed and gazed on her, and joy and tenderness almost more than human thrilled through him, and the storm was no storm to him either; he forgot the past, despised the future, and in the delirium of his joy blessed the sea and the wind, and wished for nothing but, instead of the Channel, a boundless ocean, and to sail upon it thus, her bosom tenderly grazing him, and her lovely head resting on his shoulder, for ever, and ever, and ever.

Thus they sailed on two hours and more, and Jack now began to nod.

All of a sudden Lucy awoke, and, opening her eyes, surprised David gazing at her with tenderness unspeakable. Awaking possessed with the notion that she was sleeping at home on a bed of down, she looked dumfounded an instant; but David's eyes soon sent the blood into her cheek. Her whole supple person turned eel-like, and she glided quickly, but not the least bruskly, from him; the latter might have seemed discourteous.

"Oh, Mr. Dodd," she cried, "what am I doing?"

"You have been getting a nice sleep, thank Heaven."

"Yes, and making use of you even in my sleep; but we all impose on your goodness."

"Why did you awake? You were happy; you felt no care, and I was happy seeing you so."

Lucy's eyes filled. "Kind, true friend," she murmured, "how can I ever thank you as I ought? I little deserved that you should watch over my safety as you have done, and, alas! risk your own. Any other but you would have borne me malice, and let me perish, and said, 'It serves her right.'"

"Malice! Miss Lucy. What for, in Heaven's name?"

"For—for the affront I put upon you; for the—the honor I declined."

"Hate cannot lie alongside love in a true heart."

"I see it cannot in a noble one. And then you are so generous. You have never once recurred to that unfortunate topic; yet you have gained a right to request me—to reconsider—Mr. Dodd, you have saved my life!!"

"What! do you praise me because I don't take a mean advantage? That would not be behaving like a man."

"I don't know that. You overrate your sex—and mine. We don't deserve such generosity. The proof is, we reward those who are not so—delicate."

"I don't trouble my head about your sex. They are nothing to me, and never will be. If you think I have done my duty like a man, and as much like a gentleman as my homely education permits, that is enough for me, and I shall sail for China as happy as anything on earth can make me now."

Lucy answered this by crying gently, silently, tenderly.

"Don't ye cry. Have I said something to vex you?"

"Oh no, no."

"Are you alarmed still?"

"Oh, no; I have such faith in you."

"Then go to sleep again, like a lamb."

"I will; then I shall not tease you with my conversation."

"Now there is a way to put it."

"Forgive me."

"That I will, if you will take some repose. There, I will lash you to my arm with this handkerchief; then you can lie the other way, and hold on by the handkerchief—there."

She closed her eyes and fell apparently to sleep, but really to thinking.

Then David nudged Jack, and waked him. "Speak low now, Jack."

"What is it, sir?"

"Land ahead."

Jack looked out, and there was a mountain of jet rising out of the sea, and, to a landsman's eye, within a stone's throw of them.

"Is it the French coast, sir? I must have been asleep."

"French coast? no, Channel Island—smallest of the lot."

"Better give it a wide berth, sir. We shall go smash like a teacup if we run on to one of them rocky islands."

"Why, Jack," said David, reproachfully, "am I the man to run upon a leeshore, and such a night as this?"

"Not likely. You will keep her head for Cherbourg or St. Malo, sir; it is our only chance."

"It is not our only chance, nor our best. We have been running a little ahead of this gale, Jack; there is worse in store for us; the sea is rolling mountains high on the French coast this morning, I know. We are like enough to be pooped before we get there, or swamped on some harbor-bar at last."

"Well, sir, we must take our chance."

"Take our chance? What! with heads on our shoulders, and an angel on board that Heaven has given us charge of? No, I sha'n't take my chance. I shall try all I know, and hang on to life by my eyelids. Listen to me. 'Knowledge is gold;' a little of it goes a long way. I don't know much myself, but I do know the soundings of the British Channel. I have made them my study. On the south side of this rocky point there is forty fathoms water close to the shore, and good anchorage-ground."

"Then I wish we could jump over the thundering island, and drop on the lee side of it; but, as we can't, what's the use?"

"We may be able to round the point."

"There will be an awful sea running off that point, sir."

"Of course there will. I mean to try it, for all that."

"So be it, sir; that is what I like to hear. I hate palaver. Let one give his orders, and the rest obey them. We are not above half a mile from it now."

"You had better wake the landsman. We must have a third hand for this."

"No," said a woman's voice, sweet, but clear and unwavering. "I shall be the third hand."

"Curse it," cried David, "she has heard us."

"Every word. And I have no confidence in Mr. Talboys; and, believe me, I am more to be trusted than he is. See, my cowardice is all worn out. Do but trust me, and you shall find I want neither courage nor intelligence."

David eyed her keenly, and full in the face. She met his glance calmly, with her fine nostrils slightly expanding, and her compressed lip curving proudly.

"It is all right, Jack. It is not a flash in the pan. She is as steady as a rock." He then addressed her rapidly and business-like, but with deference. "You will stand by the helm on this side, and the moment I run forward, you will take the helm and hold it in this position. That will require all your strength. Come, try it. Well done."

"How the sea struggles with me! But I am strong, you see," cried Lucy, her brow flushed with the battle.

"Very good; you are strong, and, what is better, resolute. Now, observe me: this is port, this is starboard, and this is amidships."

"I see; but how am I to know which to do?"'

"I shall give you the word of command."

"And all I have to do is to obey it?"

"That is all; but you will find it enough, because the sea will seem to fight you. It will shake the boat to make you leave go, and will perhaps dash in your face to make you leave go."

"Forewarned, forearmed, Mr. Dodd. I will not let go. I will hold on by my eyelids sooner than add to your danger."

"Jack, she is on fire; she gives me double heart."

"So she does me. She makes it a pleasure."

They were now near enough the point to judge what they had to do, and the appearance of the sea was truly terrible; the waves were all broken, and a surge of devouring fire seemed to rage and roar round the point, and oppose an impassable barrier between them and the inky pool beyond, where safety lay under the lee of the high rocks.

"I don't like it," said David. "It looks to me like going through a strip of hell fire."

"But it is narrow," said Lucy.

"That is our chance; and the tide is coming in. We will try it. She will drench us, but I don't much think she will swamp us. Are you ready, all hands?"

"Oh! please wait a minute, till I do up my hair."

"Take a minute, but no more."

"There, it is done. Mr. Dodd, one word. If all should fail, and death be inevitable, tell me so just before we perish, and I shall have something to say to you. Now, I am ready."

"Jump forward, Jack."

"Yes, sir."

"Stand by to jibe the foresail."

"Ay, ay, sir."

"See our sweeps all clear."

"Ay."

David now handled the main sheet, and at the same time looked earnestly at Lucy, who met his eye with a look of eager attention.

"Starboard a little. That will do. Steady—steady as you go," As the boat yielded to the helm, Jack gathered in on the sheet, took two turns round the cleat, and eased away till the sail drew its best: so far so good. Both sails were now on the same side of the boat, the wind on her port quarter; but now came the dangerous operation of coming to the wind, in a rough and broken sea, among the eddies of wind and tide so prevalent off headlands. David, with the main sheet in his right hand, directed Lucy with his left as well as his voice.

"Starboard the helm—starboard yet—now meet her—so!" and, as she rounded to Jack and he kept hauling the sheets aft, and the boat, her course and trim altered, darted among the breakers like a brave man attacking danger. After the first plunge she went up and down like a pickax, coming down almost where she went up; but she held her course, with the waves roaring round her like a pack of hell-hounds.

More than half the terrible strip was passed. "Starboard yet," cried David; and she headed toward the high mainland under whose lee was calm and safety. Alas! at this moment a snorter of a sea broke under her broadside, and hove her to leeward like a cork, and a tide eddy catching her under the counter, she came to more than two points, and her canvas, thus emptied, shook enough to tear the masts out of her by the board.

"Port your helm! PORT! PORT!" roared David, in a voice like the roar of a wounded lion; and, in his anxiety, he bounded to the helm himself; but Lucy obeyed orders at half a word, and David, seeing this, sprang forward to help Jack flatten in the foresheet. The boat, which all through answered the helm beautifully, fell off the moment Lucy ported the helm, and thus they escaped the impending and terrible danger of her making sternway. "Helm amidships!" and all drew again: the black water was in sight. But will they ever reach it? She tosses like a cork. Bang! A breaker caught her bows, and drenched David and Jack to the very bone. She quivered like an aspen-leaf but held on.

"Starboard one point," cried David, sitting down, and lifting an oar out from the boat; but just as Lucy, in obeying the order, leaned a little over the lee gunwale with the tiller, a breaker broke like a shell upon the boat's broadside abaft, stove in her upper plank, and filled her with water; some flew and slapped Lucy in the face like an open hand. She screamed, but clung to the gunwale, and griped the helm: her arm seemed iron, and her heart was steel. While she clung thus to her work, blinded by the spray, and expecting death, she heard oars splash into the water, and mellow stentorian voices burst out singing.

In amazement she turned, squeezed the brine out of her eyes, and looked all round, and lo! the boat was in a trifling bobble of a sea, and close astern was the surge of fire raging, and growling, and blazing in vain, and the two sailors were pulling the boat, with superhuman strength and inspiration, into a monster mill-pool that now lay right ahead, black as ink and smooth as oil, singing loudly as they rowed:

> "Cheerily oh oh! (pull) cheerily oh oh! (pull)
>
> To port we go oh (pull), to port we go (pull)."

FLARE!! a great flaming eye opened on them in the center of the universal blackness.

"Look! look!" cried Lucy; "a fire in the mountain."

It was the lantern of a French sloop anchored close to the shore. The crew had heard the sailors' voices. At sight of it David and Jack cheered so lustily that Talboys crawled out of the water and glared vaguely. The sailors pulled under the sloop's lee quarter: a couple of ropes were instantly lowered, the lantern held aloft, ruby heads and hands clustered at the gangway, and in another minute the boat's party were all upon deck, under a hailstorm of French, and the boat fast to her stern.

CHAPTER XIX.

THE skipper of the ship, hearing a commotion on deck, came up, and, taking off his cap, made Lucy a bow in a style remote from an English sailor's. She courtesied to him, and, to his surprise, addressed him in Parisian French. When he learned she was from England, and had rounded that point in an open boat, he was astonished.

"Diables d'Anglais!" said he.

The good-natured Frenchman insisted on Lucy taking sole possession of his cabin, in which was a cheerful stove. His crew were just as kind to David, Jack, and Talboys. This latter now resumed his right place—at the head of mankind; being the only one who could talk French, he interpreted for his companions. He improved upon my narrative in one particular: he led the Frenchmen to suppose it was he who had sailed the boat from England, and weathered the point. Who can blame him?

Dry clothes were found them, and grog and beef.

While employed on the victuals, a little Anglo-Frank, aged ten, suddenly rolled out of a hammock and offered aid in the sweet accents of their native tongue. The sound of the knives and forks had woke the urchin out of a deep sleep. David filled the hybrid, and then sent him to Lucy's cabin to learn how she was getting on. He returned, and told them the lady was sitting on deck.

"Dear me," said David, "she ought to be in her bed." He rose and went on deck, followed by Mr. Talboys. "Had you not better rest yourself?" said David.

"No, thank you, Mr. Dodd; I had a delicious sleep in the boat."

Here Talboys put in his word, and made her a rueful apology for the turn his pleasure-excursion had taken.

She stopped him most graciously.

"On the contrary, I have to thank you, indirectly, for one of the pleasantest evenings I ever spent. I never was in danger before, and it is delightful. I was a little frightened at first, but it soon wore off, and I feel I should shortly revel in it; only I must have a brave man near just to look at, then I gather courage from his eye; do I not now, Mr. Dodd?"

"Indeed you do," said David, simply enough.

Lucy Fountain's appearance and manner bore out her words. Talboys was white; even David and Jack showed some signs of a night of watching and anxiety; but the young lady's cheek was red and fresh, her eye bright, and she shone with an inspired and sprightly ardor that was never seen, or never observed in her before. They had found the way to put her blood up, after all

—the blood of the Funteyns. Such are thoroughbreds: they rise with the occasion; snobs descend as the situation rises. See that straight-necked, small-nosed mare stepping delicately on the turnpike: why, it is Languor in person, picking its way among eggs. Now the hounds cry and the horn rings. Put her at timber, stream, and plowed field in pleasing rotation, and see her now: up ears; open nostril; nerves steel; heart immovable; eye of fire; foot of wind. And ho! there! What stuck in that last arable, dead stiff as the Rosinantes in Trafalgar Square, all but one limb, which goes like a water-wagtail's? Why, by Jove! if it isn't the hero of the turnpike road: the gallant, impatient, foaming, champing, space-devouring, curveting cocktail.

Out of consideration for her male companions' infirmities, and observing that they were ashamed to take needful rest while she remained on deck, Lucy at length retired to her cabin.

She slept a good many hours, and was awakened at last by the rocking of the sloop. The wind had fallen gently, but it had also changed to due east, which brought a heavy ground-swell round the point into their little haven. Lucy made her toilet, and came on deck blooming like a rose. The first person she encountered was Mr. Talboys. She saluted him cordially, and then inquired for their companions.

"Oh, they are gone."

"Gone! What do you mean?"

"Sailed half an hour ago. Look, there is the boat coasting the island. No, not that way—westward; out there, just weathering that point Don't you see?"

"Are they making a tour of the island, then?"

Here the little Anglo-Frank put in his word. "No, ma'ainselle, gone to catch sheep bound for ze East Indeeze."

"Gone! gone! for good?" and Lucy turned very pale. The next moment offended pride sent the blood rushing to her brow. "That is just like Mr. Dodd; there is not another gentleman in the world would have had the ill-breeding to go off like that to India without even bidding us good-morning or good-by. Did he bid you good-by, Mr. Talboys?"

"No."

"There, now, it is insolent—it is barbarous." Her vexation at the affront David had put on Mr. Talboys soon passed into indignation. "This was done to insult —to humiliate us. A noble revenge. You know we used sometimes to quiz him a little ashore, especially you; so now, out of spite, he has saved our lives, and then turned his back arrogantly upon us before we could express our gratitude; that is as much as to say he values us as so many dogs or cats, flings us our lives haughtily, and then turned his back disdainfully on us. Life is not worth having when given so insultingly."

Talboys soothed the offended fair. "I really don't think he meant to insult us; but you know Dodd; he is a good-natured fellow, but he never had the slightest pretension to good-breeding."

"Don't you think," replied the lady, "it would be as well to leave off detracting from Mr. Dodd now that he has just saved your life?"

Talboys opened his eyes. "Why, you began it."

"Oh, Mr. Talboys, do not descend to evasion. What I say goes for nothing. Mr. Dodd and I are fast friends, and nobody will ever succeed in robbing me of my esteem for him. But you always hated him, and you seize every opportunity of showing your dislike. Poor Mr. Dodd! He has too many great virtues not to be envied—and hated."

Talboys stood puzzled, and was at a loss which way to steer his tongue, the wind being so shifty. At last he observed a little haughtily that "he never made Mr. Dodd of so much importance as all this. He owned he had quizzed him, but it was not his intention to quiz him any more; for I do feel under considerable obligations to Mr. Dodd; he has brought us safe across the Channel; at the same time, I own I should have been more grateful if he had beat against the wind and landed us on our native coast; the lugger is there long before this, and our boat was the best of the two."

"Absurd!" replied Lucy, with cold hauteur. "The lugger had a sharp stern, but ours was a square stern, so we were obliged to run; if we had beat, we should all have been drowned directly."

Talboys was staggered by this sudden influx of science; but he held his ground. "There is something in that," said he; "but still, a—a———"

"There, Mr. Talboys," said the young lady suddenly, assuming extreme languor after delivering a facer, "pray do not engage me in an argument. I do not feel equal to one, especially on a subject that has lost its interest. Can you inform me when this vessel sails?"

"Not till to-morrow morning."

"Then will you be so kind as to borrow me that little boat? it is dangling from the ship, so it must belong to it. I wish to land, and see whether he has cast us upon an in- or an uninhabited island."

The sloop's boat speedily landed them on the island, and Lucy proposed to cross the narrow neck of land and view the sea they had crossed in the dark. This was soon done, and she took that opportunity of looking about for the lateen, for her mind had taken another turn, and she doubted the report that David had gone to intercept the East-Indiaman. A short glance convinced her it was true. About seven miles to leeward, her course west-northwest, her hull every now and then hidden by the waves, her white sails spread like a bird's, the lateen was flying through the foam at its fastest rate. Lucy gazed at her so long and steadfastly that Talboys took the huff, and strolled along the cliff.

When Lucy turned to go back, she found the French skipper coming toward her with a scrap of paper in his hand. He presented it with a low bow; she took it with a courtesy. It was neatly folded, though not as letters are folded ashore, and it bore her address. She opened it and read:

"It was not worth while disturbing your rest just to see us go off. God bless you, Miss Lucy! The Frenchman is bound for ——, and will take you safe; and mind you don't step ashore till the plank is fast.

"Yours, respectfully,

"DAVID DODD."

That was all. She folded it back thoughtfully into the original folds, and turned away. When she had gone but a few steps she stopped and put her rejected lover's little note into her bosom, and went slowly back to the boat, hanging her sweet head, and crying as she went.

CHAPTER XX.

MR. FOUNTAIN remained in the town waiting for his niece's return. Six o'clock came—no boat. Eight o'clock—no boat, and a heavy gale blowing. He went down to the beach in great anxiety; and when he got there he soon found it was shared to the full by many human beings. There were little knots of fishermen and sailors discussing it, and one poor woman, mother and wife, stealing from group to group and listening anxiously to the men's conjectures. But the most striking feature of the scene was an old white-haired man, who walked wildly, throwing his arms about. The others rather avoided him, but Mr. Fountain felt he had a right to speak to him; so he came to him, and told him "his niece was on board; and you, too, I fear, have some one dear to you in danger."

The old man replied sorrowfully that "his lovely new boat was in danger—in such danger that he should never see her again;" then added, going suddenly into a fury, that "as to the two rascally bluejackets that were on board of her, and had borrowed her of his wife while he was out, all he wished was that they had been swamped to all eternity long ago, then they would not have been able to come and swamp his dear boat."

Peppery old Fountain cursed him for a heartless old vagabond, and joined the group whose grief and anxiety were less ostentatious, being for the other boat that carried their own flesh and blood. But all night long that white-haired old man paced the shore, flinging his arms, weeping and cursing alternately for his dear schooner.

Oh holy love—of property! how venerable you looked in the moonlight, with your white hairs streaming! How well you imitated, how close you rivaled, the holiest effusions of the heart, and not for the first time nor the last.

"My daughter! my ducats! my ducats! my daughter!" etc.

The morning broke; no sign of either boat. The wind had shifted to the east, and greatly abated. The fishermen began to have hopes for their comrades; these communicated themselves to Mr. Fountain.

It was about one o'clock in the afternoon when this latter observed people streaming along the shore to a distant point. He asked a coastguard man, whom he observed scanning the place with a glass, "What it was?"

The man lowered his voice and said, "Well, sir, it will be something coming ashore, by the way the folk are running."

Mr. Fountain got a carriage, and, urging the driver to use speed, was hastily conveyed by the road to a part whence a few steps brought him down to the sea. He thrust wildly in among the crowd.

"Make way," said the rough fellows: they saw he was one of those who had the best right to be there.

He looked, and there, scarce fifty yards from the shore, was the lugger, keel uppermost, drifting in with the tide. The old man staggered, and was supported by a beach man.

When the wreck came within fifteen yards of the shore, she hung, owing to the under suction, and could get neither way. The cries of the women broke out afresh at this. Then half a dozen stout fellows swam in with ropes, and with some difficulty righted her, and in another minute she was hauled ashore.

The crowd rushed upon her. She was empty! Not an oar, not a boat-hook—nothing. But jammed in between the tiller and the boat they found a purple veil. The discovery was announced loudly by one of the females, but the consequent outcry was instantly hushed by the men, and the oldest fisherman there took it, and, in a sudden dead and solemn silence, gave it with a world of subdued meaning to Mr. Fountain.

CHAPTER XXI.

MR. FOUNTAIN'S grief was violent; the more so, perhaps, that it was **not** pure sorrow, but heated with anger and despair. He had not only lost the creature he loved better than anyone else except himself, but all his plans and all his ambition were upset forever. I am sorry to say there were moments when he felt indignant with Heaven, and accused its justice. At other times the virtues of her he had lost came to his recollection, and he wept genuine tears. Now she was dead he asked himself a question that is sometimes reserved for that occasion, and then asked with bitter regret and idle remorse at its postponement, "What can I do to show my love and respect for her?" The poor old fellow could think of nothing now but to try and recover her body from the sea, and to record her virtues on her tomb. He employed six men to watch the coast for her along a space of twelve miles, and he went to a marble-cutter and ordered a block of beautiful white marble. He drew up the record of her virtues himself, and spelled her "Fontaine," and so settled that question by brute force.

Oh, you may giggle, but men are not most sincere when they are most reasonable, nor most reasonable when most sincere. When a man's heart is in a thing, it is in it—wise or nonsensical, it is all one; so it is no use talking.

I lack words to describe the gloom that fell on Mr. Bazalgette's home when the sad tidings reached it. And, indeed, it would be trifling with my reader to hang many more pages with black when he and I both know Lucy Fontaine is alive all the time.

Meantime the French sloop lay at her anchor, and Lucy fretted with impatience. At noon the next day she sailed, and, being a slow vessel, did not anchor off the port of —— till daybreak the day after. Then she had to wait for the tide, and it was nearly eleven o'clock when Lucy landed. She went immediately to the principal inn to get a conveyance. On the road, whom should she meet but Mr. Hardie. He gave a joyful start at sight of her, and with more heart than she could have expected welcomed her to life again. From him she learned all the proofs of her death. This made her more anxious to fly to her aunt's house at once and undeceive her.

Mr. Hardie would not let her hire a carriage; he would drive her over in half the time. He beckoned his servant, who was standing at the inn door, and ordered it immediately. "Meantime, Miss Fountain, if you will take my arm, I will show you something that I think will amuse you, though we have found it anything but amusing, as you may well suppose." Lucy took his arm somewhat timidly, and he walked her to the marble-cutter's shop. "Look there," said he. Lucy looked and there was an unfinished slab on which she read these words:

Sacred to the Memory

OF

LUCY FONTAINE,

WHO WAS DROWNED AT SEA ON THE

10TH SEPT., 18—.

> As her beauty endeared her to all eyes,
>
> So her modesty, piety, docilit

At this point in her moral virtues the chisel had stopped. Eleven o'clock struck, and the chisel went for its beer; for your English workman would leave the d in "God" half finished when strikes the hour of beer.

The fact is that the shopkeeper had newly set up, was proud of the commission, and, whenever the chisel left off, he whipped into the workshop and brought the slab out, pro tem., into his window for an advertisement.

Hardie pointed it out to Lucy with a chuckle. Lucy turned pale, and put her hand to her heart. Hardie saw his mistake too late, and muttered excuses.

Lucy gave a little gasp and stopped him. "Pray say no more; it is my fault; if people will feign death, they must expect these little tributes. My uncle has lost no time." And two unreasonable tears swelled to her eyes and trickled one after another down her cheeks; then she turned her back quickly on the thing, and Mr. Hardie felt her arm tremble. "I think, Mr. Hardie," said she presently, with marked courtesy, "I should, under the circumstances, prefer to go home alone. My aunt's nerves are sensitive, and I must think of the best way of breaking to her the news that I am alive."

"It would be best, Miss Fountain; and, to tell the truth, I feel myself unworthy to accompany you after being so maladroit as to give you pain in thinking to amuse you."

"Oh, Mr. Hardie," said Lucy, growing more and more courteous, "you are not to be called to account for my weakness; that would be unjust. I shall have the pleasure of seeing you at dinner?"

"Certainly, since you permit me."

He put Lucy into the carriage and off she drove. "Come," thought Mr. Hardie, "I have had an escape; what a stupid blunder for me to make! She is not angry, though, so it does not matter. She asked me to dinner."

Said Lucy to herself: "The man is a fool! Poor Mr. Dodd! he would not have shown me my tombstone—to amuse me." And she dismissed the subject from her mind.

She sent away the carriage and entered Mr. Bazalgette's house on foot. After some consideration she determined to employ Jane, a girl of some tact, to break her existence to her aunt. She glided into the drawing-room unobserved, fully expecting to find Jane at work there for Mrs. Bazalgette. But the room was empty. While she hesitated what to do next, the handle of the door was turned, and she had only just time to dart behind a heavy window-curtain, when it opened, and Mrs. Bazalgette walked slowly and silently in, followed by a woman. Mrs. Bazalgette seated herself and sighed deeply. Her companion kept a respectful silence. After a considerable pause, Mrs. Bazalgette said a few words in a voice so thoroughly subdued and solemn, and every now and then so stifled, that Lucy's heart yearned for her, and nothing but the fear of frightening her aunt into a hysterical fit kept her from flying into her arms.

"I need not tell you," said Mrs. Bazalgette, "why I sent for you. You know the sad bereavement that has fallen on me, but you cannot know all I have lost in her. Nobody can tell what she was to all of us, but most of all to me. I was her darling, and she was mine." Here tears choked Mrs. Bazalgette's words, for a while. Recovering herself, she paid a tribute to the character of the deceased. "It was a soul without one grain of selfishness; all her thoughts were for others, not one for herself. She loved us all—indeed, she loved some that were hardly worthy of so pure a creature's love; but the reason was, she had no eye for the faults of her friends; she pictured them like herself, and loved her own sweet image in them. And such a temper! and so free from guile. I may truly say her mind was as lovely as her person."

"She was, indeed, a sweet young lady," sighed the woman.

"She was an angel, Baldwin—an angel sent to bear us company a little while, and now she is a saint in Heaven."

"Ah! ma'am, the best goes first, that is an old saying."

"So I have heard; but my niece was as healthy as she was lovely and good. Everything promised long life. I hoped she would have closed my eyes. In the bloom of health one day, and the next lying cold, stark, and drenched!! Oh, how terrible! Oh, my poor Lucy! oh! oh! oh!"

"In the midst of life we are in death, ma'am. I am sure it is a warning to me, ma'am, as well as to my betters."

"It, is, indeed, Baldwin, a warning to all of us who have lived too much for vanities, to think of this sweet flower, snatched in a moment from our bosoms and from the world; we ought to think of it on our knees, and remember our own latter end. That last skirt you sent me was rather scrimped, my poor Baldwin."

"Was it, ma'am?"

"Oh, it does not matter; I shall never wear it now; and, under such a blow as this, I am in no humor to find fault. Indeed, with my grief I neglect my household and my very children. I forget everything; what did I send for you for?" and she looked with lack-luster eyes full in Mrs. Baldwin's face.

"Jane did not say, ma'am, but I am at your orders."

"Oh, of course; I am distracted. It was to pay the last tribute of respect to her dear memory. Ah! Baldwin, often and often the black dress is all; but here the heart mourns beyond the power of grief to express by any outward trappings. No matter; the world, the shallow world, respects these signs of woe, and let mine be the deepest mourning ever worn, and the richest. And out of that mourning I shall never go while I live."

"No, ma'am," said Baldwin soothingly.

"Do you doubt me?" asked the lady, with a touch of sharpness that did not seemed called for by Baldwin's humble acquiescence.

"Oh, no, ma'am; it is a very natural thought under the present affliction, and most becoming the sad occasion. Well, ma'am, the deepest mourning, if you please, I should say cashmere and crape."

"Yes, that would be deep. Oh, Baldwin, it is her violent death that kills me. Well?"

"Cashmere and crape, ma'am, and with nothing white about the neck and arms."

"Yes; oh yes; but will not that be rather unbecoming?"

"Well, ma'am—" and Baldwin hesitated.

"I hardly see how I could wear that, it makes one look so old. Now don't you think black glace silk, and trimmed with love-ribbon, black of course, but scalloped—"

"That would be very rich, indeed, ma'am, and very becoming to you; but, being so near and dear, it would not be so deep as you are desirous of."

"Why, Baldwin, you don't attend to what I say; I told you I was never going out of mourning again, so what is the use of your proposing anything to me that I can't wear all my life? Now tell me, can I always wear cashmere and crape?"

"Oh no, ma'am, that is out of the question; and if it is for a permanency, I don't see how we could improve on glace silk, with crape, and love-ribbons. Would you like the body trimmed with jet, ma'am?"

"Oh, don't ask me; I don't know. If my darling had only died comfortably in her bed, then we could have laid out her sweet remains, and dressed them for her virgin tomb."

"It would have been a satisfaction, ma'am."

"A sad one, at the best; but now the very earth, perhaps, will never receive her.

Oh yes, anything you like—the body trimmed with jet, if you wish it, and let me see, a gauze bodice, goffered, fastened to the throat. That is all, I think; the sleeves confined at the wrist just enough not to expose the arm, and yet look light—you understand."

"Yes, ma'am."

"She kissed me just before she went on that fatal excursion, Baldwin; she will never kiss me again—oh! oh! You must call on Dejazet for me, and bespeak me a bonnet to match; it is not to be supposed I can run about after her trumpery at such a time; besides, it is not usual."

"Indeed, ma'am, you are in no state for it; I will undertake any purchases you may require."

"Thank you, my good Baldwin; you are a good, kind, feeling, useful soul. Oh, Baldwin, if it had pleased Heaven to take her by disease, it would have been bad enough to lose her; but to be drowned! her clothes all wetted through and through; her poor hair drenched, too; and then the water is so cold at this time of year—oh! oh! Send me a cross of jet, and jet beads, with the dress, and a jet brooch, and a set of jet buttons, in case—besides—oh! oh! oh!—I expect every moment to see her carried home, all pale and wetted by the nasty sea—oh! oh!—and an evening dress of the same—the newest fashion. I leave it to you; don't ask me any questions about it, for I can't and won't go into that. I can try it on when it is made—oh! oh! oh!—it does not do to love any creature as I loved my poor lost Lucy—and a black fan—-oh! oh!—and a dozen pair of black kid gloves—oh!—and a mourning-ring—and—"

"Stop, aunt, or your love for me will be your ruin!" said Lucy, coldly, and stood suddenly before the pair, looking rather cynical.

"What, Lucy! alive! No, her ghost—ah! ah!"

"Be calm, aunt; I am alive and well. Now, don't be childish, dear; I have been in danger, but here I am."

Mrs. Bazalgette and Mrs. Baldwin flew together, and trembled in one another's arms. Lucy tried to soothe them, but at last could not help laughing at them. This brought Baldwin to her senses quicker than anything; but Mrs. Bazalgette, who, like many false women, was hysterical, went off into spasms —genuine ones. They gave her salts—in vain. Slapped her hands—in vain.

Then Lucy cried to Baldwin, "Quick! the tumbler; I must sprinkle her face and bosom."

"Oh, don't spoil my lilac gown!" gasped the sufferer, and with a mighty effort she came to. She would have come back from the edge of the grave to shield silk from water. Finally she wreathed her arms round Lucy, and kissed her so tenderly, warmly and sobbingly, that Lucy got over the shock of her shallowness, and they kissed and cried together most joyously, while Baldwin, after a heroic attempt at jubilation, retired from the room with a face as long as your arm. A bas les revenants!! She went to the housekeeper's room. The housekeeper persuaded her to stay and take a bit of dinner, and soon after dinner she was sent for to Mrs. Bazalgette's room.

Lucy met her coming out of it. "I fear I came mal apropos, Mrs. Baldwin; if I had thought of it, I would have waited till you had secured that munificent order."

"I am much obliged to you, miss, I am sure; but you were always a considerate young lady. You'll be glad to learn, miss, it makes no difference; I have got the order; it is all right."

"That is fortunate," replied Lucy, kindly, "otherwise I should have been tempted to commit an extravagance with you myself. Well, and what is my aunt's new dress to be now?"

"Oh, the same, miss."

"The same? why, she is not going into mourning on my return? ha! ha!"

"La bless you, miss, mourning? you can't call that mourning—glace silk and love-ribbons scalloped out, and cetera. Of course it was not my business to tell her so; but I could not help thinking to myself, if that is the way my folk are going to mourn for me, they may just let it alone. However, that is all over now; and your aunt sent for me, and says she, 'Black becomes me; you will make the dresses all the same.'" And Baldwin retired radiant.

Lucy put her hand to her bosom. "Make the dresses all the same—all the same, whether I am alive or dead. No, I will not cry; no, I will not. Who is worth a tear? what is worth a tear? All the same. It is not to be forgotten—nor forgiven. Poor Mr. Dodd!!"

Mr. Fountain learned the good news in the town, so his meeting with Lucy was one of pure joy. Mr. Talboys did not hear anything. He had business up in London, and did not stay ten minutes in ——.

The house revived, and jubilabat, jubilabat. But after the first burst of triumph things went flat. David Dodd was gone, and was missed; and Lucy was changed. She looked a shade older, and more than one shade graver; and, instead of living solely for those who happened to be basking in her rays, she was now and then comparatively inattentive, thoughtful, and distraite.

Mr. Fountain watched her keenly; ditto Mrs. Bazalgette. A slight reaction had taken place in both their bosoms. "Hang the girl! there were we breaking our hearts for her, and she was alive." She had "beguiled them of their tears."—Othello. But they still loved her quite well enough to take charge of her fate.

A sort of itch for settling other people's destinies, and so gaining a title to their curses for our pragmatical and fatal interference, is the commonest of all the forms of sanctioned lunacy.

Moreover, these two had imbibed the spirit of rivalry, and each was stimulated by the suspicion that the other was secretly at work.

Lucy's voluntary promise in the ballroom was a double sheet-anchor to Mr. Fountain. It secured him against the only rival he dreaded. Talboys, too, was out of the way just now, and the absence of the suitor is favorable to his success, where the lady has no personal liking for him. To work went our Machiavel again, heart and soul, and whom do you think he had the cheek, or, as the French say, the forehead, to try and win over?—Mrs. Bazalgette.

This bold step, however, was not so strange as it would have been a month ago. The fact is, I have brought you unfairly close to this pair. When you meet them in the world you will be charmed with both of them, and recognize neither. There are those whose faults are all on the surface: these are generally disliked; there are those whose faults are all at the core: they charm creation. Mrs. Bazalgette is allowed by both sexes to be the most delightful, amiable woman in the county, and will carry that reputation to her grave. Fountain is "the jolliest old buck ever went on two legs." I myself would rather meet twelve such agreeable humbugs—six of a sex—at dinner than the twelve apostles, and so would you, though you don't know it. These two, then, had long ere this found each other mighty agreeable. The woman saw the man's vanity, and flattered it. The man the woman's, and flattered it. Neither saw— am I to say?—his own or her own, or what? Hang language!!! In short, they had long ago oiled one another's asperities, and their intercourse was smooth and frequent: they were always chatting together—strewing flowers of speech over their mines and countermines.

Mr. Fountain, then, who, in virtue of his sex, had the less patience, broke ground.

"My dear Mrs. Bazalgette, I would not have missed this visit for a thousand pounds. Certainly there is nothing like contact for rubbing off prejudices. I little thought, when I first came here, the principal attraction of the place would prove to be my fair hostess."

"I know you were prejudiced, my dear Mr. Fountain. I can't say I ever had any against you, but certainly I did not know half your good qualities. However, your courtesy to me when I invaded you at Font Abbey prepared me for your real character; and now this visit, I trust, makes us friends."

"Ah! my dear Mrs. Bazalgette, one thing only is wanting to make you my benefactor as well as friend—if I could only persuade you to withdraw your powerful opposition to a poor old fellow's dream."

"What poor old fellow?"

"Me."

"You? why, you are not so very old. You are not above fifty."

"Ah! fair lady, you must not evade me. Come, can nothing soften you?"

"I don't know what you mean, Mr. Fountain"; and the mellifluous tones dried suddenly.

"You are too sagacious not to know everything; you know my heart is set on marrying my niece to a man of ancient family."

"With all my heart. You have only to use your influence with her. If she consents, I will not oppose."

"You cruel little lady, you know it is not enough to withdraw opposition; I can't succeed without your kind aid and support."

"Now, Mr. Fountain, I am a great coward, but, really, I could almost venture to scold you a little. Is not a poor little woman to be allowed to set her heart on things as well as a poor old gentleman who does not look fifty? You know my poor little heart is bent on her marrying into our own set, yet you can ask me to influence her the other way—me, who have never once said a word to her for my own favorites! No; the fairest, kindest, and best way is to leave her to select her own happiness."

"A fine thing it would be if young people were left to marry who they like," retorted Fountain. "My dear lady, I would never have asked your aid so long as there was the least chance of her marrying Mr. Hardie; but, now that she has of her own accord declined him—"

"What is that? declined Mr. Hardie? when did he ever propose for her?"

"You misunderstand me. She came to me and told me she would never marry him."

"When was that? I don't believe it."

"It was in the ball-room."

Mrs. Bazalgette reflected; then she turned very red. "Well, sir," said she, "don't build too much on that; for four months ago she made me a solemn promise she would never marry any lover you should find her, and she repeated that promise in your very house."

"I don't believe it, madam."

"That is polite, sir. Come, Mr. Fountain, you are agitated and cross, and it is no use being cross either with me or with Lucy. You asked my co-operation. You gentlemen can ask anything; and you are wise to do these droll things; that is where you gain the advantage over us poor cowards of women. Well, I will co-operate with you. Now listen. Lucy's penchant is neither for Mr. Hardie, nor

Mr. Talboys, but for Mr. Dodd."

"You don't mean it?"

"Oh, she does not care much for him; she has refused him to my knowledge, and would again; besides, he is gone to India, so there is an end of him.She seems a little languid and out of spirits; it may be because he is gone. Now, then, is the very time to press a marriage upon her."

"The very worst time, surely, if she is really such an idiot as to be fretting for a fellow who is away."

Mrs. Bazalgette informed her new ally condescendingly that he knew nothing of the sex he had undertaken to tackle.

"When a cold-blooded girl like this, who has no strong attachment, is out of spirits, and all that sort of thing, then is the time she falls to any resolute wooer. She will yield if we both insist, and we will insist. Only keep your temper, and let nothing tempt you to say an unkind word to her."

She then rang the bell, and desired that Miss Fountain might be requested to come into the drawing-room for a minute.

"But what are you going to do?"

"Give her the choice of two husbands—Mr. Talboys or Mr. Hardie."

"She will take neither, I am afraid."

"Oh, yes, she will."

"Which?"

"Ah! the one she dislikes the least."

"By Jove, you are right—you are an angel." And the old gentleman in his gratitude to her who was outwitting him, and vice versa, kissed Mrs. Bazalgette's hand with great devotion, in which act he was surprised by Lucy, who floated through the folding-doors. She said nothing, but her face volumes.

"Sit down, love."

"Yes, aunt."

She sat down, and her eye mildly bored both relatives, like, if you can imagine a gentle gimlet, worked by insinuation, not force.

Then the favored Fountain enjoyed the inestimable privilege of beholding a small bout of female fence.

The accomplished actress of forty began.

The novice held herself apparently all open with a sweet smile, the eye being the only weapon that showed point.

"My love, your uncle and I, who were not always just to one another, have been united by our love for you."

"So I observed as I came in—ahem!"

"Henceforth we are one where your welfare is concerned, and we have something serious to say to you now. There is a report, dearest, creeping about that you have formed an unfortunate attachment—to a person beneath you."

"Who told you that, aunt? Name, as they say in the House."

"No matter; these things are commonly said without foundation in this wicked world; but, still, it is always worth our while to prove them false, not, of course, directly—'qui s'excuse s'accuse'—but indirectly."

"I agree with you, and I shall do so in my uncle's presence. You were present, aunt—though uninvited—when the gentleman you allude to offered me what I consider a great honor, and you heard me decline it; you are therefore fully able to contradict that report, whose source, by the by, you have not given me, and of course you will contradict it."

Mrs. Bazalgette colored a little. But she said affectionately: "These silly rumors are best contradicted by a good marriage, love, and that brings me to something more important. We have two proposals for you, and both of them excellent ones. Now, in a matter where your happiness is at stake, your uncle and I are determined not to let our private partialities speak. We do press you to select one of these offers, but leave you quite free as to which you take. Mr. Talboys is a gentleman of old family and large estates. Mr. Hardie is a wealthy, and able, and rising man. They are both attached to you; both excellent matches.

"Whichever you choose your uncle and I shall both feel that an excellent position for life is yours, and no regret that you did not choose our especial favorite shall stain our joy or our love." With this generous sentiment tears welled from her eyes, whereat Fountain worshiped her and felt his littleness.

But Lucy was of her own sex, and had observed what an unlimited command of eye-water an hysterical female possesses. She merely bowed her head graciously, and smiled politely. Thus encouraged to proceed, her aunt dried her eyes with a smile, and with genial cheerfulness proceeded: "Well, then, dear, which shall it be—Mr. Talboys?"

Lucy opened her eyes so innocently. "My dear aunt, I wonder at that question from you. Did you not make me promise you I would never marry that gentleman, nor any friend of my uncle's?"

"And did you?" cried Fountain.

"I did," replied the penitent, hanging her head. "My aunt was so kind to me about something or other, I forget what."

Fountain bounced up and paced the room.

Mrs. Bazalgette lowered her voice: "It is to be Mr. Hardie, then?"

"Mr. Hardie!!!" cried Lucy, rather loudly, to attract her uncle's attention.

"Oh, no, the same objection applies there; I made my uncle a solemn promise not to marry any friend of yours, aunt. Poor uncle! I refused at first, but he looked so unhappy my resolution failed, and I gave my promise. I will keep it, uncle. Don't fear me."

It caused Mrs. Bazalgette a fierce struggle to command her temper. Both she and Fountain were dumb for a minute; then elastic Mrs. Bazalgette said:

"We were both to blame; you and I did not really know each other. The best thing we can do now is to release the poor girl from these silly promises, that stand in the way of her settlement in life."

"I agree, madam."

"So do I. There, Lucy, choose, for we both release you."

"Thank you," said Lucy gravely; "but how can you? No unfair advantage was taken of me; I plighted my word knowingly and solemnly, and no human power can release persons of honor from a solemn pledge. Besides, just now you would release me; but you might not always be in the same mind. No, I will keep faith with you both, and not place my truth at the mercy of any human being nor of any circumstance. If that is all, please permit me to retire. The less a young lady of my age thinks or talks about the other sex, the more time she has for her books and her needle;" and, having delivered this precious sentence, with a deliberate and most deceiving imitation of the pedantic prude, she departed, and outside the door broke instantly into a joyous chuckle at the expense of the plotters she had left looking moonstruck in one another's faces. If the new allies had been both Fountain, the apple of discord this sweet novice threw down between them would have dissolved the alliance, as the sly novice meant it to do; but, while the gentleman went storming about the room ripe for civil war, the lady leaned back in her chair and laughed heartily.

"Come, Mr. Fountain, it is no use your being cross with a female, or she will get the better of you. She has outwitted us. We took her for a fool, and she is a clever girl. I'll—tell—you—what, she is a very clever girl. Never mind that, she is only a girl; and, if you will be ruled by me, her happiness shall be secured in spite of her, and she shall be engaged in less than a week."

Fountain recognized his superior, and put himself under the lady's orders—in an evil hour for Lucy.

The poor girl's triumph over the forces was but momentary; her ground was not tenable. The person promised can release the person who promises— volenti non fit injuria. Lucy found herself attacked with female weapons, that you and I, sir, should laugh at; but they made her miserable. Cold looks; short answers; solemnity; distance; hints at ingratitude and perverseness; kisses intermitted all day, and the parting one at night degraded to a dignified ceremony. Under this impalpable persecution the young thoroughbred, that had steered the boat across the breakers, winced and pined.

She did not want a husband or a lover, but she could not live without being loved. She was not sent into the world for that. She began secretly to hate the two gentlemen that had lost her her relations' affection, and she looked round to see how she could get rid of them without giving fresh offense to her dear aunt and uncle. If she could only make it their own act! Now a man in such a case inclines to give the obnoxious parties a chance of showing themselves generous and delicate; he would reveal the whole situation to them, and indicate the generous and manly course; but your thorough woman cannot do this. It is physically as well as morally impossible to her. Misogynists say it is too wise, and not cunning enough. So what does Miss Lucy do but turn round and make love to Captain Kenealy? And the cold virgin being at last by irrevocable fate driven to love-making, I will say this for her, she did not do it by halves. She felt quite safe here. The good-natured, hollow captain was fortified against passion by self-admiration. She said to herself: "Now here is a peg with a military suit hanging to it; if I can only fix my eyes on this piece of wood and regimentals, and make warm love to it, the love that poets have dreamed and romances described, I may surely hope to disgust my two admirers, and then they will abandon me and despise me. Ah! I could love them if they would only do that."

Well, for a young lady that had never, to her knowledge, felt the tender passion, the imitation thereof which she now favored that little society with was a wonderful piece of representation. Was Kenealy absent, behold Lucy uneasy and restless; was he present; but at a distance, her eye demurely devoured him; was he near her, she wooed him with such a god-like mixture of fire, of tenderness, of flattery, of tact; she did so serpentinely approach and coil round the soldier and his mental cavity, that all the males in creation should have been permitted to defile past (like the beasts going into the ark), and view this sweet picture a moment, and infer how women would be wooed, and then go and do it. Effect:

Talboys and Hardie mortified to the heart's core; thought they had altogether mistaken her character. "She is a love-sick fool."

On Bazalgette: "Ass! Dodd was worth a hundred of him."

On Kenealy: made him twirl his mustache.

On Fountain: filled him with dismay. There remained only one to be hoodwinked.

SCENA.

A letter is brought in and handed to Captain Kenealy. He reads it, and looks a little—a very little—vexed. Nobody else notices it.

Lucy. "What is the matter? Oh, what has occurred?"

Kenealy. "Nothing particulaa."

Lucy. "Don't deceive us: it is an order for you to join the horrid army." (Clasps her hands.) "You are going to leave us."

Kenealy. "No, it is from my tailaa. He waunts to be paed." (Glares astonished.)

Lucy. "Pay the creature, and nevermore employ him."

Kenealy. "Can't. Haven't got the money. Uncle won't daie. The begaa knows I can't pay him, that is the reason why he duns."

Lucy. "He knows it? then what business has he to annoy you thus? Take my advice. Return no reply. That is not courteous. But when the sole motive of an application is impertinence, silent contempt is the course best befitting your dignity."

Kenealy (twirling his mustache). "Dem the fellaa. Shan't take any notice of him."

Mrs. Bazalgette (to Lucy in passing). "Do you think we are all fools?"

Ibi omnis effusus amor; for La Bazalgette undeceived her ally and Mr. Hardie, and the screw was put harder still on poor Lucy. She was no longer treated like an equal, but made for the first time to feel that her uncle and aunt were her elders and superiors, and, that she was in revolt. All external signs of affection were withdrawn, and this was like docking a strawberry of its water. A young girl may have flashes of spirit, heroism even, but her mind is never steel from top to toe; it is sure to be wax in more places than one.

"Nobody loves me now that poor Mr. Dodd is gone," sighed Lucy. "Nobody ever will love me unless I consent to sacrifice myself. Well, why not? I shall never love any gentleman as others of my sex can love. I will go and see Mrs. Wilson."

So she ordered out her captain, and rode to Mrs. Wilson, and made her captain hold her pony while she went in. Mrs. Wilson received her with a tenor scream of delight that revived Lucy's heart to hear, and then it was nothing but one broad gush of hilarity and cordiality—showed her the house, showed her the cows, showed her the parlor at last, and made her sit down.

"Come, set ye down, set ye down, and let me have a downright good look at ye. It is not often I clap eyes on ye, or on anything like ye, for that matter. Aren't ye well, my dear?"

"Oh yes."

"Are ye sure? Haven't ye ailed anything since I saw ye up at the house?"

"No, dear nurse."

"Then you are in care. Bless you, it is not the same face—to a stranger, belike, but not to the one that suckled you. Why, there is next door to a wrinkle on your pretty brow, and a little hollow under your eye, and your face is drawn like, and not half the color. You are in trouble or grief of some sort, Miss Lucy; and—who knows?—mayhap you be come to tell it your poor old nurse. You might go to a worse part. Ay! what touches you will touch me, my nursling dear, all one as if it was your own mother."

"Ah! you love me," cried Lucy; "I don't know why you love me so; I have not deserved it of you, as I have of others that look coldly on me. Yes, you love me, or you would not read my face like this. It is true, I am a little—Oh, nurse, I am unhappy;" and in a moment she was weeping and sobbing in Mrs. Wilson's arms.

The Amazon sat down with her, and rocked to and fro with her as if she was still a child. "Don't check it, my lamb," said she; "have a good cry; never drive a cry back on your heart"; and so Lucy sobbed and sobbed, and Mrs. Wilson rocked her.

When she had done sobbing she put up a grateful face and kissed Mrs. Wilson. But the good woman would not let her go. She still rocked with her, and said, "Ay, ay, it wasn't for nothing I was drawed so to go to your house that day. I didn't know you were there; but I was drawed. I WAS WANTED. Tell me all, my lamb; never keep grief on your heart; give it a vent; put a part on't on me; I do claim it; you will see how much lighter your heart will feel. Is it a young man?"

"Oh no, no; I hate young men; I wish there were no such things. But for them no dissension could ever have entered the house. My uncle and aunt both loved me once, and oh! they were so kind to me. Yes; since you permit me, I will tell you all."

And she told her a part.

She told her the whole Talboys and Hardie part.

Mrs. Wilson took a broad and somewhat vulgar view of the distress.

"Why, Miss Lucy," said she, "if that is all, you can soon sew up their stockings. You don't depend on them, anyways: you are a young lady of property."

"Oh, am I?"

"Sure. I have heard your dear mother say often as all her money was settled on you by deed. Why, you must be of age, Miss Lucy, or near it."

"The day after to-morrow, nurse."

"There now! I knew your birthday could not be far off. Well, then, you must wait till you are of age, and then, if they torment you or put on you, 'Good-morning,' says you; 'if we can't agree together, let's agree to part,' says you."

"What! leave my relations!!"

"It is their own fault. Good friends before bad kindred! They only want to make a handle of you to get 'em rich son-in-laws. You pluck up a sperrit, Miss Lucy. There's no getting through the world without a bit of a sperrit. You'll get put upon at every turn else; and if they don't vally you in that house, why, off to another; y'ain't chained to their door, I do suppose."

"But, nurse, a young lady cannot live by herself: there is no instance of it."

"All wisdom had a beginning. 'Oh, shan't I spoil the pudding once I cut it?' quoth Jack's wife."

"What would people say?"

"What could they say? You come to me, which I am all the mother you have got left upon earth, and what scandal could they make out of that, I should like to know? Let them try it. But don't let me catch it atween their lips, or down they do go on the bare ground, and their caps in pieces to the winds of heaven;" and she flourished her hand and a massive arm with a gesture free, inspired, and formidable.

"Ah! nurse, with you I should indeed feel safe from every ill. But, for all that, I shall never go beyond the usages of society. I shall never leave my aunt's house."

"I don't say as you will. But I shall get your room ready this afternoon, and no later."

"No, nurse, you must not do that."

"Tell'ee I shall. Then, whether you come or not, there 'tis. And when they put on you, you have no call to fret. Says you, 'There's my room awaiting, and likewise my welcome, too, at Dame Wilson's; I don't need to stand no more nonsense here than I do choose,' says you. Dear heart! even a little foolish, simple thought like that will help keep your sperrit up. You'll see else—you'll see."

"Oh, nurse, how wise you are! You know human nature."

"Well, I am older than you, miss, a precious sight; and if I hadn't got one eye open at this time of day, why, when should I, you know?"

After this, a little home-made wine forcibly administered, and then much kissing, and Lucy rode away revivified and cheered, and quite another girl. Her spirits rose so that she proposed to Kenealy to extend their ride by crossing the country to ——. She wanted to buy some gloves.

"Yaas," said the assenter; and off they cantered.

In the glove-shop who should Lucy find but Eve Dodd. She held out her hand, but Eve affected not to observe, and bowed distantly. Lucy would not take the hint. After a pause she said:

"Have you any news of Mr. Dodd?"

"I have," was the stiff reply.

"He left us without even saying good-by."

"Did he?"

"Yes, after saving all our lives. Need I say that we are anxious, in our turn, to hear of his safety? It was still very tempestuous when he left us to catch the great ship, and he was in an open boat."

"My brother is alive, Miss Fountain, if that is what you wish to know."

"Alive? is he not well? has he met with any accident? any misfortune? is he in the East Indiaman? has he written to you?"

"You are very curious: it is rather late in the day; but, if I am to speak about my brother, it must be at home, and not in an open shop. I can't trust my feelings."

"Are you going home, Miss Dodd?"

"Yes."

"Shall I come with you?"

"If you like: it is close by."

Lucy's heart quaked. Eve was so stern, and her eyes like basilisks'.

"Sit down, Miss Fountain, and I will tell you what you have done for my brother. I did not court this, you know; I would have avoided your eye if I could; it is your doing."

"Yes, Miss Dodd," faltered Lucy, "and I should do it again. I have a right to inquire after his welfare who saved my life."

"Well, then, Miss Fountain, his saving your life has lost him his ship and ruined him for life."

"Oh!"

"He came in sight of the ship; but the captain, that was jealous of him like all the rest, made all sail and ran from him: he chased her, and often was near catching her, but she got clear out of the Channel, and my poor David had to come back disgraced, ruined for life, and broken-hearted. The Company will never forgive him for deserting his ship. His career is blighted, and all for one that never cared a straw for him. Oh, Miss Fountain, it was an evil day for my poor brother when first he saw your face!" Eve would have said more, for her heart was burning with wrath and bitterness, but she was interrupted.

Lucy raised both her hands to Heaven, and then, bowing her head, wept tenderly and humbly.

A woman's tears do not always affect another woman; but one reason is, they are very often no sign of grief or of any worthy feeling. The sex, accustomed to read the nicer shades of emotion, distinguishes tears of pique, tears of disappointment, tears of spite, tears various, from tears of grief. But Lucy's was a burst of regret so sincere, of sorrow and pity so tender and innocent that it fell on Eve's hot heart like the dew.

"Ah! well," she cried, "it was to be, it was to be; and I suppose I oughtn't to blame you. But all he does for you tells against himself, and that does seem hard. It isn't as if he and you were anything to one another; then I shouldn't grudge it so much. He has lost his character as a seaman."

"Oh dear!"

"He valued it a deal more than his life. He was always ready to throw THAT away for you or anybody else. He has lost his standing in the service."

"Oh!"

"You see he has no interest, like some of them; he only got on by being better and cleverer than all the rest; so the Company won't listen to any excuses from him, and, indeed, he is too proud to make them."

"He will never be captain of a ship now?"

"Captain of a ship! Will he ever leave the bed of sickness he lies on?"

"The bed of sickness! Is he ill? Oh, what have I done?"

"Is he ill? What! do you think my brother is made of iron? Out all night with you—then off, with scarce a wink of sleep; then two days and two nights chasing the Combermere, sometimes gaining, sometimes losing, and his credit and his good name hanging on it; then to beat back against wind, heartbroken, and no food on board—"

"Oh, it is too horrible."

"He staggered into me, white as a ghost. I got him to bed: he was in a burning fever. In the night he was lightheaded, and all his talk was about you. He kept fretting lest you should not have got safe home. It is always so. We care the most for those that care the least for us."

"Is he in the Indiaman?"

"No, Miss Fountain, he is not in the Indiaman," cried Eve, her wrath suddenly rising again; "he lies there, Miss Fountain, in that room, at death's door, and you to thank for it."

At this stab Lucy uttered a cry like a wounded deer. But this cry was followed immediately by one of terror: the door opened suddenly, and there stood David Dodd, looking as white as his sister had said, but, as usual, not in the humor to succumb. "Me at death's port, did you say?" cried he, in a loud tone of cheerful defiance; "tell that to the marines!!"

CHAPTER XXII.

"I HEARD your voice, Miss Lucy; I would know it among a million; so I rigged myself directly. Why, what is the matter?"

"Oh, Mr. Dodd," sobbed Lucy, "she has told me all you have gone through, and I am the wicked, wicked cause!"

David groaned. "If I didn't think as much. I heard the mill going. Ah! Eve, my girl, your jawing-tackle is too well hung. Eve is a good sister to me, Miss Lucy, and, where I am concerned, let her alone for making a mountain out of a mole-hill. If you believe all she says, you are to blame. The thing that went to my heart was to see my skipper run out his stunsel booms the moment he saw me overhauling him; it was a dirty action, and him an old shipmate. I am glad now I couldn't catch her, for if I had my foot would not have been on the deck two seconds before his carcass would have been in the Channel. And pray, Eve, what has Miss Fountain got to do with that? the dirty lubber wasn't bred at her school, or he would not have served an old messmate so.

"Belay all that, and let's hear something worth hearing. Now, Miss Lucy, you tell me—oh, Lord, Eve, I say, isn't the thundering old dingy room bright now? —you spin me your own yarn, if you will be so good. Here you are, safe and sound, the Lord be praised! But I left you under the lee of that thundering island: wasn't very polite, was it? but you will excuse, won't you? Duty, you know—a seaman must leave his pleasure for his duty. Tell me, now, how did you come on? Was the vessel comfortable? You would not sail till the wind fell? Had you a good voyage? A tiresome one, I am afraid: the sloop wasn't built for fast sailing. When did you land?"

To this fire of eager questions Lucy was in no state to answer. "Oh, no, Mr. Dodd," she cried, "I can't. I am choking. Yes, Miss Dodd, I am the heartless, unfeeling girl you think me." Then, with a sudden dart, she took David's hand and kissed it, and, both her hands hiding her blushing face, she fled, and a single sob she let fall at the door was the last of her. So sudden was her exit, it left both brother and sister stupefied.

"Eve, she is offended," said David, with dismay.

"What if she is?" retorted Eve; "no, she is not offended; but I have made her feel at last, and a good job, too. Why should she escape? she has done all the mischief. Come, you go to bed."

"Not I; I have been long enough on my beam-ends. And I have heard her voice, and have seen her face, and they have put life into me. I shall cruise about the port. I have gone to leeward of John Company's favor, but there are plenty of coasting-vessels; I may get the command of one. I'll try; a seaman never strikes his flag while there's a shot in the locker."

"Here, put me up, Captain Kenealy! Oh, do pray make haste! don't dawdle so!" Off cantered Lucy, and fanned her pony along without mercy. At the door of the house she jumped off without assistance, and ran to Mr. Bazalgette's study, and knocked hastily, and that gentleman was not a little surprised when this unusual visitor came to his side with some signs of awe at having penetrated his sanctum, but evidently driven by an overpowering excitement. "Oh, Uncle Bazalgette! Oh, Uncle Bazalgette!"

"Why, what is the matter? Why, the child is ill. Don't gasp like that, Lucy. Come, pluck up courage; I am sure to be on your side, you know. What is it?"

"Uncle, you are always so kind to me; you know you are."

"Oh, am I? Noble old fellow!"

"Oh, don't make me laugh! ha! ha! oh! oh! oh! ha! oh!"

"Confound it, I have sent her into hysterics; no, she is coming round. Ten thousand million devils, has anybody been insulting the child in my house? They have. My wife, for a guinea."

"No, no, no. It is about Mr. Dodd."

"Mr. Dodd? oho!"

"I have ruined him."

"How have you managed that, my dear?"

Then Lucy, all in a flutter, told Mr. Bazalgette what the reader has just learned.

He looked grave. "Lucy," said he, "be frank with me. Is not Mr. Dodd in love with you?"

"I will be frank with you, dear uncle, because you are frank. Poor Mr. Dodd did love me once; but I refused him, and so his good sense and manliness cured him directly."

"So, now that he no longer loves you, you love him; that is so like you girls."

"Oh, no, uncle; how ridiculous! If I loved Mr. Dodd, I could repair the cruel injuries I have done him with a single word. I have only to recall my refusal, and he—But I do not love Mr. Dodd. Esteem him I do, and he has saved my life; and is he to lose his health, and his character, and his means of honorable ambition for that? Do you not see how shocking this is, and how galling to my pride? Yes, uncle, I have been insulted. His sister told me to my face it was an evil day for him when he and I first met—that was at Uncle Fountain's."

"Well, and what am I to do, Lucy?"

"Dear Uncle, what I thought was, if you would be so kind as to use your influence with the Company in his favor. Tell them that if he did miss his ship it was not by a fault, but by a noble virtue; tell them that it was to save a fellow creature's life—a young lady's life—one that did not deserve it from him, your own niece's; tell them it is not for your honor he should be disgraced. Oh, uncle, you know what to say so much better than I do."

Bazalgette grinned, and straightway resolved to perpetrate a practical joke, and a very innocent one. "Well," said he, "the best way I can think of to meet your views will be, I think, to get him appointed to the new ship the Company is building."

Lucy opened her eyes, and the blood rushed to her cheek. "Oh uncle, do I hear right? a ship? Are you so powerful? are you so kind? do you love your poor niece so well as all this? Oh, Uncle Bazalgette!"

"There is no end to my power," said the old man, solemnly; "no limit to my goodness, no bounds to my love for my poor niece. Are you in a hurry, my poor niece? Shall we have his commission down to-morrow, or wait a month?"

"To-morrow? is it possible? Oh, yes! I count the minutes till I say to his sister, 'There, Miss Dodd, I have friends who value me too highly to let me lie under these galling obligations.' Dear, dear uncle, I don't mind being under them to you, because I love you" (kisses).

"And not Mr. Dodd?"

"No, dear; and that is the reason I would rather give him a ship than—the only other thing that would make him happy. And really, but for your goodness, I should have been tempted to—ha! ha! Oh, I am so happy now. No; much as I admire my preserver's courage and delicacy and unselfishness and goodness, I don't love him; so, but for this, he MUST have been unhappy for life, and then I should have been miserable forever."

"Perfectly clear and satisfactory, my dear. Now, if the commission is to be down to-morrow, you must not stay here, because I have other letters to write, to go by the same courier that takes my application for the ship."

"And do you really think I will go till I have kissed you, Uncle Bazalgette?"

"On a subject so important, I hardly venture to give an opin—hallo! kissing, indeed? Why, it is like a young wolf flying at horseflesh."

"Then that will teach you not to be kinder to me than anybody else is."

Lucy ran out radiant and into the garden. Here she encountered Kenealy, and, coming on him with a blaze of beauty and triumph, fired a resolution that had smoldered in him a day or two.

He twirled his mustache and—popped briefly.

CHAPTER XXIII.

AFTER the first start of rueful astonishment, the indignation of the just fired Lucy's eyes.

She scolded him well. "Was this his return for all her late kindness?"

She hinted broadly at the viper of Aesop, and indicated more faintly an animal that, when one bestows the choicest favors on it, turns and rends one. Then, becoming suddenly just to the brute creation, she said: "No, it is only your abominable sex that would behave so perversely, so ungratefully."

"Don't understand," drawled Kenealy, "I thought you would laike it."

"Well, you see, I don't laike it."

"You seemed to be getting rather spooney on me."

"Spooney! what is that? one of your mess-room terms, I suppose."

"Yaas; so I thought you waunted me to pawp."

"Captain Kenealy, this subterfuge is unworthy of you. You know perfectly well why I distinguished you. Others pestered me with their attachments and nonsense, and you spared me that annoyance. In return, I did all in my power to show you the grateful friendship I thought you worthy of. But you have broken faith; you have violated the clear, though tacit understanding that subsisted between us, and I am very angry with you. I have some little influence left with my aunt, sir, and, unless I am much mistaken, you will shortly rejoin the army, sir."

"What a boa! what a dem'd boa!"

"And don't swear; that is another foolish custom you gentlemen have; it is almost as foolish as the other. Yes, I'll tell my aunt of you, and then you will see."

"What a boa! How horrid spaiteful you are."

"Well, I am rather vindictive. But my aunt is ten times worse, as her deserter shall find, unless—"

"Unless whawt?"

"Unless you beg my pardon directly." And at this part of the conversation Lucy was fain to turn her head away, for she found it getting difficult to maintain that severe countenance which she thought necessary to clothe her words with terror, and subjugate the gallant captain.

"Well, then, I apolojaize," said Kenealy.

"And I accept your apology; and don't do it again."

"I won't, 'pon honaa. Look heah; I swear I didn't mean to affront yah; I don't waunt yah to mayrry me; I only proposed out of civility."

"Come, then, it was not so black as it appeared. Courtesy is a good thing; and if you thought that, after staying a month in a house, you were bound by etiquette to propose to the marriageable part of it, it is pardonable, only don't do it again, please."

"I'll take caa—I'll take caa. I say your tempaa is not—quite—what those other fools think it is—no, by Jove;" and the captain glared.

"Nonsense: I am only a little fiendish on this one point. Well, then, steer clear of it, and you will find me a good crechaa on every other."

Kenealy vowed he would profit by the advice.

"Then there is my hand: we are friends again."

"You won't tell your aunt, nor the other fellaas?"

"Captain Kenealy, I am not one of your garrison ladies; I am a young person who has been educated; your extra civility will never be known to a soul: and you shall not join the army but as a volunteer."

"Then, dem me, Miss Fountain, if I wouldn't be cut in pieces to oblaige you. Just you tray me, and you'll faind, if I am not very braight, I am a man of honah. If those ether begaas annoy you, jaast tell me, and I'll parade 'em at twelve paces, dem me."

"I must try and find some less insane vent for your friendly feelings; and what can I do for you?"

"Yah couldn't go on pretending to be spooney on me, could yah?"

"Oh, no, no. What for?"

"I laike it; makes the other begaas misable."

"What worthy sentiments! it is a sin to balk them. I am sure there is no reason why I should not appear to adore you in public, so long as you let me keep my distance in private; but persons of my sex cannot do just what they would like.

We have feelings that pull us this way and that, and, after all this, I am afraid I shall never have the courage to play those pranks with you again; and that is a pity, since it amused you, and teased those that tease me."

In short, the house now contained two "holy alliances" instead of one. Unfortunately for Lucy, the hostile one was by far the stronger of the two; and even now it was preparing a terrible coup.

This evening the storm that was preparing blew good to one of a depressed class, which cannot fail to gratify the just.

Mrs. Bazalgette. "Jane, come to my room a minute; I have something for you. Here is a cashmere gown and cloak; the cloak I want; I can wear it with anything; but you may have the gown."

"Oh, thank you, mum; it is beautiful, and a'most as good as new. I am sure, mum, I am very much obliged to you for your kindness."

"No, no, you are a good girl, and a sensible girl. By the by, you might give me your opinion upon something. Does Miss Lucy prefer any one of our guests? You understand me."

"Well, mum, it is hard to say. Miss Lucy is as reserved as ever."

"Oh, I thought she might—ahem!"

"No, mum, I do assure you, not a word."

"Well, but you are a shrewd girl; tell me what you think: now, for instance, suppose she was compelled to choose between, say Mr. Hardie and Mr. Talboys, which would it be?"

"Well, mum, if you ask my opinion, I don't think Miss Lucy is the one to marry a fool; and by all accounts, there's a deal more in Mr. Hardies's head than what there isn't in Mr. Talboysese's."

"You are a clever girl. You shall have the cloak as well, and, if my niece marries, you shall remain in her service all the same."

"Thank you kindly, mum. I don't desire no better mistress, married or single; and Mr. Hardies is much respected in the town, and heaps o' money; so miss and me we couldn't do no better, neither of us. Your servant, mum, and thanks you for your bounty"; and Jane courtesied twice and went off with the spoils.

In the corridor she met old Fountain. "Stop, Jane," said he, "I want to speak to you."

"At your service, sir."

"In the first place, I want to give you something to buy a new gown"; and he took out a couple of sovereigns. "Where am I to put them? in your breast-pocket?"

"Put them under the cloak, sir," murmured Jane, tenderly. She loved sovereigns.

He put his hand under the heap of cashmere, and a quick little claw hit the coins and closed on them by almighty instinct.

"Now I want to ask your opinion. Is my niece in love with anyone?"

"Well, Mr. Fountains, if she is she don't show it."

"But doesn't she like one man better than another?"

"You may take your oath of that, if we could but get to her mind."

"Which does she like best, this Hardie or Mr. Talboys? Come, tell me, now."

"Well, sir, you know Mr. Talboys is an old acquaintance, and like brother and sister at Font Abbey. I do suppose she have been a scare of times alone with him for one, with Mr. Hardie's. That she should take up with a stranger and jilt an old acquaintance, now is it feasible?"

"Why, of course not. It was a foolish question; you are a young woman of sense. Here's a 5 pound note for you. You must not tell I spoke to you."

"Now is it likely, sir? My character would be broken forever."

"And you shall be with my niece when she is Mrs. Talboys."

"I might do worse, sir, and so might she. He is respected far and wide, and a grand house, and a carriage and four, and everything to make a lady comfortable. Your servant, sir, and wishes you many thanks."

"And such as Jane was, all true servants are."

The ancients used to bribe the Oracle of Delphi. Curious.

CHAPTER XXIV.

Lucy's twenty-first birthday dawned, but it was not to her the gay exulting day it is to some. Last night her uncle and aunt had gone a step further, and, instead of kissing her ceremoniously, had evaded her. They were drawing matters to a climax: once of age, each day would make her more independent in spirit as in circumstances. This morning she hoped custom would shield her from unkindness for one day at least. But no, they made it clear there was but one way back to their smiles. Their congratulations at the breakfast-table were cold and constrained; her heart fell; and long before noon on her birthday she was crying. Thus weakened, she had to encounter a thoroughly prepared attack. Mr. Bazalgette summoned her to his study at one o'clock, and there she found him and Mrs. Bazalgette and Mr. Fountain seated solemnly in conclave.

The merchant was adding up figures.

"Come, now, business," said he. "Dick has added them up: his figures are in that envelope; break the seal and open it, Lucy. If his total corresponds with mine, we are right; if not, I am wrong, and you will all have to go over it with me till we are right." A general groan followed this announcement. Luckily, the sum totals corresponded to a fraction.

Then Mr. Bazalgette made Lucy a little speech.

"My dear, in laying down that office which your amiable nature has rendered so agreeable, I feel a natural regret on your account that the property my colleague there and I have had to deal with on your account has not been more important. However, as far as it goes, we have been fortunate. Consols have risen amazingly since we took you off land and funded you. The rise in value of your little capital since your mother's death is calculated on this card. You have, also, some loose cash, which I will hand over to you immediately. Let me see—eleven hundred and sixty pounds and five shillings. Write your name in full on that paper, Lucy."

He touched a bell; a servant came. He wrote a line and folded it, inclosing Lucy's signature.

"Let this go to Mr. Hardie's bank immediately. Hardie will give you three per cent for your money. Better than nothing. You must have a check-book. He sent me a new one yesterday. Here it is; you shall have it. I wonder whether you know how to draw a check?"

"No, uncle."

"Look here, then. You note the particulars first on this counter-foil, which thus serves in some degree for an account-book. In drawing the check, place the sum in letters close to these printed words, and the sum in figures close to the pound. For want of this precaution, the holder of the check has been known to turn a 10 pound check into 110 pounds."

"Oh how wicked!"

"Mind what you say. Dexterity is the only virtue left in England; so we must be on our guard, especially in what we write with our name attached."

"I must say, Mr. Bazalgette, you are unwise to put such a sum of money into a young girl's hands."

"The young girl has been a woman an hour and ten minutes, and come into her property, movables, and cash aforesaid."

"If you were her real friend, you would take care of her money for her till she marries."

"The eighth commandment, my dear, the eighth commandment, and other primitive axioms: suum cuique, and such odd sayings: 'Him as keeps what isn't hisn, soon or late shall go to prison,' with similar apothegms. Total: let us keep the British merchant and the Newgate thief as distinct as the times permit. Fountain and Bazalgette, account squared, books closed, and I'm off!"

"Oh, uncle, pray stay!" said Lucy. "When you are by me, Rectitude and Sense seem present in person, and I can lean on them."

"Lean on yourself; the law has cut your leading-strings. Why patch 'em? It has made you a woman from a baby. Rise to your new rank. Rectitude and Sense are just as much wanted in the town of ——, where I am due, as they are in this house. Besides, Sense has spoken uninterrupted for ten minutes; prodigious! so now it is Nonsense's turn for the next ten hours." He made for the door; then suddenly returning, said: "I will leave a grain of sense, etc., behind me. What is marriage? Do you give it up? Marriage is a contract. Who are the parties? the papas and mammas, uncles and aunts? By George, you would think so to hear them talk. No, the contract is between two parties, and these two only. It is a printed contract. Anybody can read it gratis. None but idiots sign a contract without reading it; none but knaves sign a contract which, having read, they find they cannot execute. Matrimony is a mercantile affair; very well, then, import into it sound mercantile morality. Go to market; sell well; but, d—n it all, deliver the merchandise as per sample, viz., a woman warranted to love, honor and obey the purchaser. If you swindle the other contracting party in the essentials of the contract, don't complain when you are unhappy. Are shufflers entitled to happiness? and what are those who shuffle and prevaricate in a church any better than those who shuffle and prevaricate in a counting-house?" and the brute bolted.

"My husband is a worthy man," said Mrs. Bazalgette, languidly, "but now and then he makes me blush for him."

"Our good friend is a humorist," replied Fountain, good-humoredly, "and dearly loves a paradox"; and they pooh-poohed him without a particle of malice.

Then Mrs. Bazalgette turned to Lucy, and hoped that she did her the justice to believe she had none but affectionate motives in wishing to see her speedily established.

"Oh no, aunt," said Lucy. "Why should you wish to part with me? I give you but little trouble in your great house."

"Trouble, child? you know you are a comfort to have in any house."

This pleased Lucy; it was the first gracious word for a long time. Having thus softened her, Mrs. Bazalgette proceeded to attack her by all the weaknesses of her sex and age, and for a good hour pressed her so hard that the tears often gushed from Lucy's eyes over her red cheeks. The girl was worn by the length of the struggle and the pertinacity of the assault. She was as determined as ever to do nothing, but she had no longer the power to resist in words. Seeing her reduced to silence, and not exactly distinguishing between impassibility and yielding, Mrs. Bazalgette delivered the coup-de-grace.

"I must now tell you plainly, Lucy, that your character is compromised by being out all night with persons of the other sex. I would have spared you this, but your resistance compels those who love you to tell you all. Owing to that unfortunate trip, you are in such a situation that you must marry."

"The world is surely not so unjust as all this," sighed Lucy.

"You don't know the world as I do," was the reply. "And those who live in it cannot defy it. I tell you plainly, Lucy, neither your uncle nor I can keep you any longer, except as an engaged person. And even that engagement ought to be a very short one."

"What, aunt? what, uncle? your house is no longer mine?" and she buried her head upon the table.

"Well, Lucy," said Mr. Fountain, "of course we would not have told you this yesterday. It would have been ungenerous. But you are now your own mistress; you are independent. Young persons in your situation can generally forget in a day or two a few years of kindness. You have now an opportunity of showing us whether you are one of that sort."

Here Mrs. Bazalgette put in her word. "You will not lack people to encourage you in ingratitude—perhaps my husband himself; but if he does, it will make a lasting breach between him and me, of which you will have been the cause."

"Heaven forbid!" said Lucy, with a shudder. "Why should dear Mr. Bazalgette be drawn into my troubles? He is no relation of mine, only a loyal friend, whom may God bless and reward for his kindness to a poor fatherless, motherless girl. Aunt, uncle, if you will let me stay with you, I will be more kind, more attentive to you than I have been. Be persuaded; be advised. If you succeeded in getting rid of me, you might miss me, indeed you might. I know all your little ways so well."

"Lucy, we are not to be tempted to do wrong," said Mrs. Bazalgette, sternly. "Choose which of these two offers you will accept. Choose which you please. If you refuse both, you must pack up your things, and go and live by yourself, or with Mr. Dodd."

"Mr. Dodd? why is his name introduced? Was it necessary to insult me?" and her eyes flashed.

"Nobody wishes to insult you, Lucy. And I propose, madam, we give her a day to consider."

"Thank you, uncle."

"With all my heart; only, until she decides, she must excuse me if I do not treat her with the same affection as I used, and as I hope to do again. I am deeply wounded, and I am one that cannot feign."

"You need not fear me, aunt; my heart is turned to ice. I shall never intrude that love on which you set no value. May I retire?"

Mrs. Bazalgette looked to Mr. Fountain, and both bowed acquiescence. Lucy went out pale, but dry-eyed; despair never looked so lovely, or carried its head more proudly.

"I don't like it," said Mr. Fountain. "I am afraid we have driven the poor girl too hard."

"What are you afraid of, pray?"

"She looked to me just like a woman who would go and take an ounce of laudanum. Poor Lucy! she has been a good niece to me, after all;" and the water stood in the old bachelor's eyes.

Mrs. Bazalgette tapped him on the shoulder and said archly, but with a tone that carried conviction, "She will take no poison. She will hate us for an hour; then she will have a good cry: to-morrow she will come to our terms; and this day next year she will be very much obliged to us for doing what all women like, forcing her to her good with a little harshness."

CHAPTER XXV.

SAID Lucy as she went from the door, "Thank Heaven, they have insulted me!"

This does not sound logical, but that is only because the logic is so subtle and swift. She meant something of this kind: "I am of a yielding nature; I might have sacrificed myself to retain their affection; but they have roused a vice of mine, my pride, against them, so now I shall be immovable in right, thanks to my wicked pride. Thank Heaven, they have insulted me!" She then laid her head upon her bed and moaned, for she was stricken to the heart. Then she rose and wrote a hasty note, and, putting it in her bosom, came downstairs and looked for Captain Kenealy. He proved to be in the billiard-room, playing the spotted ball against the plain one. "Oh, Captain Kenealy, I am come to try your friendship; you said I might command you."

"Yaas!"

"Then will you mount my pony, and ride with this to Mrs. Wilson, to that farm where I kept you waiting so long, and you were not angry as anyone else would have been?"

"Yaas!"

"But not a soul must see it, or know where you are gone."

"All raight, Miss Fountain. Don't you be fraightened; I'm close as the grave, and I'll be there in less than haelf an hour."

"Yes; but don't hurt my dear pony either; don't beat him; and, above all, don't come back without an answer."

"I'll bring you an answer in an hour and twenty minutes." The captain looked at his watch, and went out with a smartness that contrasted happily with his slowness of speech.

Lucy went back to her own room and locked herself in, and with trembling hands began to pack up her jewels and some of her clothes. But when it came to this, wounded pride was sorely taxed by a host of reminiscences and tender regrets, and every now and then the tears suddenly gushed and fell upon her poor hands as she put things out, or patted them flat, to wander on the world.

While she is thus sorrowfully employed, let me try and give an outline of the feelings that had now for some time been secretly growing in her, since without their co-operation she would never have been driven to the strange step she now meditated.

Lucy was a very unselfish and very intelligent girl. The first trait had long blinded her to something; the second had lately helped to open her eyes.

If ever you find a person quick to discover selfishness in others, be sure that person is selfish; for it is only the selfish who come into habitual collision with selfishness, and feel how sharp-pointed a thing it is. When Unselfish meets Selfish, each acts after his kind; Unselfish gives way, Selfish holds his course, and so neither is thwarted, and neither finds out the other's character.

Lucy, then, of herself, would never have discovered her relatives' egotism. But they helped her, and she was too bright not to see anything that was properly pointed out to her.

When Fountain kept showing and proving Mrs. Bazalgette's egotism, and Mrs. Bazalgette kept showing and proving Mr. Fountain's egotism, Lucy ended by seeing both their egotisms, as clearly as either could desire; and, as she despised egotism, she lost her respect for both these people, and let them convince her they were both persons against whom she must be on her guard.

This was the direct result of their mines and countermines heretofore narrated, but not the only result. It followed indirectly, but inevitably, that the present holy alliance failed. Lucy had not forgotten the past; and to her this seemed not a holy, but an unholy, hollow, and empty alliance.

"They hate one another," said she, "but it seems they hate me worse, since they can hide their mutual dislike to combine against poor me."

Another thing: Lucy was one of those women who thirst for love, and, though not vain enough to be always showing they think they ought to be beloved, have quite secret amour propre enough to feel at the bottom of their hearts that they were sent here to that end, and that it is a folly and a shame not to love them more or less.

If ever Madame Ristori plays "Maria Stuarda" within a mile of you, go and see her. Don't chatter: you can do that at home; attend to the scene; the worst play ever played is not so unimproving as chit-chat. Then, when the scaffold is even now erected, and the poor queen, pale and tearful, palpitates in death's grasp, you shall see her suddenly illumined with a strange joy, and hear her say, with a marvelous burst of feminine triumph,

"I have been amata molto!!!"

Uttered, under a scaffold, as the Italian utters it, this line is a revelation of womanhood.

The English virgin of our humbler tale had a soul full of this feeling, only she had never learned to set the love of sex above other loves; but, mark you, for that very reason, a mortal insult to her heart from her beloved relatives was as mortifying, humiliating and unpardonable as is, to other high-spirited girls, an insult from their favored lover.

What could she do more than she had done to win their love? No, their hearts were inaccessible to her.

"They wish to get rid of me. Well, they shall. They refuse me their houses. Well, I will show them the value of their houses to me. It was their hearts I clung to, not their houses."

A tap came to Lucy's door.

"Who is that? I am busy."

"Oh, miss!" said an agitated voice, "may I speak to you—the captain!"

"What captain?" inquired Lucy, without opening the door.

"Knealys, miss.

"I will come out to you. Now. Has Captain Kenealy returned already?"

"La! no, miss. He haven't been anywhere as I know of. He had them about him as couldn't spare him."

"Something is the matter, Jane. What is it?"

Jane lowered her voice mysteriously. "Well, miss, the captain is—in trouble."

"Oh, dear, what has happened?"

"Well, the fact is, miss, the captain's—took"

"I cannot understand you. Pray speak intelligibly."

"Arrested, miss."

"Captain Kenealy arrested! Oh, Heaven! for what crime?"

"La, miss, no crime at all—leastways not so considered by the gentry. He is only took in payment of them beautiful reg-mentals. However, black or red, he is always well put on. I am sure he looks just out of a band-box; and I got it all out of one of the men as it's a army tailor, which he wrote again and again, and sent his bill, and the captain he took no notice; then the tailor he sent him a writ, and the captain he took no notice; then the tailor he lawed him, but the captain he kep' on a taking no more notice nor if it was a dog a barking, and then a putting all them ere barks one after another in a letter, and sending them by the post; so the end is, the captain is arrested; and now he behooves to attend a bit to what is a going on around an about him, as the saying is, and so he is waiting to pay you his respects before he starts for Bridewell."

"My fatal advice! I ruin all my friends."

"Keep dark," says he; "don't tell a soul except Miss Fountain."

"Where is he? Oh?"

Jane offered to show her that, and took her to the stable yard. Arriving with a face full of tender pity and concern, Lucy was not a little surprised to find the victim smoking cigars in the center of his smoking captors. The men touched their hats, and Captain Kenealy said: "Isn't it a boa, Miss Fountain? they won't let me do your little commission. In London they will go anywhere with a fellaa."

"London ye knows," explained the assistant, "but this here is full of hins and houts, and folyidge."

"Oh, sir," cried Lucy to the best-dressed captor, "surely you will not be so cruel as to take a gentleman like Captain Kenealy to prison?"

"Very sorry, marm, but we 'ave no hoption: takes 'em every day; don't we, Bill?"

Bill nodded.

"But, sir, as it is only for money, can you not be induced by—by—money—"

"Bill, lady's going to pay the debtancosts. Show her the ticket. Debt eighty pund, costs seven pund eighteen six."

"What! will you liberate him if I pay you eighty-eight pounds?"

"Well, marm, to oblige you we will; won't we, Bill?"

He winked. Bill nodded.

"Then pray stay here a minute, and this shall be arranged to your entire satisfaction"; and she glided swiftly away, followed by Jane, wriggling.

"Quite the lady, Bill."

"Kevite. Captn is in luck. Hare ve to be at the vedding, capn?"

"Dem your impudence! I'll cross-buttock yah!"

"Hold your tongue, Bill—queering a gent. Draw it mild, captain. Debtancosts ain't paid yet. Here they come, though."

Lucy returned swiftly, holding aloft a slip of paper.

"There, sir, that is a check for 90 pounds; it is the same thing as money, you are doubtless aware." The man took it and inspected it keenly.

"Very sorry, marm, but can't take it. It's a lady's check."

"What! is it not written properly?"

"Beautiful, marm. But when we takes these beautiful-wrote checks to the bank, the cry is always, 'No assets.'"

"But Uncle Bazalgette said everybody would give me money for it."

"What! is Mr. Bazalgette your uncle, marm? then you go to him, and get his check in place of yours, and the captain will be free as the birds in the hair."

"Oh, thank you, sir," cried Lucy, and the next minute she was in Mr. Bazalgette's study. "Uncle, don't be angry with me: it is for no unworthy purpose; only don't ask me; it might mortify another; but would you give me a check of your own for mine? They will not receive mine."

Mr. Bazalgette looked grave, and even sad; but he sat quietly down without a word, and drew her a check, taking hers, which he locked in his desk. The tears were in Lucy's eyes at his gravity and his delicacy. "Some day I will tell you," said she. "I have nothing to reproach myself, indeed—indeed."

"Make the rogue—or jade—give you a receipt," groaned Bazalgette.

"All right, marm, this time. Captain, the world is hall before you where to chewse. But this is for ninety, marm;" and he put his hand very slowly into his pocket.

"Do me the favor to keep the rest for your trouble, sir."

"Trouble's a pleasure, marm. It is not often we gets a tip for taking a gent. Ve are funk shin hairies as is not depreciated, mam, and the more genteel we takes 'em the rougher they cuts; and the very women no more like you nor dark to light; but flies at us like ryal Bengal tigers, through taking of us for the creditors."

"Verehas we hare honly servants of the ke veen;" suggested No. 2, hashing his mistress's English.

"Stow your gab, Bill, and mizzle. Let the captain thank the lady. Good-day, marm."

"Oh, my poor friend, what language! and my ill advice threw you into their company!"

Captain Kenealy told her, in his brief way, that the circumstance was one of no import, except in so far as it had impeded his discharge of his duty to her. He then mounted the pony, which had been waiting for him more than half an hour.

"But it is five o'clock," said Lucy; "you will be too late for dinner."

"Dinner be dem—d," drawled the man of action, and rode off like a flash.

"It is to be, then," said Lucy, and her heart ebbed. It had ebbed and flowed a good many times in the last hour or two.

Captain Kenealy reappeared in the middle of dinner. Lucy scanned his face, but it was like the outside of a copy-book, and she was on thorns. Being too late, he lost his place near her at dinner, and she could not whisper to him. However, when the ladies retired he opened the door, and Lucy let fall a word at his feet: "Come up before the rest."

Acting on this order, Kenealy came up, and found Lucy playing sad tunes softly on the piano and Mrs. Bazalgette absent. She was trying something on upstairs. He gave Lucy a note from Mrs. Wilson. She opened it, and the joyful color suffused her cheek, and she held out her hand to him; but, as she turned her head away mighty prettily at the same time, she did not see the captain was proffering a second document, and she was a little surprised when, instead of a warm grasp, all friendship and no love, a piece of paper was shoved into her delicate palm. She took it; looked first at Kenealy, then at it, and was sore puzzled.

The document was in Kenealy's handwriting, and at first Lucy thought it must be intended as a mere specimen of caligraphy; for not only was it beautifully written, but in letters of various sizes. There were three gigantic vowels, I. O. U. There were little wee notifications of time and place, and other particulars of medium size. The general result was that Henry Kenealy O'd Lucy Fountain ninety pound for value received per loan. Lucy caught at the meaning. "But, my dear friend," said she, innocently, "you mistake. I did not lend it you; I meant to give it you. Will you not accept it? Are we not friends?"

"Much oblaiged. Couldn't do it. Dishonable."

"Oh, pray do not let me wound your pride. I know what it is to have one's pride wounded; call it a loan if you wish. But, dear friend, what am I to do with this?"

"When you want the money, order your man of business to present it to me, and, if I don't pay, lock me up, for I shall deserve it."

"I think I understand. This is a memorandum—a sort of reminder."

"Yaas."

"Then clearly I am not the person to whom it should be given. No; if you want to be reminded of this mighty matter, put this in your desk; if it gets into mine, you will never see it again; I will give you fair warning. There—hide it— quick—here they come."

They did come, all but Mr. Bazalgette, who was at work in his study. Mr. Talboys came up to the piano and said gravely, "Miss Fountain, are you aware of the fate of the lugger—of the boat we went out in?"

Indeed I am. I have sent the poor widow some clothes and a little money."

"I have only just been informed of it," said Mr. Talboys, "and I feel under considerable obligations to Mr. Dodd."

"The feeling does you credit."

"Should you meet him, will you do me the honor to express my gratitude to him?"

"I would, with pleasure, Mr. Talboys, but there is no chance whatever of my seeing Mr. Dodd. His sister is staying in Market Street, No. 80, and if you would call on them or write to them, it would be a kindness, and I think they would both feel it."

"Humph!" said Talboys, doubtfully. Here a servant stepped up to Miss Fountain. "Master would be glad to see you in his study, miss."

"I have got something for you, Lucy. I know what it is, so run away with it, and read it in your own room, for I am busy." He handed her a long sealed packet. She took it, trembling, and flew to her own room with it, like a hawk carrying off a little bird to its nest. She broke the enormous seal and took out the inclosure. It was David Dodd's commission. He was captain of the Rajah, the new ship of eleven hundred tons' burden.

While she gazes at it with dilating eye and throbbing heart, I may as well undeceive the reader. This was not really effected in forty-eight hours. Bazalgette only pretended that, partly out of fun, partly out of nobility. Ever since a certain interview in his study with David Dodd, who was a man after his own heart, he had taken a note, and had worked for him with "the Company;" for Bazalgette was one of those rare men who reduce performance to a certainty long before they promise. His promises were like pie-crust made to be eaten, and eaten hot.

Lucy came out of her room, and at the same moment issued forth from hers

Mrs. Bazalgette in a fine new dress. It was that black glace; silk, divested of gloom by cheerful accessories, in which she had threatened to mourn eternally Lucy's watery fate. Fire flashed from the young lady's eyes at the sight of it. She went down to her uncle, muttering between her ivory teeth: "All the same —all the same;" and her heart flowed. The next minute, at sight of Mr. Bazalgette it ebbed. She came into his room, saying: "Oh, Uncle Bazalgette, it is not to thank you—that I can never do worthily; it is to ask another favor. Do, pray, let me spend this evening with you; let me be where you are. I will be as still as a mouse. See, I have brought some work; or, if you would but let me help you. Indeed, uncle, I am not a fool. I am very quick to learn at the bidding of those I love. Let me write your letters for you, or fold them up, or direct them, or something—do, pray!"

"Oh, the caprices of young ladies! Well, can you write large and plain? Not you."

"I can imitate anything or anybody."

"Imitate this hand then. I'll walk and dictate, you sit and write."

"Oh, how nice!"

"Delicious! The first is to—Hetherington. Now, Lucy, this is a dishonest, ungrateful old rogue, who has made thousands by me, and now wants to let me into a mine, with nothing in it but water. It would suck up twenty thousand pounds as easily as that blotting-paper will suck up our signature."

"Heartless traitor! monster!" cried Lucy.

"Are you ready?"

"Yes," and her eye flashed and the pen was to her a stiletto.

Bazalgette dictated, "My dear Sir—"

"What? to a cheat?"

"Custom, child. I'll have a stamp made. Besides, if we let them see we see through them, they would play closer and closer—"

"My dear Sir—In answer to yours of date 11th instant, I regret to say—that circumstances prevent—my closing—with your obliging—and friendly offer."

They wrote eight letters; and Lucy's quick fingers folded up prospectuses, and her rays brightened the room. When the work was done, she clung round Mr. Bazalgette and caressed him, and seemed strangely unwilling to part with him at all; in fact, it was twelve o'clock, and the drawing-room empty, when they parted.

At one o'clock the whole house was dark except one room, and both windows of that room blazed with light. And it happened there was a spectator of this phenomenon. A man stood upon the grass and eyed those lights as if they were the stars of his destiny.

It was David Dodd. Poor David! he had struck a bargain, and was to command a coasting vessel, and carry wood from the Thames to our southern ports. An irresistible impulse brought him to look, before he sailed, on the place that held the angel who had destroyed his prospects, and whom he loved as much as ever, though he was too proud to court a second refusal.

"She watches, too," thought David, "but it is not for me, as I for her."

At half past one the lights began to dance before his wearied eyes, and presently David, weakened by his late fever, dozed off and forgot all his troubles, and slept as sweetly on the grass as he had often slept on the hard deck, with his head upon a gun.

Luck was against the poor fellow. He had not been unconscious much more than ten minutes when Lucy's window opened and she looked out; and he never saw her. Nor did she see him; for, though the moon was bright, it was not shining on him; he lay within the shadow of a tree. But Lucy did see something—a light upon the turnpike road about forty yards from Mr. Bazalgette's gates. She slipped cautiously down, a band-box in her hand, and, unbolting the door that opened on the garden, issued out, passed within a few yards of Dodd, and went round to the front, and finally reached the turnpike road. There she found Mrs. Wilson, with a light-covered cart and horse, and a lantern. At sight of her Mrs. Wilson put out the light, and they embraced; then they spoke in whispers.

"Come, darling, don't tremble; have you got much more?"

"Oh, yes, several things."

"Look at that, now! But, dear heart, I was the same at your age, and should be now, like enough. Fetch them all, as quick as you like. I am feared to leave Blackbird, or I'd help you down with 'em."

"Is there nobody with you to take care of us?"

"What do you mean—men folk? Not if I know it."

"You are right. You are wise. Oh, how courageous!" And she went back for her finery. And certain it is she had more baggage than I should choose for a forced march.

But all has an end—even a female luggage train; so at last she put out all her lights and came down, stepping like a fairy, with a large basket in her hand.

Now it happened that by this time the moon's position was changed, and only a part of David lay in the shade; his head and shoulders glittered in broad moonlight; and Lucy, taking her farewell of a house where she had spent many happy days, cast her eyes all around to bid good-by, and spied a man lying within a few paces, and looking like a corpse in the silver sheen. She dropped her basket; her knees knocked together with fear, and she flew toward Mrs. Wilson. But she did not go far, for the features, indistinct as they were by distance and pale light, struck her mind, and she stopped and looked timidly over her shoulder. The figure never moved. Then, with beating heart, she went toward him slowly and so stealthily that she would have passed a mouse without disturbing it, and presently she stood by him and looked down on him as he lay.

And as she looked at him lying there, so pale, so uncomplaining, so placid, under her windows, this silent proof of love, and the thought of the raging sea this helpless form had steered her through, and all he had suffered as well as acted for her, made her bosom heave, and stirred all that was woman within her. He loved her still, then, or why was he here? And then the thought that she had done something for him too warmed her heart still more toward him. And there was nothing for her to repel now, for he lay motionless; there was nothing for her to escape—he did not pursue her; nothing to negative—he did not propose anything to her. Her instinct of defense had nothing to lay hold of; so, womanlike, she had a strong impulse to wake him and be kind to him—as kind as she could be without committing herself. But, on the other hand, there was shy, trembling, virgin modesty, and shame that he should detect her making a midnight evasion, and fear of letting him think she loved him.

While she stood thus, with something drawing her on and something drawing her back, and palpitating in every fiber, Mrs. Wilson's voice was heard in low but anxious tones calling her. A feather turned the balanced scale. She must go. Fate had decided for her. She was called. Then the sprites of mischief tempted her to let David know she had been near him. She longed to put his commission into his pocket; but that was impossible. It was at the very bottom of her box. She took out her tablets, wrote the word "Adieu," tore out half the leaf, and, bending over David, attached the little bit of paper by a pin to the tail of his coat. If he had been ever so much awake he could not have felt her doing it; for her hand touching him, and the white paper settling on his coat, was all done as lights a spot of down on still water from the bending neck of a swan.

"No, dear Mrs. Wilson, we must not go yet. I will hold the horse, and you must go back for me for something."

"I'm agreeable. What is it? Why, what is up? How you do pant!"

"I have made a discovery. There is a gentleman lying asleep there on the wet grass."

"Lackadaisy! why, you don't say so."

"It is a friend; and he will catch his death."

"Why, of course he will. He will have had a drop too much, Miss Lucy. I'll wake him, and we will take him along home with us."

"Oh, not for the world, nurse. I would not have him see what I am doing, oh, not for all the world!"

"Where is he?"

"In there, under the great tree."

"Well, you get into the cart, miss, and hold the reins"; and Mrs. Wilson went into the grounds and soon found David.

She put her hand on his shoulder, and he awoke directly, and looked surprised at Mrs. Wilson.

"Are you better, sir?" said the good woman. "Why, if it isn't the handsome gentleman that was so kind to me! Now do ee go in, sir—do ee go in. You will catch your death o' cold." She made sure he was staying at the house.

David looked up at Lucy's windows. "Yes, I will go home, Mrs. Wilson; there is nothing to stay for now"; and he accompanied her to the cart. But Mrs. Wilson remembered Lucy's desire not to be seen; so she said very loud, "I'm sure it's very lucky me and my niece happened to be coming home so late, and see you lying there. Well, one good turn deserves another. Come and see me at my farm; you go through the village of Harrowden, and anybody there will tell you where Dame Wilson do live. I would ask you to-night, but—" she hesitated, and Lucy let down her veil.

"No, thank you, not now; my sister will be fretting as it is. Good-morning"; and his steps were heard retreating as Mrs. Wilson mounted the cart.

"Well, I should have liked to have taken him home and warmed him a bit," said the good woman to Lucy; "it is enough to give him the rheumatics for life. However, he is not the first honest man as has had a drop too much, and taken 's rest without a feather-bed. Alack, miss, why, you are all of a tremble! What ails you? I'm a fool to ask. Ah! well, you'll soon be at home, and naught to vex you. That is right; have a good cry, do. Ay, ay, 'tis hard to be forced to leave our nest. But all places are bright where love abides; and there's honest hearts both here and there, and the same sky above us wherever we wander, and the God of the fatherless above that; and better a peaceful cottage than a palace full of strife." And with many such homely sayings the rustic consoled her nursling on their little journey, not quite in vain.

CHAPTER XXVI.

NEXT morning the house was in an uproar. Servants ran to and fro, and the fish-pond was dragged at Mr. Fountain's request. But on these occasions everybody claims a right to speak, and Jane came into the breakfast-room and said: "If you please, mum, Miss Lucy isn't in the pond, for she have taken a good part of her clothes, and all her jewels."

This piece of common sense convinced everybody on the spot except Mrs. Bazalgette. That lady, if she had decided on "making a hole in the water," would have sat on the bank first, and clapped on all her jewels, and all her richest dresses, one on the top of another. Finally, Mr. Bazalgette, who wore a somber air, and had not said a word, requested everybody to mind their own business. "I have a communication from Lucy," said he, "and I do not at present disapprove the step she has taken."

All eyes turned with astonishment toward him, and the next moment all voices opened on him like a pack of hounds. But he declined to give them any further information. Between ourselves he had none to give. The little note Lucy left on his table merely begged him to be under no anxiety, and prayed him to suspend his judgment of her conduct till he should know the whole case. It was his strong good sense which led him to pretend he was in the whole secret. By this means he substituted mystery for scandal, and contrived that the girl's folly might not be irreparable.

At the same time he was deeply indignant with her, and, above all, with her hypocrisy in clinging round him and kissing him the very night she meditated flight from his house.

"I must find the girl out and get her back;" said he, and directly after breakfast he collected his myrmidons and set them to discover her retreat.

The outward frame-work of the holy alliance remained standing, but within it was dissolving fast. Each of the allies was even now thinking how to find Lucy and make a separate peace. During the flutter which now subsided, one person had done nothing but eat pigeon-pie. It was Kenealy, captain of horse.

Now eating pigeon-pie is not in itself a suspicious act, but ladies are so sharp. Mrs. Bazalgette said to herself, "This creature alone is not a bit surprised (for Bazalgette is fibbing); why is this creature not surprised? humph! Captain Kenealy," said she, in honeyed tones, "what would you advise us to do?"

"Advertaize," drawled the captain, as cool as a cucumber.

"Advertise? What! publish her name?"

"No, no names. I'll tell you;" and he proceeded to drawl out very slowly, from memory, the following advertisement. N. B.—The captain was a great reader of advertisements, and of little else.

      "WANDERAA, RETARN.

"If L. F. will retarn—to her afflicted—relatives—she shall be received with open aams. And shall be forgotten and forgiven—and reunaited affection shall solace every wound."

"That is the style. It always brings 'em back—dayvilish good paie—have some moa."

Mr. Fountain and Mrs. Bazalgette raised an outcry against the captain's advice, and, when the table was calm again, Mrs. Bazalgette surprised them all by fixing her eyes on Kenealy, and saying quietly, "You know where she is." She added more excitedly: "Now don't deny it. On your honor, sir, have you no idea where my niece is?"

"Upon my honah, I have an idea."

"Then tell me."

"I'd rayther not."

"Perhaps you would prefer to tell me in private?"

"No; prefer not to tell at all."

Then the whole table opened on him, and appealed to his manly feeling, his sense of hospitality, his humanity—to gratify their curiosity.

Kenealy stretched himself out from the waist downward, and delivered himself thus, with a double infusion of his drawl:—

"See yah all dem—d first."

At noon on the same day, by the interference of Mrs. Bazalgette, the British army was swelled with Kenealy, captain of horse.

The whole day passed, and Lucy's retreat was not yet discovered. But more than one hunter was hemming her in.

The next day, being the second after her elopement with her nurse, at eleven in the forenoon, Lucy and Mrs. Wilson sat in the little parlor working. Mrs. Wilson had seen the poultry fed, the butter churned, and the pudding safe in the pot, and her mind was at ease for a good hour to come, so she sat quiet and peaceful. Lucy, too, was at peace. Her eye was clear; and her color coming back; she was not bursting with happiness, for there was a sweet pensiveness mixed with her sweet tranquillity; but she looked every now and then smiling from her work up at Mrs. Wilson, and the dame kept looking at her with a motherly joy caused by her bare presence on that hearth. Lucy basked in these maternal glances. At last she said: "Nurse."

"My dear?"

"If you had never done anything for me, still I should know you loved me."

"Should ye, now?"

"Oh yes; there is the look in your eye that I used to long to see in my poor aunt's, but it never came."

"Well, Miss Lucy, I can't help it. To think it is really you setting there by my fire! I do feel like a cat with one kitten. You should check me glaring you out o' countenance like that."

"Check you? I could not bear to lose one glance of that honest tender eye. I would not exchange one for all the flatteries of the world. I am so happy here, so tranquil, under my nurse's wing."

With this declaration came a little sigh.

Mrs. Wilson caught it. "Is there nothing wanting, dear?"

"No."

"Well, I do keep wishing for one thing."

"What is that?"

"Oh, I can't help my thoughts."

"But you can help keeping them from me, nurse."

"Well, my dear, I am like a mother; I watch every word of yours and every look; and it is my belief you deceive yourself a bit: many a young maid has done that. I do judge there is a young man that is more to you than you think for."

"Who on earth is that, nurse?" asked Lucy, coloring.

"The handsome young gentleman."

"Oh, they are all handsome—all my pests."

"The one I found under your window, Miss Lucy; he wasn't in liquor; so what was he there for? and you know you were not at your ease till you had made me go and wake him, and send him home; and you were all of a tremble. I'm a widdy now, and can speak my mind to men-folk all one as women-folk; but I've been a maid, and I can mind how I was in those days. Liking did use to whisper me to do so and so; Shyness up and said, 'La! not for all the world; what'll he think?'"

"Oh, nurse, do you believe me capable of loving one who does not love me?"

"No. Who said he doesn't love you? What was he there for? I stick to that."

"Now, nurse, dear, be reasonable; if Mr. Dodd loved me, would he go to sleep in my presence?"

"Eh! Miss Lucy, the poor soul was maybe asleep before you left your room."

"It is all the same. He slept while I stood close to him ever so long. Slept while I—If I loved anybody as these gentlemen pretend they love us, should I sleep while the being I adored was close to me?"

"You are too hard upon him. 'The spirit is willing but the flesh is weak.' Why, miss, we do read of Eutychus, how he snoozed off setting under Paul himself —up in a windy—and down a-tumbled. But parson says it wasn't that he didn't love religion, or why should Paul make it his business to bring him to life again, 'stead of letting un lie for a warning to the sleepy-headed ones. 'Twas a wearied body, not a heart cold to God,' says our parson."

"Now, nurse, I take you at your word. If Eutychus had been Eutycha, and in love with St. Paul, Eutycha would never have gone to sleep, though St. Paul preached all day and all night; and if Dorcas had preached instead of St. Paul, and Eutychus been in love with her, he would never have gone to sleep, and you know it."

At this home-thrust Mrs. Wilson was staggered, but the next moment her sense of discomfiture gave way to a broad expression of triumph at her nursling's wit.

"Eh! Miss Lucy," cried she, showing a broadside of great white teeth in a rustic chuckle, "but ye've got a tongue in your head. Ye've sewed up my stocking, and 'tisn't many of them can do that." Lucy followed up her advantage.

"And, nurse, even when he was wide awake and stood by the cart, no inward sentiment warned him of my presence; a sure sign he did not love me. Though I have never experienced love, I have read of it, and know all about it." [Justice des Femmes!]

"Well, Miss Lucy, have it your own way; after all, if he loves you he will find you out."

"Of course he would, and you will see he will do nothing of the kind."

"Then I wish I knew where he was; I would pull him in at my door by the scruf of the neck."

"And then I should jump out at the window. Come, try on your new cap, nurse, that I have made for you, and let us talk about anything you like except gentlemen. Gentlemen are a sore subject with me. Gentlemen have been my ruin."

"La, Miss Lucy!"

"I assure you they have; why, have they not set my uncle's heart against me, and my aunt's, and robbed me of the affection I once had for both? I believe gentlemen to be the pests of society; and oh! the delight of being here in this calm retreat, where love dwells, and no gentleman can find me. Ah! ah! Oh! What is that?"

For a heavy blow descended on the door. "That is Jenny's knock," said Mrs. Wilson; dryly. "Come in, Jenny." The servant, thus invited, burst the door open as savagely as she had struck it, and announced with a knowing grin, "A GENTLEMAN—for Miss Fountain!!"

CHAPTER XXVII.

DAVID and Eve sat together at their little breakfast, and pressed each other to eat; but neither could eat. David's night excursion had filled Eve with new misgivings. It was the act of a madman; and we know the fears that beset her on that head, and their ground. He had come home shivering, and she had forced him to keep his bed all that day. He was not well now, and bodily weakness, added to his other afflictions, bore his spirit down, though nothing could cow it.

"When are you to sail?" inquired Eve, sick-like.

"In three days. Cargo won't be on board before."

"A coasting vessel?"

"A man can do his duty in a coaster as well as a merchantman or a frigate." But he sighed.

"Would to God you had never seen her!"

"Don't blame her—blame me. I had good advice from my little sister, but I was willful. Never mind, Eve, I needn't to blush for loving her; she is worthy of it all."

"Well, think so, David, if you can." And Eve, thoroughly depressed, relapsed into silence. The postman's rap was heard, and soon after a long inclosure was placed in Eve's hand.

Poor little Eve did not receive many letters; and, sad as she was, she opened this with some interest; but how shall I paint its effect? She kept uttering shrieks of joy, one after another, at each sentence. And when she had shrieked with joy many times, she ran with the large paper round to David. "You are captain of the Rajah! ah! the new ship! ah! eleven hundred tons! Oh, David! Oh, my heart! Oh! oh! oh!" and the poor little thing clasped her arms round her brother's neck, and kissed him again and again, and cried and sobbed for joy.

All men, and most women, go through life without once knowing what it is to cry for joy, and it is a comfort to think that Eve's pure and deep affection brought her such a moment as this in return for much trouble and sorrow. David, stout-hearted as he was, was shaken as the sea and the wind had never yet shaken him. He turned red and white alternately, and trembled. "Captain of the Rajah! It is too good—it is too good! I have done nothing for it"; and he was incredulous.

Eve was devouring the inclosure. "It is her doing," she cried; "it is all her doing."

"Whose?"

"Who do you think? I am in the air! I am in heaven! Bless her—oh, God, bless her for this. Never speak against cold-blooded folk before me; they have twice the principle of us hot ones: I always said so. She is a good creature; she is a true friend; and you accused her of ingratitude!"

"That I never did."

"You did—Rajah—he! he! oh!—and I defended her. Here, take and read that: is that a commission or not? Now you be quiet, and let us see what she says. No, I can't; I cannot keep the tears out of my eyes. Do take and read it, David; I'm blind."

David took the letter, kissed it, and read it out to Eve, and she kept crowing and shedding tears all the time.

"DEAR MISS DODD—I admire too much your true affection for your brother to be indifferent to your good opinion. Think of me as leniently as you can. Perhaps it gives me as much pleasure to be able to forward you the inclosed as the receipt of it, I hope, may give you.

"It would, I think, be more wise, and certainly more generous, not to let Mr. Dodd think he owes in any degree to me that which, if the world were just, would surely have been his long ago. Only, some few months hence, when it can do him no harm, I could wish him not to think his friend Lucy was ungrateful, or even cold in his service, who saved her life, and once honored her with so warm an esteem. But all this I confide to your discretion and your justice. Dear Miss Dodd, those who give pain to others do not escape it themselves, nor is it just they should. My insensibility to the merit of persons of the other sex has provoked my relatives; they have punished me for declining Mr. Dodd's inferiors with a bitterness Mr. Dodd, with far more cause, never showed me; so you see at each turn I am reminded of his superiority.

"The result is, I am separated from my friends, and am living all alone with my dear old nurse, at her farmhouse.

"Since, then, I am unhappy, and you are generous, you will, I think, forgive me all the pain I have caused you, and will let me, in bidding you adieu, subscribe myself,

"Yours affectionately,

"It is the letter of a sweet girl, David, with a noble heart; and she has taken a noble revenge of me for what I said to her the other day, and made her cry, like a little brute as I am. Why, how glum you look!"

"Eve," said David, "do you think I will accept this from her without herself?"

"Of course you will. Don't be too greedy, David. Leave the girl in peace; she has shown you what she will do and what she won't. One such friend as this is worth a hundred lovers. Give me her dear little note."

While Eve was persuing it, David went out, but soon returned, with his best coat on, and his hat in his hand. Eve asked in some surprise where he was going in such a hurry.

"To her."

"Well, David, now I come to read her letter quietly, it is a woman's letter all over; you may read it which way you like. What need had she to tell me she has just refused offers? And then she tells me she is all alone. That sounds like a hint. The company of a friend might he agreeable. Brush your coat first, at any rate; there's something white on it; it is a paper; it is pinned on. Come here. Why, what is this? It is written on. 'Adieu.'" And Eve opened her eyes and mouth as well.

She asked him when he wore the coat last.

"The day before yesterday."

"Were you in company of any girls?"

"Not I."

"But this is written by a girl, and it is pinned on by a girl; see how it is quilted in!! that's proof positive. Oh! oh! oh! look here. Look at these two 'Adieus'— the one in the letter and this; they are the same—precisely the same. What, in Heaven's name, is the meaning of this? Were you in her company that night?"

"No."

"Will you swear that?"

"No, I can't swear it, because I was asleep a part of the time; but waking in her company I was not."

"It is her writing, and she pinned it on you."

"How can that be, Eve?"

"I don't know; I am sure she did, though. Look at this 'Adieu' and that; you'll never get it out of my head but what one hand wrote them both. You are so green, a girl would come behind you and pin it on you, and you never feel her."

While saying these words, Eve slyly repinned it on him without his feeling or knowing anything about it.

David was impatient to be gone, but she held him a minute to advise him.

"Tell her she must and shall. Don't take a denial. If you are cowardly, she will be bold; but if you are bold and resolute, she will knuckle down. Mind that; and don't go about it with such a face as that, as long as my arm. If she says 'No,' you have got the ship to comfort you. Oh! I am so happy!"

"No, Eve," said David, "if she won't give me herself, I'll never take her ship. I'd die a foretopman sooner;" and, with these parting words, he renewed all his sister's anxiety. She sat down sorrowfully, and the horrible idea gained on her that there was mania in David's love for Lucy.

CHAPTER XXVIII.

DAVID had one advantage over others that were now hunting Lucy. Mrs. Wilson had unwittingly given him pretty plain directions how to find her farmhouse; and as Eve, in the exercise of her discretion, or indiscretion, had shown David Lucy's letter, he had only to ride to Harrowden and inquire. But, on the other hand, his competitors were a few miles nearer the game, and had a day's start.

David got a horse and galloped to Harrowden, fed him at the inn, and asked where Mrs. Wilson's farm was. The waiter, a female, did not know, but would inquire. Meantime David asked for two sheets of paper, and wrote a few lines on each; then folded them both (in those days envelopes were not), but did not seal them. Mrs. Wilson's farm turned out to be only two miles from Harrowden, and the road easy to find. He was soon there; gave his horse to one of the farm-boys, and went into the kitchen and asked if Miss Fountain lived there. This question threw him into the hands of Jenny, who invited him to follow her, and, unlike your powdered and noiseless lackey, pounded the door with her fist, kicked it open with her foot, and announced him with that thunderbolt of language which fell so inopportunely on Lucy's self-congratulations.

The look Mrs. Wilson cast on Lucy was droll enough; but when David's square shoulders and handsome face filled up the doorway, a second look followed that spoke folios.

Lucy rose, and with heightened color, but admirable self-possession, welcomed David like a valued friend.

Mrs. Wilson's greeting was broad and hearty; and, very soon after she had made him sit down, she bounced up, crying: "You will stay dinner now you be come, and I must see as they don't starve you." So saying, out she went; but, looking back at the door, was transfixed by an arrow of reproach from her nursling's eye.

Lucy's reception of David, kind as it was, was not encouraging to one coming on David's errand, for there was the wrong shade of amity in it.

In times past it would have cooled David with misgivings, but now he did not give himself time to be discouraged; he came to make a last desperate effort, and he made it at once.

"Miss Lucy, I have got the Rajah, thanks to you."

"Thanks to me, Mr. Dodd? Thanks to your own high character and merit."

"No, Miss Lucy, you know better, and I know better, and there is your own sweet handwriting to prove it."

"Miss Dodd has showed you my letter?"

"How could she help it?"

"What a pity! how injudicious!"

"The truth is like the light; why keep it out? Yes; what I have worked for, and battled the weather so many years, and been sober and prudent, and a hard student at every idle hour—that has come to me in one moment from your dear hand."

"It is a shame."

"Bless you, Miss Lucy," cried David, not noting the remark.

Lucy blushed, and the water stood in her eyes. She murmured softly: "You should not say Miss Lucy; it is not customary. You should say Lucy, or Miss Fountain."

This apropos remark by way of a female diversion.

"Then let me say Lucy to-day, for perhaps I shall never say that, or anything that is sweet to say again. Lucy, you know what I came for?"

"Oh, yes, to receive my congratulations."

"More than that, a great deal—to ask you to go halves in the Rajah."

Lucy's eyebrows demanded an explanation.

"She is worth two thousand a year to her commander; and that is too much for a bachelor."

Lucy colored and smiled. "Why, it is only just enough for bachelors to live upon."

"It is too much for me alone under the circumstances," said David, gravely;

and there was a little silence.

"Lucy, I love you. With you the Rajah would be a godsend. She will help me keep you in the company you have been used to, and were made to brighten and adorn; but without you I cannot take her from your hand, and, to speak plain, I won't."

"Oh, Mr. Dodd!"

"No, Lucy; before I knew you, to command a ship was the height of my ambition—her quarter-deck my Heaven on earth; and this is a clipper, I own it; I saw her in the docks. But you have taught me to look higher. Share my ship and my heart with me, and certainly the ship will be my child, and all the dearer to me that she came to us from her I love. But don't say to me, 'Me you shan't have; you are not good enough for that; but there is a ship for you in my place.' I wouldn't accept a star out of the firmament on those terms."

"How unreasonable! On the contrary you should say, 'I am doubly fortunate: I escape a foolish, weak companion for life, and I have a beautiful ship.' But friendship such as mine for you was never appreciated; I do you injustice; you only talk like that to tease me and make me unhappy."

"Oh, Lucy, Lucy, did you ever know me—"

"There, now, forgive me; and own you are not in earnest."

"This will show you," said David, sadly; and he took out two letters from his bosom. "Here are two letters to the secretary. In one I accept the ship with thanks, and offer to superintend her when her rigging is being set up; and in this one I decline her altogether, with my humble and sincere thanks."

"Oh yes, you are very humble, sir," said Lucy. "Now—dear friend—listen to reason. You have others—"

"Excuse my interrupting you, but it is a rule with me never to reason about right and wrong; I notice that whoever does that ends by choosing wrong. I don't go to my head to find out my duty, I go to my heart; and what little manhood there is in me all cries out against me compounding with the woman I love, and taking a ship instead of her."

"How unkind you are! It is not as if I was under no obligations to you. Is not my life worth a ship? an angel like me?"

"I can't see it so. It was a greater pleasure to me to save your life, as you call it, than it could be to you. I can't let that into the account. A woman is a woman, but a man is a man; and I will be under no obligation to you but one."

"What arrogance!"

"Don't you be angry; I'll love you and bless you all the same. But I am a man, and a man I'll die, whether I die captain of a ship or of a foretop. Poor Eve!"

"See how power tries people, and brings out their true character. Since you commanded the Rajah you are all changed. You used to be submissive; now you must have your own way entirely. You will fling my poor ship in my face unless I give you—but this is really using force—yes, Mr. Dodd, this is using force. Somebody has told you that my sex yield when downright compulsion is used. It is true; and the more ungenerous to apply it;" and she melted into a few placid tears.

David did not know this sign of yielding in a woman, and he groaned at the sight and hung his head.

"Advise me what I had better do."

To this singular proposal, David, listening to the ill advice of the fiend Generosity, groaned out, "Why should you be tormented and made cry?"

"Why indeed?"

"Nothing can change me; I advise you to cut it short."

"Oh, do you? very well. Why did you say 'poor Eve'?"

"Ah, poor thing! she cried for joy when she read your letter, but when I go back she will cry for grief;" and his voice faltered.

"I will cut this short, Mr. Dodd; give me that paper."

"Which?"

"The wicked one, where you refuse my Rajah."

David hesitated.

"You are no gentleman, sir, if you refuse a lady. Give it me this instant," cried Lucy, so haughtily and imperiously that David did not know her, and gave her the letter with a half-cowed air.

She took it, and with both her supple white hands tore it with insulting precision exactly in half. "There, sir and there, sir" (exactly in four); "and there" (in eight, with malicious exactness); "and there"; and, though it seemed impossible to effect another separation, yet the taper fingers and a resolute will reduced it to tiny bits. She then made a gesture to throw them in the fire, but thought better of it and held them.

David looked on, almost amused at this zealous demolition of a thing he could so easily replace. He said, part sadly, part doggedly, part apologetically, "I can write another."

"But you will not. Oh, Mr. Dodd, don't you see?!"

He looked up at her eagerly. To his surprise, her haughty eagle look had gone, and she seemed a pitying goddess, all tenderness and benignity; only her mantling, burning cheek showed her to be woman.

She faltered, in answer to his wild, eager look. "Was I ever so rude before? What right have I to tear your letter unless I—"

The characteristic full stop, and, above all, the heaving bosom, the melting eye, and the red cheek, were enough even for poor simple David. Heaven seemed to open on him. His burning kisses fell on the sweet hands that had torn his death-warrant. No resistance. She blushed higher, but smiled. His powerful arm curled round her. She looked a little scared, but not much. He kissed her sweet cheek: the blush spread to her very forehead at that, but no resistance. As the winged and rapid bird, if her feathers be but touched with a speck of bird-lime, loses all power of flight, so it seemed as if that one kiss, the first a stranger had ever pressed on Lucy's virgin cheek, paralyzed her eel-like and evasive powers; under it her whole supple frame seemed to yield as David drew her closer and closer to him, till she hid her forehead and wet eyelashes on his shoulder, and murmured:

"How could I let you be unhappy?!"

Neither spoke for a while. Each felt the other's heart beat; and David drank that ecstasy of silent, delirious bliss which comes to great hearts once in a life.

Had he not earned it?

CHAPTER XXIX.

By some mighty instinct Mrs. Wilson knew when to come in. She came to the door just one minute after Lucy had capitulated, and, turning the handle, but without opening the door, bawled some fresh directions to Jenny: this was to enable Lucy to smooth her ruffled feathers, if necessary, and look Agnes. But Lucy's actual contact with that honest heart seemed to have made a change in her; instead of doing Agnes, she confronted (after a fashion of her own) the situation she had so long evaded.

"Oh, nurse!" she cried, and wreathed her arms round her.

"Don't cry, my lamb! I can guess."

"Cry? Oh no; I would not pay him so poor a compliment. It was to say, 'Dear nurse, you must love Mr. Dodd as well as me now.'"

The dame received this indirect intelligence with hearty delight.

"That won't cost me much trouble," said she. "He is the one I'd have picked out of all England for my nursling. When a young man is kind to an old woman, it is a good sign; but la! his face is enough for me: who ever saw guile in such a face as that. Aren't ye hungry by this time? Dinner will be ready in about a minute."

"Nurse, can I speak to you a word?"

"Yes, sure."

It was to inquire whether she would invite Miss Dodd.

"She loves her brother very dearly, and it is cruel to separate them. Mr. Dodd will be nearly always here now, will he not?"

"You may take your davy of that."

In a very few minutes a note was written, and Mrs. Wilson's eldest son, a handsome young farmer, started in the covered cart with his mother's orders "to bring the young lady willy-nilly."

The holy allies both openly scouted Kenealy's advice, and both slyly stepped down into the town and acted on it. Mr. Fountain then returned to Font Abbey. Their two advertisements appeared side by side, and exasperated them.

After dinner Mrs. Wilson sent Lucy and David out to take a walk. At the gate they met with a little interruption; a carriage drove up; the coachman touched his hat, and Mrs. Bazalgette put her head out of the window.

"I came to take you back, love."

David quaked.

"Thank you, aunt; but it is not worth while now."

"Ah!" said Mrs. Bazalgette, casting a venomous look on David; "I am too late, am I? Poor girl!"

Lucy soothed her aunt with the information that she was much happier now than she had been for a long time past. For this was a fencing-match.

"May I have a word in private with my niece?" inquired Mrs. Bazalgette, bitterly, of David.

"Why not?" said David stoutly; but his heart turned sick as he retired. Lucy saw the look of anxiety.

"Lucy," said Mrs. Bazalgette, "you left me because you are averse to matrimony, and I urged you to it; of course, with those sentiments, you have no idea of marrying that man there. I don't suspect you of such hypocrisy, and therefore I say come home with me, and you shall marry nobody; your inclination shall be free as air."

"Aunt," said Lucy, demurely, "why didn't you come yesterday? I always said those who love me best would find me first, and you let Mr. Dodd come first. I am so sorry!"

"Then your pretended aversion to marriage was all hypocrisy, was it?"

Lucy informed her that marriage was a contract, and the contracting parties two, and no more—the bride and bridegroom; and that to sign a contract without reading it is silly, and meaning not to keep it is wicked. "So," said she, "I read the contract over in the prayer-book this morning, for fear of accidents."

My reader may, perhaps, be amused at this admission; but Mrs. Bazalgette was disgusted, and inquired, "What stuff is the girl talking now?"

"It is called common sense. Well, I find the contract is one I can carry out with Mr. Dodd, and with nobody else. I can love him a little, can honor him a great deal, and obey him entirely. I begin now. There he is; and if you feel you cannot show him the courtesy of making him one in our conversation, permit me to retire and relieve his solitude."

"Mighty fine; and if you don't instantly leave him and come home, you shall never enter my house again."

"Unless sickness or trouble should visit your house, and then you will send for me, and I shall come."

Mrs. Bazalgette (to the coachman).—"Home!"

Lucy made her a polite obeisance, to keep up appearances before the servants and the farm-people, who were gaping. She, whose breeding was inferior, flounced into a corner without returning it. The carriage drove off.

David inquired with great anxiety whether something had not been said to vex her.

"Not in the least," replied Lucy, calmly. "Little things and little people can no longer vex me. I have great duties to think of and a great heart to share them with me. Let us walk toward Harrowden; we may perhaps meet a friend."

Sure enough, just on this side Harrowden they met the covered cart, and Eve in it, radiant with unexpected delight. The engaged ones—for such they had become in those two miles—mounted the cart, and the two men sat in front, and Eve and Lucy intertwined at the back, and opened their hearts to each other.

Eve. And you have taken the paper off again?

Lucy. What paper? It was no longer applicable.

CHAPTER XXX.

I HAVE already noticed that Lucy, after capitulation, laid down her arms gracefully and sensibly. When she was asked to name a very early day for the wedding, she opposed no childish delay to David's happiness, for the Rajah was to sail in six weeks and separate them. So the license was got, and the wedding-day came; and all Lucy's previous study of the contract did not prevent her from being deeply affected by the solemn words that joined her to David in holy matrimony.

She bore up, though, stoutly; for her sense of propriety and courtesy forbade her to cloud a festivity. But, when the post-chaise came to convey bride and bridegroom on their little tour, and she had to leave Mrs. Wilson and Eve for a whole week, the tears would not be denied; and, to show how perilous a road matrimony is, these two risked a misunderstanding on their wedding-day, thus: Lucy, all alone in the post-chaise with David, dissolved—a perfect Niobe—gushing at short intervals. Sometimes a faint explanation gurgled out with the tears: "Poor Eve! her dear little face was working so not to cry. Oh! oh! I should not have minded so much if she had cried right out." Then, again, it was "Poor Mrs. Wilson! I was only a week with her, for all her love. I have made a c—at's p—paw of her—oh!"

Then, again, "Uncle Bazalgette has never noticed us; he thinks me a h—h—ypocrite." But quite as often they flowed without any accompanying reason.

Now if David had been a poetaster, he would have said: "Why these tears? she has got me. Am I not more than an equivalent to these puny considerations?" and all this salt water would have burned into his vanity like liquid caustic. If he had been a poet, he would have said: "Alas! I make her unhappy whom I hoped to make happy"; and with this he would have been sad, and so prolonged her sadness, and perhaps ended by sulking. But David had two good things—a kind heart and a skin not too thin: and such are the men that make women happy, in spite of their weak nerves and craven spirits.

He gave her time; soothed her kindly; but did not check her weakness dead short.

At last my Lady Chesterfield said to him, penitently, "This is a poor compliment to you, Mr. Dodd"; and then Niobized again, partly, I believe, with regret that she was behaving so discourteously.

"It is very natural," said David, kindly, "but we shall soon see them all again, you know."

Presently she looked in his radiant face, with wet eyes, but a half-smile. "You amaze me; you don't seem the least terrified at what we have done."

"Not a bit," cried David, like a cheerful horn: "I have been in worse peril than this, and so have you. Our troubles are all over; I see nothing but happiness ahead." He then drew a sunny picture of their future life, to all which she listened demurely; and, in short, he treated her little feminine distress as the summer sun treats a mist that tries to vie with it. He soon dried her up, and when they reached their journey's end she was as bright as himself.

CHAPTER XXXI.

THEY had been married a week. A slight change, but quite distinct to an observer of her sex, bloomed in Lucy's face and manner. A new beauty was in her face—the blossom of wifehood. Her eyes, though not less modest, were less timid than before; and now they often met David's full, and seemed to sip affection at them. When he came near her, her lovely frame showed itself conscious of his approach. His queen, though he did not know it, was his vassal. They sat at table at a little inn, twenty miles from Harrowden, for they were on their return to Mrs. Wilson. Lucy went to the window while David settled the bill. At the window it is probable she had her own thoughts, for she glided up behind David, and, fanning his hair with her cool, honeyed breath, she said, in the tone of a humble inquirer seeking historical or antiquarian information, "I want to ask you a question, David: are you happy too?"

David answered promptly, but inarticulately; so his reply is lost to posterity. Conjecture alone survives.

One disappointment awaited Lucy at Mrs. Wilson's. There were several letters for both David and her, but none from Mr. Bazalgette. She knew by that she had lost his respect. She could not blame him, for she saw how like disingenuousness and hypocrisy her conduct must look to him. "I must trust to time and opportunity," she said, with a sigh. She proposed to David to read all her letters, and she would read all his. He thought this a droll idea; but nothing that identified him with his royal vassal came amiss. The first letter of Lucy's that David opened was from Mr. Talboys.

"DEAR MADAM—I have heard of your marriage with Mr. Dodd, and desire to offer both you and him my cordial congratulations.

"I feel under considerable obligation to Mr. Dodd; and, should my house ever have a mistress, I hope she will be able to tempt you both to renew our acquaintance under my roof, and so give me once more that opportunity I have too little improved of showing you both the sincere respect and gratitude with which I am,

"Your very faithful servant,

"REGINALD TALBOYS."

Lucy was delighted with this note. "Who says it was nothing to have been born a gentleman?"

The second letter was from Reginald No. 2; and, if I only give the reader a fragment of it, I still expect his gratitude, all one as if I had disinterred a fragment of Orpheus or Tiresias.

    Dear lucy.

    It is very ungust of you to go and

    Mary other peeple wen you

    Promised me. but it is mr. dod.

    So i dont so much mind i like

    Mr. dod. he is a duc. and they all

    Say i am too litle and jane says

    Sailors always end by been

    Drouned so it is only put off.

    But you reely must keep your

    Promise to me. wen i am biger

    And mr. Dod is drouned. my

    Ginny pigs—

Here a white hand drew the pleasing composition out of David's hand, and dropped it on the floor; two piteous, tearful eyes were bent on him, and a white arm went tenderly round his neck to save him from the threatened fate.

At this sight Eve pounced on the horrid scroll, and hurled it, with general acclamation, into the flames.

Thus that sweet infant revenged himself, and, like Sampson, hit hardest of all at parting—in tears and flame vanished from written fiction, and, I conclude, went back to Gavarni.

There was a letter from Mr. Fountain—all fire and fury. She was never to write or speak to him any more. He was now looking out for a youth of good family to adopt and to make a Fontaine of by act of Parliament, etc., etc. A fusillade of written thunderbolts.

There was another from Mrs. Bazalgette, written with cream—of tartar and oil —of vitriol. She forgave her niece and wished her every happiness it was possible for a young person to enjoy who had deceived her relations and married beneath her. She felt pity rather than anger; and there was no reason why Mr. and Mrs. Dodd should not visit her house, as far as she was concerned; but Mr. Bazalgette was a man of very stern rectitude, and, as she could not make sure that he would treat them with common courtesy after what had passed, she thought a temporary separation might be the better course for all parties.

I may as well take this opportunity of saying that these two egotists carried out the promise of their respective letters. Mr. Fountain blustered for a year or two, and then showed manifest signs of relenting.

Mrs. Bazalgette kept cool, and wrote, in oils, twice a year to Mrs. Dodd:

"ET GARDAIT TOUT DOUCEMENT UNE HAINE IRRECONCILIABLE."

Lucy had to answer these letters. In signing one of them, she took a look at her new signature and smiled. "What a dear, quaint little name mine is!" said she. "Lucy Dodd;" and she kissed the signature.

A Month after Marriage.

The Dodds took a house in London and Eve came up to them. David was nearly all day superintending the ship, but spent the whole evening with his wife at home. Zeal always produces irritation. The servant that is anxious for his employer's interest is sure to get into a passion or two with the deadness, indifference and heartless injustice of the genuine hireling. So David was often irritated and worried, and in hot water, while superintending the Rajah,but the moment he saw his own door, away he threw it all, and came into the house like a jocund sunbeam. Nothing wins a woman more than this, provided she is already inclined in the man's favor. As the hour that brought David approached, Lucy's spirits and Eve's used both to rise by anticipation, and that anticipation his hearty, genial temper never disappointed.

One day Lucy came to David for information. "David, there is a singular change in me. It is since we came to London. I used to be a placid girl; now I am a fidget."

"I don't see it, love."

"No; how should you, dear? It always goes away when you come. Now listen. When five o'clock comes near, I turn hot and restless, and can hardly keep from the window; and if you are five minutes after your time, I really cannot keep from the window; and my nerves se crispent, and I cannot sit still. It is very foolish. What does it mean? Can you tell me?"

"Of course I can. I am just the same when people are unpunctual. It is inexcusable, and nothing is so vexing. I ought to be—"

"Oh David, what nonsense! it is not that. Could I ever be vexed with my David?"

"Well, then, there is Eve; we'll ask her."

"If you dare, sir!" and Mrs. Dodd was carnation.

Four years after the above events

Two ladies were gossiping.

1st Lady. "What I like about Mrs. Dodd is that she is so truthful."

2d Lady. "Oh, is she?"

1st Lady. "Yes, she is indeed. Certainly she is not a woman that blurts out unpleasant things without any necessity; she is kind and considerate in word and deed, but she is always true. She has got an eye that meets you like a little lion's eye, and a tongue without guile. I do love Mrs. Dodd dearly."

Two Qui his were talking in Leadenhall Street.

1st Qui hi. "Well, so you are going out again."

2d Qui hi. "Yes; they have offered me a commissionership. I must make another lac for the children."

1st Qui hi. "When do you sail?"

2d Qui hi. "By the first good ship. I should like a good ship."

1st Qui hi. "Well, then, you had better go out with Gentleman Dodd."

2d Qui hi. "Gentleman Dodd? I should prefer Sailor Dodd. I don't want to founder off the Cape."

1st Qui hi. "Oh, but this is a first-rate sailor, and a first-rate fellow altogether."

2d Qui hi. "Then why do you call him 'Gentleman Dodd'?"

1st Qui hi. "Oh, because he is so polite. He won't stand an oath within hearing of his quarter-deck, and is particularly kind and courteous to the passengers, especially to the ladies. His ship is always full."

2d Qui hi. "Is it? Then I'll go out with 'Gentleman Dodd.'"

———————————

TO MY MALE READERS.

I SEE with some surprise that there still linger in the field of letters writers who think that, in fiction, when a personage speaks with an air of conviction, the sentiments must be the author's own. (When two of his personages give each other the lie, which represents the author? both?)

I must ask you to shun this error; for instance, do not go and take Eve Dodd's opinion of my heroine, or Mrs. Bazalgette's, for mine.

Miss Dodd, in particular, however epigrammatic she may appear, is shallow: her criticism peche par la base. She talks too much as if young girls were in the habit of looking into their own minds, like little metaphysicians, and knowing all that goes on there; but, on the contrary, this is just what women in general don't do, and young women can't do.

No male will quite understand Lucy Fountain who does not take "instinct" and "self-deception" into the account. But with those two dews and your own intelligence, you cannot fail to unravel her, and will, I hope, thank me in your hearts for leaving you something to study, and not clogging my sluggish narrative with a mass of comment and explanation.

The End.